The ORPHAN'S SONG

YOUNG ADULT NOVELS
BY LAUREN KATE

Teardrop Series

Waterfall

Teardrop

❁

Fallen Series

Unforgiven

Rapture

Fallen: Angels in the Dark

Fallen in Love

Passion

Torment

Fallen

❁

The Betrayal of Natalie Hargrove

The ORPHAN'S SONG

Lauren Kate

G. P. Putnam's Sons
New York

PUTNAM
— EST. 1838 —

G. P. Putnam's Sons
Publishers Since 1838
An imprint of Penguin Random House LLC
penguinrandomhouse.com

ISBN 9780735212572
International edition: ISBN 9780593085837

Printed in the United States of America
1 3 5 7 9 10 8 6 4 2

Book design by Katy Riegel

For Milo,
always with me

❦

The ORPHAN'S SONG

VENICE

December 1725

IN A NORTHERN notch of the Adriatic Sea, beyond allegiance to Byzantium or Rome, a thousand-year-old empire was sinking. No one noticed her descent, disguised by centuries of wealth and reputation, like her citizens, living each day behind their *carnevale* masks.

See them in their gondolas, lovers lifting disguises beneath bridges to kiss. Imagine the senator, making his vote anonymously in the halls of the Doge's Palace. And the little girl at the market buying artichokes with her mama, the black ribbon of her mask whipping in a summer wind.

In the years before the republic fell, this was the Venetian way: to make a mystery of everything, to obscure identity and life, never to look too closely at what lay underneath. For a thousand years, Venice had glittered at the center of the trading world, jewel of the Mediterranean. But when the trade routes shifted, and with them went the gold, she misheard her swan song as the music of celebration. She feasted more riotously than ever. Venice had always been sinking; why not don the masks another day and toast another pink sunset?

Except in the churches and the hospitals, where masks were forbidden. Most days, the city's sick and the city's orphans, those wards of the church, were the only bare faces in Venice.

This story begins in an orphanage, on a lonesome night in the sleepy neighborhood of Dorsoduro. There, in a nursery for foundling children, a five-year-old girl lay in bed, planning her escape.

❁

WINTER HAD THE city in its grip again, and a driving wind rattled the pane of the window with its sad view of the building next door. Even if Violetta pressed against its glass, the most she could see was a curtained window through which no one ever looked out.

As soon as the others fell asleep, she would steal to the attic. Behind crates of old vestments and broken violins, its sole, high window cleared the neighboring rooftop. She could see how Venice stretched to the horizon. She could be alone.

She waited for the last whispers to fade to breathing, for the extraordinary stillness of three dozen sleeping girls. She had a trick for keeping patient: she explored the streets of Venice in her mind. She traveled up and down her city's bridges, blinking at the trembling, gold reflection of the sun on the canal. If she focused, she could almost smell the water's brine.

Four times had she been allowed beyond the orphanage walls, to walk the stone streets in a line of orphans taking alms, chanting, and invoking saints. Violetta held fast to those memories—gondoliers crooning, street performers throwing knives and swallowing fire, sidestepping white-masked noblemen and women, so unlike the barefaced orphans that they might have been another species. How she longed to wear a mask.

The walks always ended the same way: with the prioress turning the girls back to the Zattere, the sunny stone promenade slapped by the Giudecca Canal. Then they hurried past the *traghetto* stop, where gondoliers whistled beneath the brims of their straw hats. They passed the entrance to the building's west wing, the sculpted head of a foundling boy marking the door of the male dormitory. They passed the central double doors—the public entrance, which opened to a high-ceilinged vestibule that led directly into the church. And then, too soon, they were back at the east wing, where the corresponding sculpted head of a foundling girl hung over the entrance of the only home Violetta had ever known.

In her imagination, this was the moment she broke free, took off running down the narrow *calle*, ducking past street hawkers until she found herself gloriously alone.

Until she wasn't an orphan anymore.

In her mind, she was clattering across a stone bridge wearing the painted, wooden high-heeled clogs of a patrician lady. She was masked. She was boarding a gondola, wind dancing with her cloak. She was sailing for Giudecca, for a masquerade at one of the stately palazzi across the canal.

Or maybe she was going farther. Where?

How much more was there to this city, to life, than she had been allowed to see?

Beneath her covers, Violetta ran her thumb along her right heel, where the thin blue *I* branded her a ward of the Incurables. This mark told the universe that she had no family, that she belonged nowhere but here, within this walled, Istrian stone compound at the southern edge of the city.

The Incurables was built around a large square central courtyard with a towering church in its center. Outside San Marco's Basilica, the cheisa degli Incurabili, church of the Incurables, was the most famous house of worship in Venice. Though it had earned its unsettling name in the sixteenth century from those dying of syphilis in the infirmary on the ground floor, more recently, the Incurables had become one of four hospitals renowned for a brighter function: training its foundling girls into a conservatory of musicians.

The two sexes were strangers within the Incurables. There were not only separate entrances for boys and girls, but separate worlds within: separate nurseries, dining rooms, and studies on either side of the compound's second story. Foundling boys grew up and moved on to apprenticeships; they needed no musical training. But to keep the girls off the streets, they were taught to sing and play for the church. Over time their performances deepened the church's coffers, and this money paid the best composers to instruct the next generation's most talented girls. The Incurables was made of music—the finest in the city and therefore in the world.

Violetta loved music. Her heart beat to the sacred concertos that echoed off the nursery walls, but she heard the silent mystery of her origins each day. She had been abandoned when she was two days old. No one knew where she had come from, who had brought her, or under what duress. From a young age she grasped that her caretakers—the priest and the prioress; the cook and the apothecary; even the benevolent *zie*, retired "aunts" who were themselves once foundlings—viewed her as a duty to be attended to.

The other girls sought affection from the *zie,* but Violetta couldn't fake a bond. She needed food and warmth and shelter as much as any child, but she wanted love—real love, or no love at all. This longing infected her like a disease. She knew no cure.

❋

FINALLY: A MEASURE of quiet in the nursery. Violetta's practiced ear could tell, from the cadence of communal breathing, that the others were asleep at last. She rose from bed. Her bare feet made no sound on the cold mosaic tiles as she slipped out of the nursery, down the dark hall, and up the stairs.

She closed herself in the attic, rubbed her hands on her thighs for warmth, and checked her treasures on the windowsill: the sterling soldo dropped by the priest visiting from Rome; the peacock feather blown over the walls; the chipped porcelain honey bowl, discarded by the cook and long licked clean (though she dipped her finger in it every night, sucking the memory of sweetness). And, her most prized possession, Letta.

She had rescued the doll from the cold waters of the canal behind the orphanage. A few months back the orphans had been returning from an alms walk when Violetta saw a girl in a lace coat that sparkled with gold filigree arguing with her mother over a piece of candy. Seized by anger, the girl had simply *let go* of the doll. Before anyone noticed, Violetta plucked it from the water.

She called the doll Letta, short for Violetta—though Violetta had never been given a nickname. With the doll at her breast in the attic, she pressed against the window and felt the cold night beyond. Her breath frosted the pane as she stood on her toes to look out.

The water made the night look deeper, and a range of terra-cotta roofs, pitched at all angles, stretched farther than she could imagine. She wanted to reach out and touch the vines snaking through lattices on the balcony next door. She wanted to explore every narrow alley until she made it to the sea. Some nights she tried to count the black gondolas bobbing upon the canal. Other nights she stared at the water until her eyes teared.

The city was dark, unusually quiet. It was the start of Advent, two weeks when *carnevale* paused for Christmas, as if to let Venice catch its breath. There were no operas, no balls. Mass at the Incurables drew even larger crowds than normal, because the churches of the four *ospedali* became the only places in Venice to hear music. That night, the masked revelers—generally fixtures on the Zattere—were nowhere to be seen. The *calli* were empty. Almost.

"There he is," Violetta gasped.

Down on the Zattere a man in a tricorne approached from the west. It was her favorite street performer coming up and over the bridge, now along the promenade. There was his small, spotted dog, whom Violetta had named Giacomo.

"Do you think he did well today?" she asked Letta.

What was it like to hustle in a huge piazza, your voice echoing off buildings, feeling the crowd draw near? Where did such a man go at night? Would he take Giacomo to one of the taverns Violetta had glimpsed longingly through closing doors on her walks?

"What would you order at a tavern, Letta? Brandy?" She wrinkled her nose, thinking of the vile little glass the prioress carried to bed. "I'd have *acqaioli*."

She didn't know what comprised the drink she'd overheard patrician ladies order on café steps, but she loved its opalescent sparkle and the way the women raised their masks just enough to tip it to their lips.

She imagined *acqaioli* was rain from a sweetened cloud. Someday she would taste it.

When the man and his dog passed out of sight Violetta sighed.

"They'll be back tomorrow," she told Letta, even as she yearned to break through the window, to leap down and run after them, to touch Giacomo's ears and feel his nose against her wrists. She had never touched a dog.

But then, a song—a woman's voice—brought her attention to the *calle* below her window. Violetta leaned forward, scanning the darkness. She heard music all the time, but this was different. At the Incurables, they sang to commune with God. This music pulled her close not to God but to its singer.

Low in pitch and volume, the song sounded like a secret. It was not the ditty whistled by the street performer, not the gondolier's cheeky barcarolle. This was love and sorrow stitched together so tightly Violetta could barely breathe.

When she found the woman in the moonlight, Violetta gasped. The singer was headed for the wheel.

To those walking past on the *calle*, the wheel looked discreet, a rusted metal half cylinder protruding from the base of the building's western wall. But if you pulled the heavy iron handle to set the wheel in motion, you'd expose a wooden platform, no larger than the space made by Violetta's embracing arms. On the other side, the wheel opened to the kitchen, where its contents would be discovered by the cook who came early to light the hearth.

Violetta knew the stories from before the wheel was built. Abandoned babies found frozen, blue at sunrise, outside the front gates. The wheel let mothers leave their children unexposed to rain and wind. You could keep your anonymity—and your child alive.

Violetta's birthday was in early February. She knew she would be dead if not for the wheel. The contraption tormented her, but in all her nights spying from the attic, she'd never seen it turn. Now the singer approached it and dropped to her knees. She wore no mask, only a hooded cloak with a bulge beneath it. A baby.

Don't, Violetta willed the woman. How could she not imagine her own mother at the wheel?

The woman opened her cloak, and Violetta was stunned to find her child was no baby. Relief flooded her. A boy that size would never fit inside. The woman would be forced to change her mind.

Her singing had intensified. Now Violetta could make out the words.

I am yours, you are mine . . .

Her fingers brushed fair hair from the boy's closed eyes. They traced his shoulders, his elbows, down to his hands. Held them. A throb formed in Violetta's chest, and she envied that boy for these caresses, even as she saw their end.

Tears shone on the woman's cheeks. Her note wobbled, but she kept singing, turning her face before her sorrow dampened his skin. She looked up at the heavens, and Violetta saw her. She memorized this mother's small straight nose, her round cheeks, her lips. She wore a large stone on a chain in the hollow of her throat. She was beautiful. Her features were washed in shame.

She heaved the wheel's handle to the side, laid her boy on the wood circle, and bent his knees to his chest. She rubbed his feet softly, then desperately, as if no amount of effort could warm them to her satisfaction. Her son slept on.

Violetta held Letta to the window, frozen with dread, unable to look away as the woman turned the wheel. When it stuck, the mother's palms pressed her son's shoulders, and she forced him through with a violence that shocked Violetta to her core.

"This is what mothers do," Violetta said. "This is what mothers are." Her hands shook as she set her doll back on the windowsill, then looked up to meet her own eyes in the reflection of the glass. "Never be a mother."

One

VIOLETTA!"

She spun from her bedroom window, from the seagull roosting on the terra-cotta rooftop next door. She'd been willing its wings to take flight and abandon this shadowy alley. If Violetta were a bird, she would be gliding over the ocean. She would never land on the same ship twice.

Outside, the September morning was so bright, and her sliver of sky so blue, that when she turned from the window it took a moment for her eyes to adjust to the heaving form in her doorway.

"What is it, Laura?" she asked, making room on the bed for her friend. Both girls were sixteen. They had been neighbors, sharing a wall between their single bedrooms on the second floor since they graduated from the nursery at ten. "Come, catch your breath. Take a lesson from a lazy seagull."

But it wasn't Laura's nature to catch her breath. She could worry over anything, from rain dampening a feast day to what happened to sparrow eggs when a mother bird swallowed a pebble of glass. She worried over the moisture from her palms when she played a difficult piece on the violin, drying the wood fastidiously with linen so it wouldn't warp. She worried over how to distinguish her playing from the other violinists in the music school. She worried deeply over being promoted to the *coro*, and she worried that Violetta didn't worry enough about being promoted with her. She never missed an opportunity to remind Violetta that the *coro* had space for only thirty-three women at a time, less than half the number presently training in the music school. There were only a few openings each year, as the older girls married or retired to nunneries.

Laura worried over Violetta's voice exercises and the sheet music for Violetta's librettos—too often left scattered on the floor. Over the years, Laura had gotten better at making up excuses for the prioress when Violetta was late for a lesson, but she never stopped worrying that Violetta would be caned. Their relationship was a duet: the more Laura worried, the more Violetta gave her cause to.

It wasn't that Violetta was carefree; she only seemed that way to Laura, who turned toward her worries as much as Violetta tried to escape them. It was why she spent so much time at her window, imagining herself beyond it.

Laura stuffed a loose curl back into the great brown bun of her hair. "Of course, you didn't hear."

"Hear what?" Violetta didn't know how long she'd been at the window. This happened on days when she'd had the dream.

The wheel, the woman. That song. Eleven years had passed since that night, but she remembered the dark race downstairs as if it were yesterday. She'd been the only one who knew he was there, stuck. The only one who could help. She'd never been so near a boy's alien body. He'd still been sleeping when she pulled him from the wheel.

Years later she had realized that his mother must have drugged him. That he hadn't even heard the woman's song.

Whenever Violetta dreamed that song, it rendered her waking life muted and pale. She struggled to go about her responsibilities as usual: rising at sunrise, praying aloud by rote—first the Angelus, then a prayer for suppression of heresy, one for their most pious republic, one for the benefactors and the *governati* of the Incurables, and on and on—just as all the other murmuring voices did in the rooms to the left and right of hers.

Before mass she had taken her breakfast of porridge and cream as the prioress's wide hips moved between the rough wood tables, spouting sacred readings in her corrosive whisper, daring any of them to gossip or to giggle. And then the morning had passed with three hours of music lessons—first with the full music school, second with a smaller coterie of singers, and finally with her private tutor, Giustina.

Giustina was beautiful, twenty-four, and the lead soprano in the *coro.* She was known as *bella voce* throughout the city, and even beyond the republic of Venice. Tourists traveled from across Europe, paying dearly to hear her perform. Last summer, she astonished Violetta, selecting her as one of two apprentices. Violetta still could not be sure what Giustina saw in her, but her *sottomaestra*'s patient generosity inspired her to try her best.

At the moment, she was meant to be reading the latest corrections to her sheet music, practicing her trills and *passaggios.* Giustina would test her on them later, before *compline*, the prayer at end of day. But Violetta hadn't even looked at the pages. The moment she'd been free to close herself in her room, she'd drawn near the window, felt the warmth beyond it, and let her mind fly away.

The dream song haunted her, those words she could never sing aloud.

I am yours, you are mine . . .

It had become her song. But who or what was she addressing? Sometimes she still thought of the boy she had pulled from the wheel that night. Before Violetta had left him near the embers of the kitchen hearth, tucked beneath a folded tablecloth, she had discovered the small painting clutched in his hand.

It was half a painting, really, a thin piece of wood, splintered from being shorn diagonally in half. It hung from a broken chain, as if it had once been a pendant. It featured a naked woman. Half a woman. Face and breasts and a belly covered by waves of flowing blond hair, the same shade as the boy's. Dark eyes cast into the distance, her mouth open in song against a blue sky.

The boy's mother must have kept the other half. Most orphans at the Incurables had some such token—part of a painting or a swath of patterned fabric—proof of a bond, should destiny ever reunite mother and child.

Violetta had none. She didn't believe in such fantasies.

She'd never seen that boy again, so separate were the lives of boys and girls at the Incurables. She didn't want to see him, though he was always with her. The song meant for him haunted her, gave words to the part of herself she most wanted to deny—that someone had done the same thing to her. She hoped he had no memory of his abandonment, that he never had to think upon that night. Likely by now he had moved on from the orphanage to an apprenticeship somewhere in the city.

"Violetta!" Laura took her arm. "Porpora is back."

Violetta jumped to her feet. "Why didn't you say so?"

That year, the Incurables had commissioned the famous Neapolitan composer Nicola Porpora to lead the *coro.* He was the final authority, determining which girls advanced and which did not. Even the youngest students, tiny children six years of age, straightened their shoulders and hushed their gossip at the mention of his name.

Those Porpora chose for the *coro* could look forward to years of intense collaboration with the brilliant, tightly wound composer and to regular performances before admiring crowds. The women of the *coro* enjoyed leisure time, more frequent outings, better food, and wine. Some of them received letters from important Venetians or European tourists who traveled just to see them perform. A portion of the sizeable earnings from their concerts was saved in a special dowry.

The girls not chosen for the *coro* became *figlie di commun*, the ordinary women of the orphanage. They served as nurses to the syphilitics on the first floor, or toiled in menial tasks like laundry and lace making, sewing and dyeing the thick wool cloaks that inimitable shade of midnight blue. Some became *zie* and cared for foundling babies. *Figlie di commun* worked for the orphanage until they were forty, and then they were sent to a nunnery. The only possibility of escape was to be sold off as a servant. But worst of all, the music simply stopped. There were no more opportunities to practice or perform if you were a *figlia di commun.*

This horrified Violetta. All they knew of life was music, and to have it taken away? She and Laura had pledged to each other that they would not accept this fate. Deep down, Violetta suspected that both of them knew Laura would be fine, but that Violetta, with her tendency toward daydreams, might not make the cut.

The maestro had been abroad for all of August and half of September. Lessons relaxed in his absence, but no longer. Porpora would stay on through the fall, through the festival of *carnevale*, as the *coro* prepared for their most important season of performances, Advent. For Violetta and Laura, and each of the sixty-two younger girls in the music school, Porpora's arrival meant a trial by fire.

"He wasn't meant to return until next week," Violetta said.

"He's early," Laura said. "And he wants to hear us. In the gallery."

"The gallery?" That was where the *coro* girls performed. Violetta had been in its anteroom many times, fetching sheet music for Giustina, but she'd never set foot in the special enclave that looked down over the entire church through a gilded grille. The music school girls practiced in a stifling, windowless chamber above the apothecary. It stank of the holywood tea brewing for the syphilitics downstairs.

"You're already late," Laura said, "and you're not leaving this room with your hair like that."

"What's wrong with my hair?" Violetta tugged the thick, dark rope that hung to her waist. There was no mirror in her chamber. She couldn't remember the last time she'd brushed her impossible hair.

"Leave it to me," Laura said, moving behind her, standing astride Violetta on the creaking bed, her toes nudging Violetta's thighs through her slippers. "You start warming up. Scales. And, Madonna, stockings!"

Violetta worked the scratchy wool stockings up her legs, fastening them with a ribbon just above her knee. She grumbled when Laura undid her days-old braid and pulled dense knots from her hair.

While Laura's fingers gathered and combed, Violetta straightened her back and breathed through a fibrous wall of nerves. She pulled on her tongue, flattening it between her fingers as she moved through three octaves of scales, as Giustina had taught her to do.

"When you sing," the *sottomaestra* had said, "you must think of what you want to say to the world."

When Violetta sang, she was barely confident enough to want to be heard, let alone to convey a message. She found it hard to imagine the world might be listening to her.

She turned the question back on Giustina. "What do *you* want to say to the world?"

Giustina pressed both hands to her breast and sighed. "*Love is here.*"

Violetta's eyes had pricked with tears, for she felt there was nothing higher any musician could aspire to. And she felt hopeless. She would never be able to sing something so brave and essential to the world. She wanted to see and hear the world and be inspired by it. She couldn't imagine returning the favor.

Giustina had squeezed Violetta's shoulder and said softly, "Don't worry, you'll find it."

Would she? Violetta was a soprano, but a faint one, and despite her years of practice and prayer, her voice still stretched to reach the highest notes of the complicated arias she loved best. Sometimes she felt fear holding her back. If she could only make the *coro* and relieve herself of this anxiety, her voice might come into its own. She wondered what it felt like to perfect an aria, to sing as Porpora intended—or better. But when she thought of asking Giustina, she knew this was not something one could express, much like the buried root of Violetta's own longing.

The best moments were those when she felt her voice blend with the other singers'. When she felt a part of the music instead of alone. Then Violetta longed to be nowhere else, caught in the joyful embrace of a song.

But today the dream had its grip on her, and she felt unworthy of the music. Why did the maestro have to arrive now?

At least Laura's presence was a comfort. Soon she and Violetta synchronized—as Violetta moved toward the upper registers of her scales, Laura spun her hair into a neater, tighter braid. Music was in all the girls so deeply that they made it out of everything they did: the syncopated clanks of their spoons against their bowls at dinner, the soft percussion of their footsteps to nightly confession, the tenor whistle of their piss into porcelain pots.

"Hold your notes. What's wrong with you?" Laura said as she secured Violetta's hair. She came around to stand before Violetta, smoothed a wild cowlick, nodded at her work. She touched one finger under Violetta's chin, raised it, looked into her eyes.

"You had the dream?"

Violetta nodded, quiet but not ashamed. From the years she'd slept in the nursery she knew that nightmares were common. Laura knew Violetta dreamed of one thing again and again, and that when she did, it brought great sorrow, but she had never asked Violetta for details. And Violetta had never clarified; she had never asked about Laura's own painful dreams. What would have been the point? Each girl here had so little from her time before, when she had been *figlia di mamma*—the daughter of a mother—not just *figlia degli incurabili*—a daughter of the Incurables.

For Laura, it was enough to know Violetta had the dream and that the day would be shaped by its ghost. And so Laura's hand found Violetta's, a reassuring secret music in the pressure of their palms, in the sound of their slippers as they ran for the bridge.

The bridge was a short, windowless passageway, no longer than a gondola, accessed through the third floor of the dormitory. It arced over the courtyard and connected to the church in the center, opening onto a small anteroom where the *coro* girls warmed their voices, tuned their violins, and broke in new oboe reeds before performances.

Beyond a white door at the far end of the anteroom was the treasured performance space of the *coro*: the singing gallery. A chest-high marble parapet enclosed the gallery, and, above the parapet, the famous brass grille of sculpted orange blossoms was the object of widespread fascination. The grille was intended to obscure the performers from the eyes of the church below—and vice versa—but when Violetta sat in her pew downstairs with the other music school girls and gazed up, she could discern which girl was which.

How powerful and mysterious they had looked behind those gilded orange blossoms. How she always wanted to be one of them. She suspected most parishioners spent the full mass straining to see the angels making music on the other side.

"Are you ready?" Laura asked at the door to the gallery.

Violetta's throat felt troublingly tight. She squeezed Laura's hand. "I can't believe you left rehearsal to come find me."

The corners of Laura's mouth flicked up. "We made a deal."

Laura cracked the white door open, pushed Violetta's shoulders gently forward, and the two of them slipped inside the gallery. Violetta ducked below the parapet. She did not wish to be seen by Porpora or the prioress, conducting in the nave below, until she was in her place.

How small the gallery was, only two standing rows packed tightly, the upper level for strings, woodwinds, and the organist, the lower level for singers. Violetta quickly gauged that only half the music school was there—the girls of fourteen years and older who were approaching consideration for the *coro*. Each performed for their life. And here came Violetta, like a lost dog underfoot.

Laura made their late entrance look easy, taking her place near the door where her violin was waiting. She'd picked it up and had fallen in with the music before Violetta even chose the smoothest route to her place at the front. She tried to weave between the singers. Most inched back so she could pass before them, wishing to hurry along the distraction. None of them stopped singing the "Alleluia." It was a short piece of music with violin and timpani parts that complemented a range of singers—now the contraltos, now the sopranos.

At last, she arrived at her place, third from the end, between Olivia and Reine. Olivia made room for her; Reine would not give an inch. If Reine and Violetta had disliked each other from the moment Reine arrived at the Incurables a year ago, their animosity had swelled when Giustina chose them both as her apprentices.

Reine was not Venetian. She was not even an orphan. Her rich Parisian parents had elected to send her to the Incurables. No amount of money could buy a rich girl of the republic a spot. Only foreigners were permitted to feign orphandom for a price.

She liked to provoke Violetta. "Do you dream of the whorehouse where your mother birthed you, took one look at your bug eyes, and abandoned you here?"

"My mother is music," Violetta replied with such conviction that she silenced the French girl. She strained inside to steady her voice as she spoke a portion of the truth: "In my dreams, she sings."

Reine was a marginally better singer, but she postured as if she were the *coro*'s greatest star. When the day came for Giustina to leave the *coro*, only one of them would move up.

Violetta inhaled and tried to make herself brave. She rose to stand next to Reine, opening her mouth and joining the song.

"Nei secoli dei secoli, nei secoli dei secoli. Alleluia."

Her eyes widened as she adjusted to her surroundings. Through the grille the nave was lit by broad beams of sunlight streaming through the clerestory. She saw the rows and rows of empty pews and tried to imagine singing to a thousand people. Her chest expanded with unexpected joy.

She saw the brilliant Tintoretto hanging in the apse, depicting Saint Ursula and her eleven thousand virginal maids. It was a reminder of what the Incurables girls aspired to: musicians, yes—but nothing before virgins.

And then she saw the sharp flick of the prioress's head. She noticed Violetta.

She assumed her most virginal expression, casting her eyes to the heavens. She lengthened her spine, clasped hands over her belly, puffed out her chest. She hit the notes perfectly, defiant. She'd pay for this later, but canings and humiliating public confessions had long been part of Violetta's life. It was Porpora she didn't wish to aggravate.

The guest of honor stood next to the prioress, swaying to his music, eyes mercifully closed. He was not interested in the music school students so much as he was interested in hearing his new composition. He did not know these girls' names, their voices, their special talents and limitations. He saved this attention for those chosen for the *coro*.

A bloated man in midlife, with a wispy gray wig and round, pink cheeks, their maestro didn't look like the man who would compose such astonishing music. He was no Vivaldi, whose red hair and intense gaze had arrested Violetta when she studied his portrait. She had found it sketched on the library copy of a libretto Vivaldi had written for the rival *coro* at the Ospedale della Pietà, across the Grand Canal. But then who was Violetta to judge appearances? Her own face hadn't grown to accommodate her huge dark eyes, which made her feel like a beetle when she passed her reflection in the glass. And she still didn't have any breasts.

The sopranos' notes were rising. Violetta had to arch her back to get them out. Her shoulder probed Reine's, who responded by elbowing Violetta's ribs. Violetta's voice snagged as she wheezed, but she recovered quickly, shooting Reine a dangerous look.

Now the music moved from "Alleluia" to a recitative, easier to sing. The lyrics were more like talking, and the good ones told a story. The performers seemed to relax, but as Violetta's lips moved through the memorized verses, her heart swerved to another song.

I am yours, you are mine . . .

She tried to push it away, to channel the other concentrating girls. But the dream song possessed her, weaving its way into the recitative. It wanted to be sung. From the corner of her eye, she saw spit flying from Reine's mouth, and she hated her. Reine, whose parents sent great sums of money to the school along with multipaged letters to their daughter, lace handkerchiefs misted with sickly sweet perfume. Reine, who did not know what it was like to have been abandoned. Reine, who would surely make the *coro* over her.

Another jostle of shoulders. Violetta couldn't tell whose fault it was, but she rolled her shoulder forward, edging in front of the girl. Reine rolled hers forward, edging in front of Violetta. Violetta wished deeply to be free of this gallery, of this cruel girl, of the dream song she could not unhear. And all of that eventually drove her to lift her foot and stamp down hard on Reine's rich toe.

She would have wagered almost anything that Reine would sing through the pain, plan a dark, future revenge. She never expected the French girl to scream.

The sound ripped through the cathedral. Everyone froze mid-note and turned to stare. The prioress glowered, and with a single pointed finger, evicted Violetta.

"To confession."

❈

VIOLETTA DIDN'T GO to confession. When she fled the gallery, then the anteroom, when she crossed the bridge back to the dormitory and imagined cloistering herself in Father Marché's chambers, Violetta could not breathe. She had to calm herself, and there was only one place at the Incurables to do that.

She went to the attic, but today when she got to the window, she felt trapped by the glass, oppressed by the view—all those boats on the water, all those people so much freer. She needed a greater escape.

She pressed her hands to the windowpane. When it gave a little, her fingers moved to the edge of the glass near the casement and she jiggled the pane. It came loose and she slid it out in amazement, leaning the glass against the wall beneath the window.

Brisk autumn air rushed in, inviting her outside. Did she dare?

Later, she could bear the confession booth. Later, she could add what she was about to do to her litany of sins. She moved a crate closer, stood atop it. She hoisted one foot, then another, to the sill, until she crouched upon its threshold.

She held the casement for balance as she straightened to stand on the window's exterior ledge. Her heart raced as she brought her chest level with the roof. She wiped dampness from her palms, reached up, and wrapped her fingers around the low parapet. She could see beyond it to the dominating white dome of the Santa Maria della Salute at the eastern tip of Dorsoduro. And then, she could see the horizon, that magical beyond where the magnitude of Venice condensed into a single brilliant line. Violetta wished to walk along it, the way she'd once seen an acrobat walk a cable stretched to a height of ten men, from one end of Campo Santa Margherita to the other.

She raised her right leg until her foot notched over the roof's ledge. Then she made the mistake of looking down. The sight of the drop paralyzed her. For several moments, she could not move.

But then she glimpsed the wheel, barely visible, four stories down. And she thought of that mother abandoning that boy all those years ago. The time had come to leave that night behind. Maybe she would always dream that song, but wasn't it hers by now? Why couldn't she ascend beyond what she'd seen happen at the wheel?

The wind spurred her on. She sang to it as she pulled her body higher.

I am yours, you are mine.
One more turn and I'm the sky.

When finally she reached the roof's flat top, she collapsed on her back, gazing at a sky so blue it hurt to look at. She wanted to laugh at her achievement, but the need to weep won out.

Curse her impulsiveness, her bony shoulder and tattooed heel. Had it cost her the *coro*? Could she stay up here forever?

She rose and looked around. The day was windy and bright. Sunlight sparkled on the canal and made the boats look like black gems. Down on the Zaterre, white awnings sheltered people flirting on café steps. Across the water, the island of Giudecca beckoned with its row of tall palazzi facing the promenade, each of them roofed in warm orange terra-cotta. Spires of cypress tress protruded above iron garden gates.

It was only mid-September, but the air was turning crisp. There was smoke on the wind, and rosemary and verbena from the pots in apartment windows. Underneath, always, was the salty musk of the canals.

Music filtered through the air. It was everywhere if you had the luxury to listen. For the first time, Violetta felt free to take in her city's wondrous, accidental melodies. The slap of oars against the water, the bright banter of hawkers selling watermelon on the Zattere. Here came the staccato whip of windblown bedsheets on a line. She closed her eyes and heard all of it doubled, the way everything in Venice was reflected a second time on the water, as if God had noted in the composition of the city that it was to be played *forte*, extra strong.

Brassy tones of laughter broke through and made Violetta crouch at the parapet. She glanced west, toward the next building, whose roof stood one level down. Her hiding spot was bare of any comfort, but the neighboring roof was a sumptuous *altana*—a welcoming open-air balcony made somewhat private by Arab lattices and trailing verbena. Leather awnings shaded seats for a dozen. A bronze sundial stood on a marble pedestal in the corner. A wicker table brimmed with pomades and potions, trays of grapes and apricots, crystal platters stacked with tarts.

Four women lazed on the *altana*, bleaching their hair in the sun. Their heads were covered with special wide-brimmed caps that shaded their faces but exposed their hair to the light. Violetta guessed the ladies had only a handful of years on her, but their laughter made her feel like a child. It was rich with womanly knowledge, brushed lightly with hedonism.

Had she ever heard an Incurables girl laugh with that much spirit? Not even Giustina, who could access four octaves without wheezing.

Violetta was dazzled by the elaborate rituals of their toilette. One woman, whose face was slathered with a pale blue cream, lifted lace fans from a basket, settling on a rich purple one to bat the autumn air. Another, whose hair was set in rolls above her cap, painted her nails with silver lacquer, sipping from a small crystal teacup between coats. A third rose from her chair to check the progress of the fourth woman's coiled tresses, a stack of bracelets jangling on her wrist.

"Don't touch," a man's voice warned. "She's still drying."

Now Violetta noticed the two men hovering in the shadows. They wore the powdered periwigs so fashionable among the upper class. Their pastel britches matched their silken blouses and the ribbons tied around their stockings. Violetta gaped at them, transfixed. These were *cicisbei*, a strange breed of cavalier servants particular to Venice's patrician class.

She had heard the *zie* whisper about a man who had taken a *cicisbeo* position with a wealthy noble couple. He earned seventy sequins a year for his service, more than enough for a bachelor.

But what exactly did he *do*? another *zia* wanted to know—and so had Violetta, leaning close with Laura to eavesdrop. The first *zia* explained that while the senator was occupied, the cicisbeo looked after his wife in any manner she desired.

The *zie* had laughed and Violetta had blushed without knowing exactly why. And then, on the Christmas alms walk, a combination of high tide and heavy rain had flooded the streets—and Violetta had stopped in the middle of the orphans' chant to watch a *cicisbeo* hoist a lady in his arms to cross a deluged *calle*.

She had understood from the woman's eyes and the *cicisbeo*'s hands that there was more at play than a lady's wish to keep her skirt dry. For the first time, she had seen desire's spark. She'd felt a warmth coursing through her belly that made her wish she were in that man's arms, if only to feel what it was like to be wanted in that way.

She couldn't begin to imagine what a lover might be like. Incurables girls wore the expectation of eternal virginity like a second cloak. It was part of what distinguished them from any other Venetian woman who performed onstage. Singers at operas or masquerades were considered immoral by nature of their performance; but the *coro* girls were different, singing in the image of the vestal virgins of Rome.

Well, there was one chance at sex. Occasionally, a man would ask the prioress for a meeting with a *coro* girl he'd heard at mass with the goal of taking home a bride. These meetings were a source of fascination for the younger girls, not only because they involved a man from outside the orphanage, but because, if a *coro* girl determined to marry, she left a space for one of the younger students to move up. Two men had already requested meetings with Giustina—both three times her age. She had told Violetta she was so nervous that she hadn't been able to stop giggling. To her horror, both men had left the Incurables even more committed to her. Benevolent, lovely Giustina had begged the prioress to decline their proposals. She wasn't ready to leave the *coro* yet.

But, she'd confided to Violetta, had the proposal come from the young, dark-haired gondolier whom Giustina often saw through her window as he walked to work, she would have straddled him then and there. She would have seasoned him with kisses, raised her cloak to him, and to hell with the prioress's prudish disbelief.

Giustina would never really do it—but just knowing that someone as noble and good as her *sottomaestra* also yearned for an unattainable *more* had given Violetta comfort. She'd tried to picture Giustina straddling the *traghetto* boy. She had tossed in her bed imagining the possibilities.

If any man ever requested a meeting with her, she, too, would beg the prioress to decline. The last thing in the world she wanted was to become a wife of some old man, the mother of his child. She would never marry. She would not risk doing to a child what had been done to her. Abandonment was in her blood, her one inheritance; she would not make it manifest.

On the *altana*, the *cicisbei* were refreshing drinks. Violetta memorized the way they poured chilled water, then a splash of alcohol, then a drop of something opalescent. Was this *acqaioli*? How she wanted to be over there, a tourist in that exotic realm, so close and far away.

"Lemon balm?" The *cicisbei* offered spoonfuls to sweeten the breath. They held parasols over décolletage as the women studied themselves in jeweled looking glasses. They touched up powdered cheeks and laughed at jokes. They praised the peaks of the women's hair, the coquettish placement of beauty marks, the ambergris perfuming necks.

"Marvelous." They applauded. "*Che bellezza*."

"Did you hear," one said in a voice both loud and intimate, "last night Annalisa Feltrinelli was seen at the same gambling table as her husband?"

When the women gasped, the second man tittered. "And she *stayed*. They say she played three games of backgammon against him."

"And *lost*," the first man added, powdering his own cheeks when the women weren't looking.

"Well, it's bad luck." One of the women smirked at her reflection, her natural red hair drying to a dark, desirable blond. "The only time you'll see me in society with my lord will be at his funeral."

Violetta covered her laugh with her hand. She wished Laura had heard that. The upper class in Venice was infamous for the laxity of its morals, its discreet indiscretions. The prioress tried to shelter the Incurables girls, but sex and desire were favorite topics for Laura and Violetta. At mass, they'd nudge each other, watching the roving eyes of married women free to sit away from their husbands.

But what would Laura do if Violetta brought her to the roof? Hold out a rosary and make her swear not to return, not to risk her place in the *coro* again? It was one thing to gossip, another to sneak up here alone.

"If you liked that one," a voice behind Violetta said, "stay until Fiona's had another drink."

Violetta whipped around.

She found herself facing a lanky blond boy about her age. He smiled at her as if they were in on the same joke.

Her eyes narrowed. Her shoulders drew back as they did when she prepared to sing, when she gathered all the air into her lungs.

Had he followed her up here? At whose orders? Violetta's heart was pounding, but she struggled to reconcile her sense of doom with the amusement in his startlingly blue eyes.

He didn't have the air of authority. They were the same height, and he was almost as skinny as she was, though his hands and feet were huge, like a puppy. His hair, which needed trimming, was an unusual shade for a Venetian, the flaxen blond the women on the *altana* yearned for. He wore the orphanage's light linen blouse and thin cotton britches, but he looked too old to board at the Incurables. She thought boys his age would have already left to work—but then, she didn't really know the policies of the boys' wing. They were certainly freer than those governing the girls.

All she'd ever seen of the Incurables boys were rare glimpses across the courtyard. When the girls passed beneath the loggia, the covered gallery, on the ground floor that opened to the east side of the courtyard, they were made to walk in a silent, steady line, heads forward and eyes low. Once Violetta had heard the rapid footfall of a pair of boys running unchaperoned along the loggia on the opposite side and she'd raised her head. The freedom of their young limbs stopped her in her tracks.

The prioress had barked at her, made her wear the hood of her cloak the next time they walked along the loggia, in an attempt to block her view. It hadn't stopped Violetta, whose curiosity knew no bounds. At the second offense, she'd been caned. After that, Violetta tried to let the boys dissolve back into mystery. She didn't think about them because it hurt; they got to leave the orphanage eventually, and she envied them that freedom.

Now one stood before her, and her envy turned to mistrust.

"What are you doing here?" she said.

"Didn't mean to startle you," he said. "When Fiona gets tipsy, she's a storm of advice." He spoke quickly and made oversized gestures with his hands that reminded Violetta of a maestro. "It's worth sticking around to see the show. Not that you need advice from her. I mean . . ."

"Who are you?" Violetta asked.

The skin pinched between the boy's blue eyes. It made her hear how cold and accusing she sounded.

"I'm the guy who's not going to turn you in," he said. "You can call me Mino. If you want. But you came up here to be alone. I'll leave you now. I'm sorry—"

There was something familiar about him. Maybe it was the way he spoke, without seeming to think before the words came out. It made Violetta feel closer to him than she expected, and she didn't know whether she liked it. He must be this way with everyone, as open with strangers as she was closed, sometimes even to her friends.

"Sit," she said. She was surprised by her own invitation. He planted himself next to where she had been sitting, draping long, skinny arms over the parapet. He looked so at home that Violetta saw the roof anew. She saw that it was also his. She expected this to make her feel invaded. Instead, she felt less lonely. Here was a kindred spirit on a roof. She sat down next to him. She looked at his knee, a handbreadth from hers, and she felt a flutter in her chest. Laura would think he was handsome. Violetta wasn't sure.

"What else does Fiona know?" She nodded toward the redhead, whose *cicisbeo* was sponging bleach from her hair.

Mino grinned, a smile that involved not just his mouth but his eyes and cheeks and even his ears. His commitment to the expression was so full, so bright, Violetta had to look away, as from the sun jumping out from behind a cloud.

"That depends," he said. "Are you embarking on an affair or betrothed to a man you don't love?"

"Both," Violetta said and laughed.

Mino raised his chin, angled his shoulders, and squinted one eye in a near-perfect imitation of Fiona.

"Always change gondolas three times if discretion is your wish."

He had assumed her voice so precisely that Violetta applauded, clapping her hands without irony. She felt like her five-year-old self watching a street performer. She wanted more. "All right, now I'm betrothed to a grisly old merchant with two teeth left."

Mino's eyes twinkled as he cleared his throat and hitched his voice high again. "How can you enjoy the exquisite pleasures of widowhood if you never marry?"

"Stop," Violetta begged, laughing. "That's terrifying."

"Nah," he said and glanced at her sidelong. "You're too brave to be scared by that."

"You don't know me," she said. Reckless maybe, careless certainly, but she'd never considered that she was brave. She found herself mulling over the word, enjoying it.

"You're here, aren't you?" Mino said.

"So are you."

He shook his head. "I'm not the one with a brand on my heel. I'm not the one with the musical training. I'm not the one who'll be noticed missing."

Violetta grew somber, remembering what had happened in the gallery. "They'll wish I'd go missing for good."

Mino tilted his head at her and his eyes widened. "You're the one who broke Reine's toe?"

Violetta's mouth dropped open. "It's broken? I'll never make the *coro*." She hung her head, anguished. "And they're going to make me cut my hair again."

Years ago, she'd been caught writing her own lyrics over the sheet music for a cantata. She'd had to kneel before the other girls at public confession, praying for forgiveness as the prioress hacked her hair with a kitchen knife. Since then she'd never written down her songs; she tried to push ideas for new melodies from her mind.

Today's offense was far worse than making up music. She had broken the bone of the one rich non-orphan at the Incurables. She had thrown everything away.

Mino tugged gently on her braid, a little pull toward him she could still feel after he'd let go. She looked up. He wasn't laughing anymore.

"My mother had short hair," he said in a voice suddenly soft.

"You remember her?" Violetta whispered.

"Not much, but I remember that. I remember the way it felt between my fingers." He took a breath. "Have you ever noticed people around here don't talk about mothers?"

Violetta swallowed. "Maybe there's nothing for them to say."

He looked at her. "You don't remember yours?"

"I don't think about it." She felt embarrassed and looked down.

"I'm going to find her someday," Mino said. "My mother."

"How?"

"I'll do whatever it takes," he said.

They were quiet and Violetta couldn't tell whether she pitied or admired Mino. She certainly didn't share his goal. She didn't know how to respond.

"What I meant was," he said, "you'd still look nice with short hair."

Violetta's cheeks blazed with heat.

"At least you'll never look like them." He raised his chin toward the *altana*.

Violetta realized he thought those elegant women were ridiculous. Here she'd been admiring them, envying their transformations. She didn't want to let him know.

"They spend all that time trying to look like you," she said. "Venice loves a blonde." She surprised herself by reaching out to touch him. She felt the warmth of his scalp in the sunlight, the softness of his fine hair. She'd never done anything like that. She never came near having the chance to touch a boy. But it felt so natural, she didn't want to draw away. He leaned into her touch and sought her eyes. She dropped her hand.

"Don't worry about Reine," he said, his voice quieter. "Her parents will send her a new toe. Made of gold." He put on a French accent as convincing as his Fiona. "They must make those in Paris, no?"

Violetta laughed, and it made her feel better, like she might be able to go downstairs and face what she had done. But then, she wondered—

"How did you know Reine's name?"

"We know you all," he said. "You're famous."

"The *coro* girls are famous," she corrected. The music school girls were no one, yet. In Violetta's case—especially after today—she would probably be no one forever.

"You have futures here," he said. "You're valuable to the church. We're just hungry mouths. They cram ten of us in one room and try their best not to see us until they can show us the door. But you"—he raised an eyebrow at her and it made him look unbearably handsome—"you're Violetta, assistant to the renowned soprano Giustina. Future—"

"Future nothing," she said. She couldn't believe he knew her name.

"Well, that's not very sonorous. What do your friends call you?"

He made it sound like she had so many, like together all her friends had sat down and agreed upon a nickname. Laura called her Violetta. No one else went much out of their way to speak to her at all.

But she didn't want to damage Mino's image of her, false as it was. She wanted to be the girl he'd keep looking at with such bright eyes. She said the first thing that came to mind, the name of her old doll, with whom she used to imagine escaping this place, disappearing into the night.

"You can call me Letta."

"I like it."

They stayed still, looking at each other. What would happen if she touched his hair a second time, let her fingers trail down the side of his face? His cheeks were smooth, no hint of a beard, and she liked how he looked young and innocent, like her, even if his boyish wildness gave him the air of someone older. She wanted to know more about him, to come back here and be close to him.

When Mino looked away, she felt ashamed, as if he'd seen her desires in her eyes.

"I should go," she said.

"Wait," he said.

"What?"

"Do you want to know why I come up here?"

"Not Fiona?" she teased.

"Can you keep a secret?"

When she nodded, Mino crossed the roof to a retrieve a wooden violin case. Incurables boys were not taught music. How had he learned to play? This was a violation of the order of the orphanage.

It thrilled her to think of him sneaking up here to practice. She was flattered he was taking her into his confidence.

When he opened the case and lifted the instrument, her breath caught. Tucked beneath the violin was a painting. Half a painting on a piece of wood: a woman with flowing blond hair. Violetta had seen it before—in the hand of the boy she'd rescued from the wheel.

She felt winded, as if she'd just sung a full mass. This handsome young man who'd made her laugh, made her forget her troubles for a while—*why* did he have to be the boy from the wheel?

She saw it now—the same blond hair, the slope of the nose and set of the eyes so like his mother's. He'd never opened his eyes that night, or else she would have known him sooner. He had eyes you'd remember.

Violetta had been trying for more than a decade to forget that woman and her song. Now it had caught up to her at her first taste of freedom. It had disguised itself behind a mask of intrigue, and she'd been fooled.

All this made her feel she would never escape her orphandom, no matter where she went. She wanted to leave and not see Mino again.

But he'd been kind to her. He'd made her laugh. When he looked into her eyes, she felt she might become someone new.

He began to play, the opening note a beautiful G-sharp with a gentle touch of vibrato. Right away, she could tell he was special. Such wrenching soulfulness emanated through the strings that she forgot the wheel and only listened. When the melody took shape, she froze.

Over the years she had begun to think of this music as hers, but of course it wasn't. It was his.

The song was different than she remembered. He had taken the small, simple melody and raised it into something rich and soaring. He made impassioned leaps up the scale, whirling at the highest register like a leaf in a storm.

An unsuppressible urge crept into Violetta. She began to sing.

I am yours, you are mine . . .

Somehow, she sensed the song's changes, and she embellished them, collaborating with him. Out poured a fierce, ecstatic melody she had always dreamed of singing and had never believed she could. She bared herself through her song. Mino watched her closely, following her instincts, and together they improvised a tangled melody.

Violetta didn't wonder where the next words came from. She simply let them out:

I loved you ere I said hello,
I'll love you long after you go.
Farewell is neither fare nor well.

Speak not a word that cannot tell,
That cannot tell . . .

For the first time, she understood what Giustina meant when she'd said "Love is here." That *was* what Giustina said to the world with her voice. Violetta suddenly knew that this song was what she had to say: *I am yours, World. You are mine.*

It was a vow and a surrender, a manifestation of all the love she'd ever felt but could never express. She didn't have to worry that the world wouldn't receive her love, wouldn't love her back. It was infinite. It could do anything, be anything. It could take her as she was. It wouldn't abandon her.

Tears brimmed in her eyes. Never had she felt so many things so intensely at the same time: fear and heartbreak and wonder and desire all danced within her. She leaned into these emotions, singing with every forgotten part of her soul. At the end, when Mino lifted his bow from the strings, both of them were shaking.

"How did you know?" he asked as the women of the *altana* applauded their invisible musicians. "I thought that song lived only in my heart."

He didn't remember. He didn't know his mother had sung it to him. He thought he'd made it up. Violetta struggled with how to respond. She didn't want to lie to him, but how could she tell him about his mother? He'd want to know everything, and she was not prepared to part with the memory. It was hers, too.

And then there was the matter of her voice, which had blossomed through this song. She should have been proud, but she feared she would never again be able to re-create that sound, not with any song but this one. She couldn't sing this to Porpora.

Before she lost her nerve, she stepped close and put her arms around Mino. She leaned her head against his and held him, feeling his arms come around her. Her cheek to his, she gazed beyond his shoulder to the horizon.

For years, each of them had nurtured this music privately within them. Now Violetta could almost *see* how the song had entered into the world. They'd let it out, a physical force, a subtle shift of light and sky.

It was everywhere. How far would it go?

Two

MEETING LETTA CHANGED Mino. From the moment they played together, he felt he would do anything for her. Every day for weeks afterward he brought his violin to the roof at the same hour, hoping to see her. His skin browned as he lingered, practicing his vibrato under the September sun. Would she come again? He stayed until the cook expected him to serve supper to the boys. He climbed back through the attic window unwillingly.

He couldn't stop thinking about her. He could confide in no one.

By October, the weather turned cold and dark gray. *Carnevale* began on Sunday. Though its celebration never entered the Incurables, you could still breathe it in the air, like the complicated sweetness of the canals. You could feel the city's pulse quickening, even through these walls.

Up on the roof, Mino shivered, tuning his violin absently, entranced by sunlight on the dome of Il Redentore across the Giudecca Canal.

"It's like someone polished a piece of the moon and stuck it on that church." The voice startled him.

He turned, and it was Letta, at his side. His heart raced. His desire to draw closer to her made him speechless. She was all he'd thought about for weeks, and now that she stood before him, he knew his memory did her an injustice. She was as beautiful as he remembered, with her bright smile and large eyes. Her dark hair had been cut short, as she'd feared, punishment for breaking the French girl's toe. Mino liked the way it looked. But it was more than that, there was something altogether *more* to her in person: she seemed free despite every restriction of life at the Incurables. Mino got the feeling she'd been born with a spirit so big nothing could constrain it. He'd never met anyone like her.

"How old are you?" she asked.

She seemed to tower over him, and Mino straightened, embarrassed, even though he'd grown a handbreadth since the new year. He'd always been small for his age.

"I'll be sixteen this month," he said. "Or so it says on my birth card. Do you know your birthday?"

She looked across the water. "Close enough. Only because I was so young when I arrived."

How young? he wanted to know. *Who would leave you?*

"I turned sixteen in February," she said. "Do you have an apprenticeship? I heard some boys get to leave as young as twelve."

Mino wondered what else she'd heard about the dozen foundling boys who lived on his side of the Incurables. Letta spoke like leaving here was a privilege, but only the troublesome boys had apprenticeships hastily arranged by Father Marché before they turned thirteen, a way to move them out. Father liked Mino, and so did Esmeralda, the cook, and the younger boys, whom he taught woodworking to by day and forbidden card games by candlelight in the dormitory. There was no urgency to be rid of Mino, and he'd been glad of that—until now, when his lack of apprenticeship made him feel like a child. Letta made him want to be a man.

But then, if he had an apprenticeship, he wouldn't be here with her now.

"Father Marché wants a position at the *squero* for me," he said, "but I wouldn't start for another year." The boatyard in Dorsoduro made most of the gondolas in Venice. Mino had been there only once, to meet the foreman.

"Is that what you want?" Letta asked.

"It's a good position," he said. *Unheard of for an orphan*, Father Marché said. It would be a rise well above Mino's station. "I like intricate projects."

He looked down at his violin, and wanted to tell her how he'd discovered it in the attic when he was eight years old. It had seemed to him a barely living thing in need of care. The strings were broken, and the neck had been snapped nearly in two. The ebony fingerboard hung on by a few splintery shards of wood, and there was a gash in the lower bout. It looked as if it had been bashed against a wall. Mino took it into his arms and adopted it. He borrowed tools from Father Marché when they wouldn't be missed. Alone on this roof, he took the whole thing apart and taught himself to put it back together again. He restored the neck, pitching it at a higher angle than before, so the strings now arched like an elegant Venetian bridge over a canal. He'd patched the hole in the bout. The only wood he could find was a lighter grain, so you could still see where he reset it with resin, but Mino liked the visible imperfection, the way it honored the instrument's life. Over the years, he had tinkered continually, shaping the violin into many different incarnations. Each had a voice slightly but essentially different from the rest.

He wanted to tell Letta all of this, but when he looked at her, she was watching the water, melancholy in her eyes.

"Do you want to play again?" he asked, raising his violin. He wanted to bring back her smile.

"I shouldn't," she said, but her gaze and body twisted toward his violin.

"Why not?"

"Because I want to." She smiled at him. It made him stiffen everywhere. He felt transparent before her.

"Most of the things I want get me into trouble here," she said.

Was she flirting? He dared not dream so boldly. "I thought you wanted to make the *coro*."

When Letta tossed her head, her dark hair shone. "I want to make music. I want to sing my way to the horizon. The *coro* is the closest I can get." She looked out, her gaze searching the distance as she leaned against the parapet. "How do you reach the horizon, do you think?"

Mino followed her gaze to the thin blue line where sky met sea. "Keep going?"

"It's easy for you. I bet you don't have a tenth of the rules we do."

"There are still things I want." He wanted her to turn from the view, to him.

"Like what?" she whispered.

How could he tell her how she'd filled his mind for weeks? Where would he start? He looked down at the Zaterre, at a party of maskers clinking glasses on the café patio. Their laughter filtered up like smoke.

"I'd like to be down there," he said, "dressed for *carnevale*."

Letta leaned closer. Their shoulders touched and neither moved away.

"I want a *bauta*," she said.

"Me too." Foundlings at the Incurables were sheltered from nearly all the simple pleasures of childhood, but they still knew about the costumes, the masks, the great lure and art of concealment. Behind a *bauta*, you could be anyone. Paupers could flirt with noblewomen. Senators could kiss fishermen's daughters. The Venetian *bauta* covered the entire face, with holes just for the eyes and a sculpted nose. The bottom of the mask protruded far enough that the wearer could eat and drink beneath it. The fashion had become so admired, at once elegant and discreet, that most Venetians wore them year-round, all but the days expressly forbidden by the sumptuary laws of the republic. Every year the laws changed, depending on the way the Great Council voted. One year there might be twenty forbidden days; the next year there might be twenty-four, but for the rest, whomsoever desired could wear masks out on the street, in the markets, at the masquerades. Mino vowed somehow, someday to get masks for them both.

I am yours, you are mine . . .

Her voice arrived suddenly and filled him with joy. He scrambled to meet her with his bow. He held her gaze as they played. The last note of their song left Mino trembling.

Letta didn't embrace him like the first time. Though he longed to reach for her, shyness kept his arms at his sides.

"Is that the only song you know?" she asked.

"I can learn others."

"When I was younger, I used to make up songs, but . . ." She looked down at her hands, and Mino saw the scars on her palms.

He'd seen other boys caned for stealing food or missing mass, but no violence had befallen him at the Incurables. "Up here, no one would know."

"Do you ever come at night?"

He took her hand and squeezed a promise. "Tonight."

ALL THROUGH THAT winter and the following spring, Letta met Mino on the moonlit roof once a week. By May, it was warm enough to meet without first donning the musty robes from the attic crates, and the sight of her climbing up in just her nightgown made Mino gulp.

It wasn't that Letta was the first beautiful girl he'd seen; Incurables boys were naïve relative to the rest of Venice, but they weren't blind. From an early age, he'd been transfixed by the *coro* singers up in the gallery of the church. Even through the brass grille, you could see lips flash and dark eyes shine.

During his walk to his first training at the *squero* in June, the women with their feathered hats and sweet colognes had made his head spin. He knew what all Venetian men knew: that you could experience a woman's radiance through her mask. It was in the way she walked, in her laughter, and her carriage. It was in her hands. He knew that men had to earn the gift of a woman's bare face. He could imagine the thrill of getting a woman to lift her mask, but he did not desire any radiance but Letta's.

Tonight she vibrated with inspiration in the cooling September air as she came close to him on the roof, nodding at his violin. "Play an A-sharp chord."

He did, concentrating on her word, *sharp*, knifing his bow hard and true, as if slaying a dragon.

She wore the pride of a new song in her eyes as she began:

"*Who*"—she held the note, so Mino held it, too, patiently in his chord. *"Who named the moon?"*

He followed her to C-sharp minor as her song unfurled.

"Who named the heart?"

D-sharp minor now.

"Who asked the poet to turn her pain to art?"

"Beautiful, Letta!" he called, still playing, beaming at her.

"The man who named the beasts stopped too late to start. It was me." Her voice softened near the end of the refrain, eyes closed and hand on heart. Mino stabbed his violin with the most forceful E-sharp 7th of his life. *"Only Eve."*

When she finished the last deep note, she paused, eyes still closed. She looked so peaceful, like a visiting angel. Then she opened her eyes and burst out laughing.

Mino started laughing, too, the deep, abandoned laugh only these collaborations on the roof brought forth, when they channeled something holy and strong. And then she hugged him and he stilled.

"Oh, Mino."

He never dared break an embrace with Letta, unsure when one would come again.

She pulled back and sighed in blissful pride.

"I got the apprenticeship at the *squero*," he said casually, rubbing a bit of resin up his bow. He'd been aching to tell her all week, waiting for this meeting on the roof.

"Mino!" Her eyes lit with excitement—then flickered with sadness, which she tried to hide, looking away. "I'm happy for you."

"Come with me when I go," he said, putting his violin down, taking her hands.

She laughed, just as he thought she would, and he was too nervous to insist on his earnestness. If they could be together he'd do anything, give up this post, leave the republic, go anywhere. For her.

"Fairy tales," she said.

"Letta," he said, but she flinched away.

"Good night, Mino. Congratulations."

ONE MONTH LATER, just over a year since their first accidental meeting on the roof, Mino paced the stairwell to the second floor of the boys' dormitory in the west wing. It was cold for early October. A penetrating dampness gripped the shadowy corners and old stone walls of the Incurables. Raindrops fell through a gap in the roof onto the mossy stone near his feet, setting an anxious tempo for his troubled mind.

He gripped his half token, his thumb rubbing the painted woman's chipped hair. His nails were chewed to the quick, his stockings slipping from the ribbons tied at his knees. He scarcely noticed. He was deep in a fantasy conversation.

"It isn't much . . ." he tried beneath his breath, flipping his blond hair from his eyes. *Be honest.*

"It's nothing really . . ."

Madonna, he hated how flimsy he sounded.

"You deserve more."

Closer.

"And one day, we'll have it."

Mino had felt the first seed of this plan the day he met Letta. By now, they had a thousand private jokes. They had shared a dozen dreams of the horizon. He'd begun to understand what she meant when she said she wanted more. Mino wanted more now, too. But where Letta's desire was infinite to the point of being unknowable, Mino wanted one thing. He wanted it with all his heart. So absolute was Mino's love for Letta, he felt it defined him.

Over the past year, he'd watched her blossom from a thin, angular girl of sixteen, with pretty black eyes and a wild mane of dark hair, into a self-possessed young woman. Her eyes, still large and spellbinding, were no longer the first thing you noticed about her. There was an inner light within Letta that she let show more and more. It lit her pale skin, her small lips, her soft words, and impulsive mannerisms. It illuminated Mino and made him feel as if he shone, too.

"Someday"—he practiced in the stairwell—"we'll reach the horizon."

There. That's what he would say. Rehearsing the words in his mind, he hurried from the stairwell. He was late for his appointment with Father Marché, who wished to discuss some final details of Mino's apprenticeship before he left for the *squero*. Mino would spend the afternoon at the gondola maker's before returning to the Incurables in time for vespers.

Tonight he would leave his parting gift for Letta on the roof, the scroll of good paper tied with a ribbon, on which he had written the score and lyrics of the first song they'd performed together. Drawing those notes, spelling out the words he knew so well, he had imagined her reading them after he left. He hoped she would sense through the old lyrics a new promise that this was not the end. Soon he would ask her to join him outside the *ospedale*'s walls, but first he had to prepare a life he could be proud of, one that could offer her the freedom she deserved.

In the morning he would walk out of the Incurables with only the clothes on his back and one spare set. He had already sneeked his violin out; it sat in his new apartment. His other possessions of value all fit in his pocket or beneath his cloak: his half token from his mother, the two *bauta* purchased the week before, and the gold wedding band he hoped to give Letta. The first time he returned to the Incurables after visiting his new apartment, he had seen the gold band winking from the side of the street and it had felt like fate, a confirmation of his plan.

With his first payment from the *squero* he had gone straight to the shop on the Fondamenta Priuli. The cost for the *bauta* was only a few soldi, but it had felt like a fortune. He had never spent money before, never had a soldo to spend. And yet, he would have paid anything for the masks to see Letta's face when he made this simple dream come true for her.

As soon as he could afford it, he would buy them both black tricornes to secure their masks, and then the black wool capes known as *tabarri.* Then they would truly be ready to experience *carnevale* like Venetians.

All week Mino had slept upon his treasures, laying his face against the masks' curved forms through the down of his pillow, fitting himself into them like a lover, his hand clutched around the ring. One day soon, he would bring them out.

❃

At last it was Sunday, the start of *carnevale,* one week since he had left the Incurables. This morning the music school girls would take their annual outing to hear the *coro* perform at another *sestieri*'s church, and Mino would seize the chance to find Letta and make his love plain.

He woke early, wandered from his apartment nearly all the way back to the Incurables. He wanted to trace the steps she'd take on her way to him.

He skirted the busy Zattere, turning north and veering in the direction of the city's center, San Marco. He walked in the eternal twilight of the alleys carved between the leaning, high-walled buildings. The *calli* were narrow. The city hugged him, only a sliver of sky visible over the buildings as he passed merchants offering stewed pears, knife sharpening, and cat castration.

When Mino used to take this route to the *squero*, he left himself double the time he needed to get there. The women on their stoops always held him up with some urgent request: one needed a long arm to help hang her washing, another a strong hand to lop off the tough stem of her winter squash, a third might want his opinion on the price of watermelon. Mino enjoyed obliging these women as much as he enjoyed the dim light of the alleys; the lack of sky above; the secret, hidden feeling of his city. Today he wore his mask and hummed to himself as he wound along the narrow *calli*, threading north and west, over wooden bridges, under low stone passageways, thrilled by the thought of finding new paths to get lost along with Letta. He heard their music all around him.

When he veered left at the café on the corner of rio Terà, the *calle* stopped short and opened wide onto the magnificent broad day of Campo Santa Margherita. The huge square was paved in white stone, surrounded by shops and apartments. It was one of the largest squares in Venice, could hold a thousand people during parades. A dozen entrances rendered it bright with constantly changing crowds, all masked, all rushing together in a great pastel tide. The air smelled like roasting fowl and cinnamon-spiced nuts.

It reminded Mino of a moment near the end of his favorite of Porpora's motets, when the full *coro* came together in a single note of glory. Music as big as the heavens. That moment, that music, was what it felt like to arrive on the Campo Santa Margherita.

This was where he would wait for her.

It was only midmorning, but already, *carnevale* was a force on the streets. The costumed masquerades would last six months. During Mino's youth, cloistered in the Incurables, these months had seemed endless. Now half a year seemed hardly long enough to celebrate his independence. He knew that once *carnevale* ended there were many other feasts to fill the year. In May, he would finally get to go to San Marco to watch the doge throw a ring into the Adriatic on Ascension Day, the symbolic anniversary of Venice's marriage to the sea. And come September, the annual Historical Regatta would be the highlight of his work at the boatyard. But no festival compared to *carnevale*. Full of risk and pleasure, it was the right moment to begin the rest of his life with Letta.

His white mask covered his face, and when he looked to the left, to the right, his restricted vision felt somehow wider. He had capped the mask with a new black tricorne. He held the second mask in his hand, the ring in his coat pocket.

An eternity passed before he saw them, the sea of girls dressed in matching blue cloaks, a spectacle of youth, bare faces in a city of masks. The silver-haired prioress walked in front, arms folded before her, her eyes cast modestly low. She led her charges toward the Basilica dei Frari, where they would watch the *coro* perform before the feast.

Walking in line, the music school girls were chanting, their beautiful low voices attracting gazes. Here was Reine, who'd limped for a year after her toe was broken before she finally gave it up. He didn't see Letta. Her dark hair would be under her white cotton bonnet, just like the other girls'. He imagined her at the rear of the pack, annoyed at being let outside only to be marched into another church.

She loved Venice's nighttime glow—the candles flickering through curtained apartment windows, the lanterns bobbing from gondolas on the canals. She had memorized the differences between the horizons to the north, south, east, and west. She dreamed of walking on those lines—but she couldn't bear walking *in* one. She found the chaperoned outings outside the Incurables unbearably rigid, at odds with the city. She always returned from them in a foul mood. But maybe not today.

Now they were close upon him, and Mino pressed his back against the stone of a building, nervous.

And then, there she was, her face was as bright and clear to Mino as the first notes of an aria. Violetta's dark eyes were enchanting beneath her ebony hair, now just long enough to gather in a short braid. Half of it fell out and brushed her cheeks, but she didn't seem to notice.

She was neither tall nor short, neither noticeably thin nor heavy—and yet, she was so different from other girls, even in her matching clothes, even with her gaze on the cobblestones. She walked among them but was not of them. Her spine was straighter, her shoulders looser. For several steps, her eyes were closed, and he realized she was writing music in her mind. He counted her steps. She was dancing, her slippered feet gliding in time to a song only she could hear.

She passed without seeing him, turned the corner of rio Terà, and for an instant this felt like a horrible omen. But he had a plan, a vision for how today should go.

He moved between pairs of lovers, caught up to the sea of Incurables girls just as they entered the open *campo*. Pigeons scattered. Café tables of masked patrons lingered over crystal goblets of *acqaioli*. Church bells rang from the medieval stone tower of Santa Margherita at the far north corner. For a moment, the prioress let them pause and marvel at the singularly Venetian spectacle of costumed men, women, and children at ten o'clock on a Sunday morning.

Mino heard the gasps of the youngest girls. He felt their wonder coming off them like a glare. He wasted no time. For a few more moments, no one would notice him. He found Letta at the back of the crowd.

He took her hand, squeezed. She looked over her shoulder at him as if she knew his touch before the sight of him.

"It's me," he said and gave her hand a tug. He'd meant to be smiling and mischievous as he slipped the second mask into her hand. But beneath his mask his face was strained in terror.

"Let's go," he managed to croak, and God love her, she didn't even look back.

As soon as they'd hurried around a corner, he drew her into an alcove under a tiny marble Madonna.

"What are we doing?" she asked, laughing.

"You'll see." He held the second mask up and she grinned.

"How did you find me at the moment I most needed to be free?"

"Because I know you." He pressed the *bauta* to her face. He reached his hands around the back of her head and tied the knot. He felt her breath and silken hair on his arm as he tied the bow. He stood back to look at her. The sight of her—disguised to everyone but him—moved Mino almost to tears. "It's perfect."

She touched the waxed linen surface above her cheek, ran her fingers over the raised nose and the eyeholes.

"I can't believe this," she said. "Thank you."

"Turn your cloak inside out," he said. "It will be less noticeable." He helped her so that its brilliant blue was on the inside, and the more mundane navy wool was exposed. She was radiant. He wanted to kiss her but knew he must wait. From here it was a three-minute walk to his apartment. He had rented it in anticipation of this moment. He yearned to get there, to show her, to close the door behind her and feel, at last, at home.

But he knew how she was feeling, to have only just broken free. Her first time outside on her own. She'd need to run, to breathe, to wonder. So instead of pointing her in the direction of calle de le Pazienza, Mino said, "Which way should we go?"

This delighted her. He could see her smile arrive in the slight tilt of the mask. She took his hand and started running. The wind on Mino's skin, the strength in the knot of their fingers, and the pounding of his heart produced a joy he'd never known. They were doing it. They were free, together. They never had to go back.

"Duck!" Letta shouted, laughing as they barely dodged a smoking bucket of grilled fish being lowered from a window by a rope. A hawker caught the bucket just before it hit them, baring his fileting knife at them in annoyance.

When they passed a *magazzen*, the humblest of taverns that smelled of cheap, sweet liquor, Letta turned to him, pressed close. "Should we take a drink?"

He wasn't used to her sounding nervous when she laughed.

"Not there," Mino said. He had a bottle of better wine in his apartment. He had a toast in mind. "Let's keep going," he said, and she nodded. Her feet flew.

They ran until they reached the elegant stone bridge at Ca' Foscari. There both of them stopped. They were out of breath, but there was something else that held them back. For Mino it was a sense that to cross a bridge together meant something, and they would arrive on the other side different.

There were five wide stone steps leading up the bridge, five more leading down the other side. In the center, on the short, flat stretch of stone, a dozen other masked Venetians lingered to take in the view.

Violetta pulled him up the steps, and at the bridge's center, she leaned against the parapet. Wind whipped her hair. She squeezed his hand, and he tried to see the view through her eyes. She was looking north, where this minor canal ended in the Grand Canal, the central artery that pulsed through Venice, separating Dorsoduro from the city's other neighborhoods. If the minor canals were violin solos, the Grand Canal was a full orchestra—a dozen times broader, faster, holding hundreds of passing ships in her arms. It was lined on either side by the finest palazzi, offering the most prized view in the city.

They could hop from the bridge into a gondola now. They could reach the Grand Canal in minutes. Was this what she was thinking? How much farther they could go?

With her face obscured behind her *bauta*, Mino was more aware of her slender wrists, her graceful neck, the way she stood with her toes pointed out. He could not wait to raise her *bauta* in the sanctuary of his apartment, where they wouldn't have to worry about being seen.

"Marvelous," she whispered, shaking her head. She wiped tears from her eyes, then grew worried about damaging the mask, dabbing her fingers underneath.

"Don't worry." He took out a handkerchief, tucked it under her mask.

"About what?" she said.

"Anything."

All around them Mino saw couples like them, holding hands and basking in the day, in the sun on the canal, the songs of gondoliers, and the anonymity of their masks.

He wanted to do it now. He wanted to take her in his arms and kiss her with all the love in his heart. He wanted to tell her what he planned for them. It took everything he had to resist doing it now, here, forever.

That might scare her. He could not act impulsively, that was Letta's territory. He had made his plans with her in mind—every little oddity accounted for. He would do it as he planned.

"This is worth tenfold whatever punishment the prioress concocts," Letta said. "Where did you get the masks? They look practically new."

"There's more," he said.

She tilted her head at him in a way she never had before. That alone was worth it.

He took her hand and they ran back down the bridge, back through the narrow *calli*. Mino led the way, avoiding Campo Santa Margherita. By now the girls were gathered inside. The *coro* was singing in the nave, behind the brass grille. If Mino had not escaped with Violetta, she would have been packed in a pew, miserably aware of life vibrating outside.

But she was with him. They stopped before number twenty-six and Mino took out his key.

He said nothing about what the place was, and he felt her curiosity as he opened the door and nodded for her to go in. He led her up the staircase to the fourth floor.

The apartment had been arranged for him by Sior Baldona, the foreman at the *squero* and the head of its guild. The first time Mino had seen it, it had seemed impossibly luxurious, even though the ceilings were low and it was a quarter of the size of the dormitory where he slept at the Incurables. This was all his. It could be theirs. It had a small hearth with a stove on which to fit a cast-iron kettle. It had three rooms—a bedroom, a small study, and a main central room—and each had its own window. One looked west over a small canal, one looked down on the *calle* and the corner café. The bedroom window faced only a close neighboring building, but was Mino's favorite because of the fragrant potted jasmine he could breathe in when he slid up the pane. He could picture Letta there.

When he had labored over cleaning his apartment, when he had strewn it with gathered jasmine petals that morning, he had imagined her happy beneath its roof.

Now he saw it in a different light. Was it enough?

Violetta was wandering the apartment, touching the small hearth in the alcove, peering into the room where a little desk and chair sat. He had imagined her sitting there, reading or writing music, singing. Could she imagine the same? She leaned against the doorframe of the bedroom and studied the narrow cot, the table with the books, the window. She saw Mino's violin and this seemed to startle her. After that she noticed the flowers, all the blossoms he had placed atop the bed.

She turned to him, taking off her mask. Her beauty staggered him, but she looked hurt, her lips parted and her eyes softened into sadness.

"Mino?"

He realized she still thought he had left her when he left the Incurables. He flung off his own mask and took her in his arms. "Yes. It's mine."

"Congratulations." Her voice was as strained as her body, which pressed back against his arms.

"Letta, that light in your eyes when I held up your mask," he said, "that's all I want from my life."

She looked down. "Don't get used to it," she said. "After today, they'll probably never allow me outside the walls again." She raised a hand to his cheek. "It will have been worth it. I'm happy for you. Now I'll be able to imagine you here."

"Don't go back," he said, reaching for her hands. "Stay here. With me."

She laughed. "And do what?"

"What do you mean?" They would be together. What did it matter what she did?

"All I know is music," she said. "If I don't join the *coro*, I can't sing in Venice."

She could sing here, with him. He almost said that aloud, but then he heard how ridiculous it was. Of all the things Mino had worried over, the restrictive Venetian law forbidding orphans from singing outside their hospital had not been one of them. He swayed where he stood.

Of course, he knew of Letta's talent; he had seen the way she lived through singing, but he had never seen her perform before an audience. When she complained of her rehearsals with the maestro, he must not have heard that there was wonder in the experience, too. He had thought it was just singing that brought her joy. He had thought the *coro* life was the best she could imagine at the Incurables. He had thought they could play together, here, and be happy. For Mino was happiest when he played with her. Now he saw it wasn't enough.

"There must be ways," he said quickly. "I'll help you find them."

"Mino, the punishment for a *coro* girl singing outside the Incurables—"

"I know," he said. *Coro* girls took strict vows pledging their allegiance to their hospital. Mino had never heard of a *coro* girl caught performing elsewhere, but he knew such a case would be taken up by the government. The Venetian Republic had come to rely on *coro* voices funding its churches, not private hands. So a *coro* girl—and anyone who hired her—might face heavy fines and a hearing before Venice's ultimate judges, the merciless Council of Ten. The Ten were quick to imprison; terrible things happened in Venetian prisons.

But Violetta hadn't taken those vows.

"You're not in the *coro* yet," he said. "Disguised, you might sing anywhere. If anyone can outsmart the authorities, it's you."

She laughed, an odd sound he didn't trust. "This was fun, Mino. A great goodbye. I'll never forget it—"

"Letta. I love you. I always have." His voice was shivery, unrecognizable. He was wrought with nerves, but he knew if he didn't say it now, he'd lose his chance. He stepped close and put his arms around her. He pressed his lips to hers, more lightly than he wanted to. He pulled away before he could tell how she'd responded to the kiss. "Will you marry me?"

She gaped at him. For once she had nothing to say. He was expecting this. He would persevere. How many times before had one convinced the other to take a risk? This was what they did.

But then, Mino hadn't been expecting this change in her eyes. They lost their light. He'd thought she would feel comforted by the apartment, by his practicality. She could go on being Letta, wild and free, and he would keep her safe.

"You feel guilty about leaving me there. But this"—she gestured at the apartment, at the flowers—"this is foolishness."

"You don't love me," he said.

"I do love you," she replied, hotly, and Mino hung his head.

Love, as Mino felt it, meant taking your beloved in your arms, tipping her lips to yours, and saying *I love you* with all of yourself.

"There's one part of my life I didn't want to change, Mino, and it was you. And it's changed." She sighed. "Marry someone better than me."

"There is no such thing."

She was crying now, silent tears she wiped before they spilled down her cheeks. "I can't give you what you want."

He understood. "Children."

"I can't."

"Letta—"

"I would fail them," she said firmly. "I would fail you, too."

"I don't believe you. How many times have you sung those words to me?"

"They weren't my words."

He stared at her. What did she mean?

"I've never hidden myself from you," she said, trembling now. "I am not a wife. I cannot be a mother—"

"Not all mothers are terrible. My mother loved me. There's not much I remember of her, but I know that to be true. I believe she had no choice." Without realizing it, his hand had gone into his pocket and pulled out his half token. He fingered the silver chain, studied the painted woman, wishing for guidance from her more than ever. He still believed he'd reunite with his mother somehow, one day. Now that he was out of the Incurables, he would find her.

He noticed Letta looking coldly at the token in his hands. It had always seemed to annoy her when he took it out.

"What if you're wrong?" she asked.

Tears welled in his eyes. "People need family, Letta. They need love. You don't have to fear it. Not with me."

She turned away. "You're wrong about everything," she told him, and her voice was like the winter wind. With her back still to him, she said, "How do you think I knew that song, Mino? It's not our song. It was hers."

He touched her shoulder, turned her to him, tipped her chin up with his finger until he could meet her gaze. In her huge, dark eyes Mino saw resolution. But there was also something new—fear.

"I heard your mother sing it. I saw her, that night."

His hands fell away from her. He had felt those words rising through Letta's breast before her lips spoke it, but he didn't understand. Was she lying? What could she possibly know? These questions were too big for him to fathom.

"Mino," she said, reaching for him. "Let me explain."

He shook his head and it hit him: she'd said no. She had not even considered his proposal. Worse, she had used his mother to push him away.

The apartment seemed to cave in around him. He couldn't stay. He turned for the door.

❂

MAMMA? HE COULDN'T see her face. Surely he used to know it, but he couldn't summon it anymore. She was sky behind sifting clouds to him. She was silt at the bottom of the canal. For a long time now, when he looked for her, there was only an atmosphere of doom.

Was it true what Letta had told him? Had she heard his mother's song? Could she have told him even the smallest detail about her? Could she have helped Mino search for her, to find some trace of the family he desperately desired?

He had a horrible sense that Letta's words *were* true, for how else would she know that song? But then, why had she never told him until now? She knew how much he longed to find his mother.

If she'd lied—was that worse? Either way, she did not love him. She had given no thought to his proposal before she turned him down.

A hard rain arrived without warning. It shocked him out of his thoughts and made him aware he had walked back to the Incurables. To the west wall, to the wheel. He fell on his knees and began to weep. Harsh, choking sobs racked through him as he leaned his head against the stone.

The rain came down. He grabbed the metal handle. Was this what his mother had done that night? Where was the one who'd given him life? Why didn't Letta love him enough?

"Who's there?" a voice called from within the kitchen.

Suddenly Mino felt how cold he was. He looked in, saw eyes on the other side. Reine, the French girl.

"I heard a noise." She squinted. "You're the boy who just left for the *squero*—"

"Let me in." He still had the cook's key, which opened the door from the kitchen to the outside. He passed it through the wheel.

After several moments struggling with the key, she let him in, opening the door shyly, jumping back when he pushed past her. He could barely stand through his grief.

"Are you all right?" Her fingers felt his coat. "You're soaked."

"What are you doing on this side of the hospital?" he asked as she slid the cloak down his arms, draping it over a chair.

"Did you hear Violetta's run off? We all have to look for her."

"I didn't hear," Mino said numbly, sinking into the chair. Had anyone connected him to Letta? They saw each other only on the roof. No one knew of their friendship.

"It's like her to ruin the one day the rest of us get to go outside," Reine said. Mino looked up. Reine thought she was suffering at Letta's hands.

"You don't look well, Mino," she said. "Do you want a drink?"

"Nothing," he said.

He didn't know she knew his name. Her hair was loose from its braid, and it was rain damp, too, but her cloak was dry. Some of the other boys spoke about Reine, how beautiful she was, how different from the other girls, because she had money, because she had parents. She moved differently, spoke differently. But Letta had also spoken of her over the years, and what Mino felt most strongly was that Reine lacked the capacity to love anything as Mino loved Letta. Love took imagination.

"I've wanted to meet you," Reine shocked him by whispering close to his lips.

Mino stayed still. He hurt so much he did not feel on solid ground. He noticed her arms coming close, her chin tilting up. Her face approaching his.

She kissed him. And in his unmoored state, he rose to his feet and kissed her back. He wanted to lose himself in another. He put his hands on her hips, her waist. He held fast and kissed deeply, blindly, even as his heart said no. He should have been kissing the woman he loved, not this stranger who smelled of sweet cologne. Her shoulders were wider, her bearing denser than Letta's. But she felt sturdy, like something he could hold on to. She drew him against the wall, loosening the ties of her cloak and sliding her body free. Her legs wrapped around him and her body shifted until he held her aloft with his hands under her thighs.

"You found a taker."

Mino dropped Reine and spun around.

Letta. What had he done? The disgust on her face made her unrecognizable. She looked vicious—eyes narrowed, jaw clenched, face washed of color. Regret coursed through Mino. How could he have kissed Reine?

"Letta—"

"I saw her," Letta said, her voice slow and low. "I saw your mother put you in the wheel."

He wanted to wake from this nightmare back into his dreams, but Letta's gaze locked him in place. She was another person.

"I've never seen such relief as I saw in your mother's face leaving you."

Something twisted inside Mino. He stared at her in horror, in rage, as she pulled something from her cloak pocket. It was the score he'd written with their song, his promise to her left on the roof.

I am yours, you are mine . . .

Now her hands tore at it, shredding the paper and tossing it into the kitchen's hearth. There was such anger in her eyes as it burned, anger so dark Mino thought he might never know its depths. For once, he did not want to try. It took such energy to know Letta. He had loved that about her. But now, he was exhausted. He wanted to disappear. His hand went to the half token in his pocket. His fingers wrapped around it.

Slowly he became aware of footsteps coming closer.

"We found her!" Reine shouted, and Mino wrested his gaze from Letta to follow Reine's waving arm. The prioress ran down the hallway toward them, surrounded by a chorus of maestri and *zie*. "Here she is. Here's Violetta."

Letta watched the prioress advancing, then her eyes darted toward the exits in the room. She met his gaze and raised an eyebrow. Yesterday he would have thought she was suggesting the two of them run together. Today, he saw the dark flash in her eyes, and he knew she didn't love him.

When the prioress's arms closed around her, Letta gave less of a fight than Mino expected. She slackened. She didn't even look at him as they led her away.

He left the Incurables. He could never return.

Three

Three weeks of solitary meals. Five weeks of scrubbing floors. Shorn hair, again. Public confession before the other girls each night. No alms walks or outings for a year. Her name in the maestro's probation book, again. Violetta's punishment touched every part of her days. But it could not touch her.

"Why did you do it?" Laura asked, coming to her bed that night. She knew only that Violetta had slipped away from the group, missed the *coro* performance, and returned hours later. Mino had always been Violetta's secret.

"I thought it would be worth it."

"Was it?" Laura asked, aghast.

Violetta saw the bridge at Ca' Foscari in her mind. She saw the view of the Grand Canal and felt Mino at her side. "At first it was the best day of my life."

She couldn't bear to tell Laura anything more. Only Reine knew something had passed between Violetta and Mino. Violetta expected the French girl to betray her at the first chance, but the secret stayed between them. Perhaps because Reine could have been expelled for kissing Mino. Violetta did not like sharing a secret with the French girl. She wanted the pain of him to herself.

She made herself ill remembering her last words to him, hearing them over and over as she carried her bucket up and down the stairs, as she ate her lonely soup, as she sat in the confessional before the priest.

"Bless me, Father, for I have sinned." She leaned on the partition, feeling the dampness at her forehead and her breast from the holy water's anointment. "It has been one month since my last confession."

"And what sins have you committed since then?" Father Marché's question was so familiar, his cadence always precisely the same, kind but tired, a little bored.

Violetta always gave her rote response: acts of laziness and selfishness, disobeying the prioress, taking the Lord's name in vain. Not today. Her words choked her. She could hardly get them out.

"I have lied to a friend."

Father looked at her through the grate. He'd never done that. "This weighs on you."

She nodded; tears spilled from her eyes. "It is unforgivable."

"Nothing is unforgivable with penance and contrition," he said with a kind of faith Violetta could not muster. He went on about Hail Marys; she said them aloud in a daze. He gave her absolution, but it did nothing to ease her mind or heart. As she left the confessional, she felt diseased by her own actions.

Mino thought she didn't care. But apart from music, he was the best thing in her life. When they played together on the roof, Violetta knew that joy was real. Still, their paths had to diverge. There was no way around it. She had always known there was a limit to their friendship.

Mino would go on to have a life beyond the Incurables. Violetta could not. She wanted a brilliant future for him, full of the family he longed for and deserved. She couldn't give him that. She would not bring children into this difficult world.

She had seen a mother abandon her son. She had been abandoned. Caring for a child was a greater responsibility than she was built for—and an even greater leap of faith. She would not be a mother worth having, so she could not be a mother at all.

His proposal had surprised her. He couldn't know how seeing him in the wheel had shaped her. She should have told him what she'd seen of his mother sooner, but she didn't want that night to haunt him. And neither had she wanted to revisit it, to answer questions. She knew he longed to find his mother, still carried that half token. Violetta did not know his mother's fate, but her instinct told her his search would not end happily.

He had to make his own way in the world. She had wanted him to find everything he wanted, to never worry about her or this place. To remember her with affection.

She'd ruined that and it shattered her. She regretted deeply tearing up his letter, their song.

Dark and rainy weeks dragged by before she found a clear night to escape to the roof. She paused in the attic, clutching Letta, afraid to go on. His baritone laughter, his dulcet violin, his hair in his eyes as he gazed across the water at Giudecca—these had become as much a part of the view as the dome of Salute and the palazzi across the water, the white pillars of Il Redentore. Lanterns lit the gondolas going to and from Giudecca, silhouetting the oarsmen in their dark cloaks and heavy scarves. As she climbed out the window, she smelled the afternoon's rain on the *calli*. How could she stand it without him?

The wind cut cold across the water and the sky was filmed with thin, fast clouds. She drew her cloak closer about her.

Christmas was coming. *Carnevale* would soon wind down for its December pause. During the two weeks of Advent, Venetians would flood the Incurables. It was a merry time of year at the hospital, but Violetta could not feel the season's joy.

She intended to stay on the roof until she stopped expecting Mino's arm to fall around her waist, stopped listening for his jokes about the passersby below. She was glad of the darkness, the *calli* blending together below. The night made it impossible to look for the route she had taken between Mino's apartment and here. Now part of her wondered why she had returned, why she hadn't headed for the horizon?

The roof throbbed with his absence. She fell to her knees and sobbed. She would come back tomorrow. She would try again to make it hers.

FEVER CAME TO the Incurables in early December. First Laura complained of sweats and heart palpitations. Then Olivia fell gravely ill. Soon most of the girls on Violetta's floor were sick. She hoped the disease would infect her, too—that something else beside Mino's absence would take hold and lay her low.

By the twelfth day of December, lessons reminded Violetta of a capon carcass picked clean. She heard only holes in the music—where Laura's violin should have been during the first allegro, where the missing contralto singers made the sopranos sound indolent, as if the ten of them shared a single lung. They performed a pitiful imitation of Porpora's oratorio. At least no one besides the prioress would have to hear them.

In the year since she had first sung with Mino on the roof, Violetta had tried to replicate that sound in her music lessons. But even as she worked with Giustina on her range and flexibility, even as she improved, she never could find the grace that came so easily with Mino. Since he'd left, it had only gotten worse. Her voice sounded as clumsy as when she was a child.

Reine, healthy as ever, had been given the aria that morning. It was Giustina's part, but neither Reine nor Violetta could approach their mentor's angelic tones. Violetta tried not to listen. Before she had hated the French girl for her wealth, snobbery, and family. Now Reine also embodied Violetta's deepest regret. She couldn't look at Reine without seeing Mino's devastated face.

She had believed him and his love when he proposed—even if she couldn't accept. Then she had seen the passion in his lips and hands on Reine. She had felt a fool. Though what she had done was worse. The priest may have absolved her, but she knew her lie was unforgivable.

Reine's voice snagged on a note in an ascending melisma, and the prioress rapped her podium. "Again," she commanded sharply.

Now that Violetta had started thinking of Mino, it was hard to stop. She was getting better at pushing him from her thoughts, but still he found ways in. Yesterday she'd breathed in the scent of lemon in the courtyard, and instantly she was standing atop the ponte Foscari, gazing with him at the Grand Canal, smelling the cologne of a woman to their left. She hadn't even remembered that woman—nor anyone else on the bridge that day—until she smelled the lemon and was back there with Mino. If only they could have stayed in that moment, before they'd ever hurt each other.

❋

AFTER LESSONS, the prioress approached Violetta and handed her a beaked white mask, the ones the doctors wore during plague. Its beak was filled with disinfecting essences, meant to block the vapors of the sick.

"Laura wants to see you."

Violetta raced down to the infirmary, fearing the worst. She could count on one hand the number of times she had been inside the hospital's infirmary. The syphilitics there were kept almost as separated from the music school girls as the boys were. Violetta stopped at the door to put on the mask, tying the ribbons over the back of her shorn hair. She could not help but think of Mino tying the ribbon of her mask on that doomed afternoon.

She pushed into the room, dizzied by the stench of the steaming holywood tea that made the patients sweat. In the back corner, at least a dozen fevered orphan girls lay sequestered. The atmosphere was doleful and uncomfortably hot, though most of the patients shivered.

An overwhelmed nurse in a beaked mask made harried rounds among the beds, the syphilitics, and the girls. Violetta felt for her. She was a *figlia di commun*, someone who used to be in the music school but had never progressed to the *coro*. She'd likely die here, catching the worst of one sickness or another. Another failed musician would take her place.

When Violetta spotted Laura, she rushed to her, relieved to find her propped on two pillows, alert. Her curly hair looked dirty and her skin was pale.

"You look wonderful," Violetta said.

"I look like death. How were lessons?"

"Curse lessons," Violetta said. "Do you want me to bring your violin?"

Laura licked chapped lips, swallowed. "Olivia died this morning."

Violetta gasped. Olivia saved breakfast for Violetta when she was late. Both girls had been born the same winter. Violetta had known her all her life.

Laura whispered, "I'm next."

Violetta took Laura's shoulders. "You will not die. I need you."

Laura's eyes dampened. Violetta's did, too. At last, a smile cracked Laura's lips. "God knows that's true."

Both girls laughed. It was an anguished sound, and soon tears rolled down their cheeks.

Then Laura grew quiet, looking over Violetta's shoulder. Violetta followed her gaze. They were carrying another girl in.

"Giustina," Violetta whispered, standing up.

"Go," Laura said.

Violetta rushed to her *sottomaestra*, who slipped in and out of consciousness as the nurses brought in another cot. Giustina's skin was deep crimson. She writhed, gripped by a fever dream. Violetta felt the heat radiating from her body.

Kneeling beside Giustina, Violetta began to hum the aria from Porpora's oratorio. Giustina didn't open her eyes, but she stilled. Violetta stroked her hair, now singing the words, now a little louder, feeling her way through the song like a prayer. She closed her own eyes and imagined herself up on the roof, surrendering with a quiet intensity to the crescendo of high notes at the song's end.

She opened her eyes to the sound of applause. It was a syphilitic patient a few beds down, a woman not much older than Violetta, with bright green eyes.

"I love a skillful crescendo," she said, her own voice surprisingly smooth, so quiet Violetta had to lean closer. "I used to go to the opera twice a week." She winced, closing her eyes for a moment to catch her breath before continuing. "Sometimes we hear your music through the walls. If what you just sang can't heal your friend, I don't know what can." She made the sign of the cross.

Violetta was moved, imagining this frail woman in her previous life, filled with operas and excitement. How odd to have both lived beneath this roof and never seen each other before. "I'll come back tomorrow."

The woman smiled wryly. "I'll be here."

Violetta looked down at Giustina, who was sleeping peacefully. In the corner, Laura was, too.

"Love is here," Violetta whispered to her *sottomaestra*.

As she stepped into the courtyard, someone touched her shoulder. She turned to see a tall man removing his own beaked mask. It was Porpora.

"You're in the music school," he said, his voice a rich baritone. "Giustina is your *sottomaestra*, is she not?"

"Yes, Maestro," she said, her heart racing. He had never spoken to her directly. Had he heard her singing in there? The thought was mortifying. She hadn't even been sitting up straight.

"She's taught you well," he said.

"She's a good teacher. She trained Reine, too." The words rushed out, and she hated that she'd brought up the French girl, but she didn't want Porpora to lose esteem for Giustina, thinking she wasted time on Violetta's mediocre talent. At least Reine had an air of stardom.

"Come," Porpora said. "Let us pray for Giustina's recovery. Then you and I shall discuss a new aria."

⁂

THE COPYIST BROUGHT in two sheets of paper so fresh the ink still shone. Violetta sat across from the maestro in his office, reading his recent music, her spine straight as a violin's bow. She was afraid to break whatever spell had seated Porpora across from her. Any graceless word or movement might alert him to his mistake.

Porpora was efficient but he was not tidy. Papers and books of music overflowed out of his desk. An oboe sat in the corner next to a pair of red silk slippers. The air smelled like anise and dust. Violetta wondered what he went home to at night. Where did he take off his wig? Did he have a wife and children? What was *he* trying to say with his music?

He was speaking intimately of how she must perform his new aria at Sunday's mass. Violetta? Singing the aria. With the *coro*. Before an audience of a thousand people. She worked to appear at ease.

"During Advent," Porpora said, looking at his music, "everything anticipates the coming of the savior. It is a time of intensity and expectation, the perfect mood for the music I have written. But most of the people you will sing to Sunday are coming back to mass after six weeks of *carnevale*'s abandon. And now they will make no more masquerades until after Christmas. They are in mourning."

Porpora laughed, and Violetta made a laugh-like sound. She was so nervous that if he had waddled like a pigeon she would have done the same.

"It is your job to give them anticipation. Anticipate Christ . . . anticipate the resurgence of reveling after Christmas. Remind them that this is not goodbye to joy. *Carnevale* is a lover, but God is home. Your voice must welcome them home."

"It's an odd metaphor for an orphan, *sior*," Violetta said and he looked at her sharply. "I take your meaning," she added quickly. She would not miss the chance to sing with the *coro*.

"Perhaps you're right," Porpora said, setting down the music and tilting his head toward her. "Do you have a better metaphor?"

"Maybe *carnevale* is a dream, and God is wakefulness. Maybe your music is the lark that draws the soul from one to the other."

He looked at her. "Maybe you are the lark."

She dropped her eyes. She was no lark and they both knew it. There was only one Giustina. But other birds could be counted on to squawk in the morning. She could at least do that.

She scanned the score. The aria was da capo, not long but quite high, meandering outside her comfortable tonality. She grew nervous reading the first section, imagining her voice finding its high notes. The next section was lower but faster. And then the return to the beginning. She could hear Giustina making this music soar. It seemed a shame to waste on Violetta.

"Would you like to practice?" Porpora asked. His mouth turned up at the corners when he registered her shock.

She stood, smoothed her dress. She cleared her throat and hoped he didn't see her shaking as she straightened her shoulders and thought of all Giustina had taught her:

Your ribs are a cage; your mouth is a door that frees your voice.
A note is a traveler whose mind is on her next stop.
Bravery buys more than talent.

Violetta did not think about singing in front of the entire church on Sunday. She was only here, in this room, with nothing but the maestro and Giustina's training and a crisp new sheet of music. She filled her lungs and began.

The beginning was wonderful, a C-sharp minor surprisingly suited to her voice, smooth and connected with long legato phrasing. She devoted herself to it, and when she reached the next section, with its contrasting staccatos and major notes, she focused on her breath and was rewarded by hitting the fastest ones passably on key. She and Porpora had not discussed how she would embellish the ritornello of the first lines, but when she returned to them, she sang forte, with a grand series of improvised trills. She did her best, and only when it was over did she feel herself to be inadequate. She said a quick, silent prayer for Giustina's recovery.

She could perceive neither pleasure nor disappointment in the maestro's eyes. "Is that the best you can do?"

"It was my first attempt," she stammered.

"You will improve on the timing and mechanics of the notes, but what I mean is here." He stood up, came close, tapped a finger in the center of her chest. "Can you do better here?"

❊

For three days, Violetta forsook the roof. She was under constant supervision—treated like a Murano glass candelabra that had to be overseen with great attention. It was stifling, and she wished for a moment to herself, but there were new pleasures, too. She was given a temporary assistant, a young girl of nine called Helena, who had recently joined the music school. Each day Helena escorted Violetta to and from a meeting with Porpora. Walking with the young girl up those stairs and into that office made Violetta feel important. Something to aspire to again, once Giustina recovered and these days were but a memory.

Over the course of the week, as more *coro* girls fell ill, several more music school girls were moved into their place at rehearsals. Reine was among them. She and Violetta ignored each other at the *coro* dining table. None of them got comfortable in their new positions, for once the fever left the Incurables, the old order would return. Giustina would take her place as the first soprano, and Violetta would be lucky to find herself back on the roof.

For now, she felt buoyant and eager, recommitted to her singing. In a state of pleasant panic, she pressed thoughts of Mino down inside her and gave herself over to the music.

She worked with Luisa, who played the basso continuo on the harpsichord, the backbone of the *coro*. Violetta sang while Luisa built the accompaniment into something even stronger than what Porpora had written. Violetta donned the sick mask again to visit Laura and Giustina in the infirmary.

Laura was improving, eating again and drinking diluted wine mixed with allspice, but Giustina was still feverish and barely speaking.

"Perhaps next week," Helena said, but Violetta knew she was lying.

They must only look as far ahead as Sunday. Violetta rehearsed with the *coro* up in the gallery, disheartened by how thin her voice sounded all alone in the great church. She must try harder, breathe deeper. She must release her fear. Or at least—as she had done that first time on the roof with Mino—she must lean into it.

If her sudden ascent to the *coro* had happened two months ago, before he left, he would have reminded her that this was what she wanted. What did he want now, wherever he was?

She prayed he liked his work, that he was happy, and that he didn't think of her.

❁

SUNDAY MORNING SHE woke from a dream of the wheel for the first time since Mino had left. This time, Violetta had been the mother with the babe beneath her cloak. The beautiful voice had been hers.

She hurried down the freezing hall to the basin, splashed cold water on her face to dispel the feeling of the dream. She must think only of her solo. Today was the day. She held the opening notes in her mind, and through her nerves, she smiled. She could do this.

She dressed, pulling on the fine white stockings and new white silk dress with a flounce at the neck and cuffs of bobbin lace sewed by the *figlie del commun*. There was nothing to do with her hair. She missed Laura. She missed Mino. She missed him so much it hurt in the pit of her stomach.

Helena brought breakfast. The porridge was steaming, served with honey and extra cream. There were two small oranges on the tray, and tea brewed from mint.

Did Mino eat alone? How odd that Violetta didn't know what he looked like when he ate, how he held a fork, whether he chewed quickly or slowly.

The dream had its hold on her. What if she indulged it, purged it? Like sweating out a fever. Her voice needed warming up anyway. She pushed her breakfast aside and moved to the window. She stood on her bed and leaned against the glass, and she sang their song.

❁

IN THE PACKED church of the Incurables, sun streamed through the clerestory in bright bands. Venetians crowded into pews in winter cloaks of crimson, peacock blue, and gray. They wore white gloves and crinkling taffeta skirts embroidered with flowers. How tiny they looked when they rose for the kyrie eleison. Between prayers, most stole glances at the *coro* behind the brass grille.

Violetta had heard *coro* girls gossip about this phenomenon—either sighing at the burden of so many eyes or giggling at the thrill of it. It was different to feel the weight of that gaze herself. She felt the physical connection these singers shared with the republic. She was one of them today. Hers was the voice of Venice.

Her palms were damp as Porpora rose before the congregation. He locked eyes with Violetta and gave the slightest nod. The orchestra began to play. She let the notes calm her. She knew this music. No one was expecting greatness. All she had to do was make it through.

First was a gloria. She sang as she always did, hitting her notes directly but lightly, not holding on too tightly or too long. In the middle of the measure she felt a strange energy coming from Reine, who sang triumphantly, as if to demonstrate that she, not Violetta, deserved the solo. Violetta turned to look at the girl for the first time since that *carnevale* day.

Reine stared at her with loathing. Violetta's eyes fell on the French girl's full, pink lips. They were perfect, lovely, the essence of expression, ideal in every way. She saw them kissing Mino, and she felt something inside of her dissolve.

She let herself see what her anger had blinded her to that day: he had not kissed Reine to make a fool of Violetta. He had kissed Reine the way a drowning man reaches for help.

She let herself admit that she *wanted* to be the one in his arms. She wanted her lips pressed to his again. She wanted to feel all that yearning coiled between them. She wanted him. For so long she had done what was necessary, her actions divorced from feelings because she didn't want to hold Mino back. Now her body rushed to reunite with her feelings, and what she felt was . . .

Love.

She had loved him all along. And she had caused him so much pain.

She wanted to weep, but it was time to sing.

The communal gloria turned and opened into her aria, like a narrow *calle* turning onto a huge piazza. She blinked at the expanse of it before her, and in the spirit of her broken heart, she began.

She did not sing as she and Porpora had discussed. She exuded hope neither for Christ's nor *carnevale*'s return, neither wakefulness nor homecoming. She sang as if every cherished thing was gone and no one would recover what was loved.

Tears streamed down her face as she moved from the B section back into the ritornello. She was heading toward the cadenza near the end, where the full orchestra would stop and she would sing the final notes a cappella. She lost herself, singing through the grille like her pain might melt it down.

At the end, instead of growing louder as she had practiced, Violetta's voice softened to piano. She felt every body in the building leaning in.

The room was silent when she finished. She noticed small movements below, and realized parishioners were wiping away tears. She left hers on her cheeks, proof that this had really happened. She felt exhausted and alive.

Everything was about to change.

Four

Mino woke up nose to nose with a black-and-white-spotted dog. He jerked away, wincing at a burning pain in his cheek. It felt cold to the touch and wet, and he realized he had rolled into an icy puddle on the cobblestones in his sleep. That told him more than he wanted to know about his state when he'd lain down. He dried his face on his shoulder and rubbed stiffness from his neck. He drew his body closer under the alcove where he'd slept.

Was it sunrise or sunset? It didn't matter. He closed his eyes against the changing light. He hated waking up on the street.

Another day, and life without Letta was still unbearable. When he'd first left the Incurables, over four months ago, Mino had been too despondent to do anything. He never went back to his apprenticeship. He had lost his apartment. All through the brutal winter, he ate where he could, slept where he could, drank as much as he could. Wherever he roamed, his heartache went with him.

The dog returned, sniffed excessively, leaving dots of dampness on

Mino's cheek. He swiped a hand, intending to push the beast onward, but he felt the matted fur, the soft ears, the warm head, which tilted automatically into Mino's palm.

"What do you want?" he asked the dog, who leaned into Mino's bad temper instead of scampering away. He felt the dog watching him with a focus that no one had fixed on Mino in months. No one saw him anymore. It was amazing how a man could disappear in plain sight.

His head throbbed. He glanced at the bottle next to him—two swallows left of something brown and treacherous. It might make him feel better to finish it off, at least for a little while, but the thought made his stomach lurch and twist. He was hungry. He tried to think when he'd last eaten.

The dog whimpered, pawed at something in front of him. Mino looked down, and there was a pair of black leather boots. They were sturdily soled, yet nothing like the work boots men wore in the *squero*. These were rich men's boots, light as slippers near the top, but with a substantial sole, ornate stitching, and a cuff at the top as wide as Mino's palm. They would reach halfway up his calves. The dog bent his head and nosed the boots closer to Mino. He gave a tiny yap, as if to say *Take them.*

Mino glanced up and down the street, but no one was looking. It was sunset; he saw that now from the manner of the people on the street. These weren't workers; they were masked aristocrats, laughing, tipsy, parties waiting around the corner. Now a boy of twelve came down the *calle* with a torch, lighting each rushlight, the plant piths soaked in grease and set in stone holders outside doorframes.

Mino winced at the sight of his slippers, pitiful, full of holes. His stockings showed through the gaps in the thin leather, disintegrating gray wool in worse shape than his shoes. A toe poked out, filthy and white with cold. He had not taken off his shoes in weeks. The contrast of these brand-new boots made him ashamed.

He tore his slippers from his feet. He rid himself of the horrid stockings, too. Gingerly he slid a foot into one of the new boots. The immediate warmth was like an embrace. He closed his eyes, pressed his foot in all the way. The boots were a bit too small, but he'd never take them off. They would stretch. They would be perfect.

He put the other one on, ran his fingers over their surfaces, then tucked his feet beneath him and hid the boots away. He was warmer already.

He met the dog's brown eyes. "You steal boots for all the tramps and make it look this easy?"

The dog circled twice and lay down at Mino's side, resting his chin on Mino's thigh. Mino had not had this much contact with another living thing in months.

"Sprezzatura," he said, thinking of the way Porpora used to ask the musicians at the Incurables to play—with a studied nonchalance that belied their efforts.

At the sound of the word, the dog barked, his chin tossed toward the sky.

"We'll call you Sprezz," Mino said, obliging as the dog rolled onto his back for a scratch. "I'm Mino."

Some nights, trying to fall asleep on the freezing *calle*, Mino thought of changing his name. It was not his given name, but his orphan name. He was gone from the orphanage now.

But he didn't remember the name his mother had called him. She felt further out of reach than ever. He laughed bitterly thinking how he had planned to use his connections through the *squeri* guild to search for her. Those were severed now, by his own recklessness.

Even if he had some way of finding her, how could Mino meet his mother in this state? On the streets, with no prospects and no means—he was nothing. He didn't deserve to find the woman he remembered. He wouldn't know where to begin if he did.

Sprezz was on his feet now, and Mino felt that the dog was compelling him to rise as well. It was late February and the sun was timid, barely warming the streets by day. Mino stood, reluctantly folding the *tabarro* cloak he used only as a blanket. The cloak had befallen him one night when he was sleeping outside the opera house, Teatro San Angelo. A pair of lovers had drawn into the alcove where he lay begging for dreams. He'd tried to make himself small, invisible, as the woman tossed the man's cloak off in a series of heated kisses and moans. The garment landed at Mino's feet. The lovers stayed warm with their endeavors for some time, and Mino had drawn the cloak over his body. When they finished, they didn't remember the cloak. They scampered off and he heard them go their separate ways without promises.

He had used the man's cloak as a blanket ever since, sometimes thinking of the sounds its previous owner had elicited from that woman, but Mino had never worn the cloak during the day. He still wore the simple clothes he'd worn at the Incurables—a white peasant's shirt, gray trousers. His tricorne had been stolen in his sleep long ago. Together with his previous pair of slippers, Mino's clothes seemed to shout that the cloak did not belong to him. It would invite more trouble than it was worth to display it before he really needed it, in the middle of the cold night.

But his new boots begged for a *tabarro*. Mino settled the cloak over his shoulders as it was meant to be worn. It draped down to his knees, covering the threadbare patches in his pants. It was so fine. You could hardly tell how filthy it was.

Mino felt brighter than he had in some time. He had a few soldi in his pocket. The lamps were coming on in the taverns on the street. He would take the dog with him and go find them both some dinner.

They walked together past the white-pillared church of San Vidal, and around the Campo Santo Stefano, its cafés full of tourists. Mino would have turned left to patronize La Mascareta, where the polenta was cheap and the wine was red, but Sprezz turned right, barking over his shoulder. *Follow me.* Mino was beginning to like this dog despite himself.

It did not take long for Mino to notice the change in how he was perceived on the street. People looked at him, and not in a bad way. He was someone worth greeting.

"Good evening, sir," a masked stranger told him, tipping his black hat.

"*Buonasera*," he replied. The boots had changed his walk. They made a marvelous clacking on the cobblestones, announcing his arrival from around the corner of a *calle*. He knew he looked hungry and in need of a bath, but any patrician worth his palazzo might look the same way as the sun set over Venice.

Sprezz stopped before a tavern, stood on his hind legs, and pressed his nose against the window. A few nights a week Mino had enough soldi for a meal at a cheap tavern, days when he was able to score work hauling refuse by the bucket to the boat bound for Burano, where it would fertilize their fields. But on his rich days, Mino only ate cheap polenta, and he never ate at a place like this. The scents from this kitchen smelled so good he could cry. He had two coins clanging in his pocket and a plan to spend them in a cheaper tavern, where the owner's wife might smile at him—a break from the glazed eyes he got the rest of the day.

The cook rapped on the window. Mino assumed he was shooing Sprezz away, but then he came outside with a bowl of fish bones and a small plate of polenta. Mino hung back, watching the cook round the corner, set both bowls in the little alley next to the restaurant, and give Sprezz a scratch on the head.

Once the cook was back inside, Sprezz barked at Mino, a summoning sound, and Mino stepped forward, amazed by the amount of tender meat clinging to the bones of the fish. He drew one to his mouth. The morsels were still warm, brightened with lemon juice and garlic. It was so good. He closed his eyes. He would stay there all night eating this.

He cleaned the bones, and Sprezz waited patiently, eating only what Mino set aside. They shared the polenta, Mino spooning it up between two fingers, Sprezz taking delicate bites, licking the clumps from his whiskers. When they finished, Mino was more satisfied than he had been in months. He remembered the soldi in his pocket and thought of what he might do with them now.

Down the *calle*, the sign for a stufe called to him. He used to love the weekly bath at the Incurables. He'd never been in a stufe before, but he'd overheard enough at taverns to know that most of the clientele at these bathhouses were courtesans, or the men who liked to watch them.

Once he'd shared a bottle of malmsey with a painter with wild, frizzy hair. The man couldn't afford to hire a body model, but he had two soldi for the stufe. He showed Mino his sketches of the women inside. Mino later saw his paintings in the window of a palazzo that looked out over the Rialto Bridge.

It was the boots that had Mino wanting to clean up. He stopped at the door of the bathhouse, looked down at the dog, who sat, then lay at the doorstep. He would wait.

"Good boy." He scratched Sprezz on the chin and went inside.

The room was dim and wet. A girl took his money and sent him to a corner to remove his clothes. Then an older woman appeared, plump and smiling. She handed him a robe and led him through a maze of candlelit hallways to a room with an octagonal stone bench in the center and steaming buckets everywhere. They were alone. She took his robe off and doused him with hot water. She held a sponge so big it required two hands as she worked over him. She was not gentle. He was not accustomed to this steady and intense touch. But she poured cool water over him, aromatic, scented with orange peels and cloves, and his skin tingled and felt brilliant and raw to the touch. He wanted someone else, someone besides this woman and her sponge, to touch him.

As he dressed he found the mask in the deep pocket of his *tabarro*. He put it on. He finally felt worthy of the *bauta*. He hadn't worn it since that day with Violetta. He knew the money spent at the stufe was worth it, that he could wear his clothes with dignity now, but he missed his coins sorely, just as he did whenever he spent them on food. He yearned for and dreaded the next shift he would do hauling turnips out of the vegetable boats at dawn, or loading mail into a *corriere* for two more soldi to throw away on nothing.

Outside Sprezz was waiting. He matched Mino's step as they walked toward Piazza San Marco.

On certain days Mino longed to hear the lovely street music in the heart of the city. On certain days he could bear it. He entered San Marco, the central square of Venice, a vast rectangular piazza framed by colonnaded loggia stretching nearly as far as the eye could see. The ground and surrounding buildings were all of the same soft gray stone, drawing the eye toward the vast gold spires and white domes of the Byzantine basilica to the east. The cafés were always crowded in San Marco. There was always music, too.

Today the evening sky was dramatic, dusky pink with voluminous purple clouds beyond the Grand Canal. It was cold but soon it would be spring. Mino and Sprezz stopped to watch a man playing violin and a woman singing along. Mino could tell they were a couple, though they never looked at each other. She had a sweet face and a pleasant voice, but Mino had heard angels sing all his life, so it was the violinist who caught his attention.

The man was very good, but his violin was terrible, too cheap to be properly tuned. Even from a distance of ten *piedi*, Mino knew that it needed thicker ebony to reinforce the bridge.

For the thousandth time, Mino wished he'd taken his violin when he left the apartment that day, but he'd fled Letta in a fit of blind horror, and the days that followed were a blur of drunken shame. By the time he remembered his instrument and went back to the apartment, the locks had been changed, and no one answered his knock. It was surely pawned by now.

If he had it still, would he play it on the street like this man, for money? The idea was too painful to entertain. What he wanted was to fix this man's violin, to fetch his pliers and his saw. He wanted fresh catgut to replace the tired strings. He wanted to teach that instrument to sing.

"You look like you're waiting for a tarantella partner," someone said at Mino's side. He turned to find two women in silk gowns. They wore smaller black masks that covered only the top halves of their faces. Their tricornes were perched at jaunty angles. They'd each perfected the flirtatious closed-lipped smirk for which Venetian women were famous.

Mino didn't know how to dance the tarantella, but for months the only words anyone had directed at him were commands to get out of the way or settle a bill. He couldn't imagine dancing, but neither could he deny the woman with the dyed blond hair outright.

"I dare not make your lover jealous, *siora*," he said, glancing left and right dramatically. "Surely you have one here?"

"How's your stamina? You might outrun him." She laughed as she touched his hair, and Mino stilled at the shocking caress. "Is this your natural color?"

He bowed, recovering. "I'm afraid it is."

"Oh, grow it long," she pleaded. "Make me a wig. I've never seen hair so fine—"

"And soft," her brunette companion added, petting Mino. "What do you do, Sior Oro?" *Mr. Gold.*

He was so taken aback by their attention, he started to say what came first into his mind. "Gondol—"

But he broke off. Once he would have been proud to speak of his apprenticeship, the apprenticeship he'd thrown away. Now that he'd been wandering Venice for nearly an entire *carnevale* season, and had listened to the talk on the streets, he knew that building gondolas was nothing in the noble world of money and masquerades.

But the women heard what they wanted, exclaiming, "A gondolier!" They saw his *tabarro*, his boots and fine blond hair, and they assumed he must work with the wealthy.

"For which family?" the blonde asked. Not just any gondolier, rowing the same route back and forth across the canal. They thought him a private employee of a noble family. Mino, who had been destitute for nearly half a year, who had never been anywhere near the rich except in passing on the *calle*. Mino, who came from nowhere.

They tilted their chins at him, and he wondered how far he could take their mistake. Letta would have known how to spin it to her advantage.

"Are you spying on someone?" he asked, teasing. Private gondoliers were believed to know everything about their employers' intimate lives.

"A lady must, if she has any wits," the brunette said. Turning to her friend, she added, "He'll never tell you anything."

Mino bowed and smiled, fully taking on the part. "It's in the guild's code. Men have been drowned for such a lack of discretion."

"All right, we won't pry," the blonde said, "but maybe you can give us some advice?" She put her hand on his chest. Mino held his breath. Her touch was the most intimate thing he'd felt in months.

"She thinks her lover is straying," the brunette said, leaning in between them.

"What a fool." Mino said the only appropriate thing.

The blonde was pleased. She drew closer and lowered her voice as, behind them, the musicians packed up.

"Every day," the woman said, "it's the same excuses. He has midnight for me, he wants me more than ever, but something is strange. At sundown, when it is time for an aperitif"—she glanced around the piazza at the masses drinking small glasses of liqueur by the fading light of day—"he's unavailable. I know he's not with his wife." She pointed over her shoulder. "She's right over there with her *cicisbeo*! No, there is somewhere he goes in Dorsoduro every day at sunset."

"Vespers," Mino said softly. To keep the boys and girls separated at the Incurables, the girls went to morning mass, while the boys attended the shorter evening service. Mino felt as if he were there now, hearing Giustina sing "Salve Regina."

The women's howls of laughter brought him back to the piazza.

"My *sior* goes to church only when the doge demands it. His god is wine and money."

"The *cori* play beautiful music," Mino said.

"Everyone knows that," the blonde said, "but he never even takes me to the opera; he's as happy with a street performer."

Mino looked around. The violinist was gone but two more were setting up, tuning their instruments. Again he wished to hold their violins, to feel with his whole body the glide of the bow. Mino had never been to the opera, but he did know of men who crossed three *sestieri* and the Grand Canal simply for the experience of the Incurables *coro.*

The brunette looked thoughtful. "Luigi Fontacari just married a singer from the Incurables. She's breathtaking. And young. Fontacari says she sings like a bird, though he's the only one who'll hear it."

"Why is that?" her friend asked.

"She signed an oath," Mino said. "A condition of accepting the dowry from the Incurables. Once the girls leave and marry, they must never sing outside the home."

"How sad," the blonde said.

The brunette nodded. "And she was famous. Imagine giving all that up." She snorted. "For old Fontacari. Pray she gets a good *cicisbeo.*"

The women laughed.

Mino leaned forward, his heart in his throat. "What is her name, this musician from the Incurables?"

"They called her Giustina, *bella voce*," the brunette said.

❋

ALL NIGHT HE wrestled with his disbelief. Giustina, married already? He tried not to think of the place in the *coro* her departure would have opened. He'd had to fight to keep from following the women as they left to spy on the blonde's married boyfriend.

He had not let himself consider how Violetta's fate might still be in flux. Now, as he wandered the moonlit piazza, it obsessed him. Had Letta progressed to the *coro* like she wanted? Or had Giustina's place gone to Reine, as Letta had long feared?

Once, he had thought that by now he would have enough money from the *squero* to move her to a larger, more comfortable home. To marry her. Even to have a child on the way, if she'd felt ready. He thought he'd have found his mother, too. Or if not *her*, at least some evidence of her existence, of his family.

Mino's dreams were meant to feel closer, instead of ever farther beyond his reach. But that hadn't happened. He didn't recognize the life he was living now.

By morning, as the sun rose over the water, he and Sprezz loitered in San Marco. Near the gold-painted basilica, where the piazza opened to face the Grand Canal, two columns towered over the square. Both had been brought from the East six centuries ago. One held up a magnificent bronze statue of a huge winged lion. He had a flowing, curly mane, a tail almost in motion, and the bearing of an angel taking flight; he was the emblem of San Marco, of the city. He was Venice, cast in metal.

The other column featured a marble sculpture of San Teodoro, a slain crocodile at his feet. He represented the republic's independence. Looking up, Mino thought of Letta.

Pale pink light shone on the canal as he sat against the base of the column. Its plinth was ringed by three stone steps, worn to seats over the years. He scratched Sprezz beneath his chin. He yearned to sleep, but his mind couldn't rest.

To whom had the *coro* spot gone—Violetta or Reine? Mino had heard the prioress whisper that Reine's tuition equaled ten times the alms the other orphans collected on their walks through the Dorsoduro. Reine would expect Giustina's spot; nothing in her life had prepared her to think otherwise.

But then, there was Violetta. She was known to be trouble, but almost everyone was drawn to her. She had always been blind to the effect she had on others. She'd once told Mino he was the only soul who cared whether she lived or died. He'd been dumb enough to take that as a compliment, intimate words from someone grateful for his love. He realized later that she meant it. She truly could not see what Mino did when he watched her through the courtyard window. She claimed Laura loved everyone, not seeing how Laura loved her best of all. She couldn't see the way the younger girls adored her, mimicking her walk and intonations. Mino knew why. Violetta was freer than any of them, and everyone wanted a taste.

He had assumed, at least, she knew how he felt about her. She used to say she knew everything Mino was thinking, and he'd believed her, taking comfort in the fact that sometimes he didn't have to speak. It emboldened him—to feel transparent and still loved. He had taken it for granted. He'd assumed she knew that if anyone were to open Mino's heart, they would find Letta's name engraved upon it.

That afternoon, his proposal had seemed a trifling detail in their romance; he'd been so certain she already knew.

He closed his eyes and heard her voice. He let it come to him. On the days they'd played together on the roof—his violin, her song—Mino wanted for nothing. How sure he had been that their future was bright.

"Nice dog."

Mino's arm snapped around Sprezz as he jolted awake. He had fallen asleep beneath the column. The day was gone. It was late afternoon and crowds of men and women sidestepped him as they moved along toward the stretch of bridges. He looked for the speaker, reclaiming his bearings, holding tight to Sprezz.

"I used to have a dog," the man said. Mino saw him standing on the dock a few feet away, leaning against a tall oar. He was wearing the black-and-white shirt and straw hat of a public gondolier. He looked as young as Mino. "Two years since Cherry died. Two years since anyone understood me." He smiled sadly, and Mino felt for him. He had known Sprezz for a single day, but would rather die than lose him now.

He loosened his grip on Sprezz. "He's friendly, if you want to say hello."

Sprezz trotted toward the man, who leaned down to pat his head. "He wants a ride," he said as Sprezz hopped into his gondola, sniffing its perimeter. "Where are you bound, little pup?"

"Come back, Sprezz," Mino called.

"It's fine." The man grinned at the sight of Sprezz standing on two paws at the gondola's helm. "Maybe you two want a ride? It's on me. I'm going to the Zattere."

Mino looked at the dog wagging his tail, at the grinning gondolier. The Zattere bordered the Incurables. The promenade was nearly an hour's walk from here, but surely far shorter by boat. He looked up at the almost setting sun. Five o'clock, he guessed. He didn't believe in luck or signs, but if they left now, he could make it to vespers. He could discover whether she'd made the *coro*. He could find a way to let it bring [illegible]n peace.

"V[illegible] not?" he said and climbed inside the boat, trying not to show how [illegible]ocking alarmed him. He had been given a basic lesson in rowing as part of his early training at the *squero*, so that he might understand how the vessels he would build worked. But that single hour on the quiet canal near the shop seemed another lifetime now. He sat down as quickly as he could on the first bench, not even making it beneath the shelter of the wooden *fèlze* where passengers were meant to sit.

Sprezz hopped up beside him, his tail wagging against Mino, who put his arm around the dog, as much to steady himself.

"I'm Mino."

"Carlo," the gondolier said, leaning to shake Mino's hand from his post at the back of the vessel. He pushed his oar off the dock to back out into the canal. He began to row. It was even colder on the water than it had been on the promenade, and Mino pulled his *tabarro* close.

He studied the small circular movements of Carlo's arms, the flexing of his torso, and the remarkable balance of his stance, memories of his lesson coming back to him. This man embodied the world Mino would have created if he'd gone to work at the *squero*. He paid very close to attention to the way Carlo's strokes hardly rippled the surface, how he leaned into the oar, his body tipped forward at such an angle that Mino was certain he would fall in. But when Mino glanced around, every gondolier passing by steered precisely that way, their chests jutting out. Rowing was a dance between gondolier and water.

Mino was unaccustomed to this hidden view of his city, a few *piedi* below the street. He saw the undersides of the *calli* he'd walked along so many times, sheathed in glowing green moss. He felt the cool blink of darkness as they passed beneath bridges. He saw how the buildings tilted forward slightly, as if reaching for one another across the water. He thought he knew the sounds of Venice, but to ride on the canals was to become part of a rhythm he'd never heard before. There were no rests in the lovely music of the water; the waves struck a chord that went on and on.

The boat entered the maelstrom of the Grand Canal, joining a matching fleet of gleaming black gondolas all moving on the water as if breathing. Carlo threaded between a hundred other vessels, whistling at friends, picking up the next line of a song someone else was crooning as they passed. Once, the helm of his boat nearly skimmed another's, and the men traded obscenities with glee.

"I'll drown your unborn children, brute," the other man shouted.

"At least my madonna isn't a whore," Carlo called back, winking at Mino. Sprezz barked his support.

The wind pummeled them, and the rocking made Mino queasy, but the sunlight warmed his skin. It made everything on the water seem to sparkle. This was the way to travel in Venice. In the life he'd dreamed of having, he would have eventually been able to afford this for Letta. But he could no more pay for a gondola ride now than he could earn her love, and when he looked again around the Grand Canal, his heart turned bitter at the sight of all the other carefree passengers.

A quarter of an hour later they arrived at the Zattere. From the water, the facade of the Incurables looked taller, bleaker, more impenetrable. So it was to Mino now. He could not go to the only home he remembered. He could enter only the public door to the church. This pained him more than he expected, a tense knot in his chest.

Carlo secured the boat, Mino thanked him and hopped off, gulping air to settle his stomach. Sprezz followed at his heels until Mino reached the entrance, then the dog circled twice and sat down outside to wait.

Mino bowed his head and entered the church. It was as crowded as ever, packed with upward of a thousand Venetians and tourists. He pulled his cloak higher, studying the tiled terrazzo as he moved for the nearest pew. He felt exposed. He wished the law allowed masks inside.

He didn't let himself look up at the brass grille. He did not wish to be witnessed, but more than that, Mino wanted to hear rather than to see Violetta's fate. He wanted to know through the music whether she had made it.

He did not anticipate that Father Marché's prayers would affect him, but the consolation they brought was immediate, like food to an empty stomach. The priest said the kyrie, led them through gloria and credo, and Mino felt sorrow that he could never be known in this place again, with all its comforting mysteries.

He closed his eyes when the music began, his body tight with nerves through the first two orchestral movements. Then her voice arrived, a sound like morning, everything rising.

Oh, Letta.

The magic of her singing filled the chapel, filled Mino until he thought he would burst. In her voice he heard the details of her life as a lead soprano. He saw her sunlit corner room, her eager assistants, the years of fame to come, the money and the suitors. He opened his eyes and forced himself to look at her.

Through the grille her pale skin shone. The movement of her lips enchanted Mino. He longed to stand up, to shout out his apologies, to climb the wall and leap over the grille. He longed to hold her, to interrupt her song with a kiss.

How quickly it was over. He sat when everyone else rose to leave. He couldn't move. When he looked up, she was gone, and he knew she'd been whisked away, first to a retiring room where younger girls would bring her tea, as Violetta had once done for Giustina.

It should have been all he needed to see, but Mino wanted more. He wanted to talk to her. He had to reach her. But how? Find the prioress and beg for a meeting like any other man who wished to see a *coro* girl?

Mino couldn't. She never wanted to see him again. And what would he say? Congratulations? She was above him now, that white dress, her hair brilliant and swept off her face in a new style. This was her destiny.

It had never been him.

He had always sensed he wasn't enough for her. He'd tried to fight it with his proposal, but he'd never really had a chance. This life was so much bigger than the one he could have offered her.

He left the church dejected, stepping outside in a daze. Dusk had fallen and the lights of Giudecca shone on the canal. Sprezz appeared at his side, and Mino patted him as he walked without knowing where he was going. He found himself back before Carlo's gondola. He wanted someone to talk to, to take him out of his head.

The gondola was there, but the gondolier wasn't. Carlo's straw hat rested on the post of the dock, and Mino picked it up, spinning it between his palms absently. Sprezz barked, and Mino looked up to see a man dressed in the red patrician vest of a senator.

"I need to get out of here. Quickly. Is this your boat?"

Mino shook his head, but when he looked up, the man tossed him a snakeskin purse. It was heavy with coins, more gold than Mino had ever held.

"What can I do for you?" Mino asked.

"Take me to La Sirena. Don't be followed." The senator was already in the gondola, seated inside the wooden *fèlze,* fanning out the wide sleeves of his robe. He drew a *bauta* from his cloak and fastened it about his face, replacing his tricorne atop it. It was Lent, so masks were prohibited on the streets, but many Venetians still carried them should the night run wild. At the neighborhood gambling houses, especially this far from the Doge's Palace in San Marco, a desire for anonymity skirted under the city's restrictive laws.

The senator seemed to relax beneath his mask and the *fèlze*. He was staring out the window, Mino realized, at a woman hurrying toward them. Mino thought of the ladies he'd met earlier and laughed to himself. In all his years growing up there, he'd never known the Incurables was a place where men could temporarily disappear.

"Go!" the senator commanded.

Mino whistled to Sprezz, who hopped on. His palms were sweating. He couldn't believe what he was about to attempt. If it worked, he would bring the boat back straightaway. He'd apologize to Carlo, split the money. He would give thanks to Saint Jude, patron of lost causes. For now he could worry about nothing but how to row. He needed that gold. He put Carlo's hat on his head. He prayed for his long-ago lesson to flow through his limbs, to guide him. He tottered toward the back of the boat.

He lifted the oar from its rowlock on the right side of the boat. He pushed off the dock post, just as Carlo had done. Sprezz ran the length of the boat, hopping up to be close to Mino. His arms were shaking, his hands freezing in the wind, knuckles white. His heart raced as he dipped the oar into the water. He tested it against the current. He had no idea where he was going, what La Sirena was, but he grasped the fundamentals: this man wanted to escape that woman. The money would be Mino's so long as he achieved that feat.

"You don't exactly have the Venetian stroke," the senator called, shaking frigid water from his boot, which Mino had soaked with a splash of his oar. Mino rowed more gently. Smaller circles, like Carlo had done. He could learn.

He might do all right if he never had to turn. But now he was approaching an intersection with another, narrower canal. Which would be more difficult: executing a turn up the calm, minor canal—or carrying on along the busy and turbulent Giudecca waterway? He didn't know how to manage either.

His choice was made for him as he heard the wailed warning of an approaching gondolier, who turned out of the narrow channel just as Mino would have passed. Mino rowed forcefully, fast circles to the right, arcing the bow in an attempt to avoid the crash. But the iron teeth of the *fèrro* at the helm of his boat sparred with the iron teeth of the other, and instantly the boats were tangled. The impact jostled Mino almost headfirst into the water. He staggered for balance, then put his arm out to catch Sprezz.

His mind went to the purse in his pocket, and he knew he was on the cusp of losing it if he didn't play the boatman. So just like Carlo, Mino began to curse the other gondolier.

"Are you steering a ship or stirring polenta with that spatula, you harlequin?" he belted out at the other man, who was savagely using his oar to extricate his boat.

"It was your whore of a mother who taught me," the man shouted back.

Mino had been moving toward the bow of his boat, coming at the *fèrro* with his own oar, but he froze, stunned by the man's words. They felt like an indictment. He had failed to find his mother, failed even to attempt it.

Fury rose in Mino, at himself, at the oarsman who dared insult his mother. He had the oar in his hands—

But at that moment, the other man loosed his *fèrro* from Mino's, sending the boats gliding apart and Mino up the narrower canal.

He heard the other gondolier go back to singing his barcarolle, as if nothing unpleasant had happened. Mino gasped for air and tried to calm himself.

He determined that if he made it off this boat, he would change his ways. He would use this money to pull himself together, to devote himself to his search for his family. That vespers service had proved once and for all that he could never have had Letta. He must instead trace love backward, to the source.

He glanced at the senator, who met Mino's eyes and chuckled.

"Boatmen," the man said to himself.

Mino exhaled, relieved to know he had not sacrificed his purse. "Where is La Sirena?" he asked.

The senator stared at him, amused. "I thought every man in Dorsoduro had darkened La Sirena's door." He pointed north toward the Grand Canal. "*Sempre dritto.*" The only Venetian direction ever given: always straight. "Curve left at rio della Toletta. It will be to the right, just past the third bridge."

On the quiet canal, away from the woman, both Mino and the senator were more relaxed. The senator settled back beneath the *fèlze*, and Mino summoned all he had learned at the *squero*. He tried to feel each one of the two hundred and eighty puzzle-like pieces of wood that formed the vessel. He knew where the boat was asymmetrical at the prow to handle the curves of the canals. He knew the heavy iron *fèrro* counterbalanced his own weight at the back. He felt a sudden sense of calm. He knew the shape of the oar, how to turn it one way, then the other. He felt how the curves of the canals were best navigated in a three-point maneuver.

Ten minutes later, they arrived on rio della Toletta. Mino rowed beneath three bridges and ducked beneath the bough of a tree. The cork oak had outgrown its small, walled garden and reached one arm almost across the canal like a bridge. Its bark was silvery and mottled, its clusters of leaves crisp and green, dotted with acorns.

Mino was exhausted. He saw the building just beyond the cork bough. It was discreet, indistinguishable from its neighbors but for a single blue glass lantern lit outside a second-story door. He propped his oar on the cobblestones to stop the boat, like he'd seen Carlo do. The senator clapped Mino on the shoulder and exited the gondola in haste.

"I am in your debt," he called back as he hurried toward a spiral staircase cast in shadows. He climbed the stairs and reached the door, glowing in the blue light.

La Sirena.

Mino knew he had to hurry back to the Zattere, to return this boat to Carlo and make amends. But as he turned the gondola back down the canal, a wooden plaque below the blue glass light of La Sirena caught his eye. It featured a fishtail, arcing up out of the water.

It was beautiful—and familiar, like something he had dreamed of long ago. He couldn't stop seeing it, even as he turned the corner and steered the boat on. He felt a compulsion to go back, to climb those stairs and enter La Sirena.

Five

Five months had passed since the December morning when Violetta performed her first aria, and ever since, she'd felt she was living another's life. Porpora had pulled her from the music school that day, promoted her to the *coro* before she'd even had time to catch her breath.

She was no longer just a charity case. She had found a purpose. But she never forgot the twisted fortune that had led her here. Had her mother not abandoned her, had she not gutted Mino with that lie, had Giustina not been so sick, Violetta would not be in this *coro*. At times, fate felt so capricious that her victory seemed like ice on the canal, soon to crack.

Her days revolved around two performances, at morning mass and vespers. On feast days or during visits from important ambassadors, sometimes a third performance was arranged. The services were short but taxing, and the other hours of her days were as regimented as ever: she awoke at the same time and said the same prayers. After mass, she waded through the morning's same long stretch of group rehearsals and private lessons, though she now tutored a pair of younger students. She gathered with the other women and girls for the same communal meals, only now she was permitted to pour herself a mug of wine. It was all the same, yet all so different, everything ornamented by her position as the *coro*'s youngest soprano. She was only eighteen; she had not dreamed of a place in the *coro* for another few years.

The first Sunday after she sang the aria, the prioress had called Violetta to her office.

It's over, she had thought. Someone had found the *bauta* in the bottom of her trunk. Or they'd changed their minds and decided to give the position to Reine. Or else she hadn't washed her dishes or tidied her room or kept up with the pages of her libretto lyrics in the specific way that a *coro* girl was expected to do. She prepared herself for further heartbreak.

"One lira for your pocket, for now," the prioress said, laying a silver coin on her desk before Violetta, "and one sequin for your dowry, for later."

Violetta stared at the silver coin on the desk, then at the gold one, disappearing into a small black purse in the prioress's hands. Slowly, Violetta reached for the silver coin, clutched it in her palm until it warmed. "For me?"

"Your earnings." The prioress nodded. "You do with it as you wish. I recommend saving, of course. I will keep your dowry here in my office." She raised the purse, then deposited it in a locked drawer in her desk. "I have a purse for each *coro* girl. Return each week, and I will dispense your pocket money."

When Violetta left the prioress's office, she'd felt the coin glowing in her hand. She wanted to run right out the front gate and spend it in the first café she crossed. She didn't know what it would buy her, how much anything cost in the city. How much was an *acqaioli*? A ride in a gondola? A lace fan from France? How much was an apartment for a week?

How much was a life outside these walls?

Soon she learned that the other *coro* girls spent their pocket money within the Incurables, on new lace collars for five lire or extra fruit for one. But Violetta kept hers in her trunk, next to her *bauta*. Over time the lire multiplied, until she traded six of them to the prioress in exchange for one gold sequin. Then another. Someday she would find a way to spend them.

In the afternoons now, between dinner and vespers, Violetta rested her voice. Porpora believed the part of the voice that spoke, not sang, thickened the tongue and thwarted singing, so it needed hours of silence each day. She gathered the notes from him, her sheet music, her cup of hot water with lemon, and a wool wrap for her neck. Even in the warming May weather she had to protect her throat. She ascended the stairs to the *coro sottomaestra*'s suite, where her red silk chaise awaited. She and Laura had moved into this double suite in the spring, after they took the *coro* vows.

They had pledged ten years of performance. They agreed to apprentice two younger girls, who would, in return, serve as their assistants. Last and most important, they promised that if they ever left the Incurables to marry, they would never play or sing in public. Violetta had spoken the vows stiffly, feeling the grip of the Incurables tighten around her. She was getting what she had long wanted, but at what cost? It made her think of Mino, and what he'd said to her when he proposed—that they might find a way around the rules, that she might perform somewhere in Venice. She had laughed at him. She wasn't laughing now.

She knew she should be grateful for her change in circumstances, but sometimes she felt the horizon slipping away. Sometimes she wanted to be back on that roof with Mino, when nothing and everything had seemed possible.

"You're in the clouds today," Laura said on a Thursday in May. After three hours of rehearsal, both girls were tired. Laura rubbed rosemary ointment over the calluses on her fingers. Violetta sipped from her steaming cup.

"Don't respond," Laura teased. "I know you're not meant to be talking. Only know that I see you, and I know something's running through your mind."

Violetta smirked at Laura, pursed her lips together dramatically. Each girl had her own large, well-furnished bedroom in their new living quarters, but they spent most of their limited leisure time in the shared parlor. It had become Violetta's favorite place, like their own private *altana*. Just Laura and her being young women alone, together. They could talk privately there—at least, when Violetta was permitted to talk.

Sometimes she felt guilty for not taking Laura into her confidence about Mino, but what happened that day still felt so raw and so private, Violetta could not speak of it aloud. It stayed within her, a wrenching secret song.

Their suite was warm. Spring had blossomed in Venice. Recently the nights smelled of jasmine, and the girls had swapped out their woolen gowns for lighter white linen blouses. Full sunlight streamed through a big window and sparkled invitingly on their view of the canal.

This room used to intimidate them. Years ago, when Violetta was first assigned to study under Giustina, she had run the new sheet music back and forth from the copyist to Giustina's parlor. Now she and Laura were the ones with servants, tiny girls with tiny voices scampering up and down the stairs at the first request.

There were irises on the mantel, wisteria blossoms on the table, a big bouquet of roses in a crystal vase on the piano. The prioress would never reveal the flowers' donors, but bouquets rained down on Laura and Violetta after each performance. Violetta didn't care whom they were from. They were a welcome burst of color for the musicians, who suddenly found themselves with little time to step outside, not even into the courtyard with its single fragrant lemon tree. When Violetta felt trapped in the Incurables, even in her new, grand chamber, she would dip her face in the flowers and inhale. For a little while, she would feel better. She would feel the pulse of life on the outside.

"I know I shouldn't say this," Laura said, looking up from her pages as Violetta smelled the roses, her finger dancing lightly across the piano's keys. "But some days I still can't shake the feeling that I'm not supposed to be here." She swallowed, her gaze flicking toward Violetta. Her hazel eyes brimmed with sadness. "Don't answer that. It was just—"

"You were always meant to be here," Violetta said. Her friend was more important than a few minutes of quiet for her voice. She knew the circumstances of Laura's promotion weighed on her, just as Violetta's did.

When the fever spread through the Incurables, Laura's violin *sottomaestra*, Ginerva, had died. Laura had come close to dying, but recently she confessed that Violetta's words—her urgent *I need you*—had brought her through the worst. Now both girls had risen to high places in the *coro*, and both of them felt guilty for it.

"Everyone knows you're meant for this," Violetta said. "Ginerva looks down and smiles to see you playing her violin." She moved to the chaise and sat down again. She took a sip from her cup and was quiet a moment, dark with thoughts of her own *sottomaestra*. Giustina had recovered from her sickness in January only to leave the Incurables in February.

"It could be worse," she said. "Ginerva could have had Giustina's luck and been married off."

"Don't say that," Laura said.

But Violetta meant it. She felt personally guilty about Giustina's situation. Had Violetta's performance during the worst of the fever not been so unexpectedly good, Porpora would have kept Giustina on as lead soprano, probably for years. She was only twenty-six. But part of a *sottomaestra*'s responsibility was to train the next girl, and now Violetta had proved herself ready—far sooner than anyone expected. Porpora liked young talent. Eighteen beat twenty-six. And just like that, with an eye toward the church's future coffers, Violetta was promoted. Giustina could have stayed on as a nonperforming maestra, or a lesser soprano in the *coro*, but she would be its star no more.

Violetta would never forget the day Giustina had summoned her to her bedside—the bed where now Violetta slept—and requested that she sing. By then Violetta had learned what she had to do, the precise feeling she had to tap into to make her voice soar, but that day, she didn't even need to think of Mino. Her sorrow for Giustina was enough. She sang her mentor's favorite aria from Hasse's opera *Allessandro nell'Indie*. She left Giustina speechless, able only to kiss Violetta's hand. Giustina had accepted her fate and her marriage with a quiet dignity that haunted Violetta.

"One day it might happen to us," she told Laura now. "Maybe we shouldn't teach our assistants as well as our *sottomaestri* taught us. We're just asking to be replaced."

"Again with this, Violetta?" Laura shook her head. "Marriage can't be that bad. What if your husband turns out kind? Think of the babies. I wouldn't mind teaching my own daughters to play violin someday."

"Not me," Violetta said, tightening her scarf. "Never."

She felt Laura's gaze on her. She picked up her music and tried to focus on her aria, aware that her cheeks were turning red. They'd had similar debates before, and Laura had always disagreed with Violetta's adamant refusal to wed. But something felt different today. The conversation was making Violetta sweat. The word *marriage* was no longer some distant fate; it was the reason Mino hated her. It was where everything between them had gone wrong.

"Do you miss him?" Laura asked. She smiled, as if to break the tension, but her eyes were curious. "You know who I mean."

Violetta's heart skipped a beat.

"How did you know?" she finally whispered, at once relieved to share her secret and devastated to speak of Mino aloud.

Laura looked down, massaged the calluses on her fingers. "I used to hear you leaving your bed in the night sometimes. Once, I followed you to the attic, watched you climb out that window. For the roof. I was so stunned, I just stood there. Then I heard a sound and I hid, and it was him, following you up a few minutes later." She looked shy when she met Violetta's gaze. "I'll never forget how gay you seemed the next morning at breakfast. I'll admit, I was jealous. And fascinated. After that, I could always tell which nights you saw him."

"Oh, Laura," Violetta said, her breath hitching, her hands pressing against her breast. "My heart is so heavy."

Laura came at once and sat beside her. She touched her forehead to Violetta's. "I know. I always wanted to know what it was like up there, with him. But you think I worry too much."

"And you were worried I would worry about your worrying?" Violetta said and both girls managed to laugh.

"I didn't want you to think I'd turn you in. But then, when you were punished, when he left, I didn't know how to tell you I understood. And now everything is so different." She looked around the parlor with a visible incredulity. "But you're still hurting." She reached for Violetta's hands. "What happened?"

Violetta let Laura's eyes warm her, as they had in earlier years. "He asked me to marry him."

Laura gasped. "Why didn't you?"

Violetta shouldn't have been stunned by the quickness of Laura's position. Laura was a born romantic. She would have said yes in Violetta's place.

"What of the *coro,* Laura?" she asked. "Would you put down your violin today and never play again?"

"What of love, Violetta? Would you put that down forever? You did love him, didn't you? Don't you?"

Violetta closed her eyes. *I was his, he was mine.* But what did it matter? She was here. She had chosen music over Mino. She had hurt him enough that she would never see him again.

"Violetta?"

"It's over now," Violetta whispered. She was grateful when their assistants, Helena and Diana, came rushing in to top up her teacup and to refresh the vases with new blooms.

❧

IN BED THAT night, Violetta couldn't stop thinking about Mino. She couldn't sleep; she did not want to dream their song. She tried to push him from her thoughts, but nothing—not Porpora's music, tomorrow's performance, not even the bath she was looking forward to in the morning—could compete with her memories. She could still call up the feeling of standing on that bridge, looking ahead at the Grand Canal. How brilliant life had felt next to Mino.

She rose from bed, went to the window, and slid up the lower sash. She leaned out and gulped the warm spring air. It felt lovely, but it wasn't enough. It wasn't enough just to watch the canal, where lantern-lit gondolas full of laughter glided by. It wouldn't even be enough to go up to the roof.

She had been out unchaperoned in this city one afternoon in her life; it couldn't be the only time.

If she'd said yes to Mino, she would have given up performing, but she might have found new richness in the world. Was he finding it? Was it changing him? She ached to consider who she might be by now if she had said yes.

She went to her armoire and selected her finest dress, the white silk gown she'd worn the day she first sang in the *coro*. How pretty it had seemed the first time she put it on, its thick cuffs of bobbin lace. Now that Violetta intended to wear it outside the Incurables, she saw only its telling simplicity. It would have to do nonetheless. She stripped off her simple nightgown and pulled the dress over her head, smoothing it down her hips. She slid her slippers on her feet.

Finally, she reached into the back of her armoire and found the white *bauta*, tied the black ribbon. Even alone in her room, she felt different, jittery, with a hungry thrill. She faced her window, held her arms out, the way she'd seen women dance with partners in the *piazzas*. She twirled, but the warm night air didn't hold her in return. She felt like a child.

She returned to the window. It was Ascension Day, the start of a two-week feast to celebrate Venice's symbolic marriage to the sea. Violetta could feel the pulsing jubilation on the street below, passing groups of young men and women like her—only free.

She took her cloak from the hook by the door. She turned it inside out. Her heart was racing.

Just one night. Just to see what it was like. Maybe she would step inside a tavern. Maybe she would flirt with a masked gentleman. An hour free on the streets tonight would last Violetta months once she returned to the Incurables' rules. It could be her new secret. She could savor its memory when she felt she couldn't breathe.

If she were discovered leaving the Incurables in the middle of the night, she would be out of the *coro*. But if she didn't follow her heart, she would lose a part of herself more important to her even than her music.

She had to try. She just couldn't be caught.

Easy enough, she heard Mino tease in her mind, goading her on.

The Zattere was two flights down. The sculpture of the orphan girl above the entrance to the dormitory formed a ledge between Violetta and the ground. She eyed the distance. The drop seemed endless. Then she remembered a conversation she'd overheard on the *altana*, about the cloth ladder a gondolier kept in his boat for when someone needed to exit a second-story tryst. She could return via the rocky, climbable ledge that reached a window in the apothecary's ground-floor store room. She was an expert at prying out the loose panes of these windows after her years in the attic. She'd discovered the entrance the afternoon of Mino's proposal.

With trembling hands she stripped her bedsheet and knotted one end to the curtain rod bolted into the wall. She gave it a tug and found it secure. She closed her eyes, made the sign of the cross, and said a prayer to the Madonna for protection before dropping one foot and then the other outside the window. Holding the ladder, she set herself free.

Every muscle in her body clenched as she slowly lowered herself down the sheet. When the toe of her slipper touched the orphan's head, a gleeful yelp escaped her lips. She got her balance. She didn't know which way she'd turn when her feet hit the ground. She couldn't wait to find out.

She wound the twisted sheet into a coil and, after three attempts, finally managed to toss it back up, through her open window. From the statue, it was only a low crouch and a leap to the street. She thought of all the times she had looked down as she climbed to the roof. Tonight, as she leaped to the cobblestoned Zattere, Violetta looked up at the stars.

Her ankle smarted when she landed, but she wasted no time worrying over it. She settled her clothes, straightened her mask, and ran.

It felt so good to move alone, independent of a tribe of orphans. Tonight the air felt alive with spring and the buildings didn't make her feel strangled but embraced. Her dress fluttered behind her, and the *bauta*'s ribbon whipped in the cool wind. She turned a corner, and ran directly into a band of costumed strangers.

"Excuse me," she said, quick to check her mask.

"There is a price to pay for that offense," a masked young man said, bowing. "You must join us."

Violetta laughed. Was he joking?

He traveled in a group of six: four young women, two young men. They passed around a bottle; a young woman tipped her mask up slightly to hold it to her lips. They commenced singing a boisterous song, complete with twirling dance steps, unlike anything Violetta had seen.

One woman's black cloak was open at the neck. Beneath it glowed an exquisite gown of pink silk, cut low and corseted with ribbons that shone in the rushlight on the *calle* corner. Violetta felt how chaste and wrong her own dress was. Even the finest clothes she owned didn't belong outside the Incurables. She felt ashamed of her inside-out cloak, how obviously it traced where she'd come from. Only her mask helped her to blend in.

"Where are you headed all alone?" the young man asked.

"I don't know," she said nervously and laughed.

"So come with us," the young woman in pink said. "We're going to a fabulous party at a palazzo next door to La Sirena."

Before Violetta could refuse, the woman linked her arm through Violetta's, and it was decided. She was going. Did it matter where?

They walked quickly, the woman's wooden-heeled, jewel-encrusted shoes clacking gaily on the cobblestones. Violetta had to hurry to keep up in her own silent leather slippers. She envied the percussion of her companion's footsteps. She wanted to make music with her body.

"What's your name?" the woman asked. She smelled of roses.

Letta was on the tip of Violetta's tongue. But she couldn't breathe aloud the name that only Mino called her. She knew she could not say *Violetta*, of course. She was newly famous for her singing at the Incurables. She'd heard people call her *Violetta, voce d'angelo*—voice of the angel—in the church, to her great astonishment.

Over the woman's shoulder, a vine of jasmine caught her eye. They were the same flowers Mino had strewn on the apartment bed that afternoon. Street flowers. Simple flowers. Of all the bouquets Violetta had received from admirers over the past few months, none had smelled so good as Mino's jasmine.

"Gelsomina," she said.

It made no difference to the woman, who wrapped painted nails around Violetta's arm and embarked again on her drunken song. Together they dashed around the corner of the *calle*. Occasional rushlights illuminated the streets. But in between these lanterns the *calli* were cast in shadows, and for long stretches Violetta could see almost nothing, not where she was going, not the company she traveled with.

It was thrilling and frightening, and when she suddenly found herself looking up at the Scuola Grandi della Carità, where the lay musicians trained, and where Violetta had gone on a dozen alms walks over the years, she could hardly believe she was still in the same city, minutes away from the Incurables. She wanted to get far away from any place she'd ever been, and at the same time, she wanted to stop and take in every bit of this night.

But she was tugged along at the pace of her new friends, who danced over bridges, forming a slender line to pass other groups almost identical to their own. Might Violetta have taken up with any of them, be headed somewhere else tonight? There was no making sense of her journey. She didn't want to try.

It was magic outside, the whole lagoon seeming to shiver in anticipation of the night ahead. She picked up the lyrics of the song and had just begun singing with hesitant merriment when the revelers stopped before a tall iron gate.

It was open, and she followed her friends inside to a courtyard garden. It was not large, maybe the size of Violetta's suite at the Incurables. In Venice, if one wanted an expansive garden, one bought a palazzo on the less densely populated island of Giudecca. But this garden was candlelit and marvelously manicured. Two tall topiary bushes were shaped like cherubs in flight.

"This way," said the woman who had taken Violetta's arm. She gestured toward the palazzo across the garden. The house was majestic, four stories of pale pink marble, chandeliers lit in every window.

Two iron torches marked the palazzo's entrance. A masked servant dressed in black and sporting a voluminous silver periwig stood at the door. At the sight of their group, to Violetta's amazement, the guard held the door wider and gestured them inside.

A current of maskers pushed her forward into a foyer. The ceilings towered over her and the intricate terrazzo floor was made of pearl and black marble. The other guests seemed to take this party's splendor for granted, as if it were commonplace. Perhaps it was.

On Violetta's left, three enormous trunks were opened wide, revealing a wealth of colorful accessories. A painted wooden plaque above them read:

DISGUISES FOR YOUR PLEASURE

Guests fell upon the trunks, rifling through them to embellish their already extravagant costumes. Violetta joined them, rising on her toes at the back of the crowd to see what she might put on.

One whole trunk contained nothing but stacks of the black mask called the *moretta*, which Violetta had seen the women on the *altana* model. It had no ribbons, no strap. It appeared a miracle that it stayed in place. But on the mask's interior, a tiny black button was fixed behind the lips, to be held between the teeth. The *moretta* rendered its wearer mute. When Violetta was younger, this had seemed alarming, but the women on the *altana* giggled over it, eroticized it. Now she began to understand. A woman could keep her voice a secret—like her breasts, like the soft inner flesh of her thighs—until she herself chose to reveal it.

Tonight Violetta's friend in the pink dress chose the *moretta,* and Violetta was tempted to take one, too, but she feared she'd forget herself, open her mouth, and drop the mask. She couldn't risk it.

She claimed a black lace fan as big as a lute, a crown woven with violet flowers, and a feathered blue sable cape, illicitly soft. She draped it over her shoulders, tied silk strings around her neck. She batted her fan in front of her mask and felt her exquisite anonymity.

Passing through the foyer, she entered a massive ballroom decorated with great globes of fragrant roses. A crowd of partygoers looked down from a second-story balcony that ringed the room. Persian carpets and candles fatter than bottles of wine gave the party a hushed atmosphere, but if you drew close enough to any group, the room was alive with laughter, booming conversations, and fast hands.

Violetta blinked in amazement. Here were all the stories from the *altana* come to life. It was the most exciting place she had ever been, better than her childhood fantasies because it was real. She was a part of it. She would never be the same.

A harp played and a soprano sang in the back corner, but Violetta was too far to hear clearly. She wove nearer, staying close to the pastel walls. She paused before a fresco of a masked Fate smiling down on a pair of mortal lovers. She sidestepped piles of guests sprawled atop one another on the furniture, which was pressed back against the wall to make room for dancing.

Women dressed as men moved through the ballroom serving drinks, extending silver trays. Violetta stared at them, wondering what it felt like to wear men's clothing, to be exciting to both sexes. Laura would have fainted by now, but Violetta wanted to touch the servers' cheeks, the beards penciled across their jaws.

"Champagne, madam?" One server bowed before her, approximating a man's deep voice. Flustered, Violetta lifted a glass and quickly took a sip. She startled as a tingle spread through her mouth. She'd never felt such a sensation. It was wonderful, the taste only a distant neighbor to the watery red wine the *coro* girls drank at dinner. This had the essence of a lemon blossom with a hint of sweetness.

Since she'd moved up to the *coro*, Violetta felt stifled by her newfound attention. At this party, she felt free. She could be foolish and drunk. No one would notice. No one would care.

She no longer saw anyone she'd come in with. They had all transformed into something else when they stepped inside.

She passed a young man in a tightly curled white wig, who sat on a tufted blue pillow on the floor, weeping with his face in his hands.

A woman leaned in to him and raised his face in her palm. She held her glass of champagne for him to sip, murmuring something. He raised his drooping *bauta* an inch and gulped the champagne like water. Then he returned to his sobbing.

"Is he all right?" Violetta asked as the woman lifted her glass to a waiter, signaling more champagne.

She smirked at Violetta. Her mask was small, concealing only her eyes, and highlighting the beauty mark painted on the dimple of her left cheek. Her lips were red with rouge, forbidden on the streets of Venice. They were mesmerizing as she opened her mouth. "He gambled away his lover tonight in a game of faro."

Violetta wondered at this—was his lover a courtesan? Did he *own* the woman? She knew she must keep her questions to herself.

Now she realized why La Sirena had sounded familiar. She had heard rumors of Dorsoduro's most exclusive casino, where money and reputations were made and lost and where trysts began behind velvet curtains. Its dark rooms eschewed the republic's strict laws forbidding jewelry and makeup and games of chance. This party must be the overflow after a night of gambling. She remembered the *altana* women saying:

"One can lose almost anything at La Sirena," Violetta said.

"Indeed," the woman said, leaning closer, speaking intimately. "But one can win almost anything, too. Last *carnevale*, my lover won two African giraffes from a sultan. He keeps them in a horse stall on the sandbars of Lido. Their flanks are so soft you can hardly stand it."

"I could have saved her in another hand," the weeping man chimed in from his pillow.

The woman leaned closer to Violetta, shook her head, and whispered, "He's really crying over the fact that it was *her* idea to put herself on the betting table when he ran out of money. And how quickly she went to the victor. Carlo didn't even have time to ask for my purse to raise his bet. Carina was already gone." Patting the man's shoulder, she said, "Give her an hour, Carlo. She'll come back to you, and better than ever. That Senator Gritti is nothing special. I should know." The woman clucked her tongue, hoisting him up under the arms. "Remember, our host reveres the lucky, not the losers. So get up and dance, or go and find yourself a tavern in which to cry."

The man straightened, lifted his mask to dry his tears. His face was young and lovely—tan skin, good teeth—but his eyes were red and miserable. He seemed to notice Violetta for the first time. He bowed extravagantly until his periwig touched the mosaic tiles of the *terrazzo*.

"Dance the furlana with me, stranger?"

Violetta wanted to focus on the music, to close her eyes and take it apart in her mind, but she felt that a man in Carlo's state should not be further disappointed, even if she was anxious about how little she knew of the dance.

"I don't know the steps," she warned him, placing her hand in his.

"Forget steps. Simply choose an emotion and hold it like a lover." He put his arms around her waist and led her to the dance floor. "Mine is agony. Ever since I fell in love with Carina, I am always the best dancer at the ball."

Violetta squeezed his hand. He looked at her, and through two masks, they understood each other.

He swept her up so that her feet barely touched the ground. Watching couples in the *campo*, dancing had always seemed to her a partnership, requiring two knowledgeable parties. But now there was no question what Violetta should do with her arms or legs or hips. Carlo moved with so much certainty, his arms tuning her as if she were an instrument. She thought of herself twirling before her window earlier that evening, and felt like a child no more.

At the harpist's side, a female singer stood tall, dressed elaborately with a red wig and a white mask. She sang not with the soft slur of the Veneto, but with an accent Violetta had never heard.

Imported, Violetta realized. Austrian or Neapolitan. The best musicians in Venice were all cloistered in the *ospedali.* To sing in an opera house or at a private party like this one, you had to come from far away.

By the middle of the song, Violetta had fallen into the rhythm, thrilled to find the dance within her. When the music ended, she felt different, more like a woman than she had before.

"That was wonderful," she said, catching her breath.

Carlo smiled sadly, still holding her in his arms. "So, what's his name?"

Violetta blinked. What had he felt through her dancing? She looked away, not wanting to think about anything but tonight.

A pair of hands covered Carlo's eyes, and he turned to face a tiny young woman with the bearing of a sparrow, dyed white-blond hair, and a black mask painted with gold.

"See how you flourish without me?" she asked teasingly, with a nod at Violetta. Laughter made the woman's mask vibrate.

"Carina," Carlo said, showering the woman's neck with kisses. "You destroy me. I can't live without you."

Carina cooed over him as he laid his head upon her breast. She smiled at Violetta.

"Does your lover collapse when you dance with another?"

The memory of Mino kissing Reine flashed before Violetta. She forced it away, but could not find the words to respond.

Carlo raised his head, as if remembering Violetta. He bowed again, kissed her palms, both cheeks of her mask.

"I shall look for you every time I hear a harp," he said.

"I'll dance with your agony anytime," Violetta said, leaving him to Carina.

But after the couple twirled away, she felt intensely alone. She drew to the side of the room, slipping under an archway to find some air. She reached a marble staircase lit with candles.

One flight up, she stood before an empty library with a glass-doored balcony. A fire glowed in the hearth. She glanced around, making sure no one could see her as she moved across the room. She turned the golden handle and stepped outside. The air was a little cooler there. She smelled the brine of the water, felt it on her skin.

Below her spread the Grand Canal. She'd never seen it so close. The only other time she'd gotten near had been standing on that bridge with Mino, and even then she'd only glimpsed a fraction of it in the distance. Now it swept below this balcony. Right beneath her feet. She looked down to the left at the curving rows of palazzi on either side of the water. She looked to the right, where the current swept out toward the lagoon. How fast and smooth the water was here. She listened to the slap of it against the mossy steps of the palazzo's dock.

Three gondolas bobbed below her, tied to posts by leather straps. She wondered who rode them, and where. The water here was as lovely as the water of the Giudecca Canal, but here, the fine homes on the other bank were close enough that Violetta could see inside their windows. Directly across was another vast ballroom with another twinkling chandelier and other masked dancers underneath it.

Were all parties as grand as the one she'd fallen into? Was it the start of the *Festa della Sensa* that called for them to be so extravagant, or was it the taste and purse of the host? Would she ever know the answer to these questions? Or would she leave here and return to the Incurables and never slip away again? It couldn't be. A girl couldn't taste champagne but a single time in her life. Tonight had to be a beginning.

Her thoughts went to Mino. Did he now live nights like this? Did he stand in rooms this fine, with views this spectacular? Did he ever think of her?

She hadn't come out tonight hoping to find him in the vast maze of Venice. She wasn't that foolish. But the chance of it had flickered through her mind.

Say she did find him. Say they recognized each other through their masks. What then?

I am yours, you are mine . . .

She sang to the Venetian night.

"You're putting that Neapolitan soprano downstairs to shame," a man said behind her. Violetta spun around, unaware she'd been heard. The man in the doorway was tall, dressed in a black robe lined with squirrel fur. Violetta noted his sleeves, which signified a man's importance. The proper greeting for a nobleman was to kiss his sleeve; the wider the sleeve, the lower to the ground the greeter had to bow. Were she to greet this man properly, her chin might touch the floor.

He wore no mask. He was the only person whose full face she had seen tonight, and she found him startlingly handsome. His hair was dark and thick, gathered with a ribbon at the nape of his neck—not like the periwigs so many men wore. His eyes sparkled the palest blue, like icicles hanging off a windowsill at dawn. He was older than Violetta, but she couldn't tell by how much. There was something magnetic about him, something deeper than his features, commanding frame, or fine clothes, and she couldn't tell what it was.

She realized he had been watching her longer than the short moments of her song. A part of her wondered whether he had seen her dance with Carlo, or had even seen her enter the party, get picked up by strangers off the street, even all the way back to the moment she gazed at the moon and felt it wasn't enough. Maybe he had seen all of that—or maybe he could glimpse it all right now. There was something unknowably perceptive in his gaze.

"I'm sorry," she said. "I thought I was alone."

He raised an eyebrow and smiled. "A masquerade is just the place to come for solitude." When she ducked her head he added, "I'm serious.

I think parties are better from a distance, looking in." He stepped closer, nodding at the window, at the party going on in the palazzo across the canal.

"Maybe everything is better from a distance," Violetta said.

Now he turned to face her, inches away. "Not you. Not your song." He reached forward gently and tried to lift her mask. "May I be so bold?"

Violetta jumped away. "No!" She slid around him, her eye on the door to leave. She had taken enough risks for one night. It was time to go.

He caught her hand, and then, feeling her anxiety, he let go.

"All right," he said. "If you don't want me to see you, how can I hear you again? Where do you sing? Don't tell me—you're the new principal at Teatro San Angelo. Everyone is comparing her to—"

"No," Violetta said. "I don't. I'm not . . . that song is just for me."

"That ought to be a crime," the man teased. "A good Venetian would alert the Council of Ten. Lucky for you, I'm not good."

She laughed despite herself and he exhaled, seeming to loosen.

"Excuse my forwardness. But your voice reminds me of someone I used to know." A smile flickered across his face, but she sensed his lightheartedness was a facade. She wanted to know what lay underneath. For a moment they stood in silence. "Would you consider coming back here sometime, singing for an audience?"

"Here? Is this your party?" she asked.

He nodded. "I can't sing to save my life. I am a patron of the arts by default. I have spent my life trying to glean how the great musicians do it."

"I've heard it said that all you need for dancing is a feeling. Perhaps the same can be said of all performing."

"Is that what you think?" he asked.

She felt him trying to get closer to her with these words. It excited her to meet a man who patronized musicians outside the Incurables, but he could do nothing for her. She was a *coro* girl now. For better or worse, she had made her choice. She must steer the conversation away from herself, lest she become tempted to dream of what might have been and give herself away.

"I think Venetians love being made to feel something intensely," she said. "We really don't care what it is."

"Maybe that's the trouble with this party," he said. She expected him to glance over his shoulder, where the rising revelry could be heard from downstairs, but he only looked at her. "I always want to create something so full of pleasure that there is room for nothing else. But my guests bring their own variety of feelings, their agonies and regrets."

As Violetta pondered his words, the clock struck twelve. A cheer rose from the ballroom. The harp music changed to an *accelerato* and was joined by a trumpet.

"Time for me to go," she said, because something about this man compelled her to stay, and that desire, more than anything else tonight, felt dangerous. She longed to experience more of the wildness of the party, but she had already taken her luck too far. Morning would come quickly. She could not risk being bleary or hoarse at rehearsal. She brushed past him, leaving the balcony.

"Will you stay, just one more moment?" The sorrow in his voice made Violetta pause at the library door. She turned and watched him walk to a desk. He opened a drawer and, after a moment, held up a white velvet pouch. He untied its strings to withdraw a large, round stone hanging from a golden chain.

It was the color of the sky just after dark, and flecked inside with an infinity of lighter blue grains that reminded Violetta of stars. The color changed completely if you shifted your angle or looked through candlelight. It took on a deeper color, a more dazzling luster.

She froze when he stepped close to her and moved to fasten it around her neck. His fingers brushed her skin and heat licked through her, rising in her cheeks.

"Anytime you change your mind," he said, "if you wish to sing for an audience of one or one thousand"—his voice was quiet, at her ear—"come and see me. Here or at my casino down the *calle.* Wear this necklace. No one will ask your name. My staff will know you by the black opal."

Six

AT MIDNIGHT ON Ascension Day, a beautiful, balmy evening in May, Mino dashed around Piazza San Marco, whisking tables and chairs out from under the patrons on the patio of the Venice Triumphant café. For the rich drinking madeira and flirting under the arches, night never fell in the piazza. But for the proprietors of the cafés, midnight marked the hour when the *sbirri* started fining establishments whose furniture still sat outside.

Floriano, the owner of the Venice Triumphant, was cunning in the most Venetian way. He saw a loophole and had hired men like Mino to swap out the wicker furniture with poultry coops and empty vegetable crates left out in a neighboring market. There was no prohibition about poultry coops in the *sbirri*'s book of laws, and so the party could go on through breakfast.

Mino had bought new clothes and begun taking rooms at boarding houses with his gold from the gondola ride three months ago. But still, like every employer who had hired Mino for small jobs since then,

Floriano shook his head when Mino showed him the painted face of his half token.

"Nothing?" Mino said, and something in his voice caused the café owner to look at him regretfully. "My mother . . ." he'd tried to explain.

"You can work here on the condition that you don't show that to my customers. That painting . . . combined with the look on your face." Floriano shook his head. "These people come here to have fun." Then he'd punched Mino lightly on the shoulder. "I hope you find her. Just not here."

Floriano paid Mino four soldi for the hour it took him to ease patrons out of their seats, replacing the chairs with various-sized crates. For the ladies, Mino laid a fine linen napkin atop to preserve their skirts, setting them back so subtly they hardly knew they had been displaced.

Before half past twelve, the party sat lower and smelled faintly of hay, but the conversations became more intimate, revolving around the latest scandals and masquerades, the French fashions that would be sold the following morning in the center of this piazza. For the next two weeks, during the *Festa della Sensa*, Venice's upper class would shop in these stalls. They would fill their wardrobes with enough Parisian couture to last until this time next year, when the stalls would come again.

Most of the women at the Venice Triumphant wanted to flirt with Mino, to stroke his bare cheek, tie their *baute* around his head to see how he'd look masked, and run long painted fingernails through his hair, but Mino eluded their grasps. This was the best money of all his cobbled-together jobs, and it demanded efficiency. Mino had promised a hundred women he'd meet them later at a party or dark tavern, but he never did, and they never held it against him. Among their class, there was always new titillation to be found around the corner.

He found close contact with the aristocracy discomfiting. It wasn't so long ago that he'd envisioned a simple life with Letta. But now that he was living on the streets, the work he could get required he serve the richest nobles in Venice. They exhausted him with their infinite masks and costumes and charades. Nothing about them seemed real. Each night, after he was paid, he felt a compulsion to roam, to leave behind the collective fantasy these rich customers shared.

Sometimes he would drop into a cheap tavern for a drink, and those evenings invariably ended in pain as he showed his half token to a stranger who neither understood nor cared. But mostly, he'd walk alone with Sprezz, only dropping into whatever bed he could rent that night when he could walk no farther.

Sprezz was waiting at the service entrance of the Venice Triumphant. Mino tossed him a half-eaten roasted pheasant wing plucked from a patron's plate. Sprezz leaped to catch it, snapping the bone up and licking the salt from his chops. They strolled toward the canal. Sprezz was always up for walking, knocking his head tenderly against Mino's knees when they paused at an intersection.

Hours earlier, as the sun set over the white dome of the basilica of La Salute, the doge had floated down the Grand Canal, waving from the deck of his majestic *bucintoro.* His ship was four times as wide as the standard gondola, decorated with garlands of flowers. Throngs of Venetians had gathered on the sea-facing promenade of San Marco, and in boats of all sizes on the Grand Canal, to see the doge. Wearing the white cambric hat he apparently never took off, he tossed the ceremonial wedding ring into the murky green water.

Mino had always found the *Festa della Sensa* romantic, a time to recommit yourself to what you loved. When he was younger, in the years just before he met Letta, these two weeks had been the time each year when he tended his violin, sneaking out to barter a few eggs for new rosin at the book printer's shop behind the Incurables. He coated his bow with the small, translucent yellow cake and relished the revived strength and control it gave his playing.

This was the first year Mino had witnessed the way the rest of Venice celebrated Ascension, had stood in the crowd on the promenade, cheering on the procession of boats. He'd watched the doge sail by, on his way to a waterfront feast near Lido. The doge's *bucintoro* was followed by a huge fleet of boats bearing flags and banners. On the decks of each, richly costumed men played fifes and trumpets. Mino wondered what it would be like to stand among them with his violin. The wind in his hair, the rhythm of the boat beneath his feet, his music sailing to these crowds. He missed playing.

He missed playing with Letta.

He thought about that golden ring in the water. He had never even taken out the ring he'd found for her. Now it was part of the lagoon. He'd thrown it into the sea the night he left the Incurables. If he'd foreseen how destitute his future was, he might have held on to it. But at the time he couldn't bear it. He'd had to free himself of the reminder of what a fool he'd been.

He could have paid a month's rent with that ring. But no, even as desperate as he was now, Mino knew he would never have pawned it. He only wished he hadn't thrown it away.

In five hours he was meant to be at the *maranzaria*, to unload the morning crates of oranges. Only one soldo, but the work was easy and quiet and Mino always left with breakfast for himself and Sprezz. He knew he should sleep, but the room he'd taken for the week was squalid, and he shared a bed with one and sometimes two Scandinavians who stank of mildew.

The breeze coming off the canal promised summer, but its fragrance of heady, night-blooming jasmine took Mino back to the apartment and that *carnevale* afternoon. He stood at the water's edge and thought of diving in to find the little gold band. He knew he would not succeed, but he dreamed of staying underneath the water, searching until his misery ended.

When he finally looked across the canal, for an instant he thought he saw a giant curved fishtail, dipping beneath the dark surface, now gone. He rubbed his eyes.

La Sirena. He hadn't thought of the casino in months, swept away by the many emotions of that day at the Incurables. Suddenly, it called to him.

He wanted to be there and couldn't say why. He wanted to drink in a dark place, in a *sestiere* far from the gaiety of San Marco. Before he knew it, he and Sprezz were crossing the Rialto Bridge. His eyes avoided its apex; all bridges now reminded him of where he had stood with Letta, where for a moment, all his dreams had seemed possible.

He wound through the *calli,* past the fortune-tellers and the pretty flower girls out too late. Twice his path dead-ended and he had to retrace his steps. Then, suddenly, there was the cork tree, whose lowest bough bridged the narrow canal. There was the staircase that spiraled from the street up to a second-story balcony, to a door lit by a blue glass lantern. There was the plaque, the upside-down fishtail as intriguing as it had been the first time Mino saw it. Only the large man at the door dissuaded Mino.

"Do we know you?" he asked as Mino approached.

Mino's lack of mask made him suspicious. He knew everyone wore them inside casinos, no matter the season or the law. He took out his *bauta* and tied it on, which only made the doorkeeper laugh.

"Do you know everyone you let in?" Mino asked.

"I know their money," the doorkeeper said.

For once Mino had six whole soldi in his pockets. Five were meant to go to Zanata, the deaf landlady, for tomorrow's rent, but it didn't matter. Mino could have a hundred soldi in his pockets, and it wouldn't impress this man, not at the door of a gambling house. Mino wished he still had the snakeskin purse from the gambler he'd brought to this door months ago. He should never have offered it to Carlo as a peace-making gesture when he returned the gondolier's boat. He could have waved it now. A purse like that, you didn't even need to see the gold inside.

"This is not a place for skulduggery," the doorkeeper said, and Mino understood that, of course, it was just the place for skulduggery. Everywhere in this city was for skulduggery, just as it was for feasting and philosophizing, for making music and making love. This was Venice, after all.

The doorkeeper's warning told him that there was money to be earned inside, and not just at the gambling tables. There were better-paying jobs than hauling oranges and chicken coops, and why shouldn't Mino find them?

"I only want a drink," he claimed, and the doorkeeper shook his head.

At that moment, two drunken men barged out the door in a roiling brawl. They cursed each other, and each other's mothers and descendants, as they fumbled past Mino and up against the railing of the bridge. More men followed, piling on, and the doorkeeper sprang into action, his immense hands seizing the back of each brawling man's neck. Threats were shouted, punches thrown, bottles smashed—a storm as violent as it was indiscriminate, and sour with fortified wine.

Mino and Sprezz, suddenly invisible, slipped inside the casino door.

La Sirena was dark, the air smoky with the singe of tobacco. The walls were tiled, the ceilings low. There was a large room filled with tables for gambling, and a raised stage at the rear with a thick black curtain behind it. The bar spanned the wall to the left of the entrance and shone with the splendor of a hundred bottles. Behind the bar, an arched doorway led into a second room with velvet seating for dining and other pleasures. Before him, only a few candles were still lit on the tables and on the bar. On the stage at the back, a woman sang something slow and melancholy, accompanied by a violinist who kept his eyes on her even as she gazed into the distance.

He made his way to the back wall to listen. The sight of them made Mino's chest ache with all he'd lost. His home. His violin. His job. And Letta. All because he'd thought they could be happy playing music together.

Nothing to do now but forget about old dreams. He would never make it in this city if his heart broke every time he heard a woman sing against a violin.

He crossed the casino, Sprezz at his heels, past a few booths of bleary men playing cards. He reached the bar. He was used to borrower's wine, a poor brew he could get on credit at the derelict *magazzens* near the Rialto. They didn't pour anything like that here. These were new bottles of Tokaj and Recioto. Whatever he ordered he would have to pay for. He met the eyes of the barmaid through her mask. She was young, and the way she held her body, the quickness of her pouring, told Mino she was scrappy. He tapped a brown bottle that looked like it would do the trick, then put the single coin he had to spare upon the bar. He hoped it would be enough.

The barmaid looked at him, and he sensed if he'd been there hours earlier she might have been gentle on him, but she was tired now and had been pushed around all night. She poured Mino a swallow and pocketed the coin.

Reluctantly, he pulled another coin from his pocket, placed it in her waiting palm. Now she topped him off.

"If you don't have enough money to play," she said, reaching over the bar to scratch Sprezz's ears, "sit near the musicians. Avoid these men." She nodded toward the only lively booth left in the casino, where five men played a loud and brutal game of cards. "Only the mongrels are still here this time of night. Everyone else has gone to Federico's party."

He didn't know who Federico was. He was interested only in his wine, which he finished too quickly. He wanted more. He was about to sit alone before the singer when one of the men in the booth called him.

"Boy—"

Mino looked up. They had finished their card game. They were too drunk to open the next bottle of wine.

"Join us. Help us." He waved a corkscrew at Mino, who crossed the bar. Six months out of the Incurables, Mino had become deft with the little metal instrument. He wanted more to drink and was lonely enough not to mind the company of mongrels. He avoided the barmaid's eyes as he sat among the men. Sprezz lay down at his feet.

"She was gone three days," a man with a lopsided white wig was saying. Turning to Mino, he explained, "My wife."

Mino had overheard stories like this from the customers at the Venice Triumphant.

"And so?" a second wigged man said, filling his glass with amber wine.

"In the end," the first man said, "I employed the inquisitor."

The men around the table murmured, shifted. Mino felt himself leaning closer.

"I was sure he would find her in bed with some fop," he said. "It's one thing to take a lover, quite another to leave your home, your family unattended."

"Three days is too long," another man agreed.

"I was ready to kill her," the man said, then shrugged with morose indifference. "She was already dead." He pulled on a long wooden pipe and puffed the smoke out slowly. "She'd fallen into a canal, washed up between the gondolas."

"The inquisitor always finds them, dead or alive," another man said as the bottle made another round of the table.

Mino swallowed his nerves. "I'm looking for someone."

The song pulsed behind him, keeping time with the quick beats of his heart. He knew there was a reason he had come here. He had felt the pull toward La Sirena from the moment he'd first seen it. He felt emboldened by this intuition that being here tonight might change something.

"My mother."

"I saw your mother." The man beside him popped Mino in the ribs with his elbow. "Last night."

"I just left her this morning," a second added, and everyone around Mino laughed.

Mino poured himself more of their wine, let their jokes glance off him. "How do I reach this inquisitor, the one who finds women, dead or alive?"

"You're an orphan?" asked a man Mino hadn't heard speak yet. He was the youngest of the group, small, with a friendlier demeanor. "Are you from an *ospedale*?"

The word piqued the interest of the others, but before any of them could ask indelicate questions about the orphan girls, he said, "I left a long time ago. I don't think about it. Only my mother."

"Do you have a half token?" the young man asked, curious.

"What's a half token?" the lopsidedly wigged man asked.

Reluctantly, Mino brought it out. He held it fast but flashed it round the table.

The man with the lopsided wig reached for it, grew annoyed when Mino wouldn't let go. He looked at it in Mino's hand, seemed to find it almost as powerful as Mino did.

"I've seen her," he said, and the others laughed. More jokes.

"No, really." He glanced up at Mino and seemed different, earnest. "I swear on my own mother's honor." Now the men around the table listened. "There is a woman in Castello who is the spitting image of this painting." He thought a moment, shook his head. "But she is older, maybe thirty-five or forty."

"This painting is at least twelve years old," Mino said hoarsely. Was it possible?

The man told him an address on the east side of the city. "Go and see her. If it is your mother, bring her back here for a drink, on me."

❦

MINO AND SPREZZ slept in a small, quiet *campo* in Castello, at the northeastern edge of the city, not far from the address he'd been given by the man in the lopsided wig.

He felt foul when he woke up, sweating in the fierce glow of the rising sun. He knew he looked awful, but he couldn't spare the money for a stufe to clean himself up. He splashed his face with water from the canal, ran wet fingers through his hair, and as he let the water trickle down his face he wondered: Was today the day? The morning was so hot but he shivered in anticipation. He brushed twigs and leaves from his cloak, spat on his boots to polish them. He combed through Sprezz's fur to pick out nits, the dog growling his protest.

"This is as good as we're going to get," he said to Sprezz, and the dog followed him around the corner, down the *calle*, to a tall and narrow building with a snarling brass lioness rapper on its door.

The woman who opened to Mino's knock was pretty, pale skinned, and ample, a few years older than Mino. Her shoulder was bare where her loose chemise had abandoned its post. When she smiled, coy and fatigued, Mino knew everything there was to know about the business of this establishment.

Hope flickered into his mind that he was mistaken—either about the address or his suspicions. He pushed it aside. No sense in deluding himself further. This was a whorehouse, and if his mother was here and a whore, so be it. She would still be his mother. Who was Mino to judge what anyone did to get by?

"We don't open until sundown, sweetness," the woman told him, leaning against the door. She extended her bare foot to stroke Sprezz along his back. The dog loved it, lifting his chin and closing his eyes.

"I'm not looking for . . . I'm looking for . . ." Mino stammered.

"Not a fuck but a lady, right?" she said smoothly, teasing him but being sweet about it. "Someone specific?"

He fumbled for the token in his pocket, expecting to place it before her eyes and have them light with recognition. He hoped to have to say nothing else. His heart raced.

She leaned forward to gaze at the painted woman's face. "Come on in."

Mino steadied himself against the doorframe. Tears pricked his eyes. He thought about turning and running. How foolish it had been not to take a bath, to buy a razor on credit, make himself appear at least a little dignified.

The woman ushered him through a shabby yet elegant parlor and into a small kitchen that smelled of coffee and yeast. She put him in a chair before a small wood table, facing a window whose sill was lined with shiny plums. She sat across from him, tugged at her chemise, and returned to peeling boiled eggs into a bowl.

"Where?" Mino whispered.

The woman put an egg on a plate and slid it to him. "Eat," she said, then poured some coffee. "Drink."

He was so hungry he could make no overtures to refuse. He ate three eggs, offered Sprezz the yolk of a fourth, and drank two strong cups of coffee. It only made him hungrier. "Thank you."

"You're an orphan," the woman said, biting into the final egg herself and chewing in a spellbindingly loud manner.

Mino nodded. She knew from his half token. But why was she still sitting here? Why not go up and fetch whoever resembled his painting and was the reason Mino had been let in?

"Real fresh out of the *ospedale*?" the woman said.

"Not so fresh," he said. Did her eyes not see how grizzled he was, how much more haggard than any orphan boy?

"Fresh, though," she said and frowned at him. "For god's sake, you're not even in on the joke."

"What joke?"

"What's your name?"

"Mino," he said. "What joke?"

"Let me guess, Mino. You were drunk last night and you showed your token to some other drunk who sent you here?"

Mino swallowed. "He swore—"

"On his own mother's honor?" She sighed, waved her hand. "Every bastard in this city tells every orphan he can that his mother is a whore, just waiting for him to go and save her. Odds are, the bastards are right about the whore part. Only not the waiting-to-be-saved part." She cracked her knuckles. "Every woman I know has babies in some *ospedale.* That painting isn't your mother, Mino. Any more than your mother is waiting for you upstairs. Whoever told you that was gulling you."

Her tone was at odds with her words. She was trying to be kind. Mino hung his head, disgusted with himself. Sprezz brought his chin to Mino's thigh and sighed.

"I want you to finish your coffee," the woman said, rising from the table and brushing eggshells from her skirt. "Then leave here before anyone else comes down those stairs." She moved to the window, her back to him. "You can't trust people, Mino. Promise you won't do it again."

He drank his coffee wordlessly. Before he rose, a cacophony of wooden-platformed footsteps clamored down the stairs. Suddenly there were two more women before him, filling the kitchen with wide red skirts, smelling of ambergris, the earthy, almost mossy, highly sought-after cologne from the east. Mino wanted to leave but he couldn't take his eyes off the three of them. He was so tired that it crossed his mind just to stay and ask for a bed, to spend the rest of his money until they kicked him out.

One of the newcomers sat in his lap, whispering to ask if she could have a sip of his coffee. "We don't open until sundown, but for you . . ."

"He's not looking for a fuck," the first woman said. "He's an orphan."

"In my experience," the whore on his lap said, "the two are not mutually exclusive."

Now Sprezz barked and snarled, and Mino looked down at him. Time to go.

"Goodbye, Mino," said the woman who'd given him the eggs. "Don't look back anymore; look ahead. Make your own family. You'll be happier."

Her words felt impossible and true. Mino rose reluctantly, squeezing himself out from under the woman on his lap, apologizing. Eventually he made his way out the door onto a street that felt blindingly bright and warm.

"What now?" he asked Sprezz. He stuffed his hands in his pockets and stopped short. He had been emptied of his last coins.

Four soldi was all he'd had, and that whore had taken it from him. He turned back to the building, banged on the door. No one answered.

Mino punched the stone frame of the brothel's entrance, then cried out in pain. He gave up.

At the entrance to a narrow *calle*, Sprezz nudged Mino toward a café. Mino sighed and felt worse as the dog pulled his charming beggar act and returned with a hefty portion of fish bones. They sat down at the water's edge together. Mino ate in shame.

Robbed. Humiliated. Back on the streets.

Letta would never have allowed anything like this happen to her. You only had to look at where she was now to know it. She was a star of the *coro*. He was just another angry fool in a city full of them.

❦

HE WENT TO see her again that night. He couldn't help himself. She may never love him back, but he could at least still have her voice. But by the time he staggered to the Incurables, vespers was over, the church emptying.

He stood before his old home in his mask, his cloak tied tight over his orphanage clothes despite the heat. He stared up at the roof and looked for her.

She wasn't that girl anymore. She would be in her private parlor, being waited on. Or she would be in a musical discussion with Porpora. She wouldn't have time for the horizon anymore.

Did she ever miss it?

He stood there until darkness settled over the building. Sprezz was sleeping at his feet, scampering after a dream.

"Is that you? Mino? Sprezz?"

Mino looked toward the voice and saw Carlo, the gondolier whose boat he had once borrowed, parked again at the Zaterre. The young man grinned and waved. "You look terrible."

"I am down on my luck," Mino admitted.

"Worse than before?" Carlo cracked a smile. He squeezed Mino's shoulder. "Last time you were down on your luck you stole my boat."

"If you can believe it, I am even worse off. Keep tight hold of your oar."

"Come on," Carlo said and stepped onto his gondola, waving Mino closer. "Hop in. I'll buy you a drink."

These were welcome words. "Anywhere but La Sirena."

"Friend," Carlo said and laughed, "where else is there to go?"

Seven

For a week after Ascension Day, Violetta would awaken with the black opal in her palm. The nights were warm, and the mornings were warmer, thick with humidity. In her sleep she would kick off her coverlet, strip bare of her nightclothes, but she wouldn't let go of the necklace. Her fingers traced the iridescent stone. Proof that night had really happened.

That music, those costumes, sipping champagne and dancing the furlana with a handsome stranger. Standing on that balcony with the promise of summer in the air and a view of the Grand Canal. Most of all, the man she'd met at the end. The man who wished to banish sorrow, who had given her the stone as a key to enter his world again.

She remembered his fastening the chain around her neck, how his hands on her skin had thrilled her. She touched the stone and closed her eyes, transporting herself back. But when she tried to recall his face, for some reason she saw Mino, his deep blue eyes watching her as he played and she sang on the roof. She saw his hair blow across his forehead; he never seemed to notice. She saw his hopeful, ready smile.

She held the stone and thought of how she used to disdain Mino's half token. She'd been so young the night she'd pulled him from the wheel, but already it had bothered her to see his hands cradling it. She'd wanted him to forget it. She knew his mother would not be back. Yet he remained attached to the token. Now she knew his attachment had been a pledge to make real his dream of finding her.

Had he done it? Violetta prayed he had. If anyone could do it, it was Mino. He was the only person she had ever met who was good at everything he turned to. He might have unearthed cousins, aunts, and uncles, a grandmother in another *sestiere* with an apartment overlooking a pretty square and garlic drying on strings in the kitchen where she'd teach Mino to cook. Violetta imagined him at a table alive with love, and saw the empty place beside him where she might have sat.

His dream, she reminded herself when she became breathless with regret. Not hers. Her dream changed all the time; its only constant was its remaining out of reach. She always seemed to want too much. She wanted the *coro* and she wanted the masquerades. She wanted Mino back and she wanted the man who'd given her the stone.

That night hadn't filled the hole inside her, only expanded it. Was this the curse of her abandonment? Would she never stop wanting more? Her true dream had to be out there somewhere. She couldn't see it yet, but when she clutched that black opal in her palm, she could almost feel it.

❋

BY THE SULTRY peak of summer, Violetta had dared to climb down from her window three more times. Each time she wore her mask and her best dress, and the opal glittering at her throat.

The second time she sneaked out, she had tugged too hard and ripped the bedsheet, plummeting toward the ground. She'd caught herself, barely, her foot gripping the ledge of the orphan's head. She'd made it to the ground eventually, but was so shaken she didn't wander far.

The next time, she wandered *too* far and got so lost in the dark, winding *calli* of Dorsoduro so long that it was nearly dawn before she made it home. She'd been sure she would never make it back before morning, that it would be the end of the *coro* and the beginning of a monastic prison sentence in a nunnery. The end of music.

She told herself to stop this nighttime wandering.

But the lure of the streets, of life, was too strong. Another sweltering week went by and she had to try again. She had to see the man from the party. There was something about him she wanted to be closer to, with her body and her heart. And so she set out with La Sirena in her mind, carefully retracing her steps from that first night. But somewhere along the maze of *calli*, she lost her nerve. She felt embarrassed by her simple dress, her old shoes and bare head. She found it easier to stay anonymous, to enter the current of another band of revelers and flow wherever they went.

When she got home, she lay in bed awhile, her head spinning pleasantly from the wine she'd drunk, the necklace still fastened at her throat. By day it stayed tucked inside her *bauta*, alongside her money at the back of her armoire, but by night, she wanted it with her. She wondered about its hold on her and why the stranger had given it to her. She wondered how much it was worth. She had passed pawnshops in Dorsoduro on alms walks, and sometimes she wondered how much she might get for this stone. What she would spend it on. Not *acqaioli* or a gondola ride.

How much did real freedom cost? What did it look like? A place where no one remembered her as an orphan? She held the stone and thought on this a long time. If she sold it, would she have enough to leave the Incurables, to start fresh in a new city, one where she could sing and live as she chose? Where she could outrun the memory of Mino? Were there such cities? She didn't know.

But she knew someone who might. The man who'd given her the opal necklace.

Tomorrow night, she'd try again. She'd don her mask and the opal. She would lose neither her courage nor her way. She would make it to La Sirena.

❁

IN THE MORNING, she felt ill before she ate breakfast. She asked for a double portion, which she'd never done before, but her stomach was churning and needed settling. She returned to her suite to warm up her voice with scales before mass. She knew she sounded cloudy as Helena brushed her hair and gossiped about the music school girls. There was a rumor another *coro* singer, Vania, would retire soon, and that Reine would take her place in the *coro*.

"Are you cross?" Helena asked. "You don't like each other."

Violetta rolled her eyes, returning to her scales. The French girl was the least of her worries. She had to be more careful about her drinking the next time she went out.

Laura had a cough, so she was made to keep her distance from Violetta. Violetta felt guiltily grateful for this; Laura was too good at reading her thoughts. She had known about the attic, about Mino, but Violetta's nighttime escapes were far more forbidden than anything she'd done before. She didn't want to put Laura in the position of having to cover for her—or report her.

In rehearsal, as they worked on Porpora's opera *Rosbale*, Violetta felt distracted, watching the sun drag across the sky through the clerestory windows. How distant the night still was, how torturous the passage of time.

❧

BY MOONLIGHT, in her mask and her simplest dress, with her necklace stowed in a pouch in her pocket, she made her fifth escape out her window.

On the warm and windy promenade, she kept apart from larger groups of revelers. But when she saw a young, elegant couple rounding the corner from the narrow calle Incurabili, she hurried to catch up to them.

"Your gown is beautiful," Violetta said, falling in step with the woman, eyeing her lavender silk skirt.

The woman stopped walking, leaned a hip toward Violetta, offering her garment up for praise. She wore no mask but at the corner of her eye, she showed off a black beauty mark known as *la passionata*. Every Venetian beauty mark signified something different, and this one meant the woman burned with passion for the particular man at her side. Some of the orphan girls, Laura among them, swooned over the romance of *la passionata*.

"I've never seen silk so fine," Violetta said.

"It's from the dressmaker at La Minada, on calle—"

"Can she make another?"

"I'm sure she could make one for you"—she glanced at Violetta's orphan's dress—"for a price."

Violetta shook her head. "Could she make another for you? I should like to have this one. Tonight."

The woman and her lover started laughing.

"How much is it worth to you?" the man teased, but when Violetta pulled out her purse and started counting sequins, his eyes widened and his laughter ceased.

"Will five do?"

"Why would you pay so much for a dress?" the woman asked, looking at Violetta with sudden distrust.

Violetta's impatience had caused her to offer too much money. She hadn't wanted to waste time haggling, but it would be worse if the woman tried to determine who Violetta was, why she had so much to spare.

Luckily, her lover was already pulling her into an alcove of a door, untying the laces of the gown's skirt. "Who cares?" he hissed.

As her fine skirt dropped to the ground, the woman spun around and glared at him, but then a brief and silent negotiation waged between their eyes, and a moment later, the woman began unpinning the top of her gown, and then the lace stomacher, handing Violetta the dozen straight pins with increasing irritation.

When the woman stood in her stays and her chemise, Violetta gave her the coins. Her beau held out his hand, offering to hold them, but the woman swiftly tucked them into the linen pocket tied around her waist. She looked at Violetta and the pale purple dress in her hands.

"Six and I'll throw in my corset."

Her lover turned his face to hide his laughter, either in greedy delight or at the thrill of his woman standing naked but for her chemise in the middle of Venice.

Violetta had long been curious how she would look and feel wearing stays. But she had no one to lace it for her, and besides, it would be challenge enough to pin the stomacher and then the gown in place on her own.

"I'd rather your kerchief," she said, gesturing at the woman's neck even as she struggled to manage the three pieces of her new garment and all its pins.

The woman shrugged. "As you like," she said, untying the airy silk scarf at her neck, taking the extra sequin in exchange. Then she was helping her beau out of his *tabarro*, which she draped over her shoulders, and the two of them hurried toward the Zaterre without another look back.

Violetta changed in the same alcove. Though she had watched the woman remove her stomacher carefully, it was far harder to pin the stiff triangular garment on straight against the fabric of her own *ospedale* gown. They never wore anything so complicated at the Incurables. She stabbed at her breast with the pins, cursing under her breath, telling herself tonight would be worth it. Eventually she moved on to the skirt, fastening the laces as tight as she could, trying to approximate the shape the stays would have given her waist. She couldn't breathe at all. But instead of loosening the skirt, Violetta remembered watching the women on the *altana* getting laced into their corsets. She looked down at her own changed form and grinned. She secured the knot. She would simply take smaller breaths.

The top of the dress was just as complicated, and by then her fingers were impatient. She might be there all night pinning herself together. What she needed was a *cicisbeo*, who would have not only pinned but offered a comb for her hair. Then she laughed at herself. How quickly she was changing.

She had no makeup, no beauty marks, no ringlets in her hair, but she had a mask and a dress whose skirt swished along the pavement.

She had a necklace that changed color at every step, and a need that propelled her forward. She found a wellhead behind which to fold her own dress, which she would need before returning to the Incurables. She followed the *calli* toward memories of his palazzo. Her heart quickened when at last she saw its grand iron gate. She gauged the nearby buildings for a sign of the casino he had told her was nearby.

A blue light at the end of the *calle* caught her eye, and she drew closer. She passed three bridges, then a remarkable tree with a silvery bough that reached up out of its red-brick-walled garden to drop leaves into the water. She'd never seen such a tree in Venice; the rare greenery in the city was usually meticulously groomed, needing to fit a confined space. This tree's need to grow out of its bounds struck a chord in Violetta.

She reached a spiral stone staircase curving from the street up to a second-story balcony. The blue light came from a glass lantern outside the door. Her hand met the smooth stone of the banister as she wound up the stairs. At the top, a doorkeeper examined her inscrutably. There was a plaque depicting a fishtail beneath the lantern, lit blue by its light. She'd come to the right place.

"Help you?" the doorkeeper said.

She raised her chin, repositioned the kerchief at her neck, and subtly showed the opal necklace. His guarded stance turned supple.

"A moment, *siora*," he said, and disappeared inside the door.

He returned quickly with a second man, twice as old and also in black. A domino covered the top half of his face. Violetta recognized him as the servant who had first greeted her at the palazzo masquerade. She remembered the twinkle in his eyes.

"*Siora*," he said with a gracious bow. "My name is Fortunato. I am at your service."

Violetta curtseyed. In any other circumstance, she would have felt the social blunder of not offering her name, but she remembered the words of the man who'd given her this necklace. The gift's purpose had been anonymity, and Violetta suspected Fortunato understood this.

"May I bring you to him?" he said.

"Don't trouble yourself," she said, suddenly nervous at how the night was accelerating. "I'll just take a moment."

He bowed again. "Should you need anything, only look for me."

She curtseyed again and passed through the door, feeling the power of the stone around her neck.

Stepping inside the casino was like stepping into a new world. It was nothing like the palazzo, where everything had been pastel, brushed gold, and reflective chandeliers. The casino was possessed of a darker mystique. Its ceiling was paneled leather, its walls tiled with painted squares depicting pairs of lovers in poses that made Violetta look twice, then blush. She pressed against them, looking for the man. Half the room wore fine patrician *vesti*, and Violetta worried she might not be able to find him in the crowd.

Suddenly, their last interaction seemed insignificant, ages ago. Would he even remember her? She touched the opal necklace. It was still there. It was real.

A chalumeau played a soulful glissando at the far side of the room, couples tangled in the corners, and card games erupted as Violetta's eyes scanned the room. She ran fingertips across a tabletop, felt a mountain range of wax from former candles. And then she saw him, at the bar, talking closely with two red-robed men. Once again, he was the only man without a mask.

She took some time to study his features at a distance. The line of his jaw, the slant of his nose, and the penetrating sparkle in his eyes felt as familiar to Violetta as her own face. It was as if she'd spent her life gazing at a portrait of him. Or as if she'd spent her life envisioning a man and had finally brought him to life.

She wished she'd come sooner. Surely she'd be less nervous had not so much time passed since they'd met. Her heart beat quickly as she crossed the room.

She was about to touch his shoulder when he turned to her and, glimpsing the necklace, smiled. He took her hand and kissed it.

"I was beginning to think you were a dream," he said.

He remembered her. She left her hand in his after the kiss.

"Mystery singer," he whispered in her ear. "Champagne?"

"Perhaps a sip," she said, remembering her first and only taste of champagne at his party. She was as amazed to be here now as she had been that night. She drew in her breath when she felt his fingers at her waist. Firm and assured, he guided her through the casino.

After spending the last month thinking of him, his touch thrilled her beyond expectation, sent a shiver coursing through her. She leaned into his hands, subtly arching her back, her whole body curving toward him like a wave about to crash. They reached a table at the back of the room and he let her go too soon.

"Please," he said, pulling out a chair.

She found herself seated across from a woman who looked like a painting. She was older than Violetta, with oiled skin beneath her black domino and a painted black *sfrontata* beauty mark on the bridge of her nose, signifying forwardness. Her stack of necklaces was so thick you could see no skin between her collarbone and her chin. She glanced up from the hand of cards she played with another man and nodded at Violetta.

"Pack my pipe, and not so poorly as last time," the woman ordered her in a dismissive tone that reminded Violetta of Reine.

Violetta's cheeks blazed. At the Incurables, she would fire back a retort, but here she needed to blend in, remain anonymous.

"Lucrezia." He put a hand over the woman's, and Violetta saw how the touch softened her. Her chin lifted and she placed her other hand atop his.

"Darling?"

Violetta felt jealous, then foolish. Had she misread the man's invitation for her to come again? She tugged at her kerchief to cover the opal necklace.

"She's not your servant," he told the woman. "She's a singer."

"Small distinction," the woman said.

He turned to Violetta with an apologetic look. "She plays Griselda in the opera at San Samuele this season. She is one of the finest contraltos in Venice, and I thought you two should meet."

"I'm not—" Violetta started to say.

"If she were a singer of consequence, Federico, I would already know her."

Federico. Violetta thought the name suited him. She toyed with it on her tongue, wanting to say it aloud.

"Perhaps you'd like to see a performance," Federico said to Violetta, sitting down between the two women. "Lucrezia is so good tickets are hard to come by, but I have a box at the theater."

"I can't," Violetta said, crestfallen.

Federico studied her. He leaned close enough that she forgot Lucrezia.

"Is it the hour?" he asked. "Too soon after sundown?"

Violetta nodded, nervous, trying to keep her secret without pushing him away.

"Because you have a family?" he said.

He wanted to know if she was married. She wanted to know the same about him. "It isn't that," she said.

"What then?" Federico said.

"Perhaps she takes exception to old men wooing her in front of their lovers," Lucrezia shot at him and puffed her pipe.

Violetta flushed but Federico was undeterred. "What then?"

"Obligations," she said.

He smiled. "What time do they rest for the night?"

"What time is it now?" She smiled back.

Federico held out his pocket watch. "Eleven."

"Then," she mused, "half past ten?"

"Perfect," Federico said. "You could catch the last act tomorrow night."

"Perhaps," she told him. *Yes.*

He smiled. Under the table, his knee touched hers, and he passed her a key.

❊

SHE VIBRATED THE next day as she sang the aria in mass. She felt the change come over the audience as her voice transformed them, gave them a collective desire to reach God. She felt like the only one in the church who wanted something else. Toward the end of the concerto, her eyes met another's through the orange-blossom grille.

Federico. He was watching her sing. In his black robe, he towered above the others in the pew, his back so straight, his chin tilted toward her. He sat very still, but his expression suggested a mind in vigorous movement.

She felt him holding his breath, felt the slick track of the tear down his cheek. He had never seen her face, she was not wearing the necklace, and yet she realized he knew it was her.

She remembered his hands around her waist the night before. She remembered the slight graze of their knees beneath the table when he'd handed her the key to his opera box. The *coro* grille made the distance between their bodies now all the more unbearable. They could see each other, almost. Desire filled her limbs, her lungs. She sang the rest of the song to him.

❦

IT WAS ONLY later that she grew fearful, as she dined silently with the other *coro* women in the downstairs hall. Everyone had praised her, Laura and Porpora most of all, but the words that normally buoyed her confidence felt small compared to her worries.

Federico now knew things about her that could destroy her. If he told anyone she'd been at his party, all she'd worked for would disappear. Was that why he had come? Would he use this information to get something from her? What could he take? She was tortured by her own stupidity for holding his gaze, for letting him know that he was right.

All afternoon, through her lessons and her meeting with Porpora, she tortured herself over whether she should go to the opera. If she did, her presence would be a confession of who she was. But if she didn't go, she might anger him. If she didn't go . . . She shook her head. There was no chance of that. Lying awake in her bed? Alone? No music or mystery for company? No chance of Federico's hands on her? She was far past accepting that fate. She was in too deep. She would go to the opera that night.

❦

TEATRO SAN SAMUELE was on the other side of the Grand Canal. Wearing the same dress she'd worn the night before, Violetta headed for a *traghetto*, whose gondoliers took groups of commoners back and forth across the water for a small price.

On her way there, winding through the *calli*, she hadn't expected to cross the bridge at Ca' Foscari. It stopped her in her tracks.

She remembered Mino at her side as she took in the joyous frenzy of the boats, the riot of colors of young men and women in masquerade attire, the smell of lemon blossom cologne, and him. How naive she'd been.

She thought about their brief kiss in the apartment. It was over before she knew it was happening. She closed her eyes and imagined kissing Federico. In her mind, the two men tangled.

A gondola passed beneath her, jarring her from her reverie. A masked man stared at her through the window in the boat's *fèlze*. She hurried down the other side of the bridge. Federico would be waiting.

She found the *traghetto* stop and paid her lire, huddling with the others on the gondola. She'd never been on a boat before. As the boatman pushed off from the dock and they began to glide across the Grand Canal, she gripped the arm of the woman in front of her, then let go sheepishly. In her haste to reach the opera, she hadn't anticipated how monumental this ride would be, how different Venice was upon the water. As she settled into the rocking, she looked around in wonder. She heard a flute playing out an open palazzo window. She smelled roasting fish and lemon in the air. She was glad for the opportunity to pause amid her beautiful escape beneath the stars.

Back on land, she hurried toward what she hoped was north. She had to ask five people for directions, and each one expected a tip. Everyone told her *sempre dritto*, always straight, which was impossible in Venice. At last, she arrived before the towering theater building. A doorkeeper asked for her ticket.

She shook her head. "I don't—"

"You need a ticket to see an opera."

Violetta held up the key uncertainly.

"Follow me," he said quickly, leading her inside and up two flights of stairs.

He brought her to a golden door, then bowed his exit. She put the key inside the lock and turned it. Before the door was open, Federico was there. No mask, just him.

"Hello," he said with great intensity.

"Hello."

For a moment, they just looked at each other. Violetta's cheeks grew hot. Below, far away, a tenor sang of love's deceit. She could feel Federico's nervousness as powerfully as her own.

"Did I go too far this morning?" he finally asked, his eyes probing her face.

She shook her head. "I went too far the night I came to your palazzo. A woman in my position, I shouldn't have—"

"Come farther," he said. "I will keep your confidence."

It was what she wanted to hear. He reached for her hand and drew her inside. He closed the door behind them. She saw they were alone. At last. She squeezed his hand and stepped closer. His words, his poise, his hand around her back as he led her to the sofa, made her heart quicken. She felt exhilarated and protected in his presence.

She leaned forward to see the stage, set with painted wood to resemble a countryside of rolling hills. She had only ever seen the country depicted in paintings. This was the closest to the world beyond Venice that she had ever been.

Her gaze swept around the opera house, taking in the spellbound audience leaning forward in their own boxes and in the rows of seats behind the orchestra. The women wore big, beautiful dresses, wigs of elaborate curls. Everyone was masked, but Violetta could tell from their posture how rapt they were by the show. She remembered something the prioress had said long ago as they passed the syphilitics' ward.

"How did they get that way?" Olivia had asked. The young orphans were not permitted in the sick room, and its mysteries caused fascination and fear.

"Loose morals," the prioress had said grimly. "The sort of women drawn to sinful temptations like the opera house. The Lord sends them back to us eventually."

Now Violetta understood how small the prioress's experiences were, how she was threatened by these liberated Venetian women. Violetta wanted to be more like them, relaxed, alluring, demanding pleasure and beauty from life.

She turned toward Federico, let her knee rub against his. She was holding her breath. She met his gaze and he smiled, reaching to touch her face. His fingers traced the edge of her *bauta*, then trailed beneath it to touch her chin. She felt the wild urge to remove the mask and let him see her, as he had that morning. But she couldn't. Certainly not here where anyone might turn their gaze from the stage.

Suddenly, Lucrezia appeared on the stage in chains, being dragged forward by two men.

"You're just in time for her finale," Federico said absently.

Violetta looked down at the singer on the stage, remembering how Lucrezia's demeanor had softened in Federico's presence.

"Are the two of you . . ." Violetta started to say. "Does she love you?"

"Once we were lovers. But I am the second-born son, not permitted to wed."

Violetta blinked. "Why not?" There was so much she didn't know.

His voice took on a hard edge. "To preserve the estate. We are a ducal house—my great-grandfather was a doge, and since then, each of his descendants has served as a voting member in the republic's Great Council. But only one son each generation takes a wife and is allowed to write his children in the noble class's Book of Names. Alas, it was not me."

"That's terrible," Violetta said. She had pitied those who left the Incurables to wed. She had always feared the bond and responsibility of motherhood. But these were her choices. What if someone had forbidden her to have a family of her own?

Perhaps no one was truly free to live on their own terms.

"It's not so bad." Federico laughed, and she wanted to know what he meant, but he pointed back to the stage, to Lucrezia, who was singing. "She's not a pleasant woman, but she's a wonderful contralto." He glanced at Violetta. "But then, you've had the finest music in the world as background all your life."

"How did you find me?" she dared to ask.

He reached for champagne, sitting on ice, and poured a glass for her. "I have long heard of the famous Violetta, *voce d'angelo*, but I haven't been to mass since my mother died. Maybe I grew tired of waiting to see you again."

"You're still leaving out the best part." She raised an eyebrow. Something told her he had not stumbled upon her performance, that his presence had been carefully determined. "*How* did you find me?"

"Are you happy there?"

His question distracted Violetta. She paused to think about it, watching Lucrezia. "It could be worse."

"Why are you here tonight? Why risk so much?"

She couldn't say it—*I want more.* She was afraid. Here, finally, was someone who might be able to help her break away. What if she really could make her dreams real?

"I want to hear you sing again," he said. "I want to put you on a stage."

"I can't. Not in Venice."

He leaned in. "Not here. The opera is too public."

"Where then?"

He smiled. "La Sirena, where we dance under the law. By day, you would sing for the Incurables. By night, come sing for me." He took her hands.

She leaned closer, breathless.

"Start with one performance a week, any day you choose. Sing anything you like. I will make you the star. I will keep your secret. I will protect you above all else." He was looking down at her thumb boldly stroking the back of his hand. It felt so much easier to convey her wishes to him with her body than her words.

"You make it sound so simple," she said.

He smiled. "We'll write up a contract. You'll make tenfold what you make at the church."

Violetta's hands stilled as she thought about this. He was serious. She had earned a little fortune in the six months she'd been singing in the *coro.* But she had spent nearly all of her pocket money on the lavender silk dress, and the rest—her dowry—was in the prioress's hands, saved for a future husband or her retirement to a nunnery at forty.

No, neither of those could be Violetta's fate. Maybe this was it, right here, with him.

"It's easier than you think," he said.

"I'm afraid," she admitted.

"I am as well," he said, surprising her. "I haven't heard a voice like yours . . ."

From the way he trailed off, Violetta expected him to add a *since*, to reference some distant time, but he didn't.

"I must think about it," she said.

"I'll be waiting," he said as onstage the curtain dropped.

Eight

On thursday evenings, La Sirena hosted unofficial gatherings for three orders of mystics. The white-bearded cabalists claimed the large center table beneath the chandelier, the Freemasons poured their wine and threw their cards at the booth nearest the barmaid, and the alchemist Rosicrucians sat at the back by the musicians.

Carlo introduced Mino to the Rosicrucians the first night they patronized La Sirena together. At first, what Mino liked most about these alchemists was their sworn enmity to the Freemasons. The leader of the Freemasons was the man who had sent Mino to the whorehouse.

But hating the Freemasons wasn't the only thing Mino and the Rosicrucians had in common. Though he could not afford to gamble with them (he always showed up at the end of their long turn at whist), he read their pamphlets and pondered the existence of an elixir of life that might cure them all. He admired the brothers' seriousness, their unprejudiced minds. He even liked their pendants—the wooden rose over the cross.

"It is not a Christian symbol," Carlo explained. "The order of the Rosicrucians predates Christianity. The cross represents the human body. The rose is what unfolds in one's consciousness over the course of one's life."

Mino liked imagining a rose slowly opening inside him. Since he'd left the Incurables, this brotherhood was the closest thing he had to a family. He liked their theory that base matter might be transformed into something nobler.

"When we speak of transmutation, do we mean only turning metal into gold?" the senior brother asked Mino over a bottle of wine. Gianni wore a bright, stiff wig and a mask too small for his large face. He had traveled to Germany, where the original manifestos of the order had been written, and he seemed to Mino to be a man of great wisdom. "Or can we attest to the transmutation of the human character, from dull to brilliant?"

"I hope both are possible," Mino said. "In my experience, metaphorical changes are often bound up with physical ones." He thought of the day he met Sprezz, and the gift of those boots. He thought of how what he'd felt for Letta in his heart had seemed to ripple through his body, too.

Mino longed to change nearly everything about himself—his loneliness, his self-worth, his dismal sleeping quarters, the length of time that had passed since he'd held a violin, his memories of that afternoon with Letta. . . .

Before he met the alchemists, he had been convinced he lacked all means to change his circumstances. But recently, especially by the end of these Thursday nights, he felt the urge to become something better growing inside him.

In late September, late in the evening, when all the bottles on the table were empty, Carlo was lamenting his love for Carina. Mino had a single soldo in his pocket, not enough to fund the evening when his friend got like this. He signaled Nadia, the barmaid, and she brought Carlo a dram of *acqaioli*.

"She promised me dinner, in an intimate café in Cannaregio, far from her husband's home," Carlo said, stirring sugar into his drink. "All day I ached to see her." He leaned close, and Mino saw the bare patch in the center of his eyebrow where he had pulled out the hair in agitation. Carlo moved to pull some more.

Mino helped his hand down. "Peace, friend. Let it be."

"When I arrived at the café," Carlo continued, "I was not the only fool. She had invited five men to dine with her."

Mino's eyes widened. Someday he would have to meet this woman, who played the men of Venice like jokers in a deck of cards. The rumor was she'd once danced the tightrope in Constantinople.

"Do you know the worst of it?" Carlo asked. "We stayed for hours, each of us, still hoping. In the end, she left alone!"

"To meet a sixth man?"

"When there is a bridge, does a man expect water underneath?" Carlo sighed. "It helps, at least, to know I'm not the only one."

Mino let himself laugh only when Carlo did. Even at his most depressed, Carlo was never beyond seeing humor in his love. Mino could not admit how he envied his friend. If only he could see Letta again.

Over his shoulder came the heavy scrape of chair legs, then the warmth of a candle drawing closer. Gianni had pulled his chair near.

"Every week it's the same, Carlo," Gianni said. "What is so noble about this woman? Are there not two dozen others right here, in this room, whose kiss could transform your misery into bliss?"

"Mino," Carlo said, reaching across him to pop a sausage in his mouth, "tell him it's impossible. Carina is an angel, and I have held her in my arms. For me there is no going back to mortal women."

"Carlo can no more kiss another woman than he could turn fire into ice," Mino said in solidarity.

"Anything is possible," Gianni said, and widened the space on his lap for a handsome and heavily perfumed courtesan.

"Not this again," she said, sitting on Gianni's knee. "Some forms are fixed. Why should your lover ever change? She has it all—the palazzo, the rich husband, the husband's mistress to keep him occupied, and a dozen fools like you." She stroked Carlo's cheek.

"They don't love her like I love her," Carlo said.

"Lucky for them." The courtesan laughed, turning to Mino. "What about you?"

"What about me?" He tensed, feeling each of their eyes on him. In the weeks since he had sat among these men, Mino had kept his past closely guarded. He skipped the gambling, arrived for the discussions, stayed to listen to the music, and left with Sprezz before the womanizing. He should have left by now. He liked these meetings on his own terms and was not ready to part with his secrets.

"What type of lover do you prefer?" the courtesan asked, leaning her elbows on the table.

"It is odd," Carlo said, squinting at Mino. "I've never seen you talk to a woman."

"A lot goes on while you are wiping away tears," Mino said.

When was the last time he had talked intimately with a woman? He exchanged pleasantries with Nadia most nights at La Sirena. He used to let the women at the Venice Triumphant flirt with him as he traded out their tables for the midnight chicken coops. He had spoken openly to that woman in the whorehouse kitchen as she fed him eggs.

She'd seemed kind and then deceived him; and ever since, he realized, he'd closed himself off even further.

Except, he still talked to Letta most nights when the moon was bright and he could feel close to her, imagining her looking up at the same sky. *Are you all right?* he would ask her. *Forgive me.* But his words were prayers, not conversation. If only he could really talk to her. Apologize. He hadn't considered what he was asking her to sacrifice that day.

"You look pale, Mino," Carlo said.

"Is he a virgin?" Gianni asked. "Is that the trouble?"

"There's a remedy for that." The courtesan laughed.

Mino wanted to leave, but all eyes were on him.

"I loved one woman," he said hoarsely. "She is dead."

Everyone burst out laughing, even Carlo, whose laughter rekindled his tears.

"It's a good thing you don't gamble," Carlo said. "You're a terrible liar, Mino."

"Come to the haberdashery and be my bookkeeper," called Marcello, the hat maker. "I've never known a man so painfully honest."

"I do need a job," Mino said. He forced himself to laugh when the others did. Not even Carlo knew how untenable Mino's situation was. It was his own choice to keep quiet about where he slept; but now, as he made friends, he was unsure how to let anyone know he needed help.

He had no money. Sprezz could scrounge up something for them to eat tomorrow morning, but it never went down easy, the shame sticking like a fish bone in the back of Mino's throat. If he were really that bad of a liar, why couldn't the Rosicrucians see through him, to his hunger and his pain?

It nagged at Mino that his whole existence felt like a lie. He had lied to the women in San Marco about being a gondolier. He had lied to the man who first brought him to La Sirena. But to speak of Letta brought Mino back to the boy he'd been that first day on the roof. Was it only her that kept him honest?

"We are pathetic," Carlo said, leaning against Mino and draping an arm around his shoulders. His eyes followed a pretty girl in a green gown weaving toward the bar. "Even Carina tells me I must find other lovers if she and I are to be happy. And I'm sure your dead lover looks down from heaven and wants you to find . . . comfort. Point and I will follow, friend. Let us try our luck tonight."

Mino's chest tightened as he looked around the casino. The women were dazzling almost without exception. He wished to talk to none of them.

His eyes found the musicians—the castrato and his tall, fair-haired accompanist—stepping down from the little stage for their break.

"The violinist," Mino said. If he were coerced into speaking to a woman tonight, he might at least have something to say to the violinist. They could discuss music, her instrument. Suddenly Mino felt pulled by an unexpected force. "Let's go."

"You have excellent taste," Carlo said and slid down from his seat. "Even better for me is her friend."

Mino wasn't looking at the friend, nor even at the woman. He was looking at the violin. It felt unlikely he would ever again possess an instrument of his own. By the time he stood before the violinist—who stood half a head taller than he with an imposing crown of white-blond hair—he was so envious he was angry.

"You play well," he growled.

"I know." She took the compliment, bored.

"Who would like more wine?" Carlo boomed behind Mino, leaning too close to the pretty young brunette seated at the table. She looked uncomfortable, Carlo miserable and desperate.

Mino turned away from them, eyeing the violin as the blonde packed it into her case. He had not been this close to one since he left his in the apartment. He clasped his hands to keep from reaching out for it. He focused on the woman, who looked lovely but exhausted. There were sweat stains on her dress and her beauty mark was smudged down her nose.

He offered a handkerchief. "May I?"

The violinist was confused but stayed still as Mino wiped the beauty mark from her face. His touch had an effect on her; she seemed to soften and a moment later lifted her mask to him. He found her far more beautiful than expected. His fingers went to his half token in his pocket and he was moved by the similarities. Was it possible there was some connection? How in the world would he raise such a topic with a stranger?

"Do you get to select the music you play here?" he asked.

"Federico chooses it," she said coolly, her mask replaced, her eyes looking past him again. "He chooses everything."

"It's a nice song," Mino said, claiming the stool across from her.

"I prefer Vivaldi. He has a marvelous opera on now at Teatro San Moisè. . . ." She looked Mino up and down, as if spotting each stain on the frayed hem of his *tabarro*. "I don't imagine you've seen it?"

"No, but I adore Vivaldi's oratorios." He had heard them sung a few times on occasional outings with the other foundlings to the rival Ospedale della Pietà. Letta and every musician she'd studied with were passionate about Vivaldi's sacred compositions.

"I like those oratorios, too." The brunette spoke up from the other side of the table, her voice both booming and frail at once, and Mino saw how desperate she was to be liberated from Carlo, who was spilling wine as he tried to refill her glass.

"Yes, she knows *all* the church music," the blonde said with great disinterest.

Mino looked at the brunette more closely. She raised her mask slowly. She had a sweet round face, and large, dark, energetic eyes. When she blinked, she reminded him of a butterfly. Her dress was plainer than most of the others at the casino, but it accented her natural, radiating beauty. Her hair, too, was very simple, unwigged, undyed, knotted in a dark chignon at the nape of her long neck. She smiled at Mino.

"My name is Ana," she said, and nodded to the blonde. "This is Stella."

Stella extended her cheek for Mino's compulsory kiss. No one did this at the Incurables; there was so much he was learning about women. He leaned in and grazed her masked cheek with the lower edge of his mask, then looked to Ana to see whether she expected the same. Slowly, she tilted her face toward his.

Maybe it was because she had removed her mask, but Mino felt compelled to remove his own before he kissed her. He set it on the table. His lips brushed her cheek. He took his time with it and felt a warm bolt through him at the supple pressure of her skin.

"My name is Mino," he said. "My friend is Carlo." He patted Carlo, who had his head down on the table.

"Is he all right?" Ana asked.

"Brokenhearted," Mino said.

Ana only nodded, and Mino realized he'd become used to women offering advice on love. He wondered about Ana's discreetness.

"Ana, I'm on my break," Stella said. "I wish to relax, not"—she waved her hand at Carlo, then at Mino—"do this."

Mino's eyes returned to her violin in the open case. He marveled at the wood, the ornate scrolls. He had never liked such large scrolls. The more modest instruments sounded warmest.

"Excuse her," Ana said. "She's very tired—"

"Damn it," Stella muttered. One of the horsehairs on her bow had come loose.

Without thought or hesitation, without turning his eyes away from Ana, Mino reached over and snapped the loose string off Stella's bow with the force required to keep all the other hairs perfectly intact.

"I am very tired, too," he said and, feeling Sprezz nuzzle against him under the table, he leaned to pat the dog's head.

Ana blinked at Mino. It took him a moment to figure out why. The motion, snapping off that horsehair, had been intuitive. But now, under her gaze, he felt himself transported back to the Incurables, to those early years when he would take his violin to the rooftop and teach himself to play.

And now he could not keep himself from asking, holding out his hands for Stella's violin: "May I?" Stella handed it to him the way a mother hands a child to a doctor, suddenly alert.

He held it close, ran his fingers over it, thought about its music and the full life it had lived—from when it was crafted for Stella as a child and the tortured howls she'd first sawed upon it to when she'd gotten this job at La Sirena and had wondered whether she was good enough; into the future, when she'd take it to an audition at Teatro San Moisè; and beyond that, to its next owner, perhaps Stella's daughter, who would feel her mother through the worn wood.

It was enough to hold the violin; Mino didn't need to play it.

"You might consider a better metal winding for your D and G strings," he finally said. "You lean on them when you play vibrato *sul ponticello*. Do they buzz?"

Mino hadn't been this candid with anyone since he'd left the Incurables, but he felt the woman needed to know this.

Ana's eyes widened as she turned to Stella. "Only yesterday you complained of buzzing in your strings."

"Different winding would completely change my tessitura," Stella said.

"Of course," Mino said, thrilled to be debating such details. "But it might be a welcome alteration, particularly when you're playing slower pieces, like a largo. And the buzzing would cease."

"What makes your buzzing cease?" Stella asked pointedly.

Mino responded perfectly in rhythm. "Like a violin, I require sure fingers."

Stella didn't laugh, but Ana did, a more musical sound than anything Mino had heard that night. Mino turned to watch her make it.

"Stella." The castrato was moving past them, barking over his shoulder for his accompanist to rejoin him.

"Give it back," Stella said, holding out her hand for Mino to return the violin. "I've wasted my entire break with you."

Mino surrendered the violin, pained by how rough Stella was with it as she hurried back up onto the stage.

At the sound of her violin, Carlo roused and moaned. He rubbed his eyes, swayed. "I must go to bed."

"Let me help you," Mino said and rose from his stool, taking Carlo under the arm.

But Carlo, even in his drunken state, glanced at Mino, then at Ana, grinned and shook his head. "Stay."

"Will you be all right on your own?" Ana asked.

"I live two blocks from here," Carlo slurred. "Not even any bridges to cross, so you don't have to worry about me drowning." He bent to kiss both of their cheeks good night.

Mino flushed as he sat back down. He should have left long ago. Why hadn't he? Yes, it had been powerful to hold that violin, but to what end? Sprezz was snoring at his feet. They were far from their regular haunts near San Marco, and Mino did not relish looking for a new corner in which to sleep in Dorsoduro.

Ana pulled her stool closer. Despite the casino crowds, it was as if they were alone.

"So," she said, curiosity lifting her voice. "Time for questions."

"All right."

She peeked beneath the table at the dog. "Who's he? He's cute."

"He's Sprezz. Short for Sprezzatura." When she tilted her head toward him, Mino gathered she wasn't familiar with the term. "It means something difficult that's made to look easy."

Her smile widened. She was enchanting. "That's a wonderful name."

"It suits him. That's what you wanted to know?"

"That's one thing," she said softly, leaning close. Mino held his breath. "Another is, who are you?"

How tiny she was. He could have put his arm around her and her shoulders would have spanned only the space between his elbow and his chest. She was young, like him, and the kind of pretty that felt out of place in this casino, no beauty marks, no rouge. Her loveliness was all in her simplicity. Mino thought he might prefer to look at her in a sunlit piazza, rather than in a hole like this, where candlelight cast flattering shadows Ana's beauty did not need. And for a moment it felt like all he wanted was to watch this young woman walk in the sunlight. The urge came out of nowhere and brought Mino both comfort and confusion.

"Fine," she said, her fingertip swirling the rim of her wineglass, which was mostly full. "I'll play. Are you a maestro? A theater composer? A private tutor?"

"I am no one," he said. Not only could he not lie to this woman, he *wanted* her to know the truth. He wanted to see the disdain in her bright eyes when she found out he slept on the street and ate scraps. Then she would expel him from his fantasy before he let it go any further. For where would it have gone? He would never see her again.

"I am nothing," he said. "A ghost."

She reached out her hand and her fingertips met his shoulders, then, gently, his cheek. "You seem so real." She tilted her head. "Who are you haunting?"

"My mother."

Ana glanced around the casino, taking him at his word. "Is she among us?"

Mino took out his half token, laid it before her on the table.

Ana glanced at it but looked more closely at him. "I don't understand."

"Have you ever seen one of these?" he asked.

She shook her head. Her fingers traced the shorn edge of the wood.

"It's a half token." He leaned closer to see it as she did. Suddenly the painting looked old to him, faded, and instead of thinking about his mother, he thought of how he was close enough to Ana to smell her skin. She smelled like oranges.

He felt dizzy. He leaned away and reached for the token.

"I have the top. My mother has the bottom. Or so I've grown up thinking."

"You're an orphan," she said quietly.

When he looked up at her, his eyes were filled with tears. He saw her through them, how she shone. And when he blinked and saw her clearly again, he expected her disappointment, her departure from this table. But she didn't move. She was crying, too.

"You mean to trace her through this token," Ana said simply, understanding.

"It's all I have," he said.

Her fingers surprised his by threading through them. "Do you remember her?"

The flash of memory assaulted him. Her short hair and the necklace she wore, the way his fingers felt winding through the chain. Now the memory was poisoned with the image of her at the wheel, relieved and running down the *calle*. Away.

A lie, Mino told himself, but his memory didn't listen.

"She was a singer," he said, now running his thumb along Ana's nail. He liked that she wore no polish. "Her voice was beautiful."

"My sister knows many musicians in Venice," Ana said. "It's a small world. Perhaps she knows someone who can help."

"That's generous," Mino said, only then realizing that Ana was nodding at Stella, who attacked her violin and glared in their direction.

"You're sisters?" he said. "You and Stella?"

"We're more alike than we seem." Ana laughed. "She's mean at first, but good-hearted once she trusts you. And she knows people."

Nadia, the barmaid, swung past their table. She didn't look happy to see Mino left behind to settle the bill. "We're closing. You owe me ten soldi."

Panic struck Mino. Carlo had left no money when he went home. Now Nadia saw his expression and whistled under her breath. "What a surprise."

"Nadia," he said. "I'll come back tomorrow—"

"With what, one?" she said. "I can't let you out the back door tonight, Mino. Federico is here." She nodded toward a tall, dark-haired gentleman who wore no mask. He must be La Sirena's owner.

Mino swallowed, realizing he had seen this man before, summoning guards to remove patrons from the casino by force. There was a clear brutality to him, one Mino wished never to confront.

But then, Ana was sifting through a purple purse, placing something in the barmaid's palm.

"We're settled," she said.

"No," Mino begged her. He was ashamed.

"Don't think of it." Ana nodded toward the door, somewhat shyly. "Let's go?"

Mino struggled for the right words. Go where? What did she mean? He felt he would go anywhere with her. "What about Stella? Shouldn't you wait?"

Ana shrugged. "She has a date."

Mino swallowed. "And you don't?"

She put her hand in his again. It was so tiny, and damp with sweat, and he liked feeling the mix of her confidence and anxiety.

"Perhaps I do." She smiled. She picked Mino's mask up off the table and tied it around his head. He did the same with hers. It was harder to tie than it should have been. He'd had too much to drink.

"Forgive me," he said. "I'm not usually so clumsy."

"It's all right, Mino." Ana seemed to understand him. "My home is close. My fire is warm. We have stayed at La Sirena long enough."

Nine

On a damp late night in September, Violetta hurried down the labyrinthine calle della Toletta wearing her mask and necklace. It was terrible to run in so tight a dress, but she would not rest until she saw that rebellious tree near the entrance to La Sirena.

She had spent nearly three months weighing Federico's offer, nervously leaning toward accepting, then backing away from the idea every time it began to feel real. Then that afternoon she had attended the farewell dinner for Vania, who, at forty, was retiring from the *coro* to the San Zaccaria nunnery. Vania's voice was still so warm and bright, but she wouldn't sing again. When Violetta embraced her, said goodbye, all she could think was *never, never, never.* Her own life could not follow the same narrow path. It was decided. And she didn't want to waste another moment letting Federico know.

When she rounded the final corner, she ran headlong into a masked pair coming from the opposite direction.

"Excuse us," the woman said. She was a head shorter than Violetta and very petite, rubbing her brow where she had smacked it upon Violetta's opal necklace.

Violetta winced. The force of the blow had caused the pointed edge of the gold collet holding the stone to stab into her breast. When she raised the stone and looked down, she saw a drop of blood on her chest.

"Are you hurt?" the woman asked, and for a moment Violetta couldn't reconcile the sting at her breast with this tiny creature before her. She wanted to berate the woman for her recklessness, to ignore that she herself had been as reckless, but then she noticed the man in his mask and *tabarro.* He was a little off-balance. He must have been drunk. Violetta understood the hurry to get the fool home and into bed.

"I'm fine," she said, more coldly than necessary. She didn't want to waste any more time on this pedestrian couple. She had to get to Federico.

She was moving past them when, at her feet, a black-and-white-spotted dog barked. A memory returned of the little dog she used to watch through the attic window when she was a girl. How she longed to meet him up close. She hadn't thought of him in years, and the sight of this dog brought her back to a simpler time, when the things she wanted did not scare her.

Moments ago, nothing could have slowed her pace. Now Violetta lowered to her knees on the cobblestones and presented her gloved palm to the dog. She felt his whiskers through the silk as he sniffed her, then the damp pressure of his tongue. She scratched his head, let her fingers linger on his ears. She wanted to ask his name.

But when she looked up at the couple, she saw the woman edging her body underneath her lover's arm. She saw how readily she shouldered the weight of her man. She saw open generosity, no judgment in the motions, in the murmured reassurances.

She tried to imagine such vulnerable tenderness between herself and Federico. There was *something* between them, but it was different, more charged. Perhaps one day, she thought, now watching the man kiss his partner's hand. The simple gesture made Violetta feel she was intruding.

"Come, Sprezzatura," the woman called the dog. "Time for bed."

The dog trotted after them, and Violetta rose to watch them go, the little family they made. She felt unexpectedly envious, and she couldn't express why. She had to admit, it was a terrific name for a dog.

She hurried across the bridge without looking back, touching the mottled bark of the tree with her fingertips as she ducked beneath it.

She should have been at La Sirena an hour ago, but just as she'd been pulling her cloak over her grown, ready to strip her bed, twist her sheet, and escape, she'd heard Laura rise in the room across the parlor. She'd heard her friend's bare feet padding on the wood. Coming closer. Violetta had untied her mask with the speed of an *accelerato.* She had kicked it and the cloak under her bed, dove back under the covers, pulled them up as high as her neck. She undid the clasp on the necklace and let it slide into her hand, beneath her pillow. She had barely closed her eyes when the door to her room creaked open.

"Violetta?"

She held her breath, not moving. She felt Laura's urge to come close, pull back the coverlet, and climb into bed as they used to do. When they were children their beds had been smaller, like the distance between their hearts. They hadn't talked much recently. But Violetta understood why Laura was there.

She'd had her nightmare of her mother.

Violetta had not been haunted by her own dream of Mino's mother in more than half a year. Her recent dreams featured Federico. They were equally hard to shake upon waking.

"Are you sleeping?" Laura asked.

Another night, Violetta would have taken her friend into her bed. They would not have to speak, only hold each other until the ache subsided enough for Laura to sleep. But not tonight. Not when she had finally determined to take Federico up on his proposal. She had the morning off tomorrow to recover. It had to be tonight.

If she let Laura in, she would see Violetta's gown, wrinkled from having been hidden in the bottom of her armoire. She'd see the slippers she wore beneath the blankets, and she would know the nature of Violetta's secret. She couldn't. Violetta had plans now that stretched across the evenings into a future she couldn't yet see.

When Laura left, Violetta felt guilty. She waited in her bed a long time, knowing how hard it would be for her friend to sleep again. She could not risk being heard when she slipped through her window.

❀

NOW SHE WORRIED she had waited too long. It was after midnight. What if Federico was gone? She had to see him tonight. She climbed the stairs, and stopped before the fishtail plaque, the candle in its blue glass.

The doorkeeper didn't recognize her in her mask, but when she moved aside the neck of her cloak and showed the opal, he bowed and opened the door. She wished Fortunato had been there; tonight she wanted a direct line to Federico.

But the casino was almost empty. A first glance showed neither the owner nor his servant.

"How can a beauty like you be alone so late in the evening?" a man said, coming up behind her, his hand sliding up her hips.

"I'm not alone," she said and swiveled away, taking in what she could of him beneath his mask. He was no taller than she, with a pale unshaven neck. He smelled of brandy.

"I'm meeting someone." The words brought a confidence to her voice.

"Everyone's gone home but the barmaid," the man said, stepping close again. "And me—"

Before he'd finished speaking, he was lifted off the ground by the neck of his *tabarro* and tossed violently to the side. He landed on a card table, then rolled off it to the floor, breaking a bottle with his fall. In his place stood Federico. As the man moaned and rolled to his knees, Federico looked at Violetta, and the violence in his eyes suddenly cleared.

"Was he bothering you?" His calmness reminded Violetta of the *Magnificat* by Johann Sebastian Bach. They used to sing it in the music school and it always struck Violetta that there was no trace of the bright and rapid second movement left when she performed the slower third.

She had not felt threatened by the man, and Federico's response seemed extreme, but Violetta was caught between being unnerved by this flash of brutality and flattered by how readily he had come to her defense.

"Is he all right?" she asked, leaning over to check on the man, bleeding through his white mask where he'd hit the table. She offered to help him up, but Federico waved two fingers in the air, and two guards arrived.

When the injured man was gone, only the barmaids remained, wiping down the tables. La Sirena had a tranquil romance about it without all its customers.

"Please don't think I make a practice of fighting," Federico said, steering Violetta toward the bar. "That man was a *confidenti* of the Ten."

Violetta knew of the Council of Ten. Within the Incurables, these judges had always been portrayed as necessarily strict arbiters of justice, but in Violetta's recent ventures out at night, she'd learned otherwise. She'd seen the crowds scatter at the sight of one of the Ten's glowing red lanterns at the bow of their gondolas. If that man was a *confidenti* of the Ten, it meant he was one of their spies. A dangerous man for a woman taking the risks she was taking.

"Thank you," she told Federico. "But you're not afraid of retribution? He was bleeding."

"I can handle the Ten, but I won't give them access to you."

He was keeping his promise to protect her identity.

"Now tell me," he said, "are you here with good news?"

"Yes." Her voice sounded small. She didn't know where her nerve had gone, but then he took her hands and it didn't matter.

"Really?" he said. "You'll sing? Here?"

"Yes," she whispered. "I came to sign."

He kissed her hands a dozen times with a happiness far purer than she'd expected. She thought of the couple she'd run into by the bridge. Someday might she and Federico care for each other as tenderly as they did?

"Contracts later," he said. "Tonight let's celebrate." He lifted a champagne bottle and two glasses in one hand, taking her arm with the other. "There's still a little starlight left before the dawn."

He led her toward the door, pausing for a whispered word with Fortunato, who bowed at the sight of Violetta. Then Federico led her out of the casino, down the stairs, under the bough of the cork tree, and along the dark canal. The night was still, the revelers finally gone to bed, merchants and guildsman getting their last moments of sleep. It felt like all of Venice belonged to Violetta and Federico.

At the third bridge, where the *calle* turned left and the Grand Canal and the tall bronze gate of Federico's palazzo came into view, he stopped in the center of the bridge and popped open the champagne. Foam spilled over the bottle. Violetta laughed as she held the glasses near to catch it.

When they were full, Federico raised his to hers with a clink.

"You'll need a name," he said.

Violetta had been thinking of this, but the one she liked was so bold it made her nervous. She sipped her champagne for courage. "What do you think about La Sirena?"

The name had come to her while staring at the blue brand of the Incurables on her heel. La Sirena would let her stay anonymous to the patrons of the casino, but it would also make her inextricable from Federico's place. The impulse to call herself after his establishment was confusing and new, but for once, she didn't fight the idea of belonging somewhere, with someone.

Now she looked at Federico and for a second she thought he flinched. But then he was pouring her more champagne and smiling. "It's perfect."

"Really?"

"Absolutely."

A gondola passed beneath the bridge, a jolt of movement in their still night.

"Your chariot," Federico said.

"Mine?"

"It will be safer for you to travel here and home again by boat." He signaled the gondolier. "That's Nicoletto. He will wait for you on the rio degli Incurabili at half past ten on nights when you perform. He will bring you home. When would you like to begin?"

Violetta worked through her obligations. Wednesday mornings generally started later for the *coro*. Mass was held in the evening that day. "Tuesday?"

"Until Tuesday, then," Federico said and kissed her hands. "At half past ten."

"Federico, wait," she said, holding fast to him before he could pull away. "There's something I must know."

"Anything."

One hand touched the opal at her breast. Above her, stars peeked through black sky. "Why did you give me this necklace?"

He gazed at it a moment, then met her eyes through her mask and smiled. "I knew that if I didn't, I'd never see you again."

"But what if I had pawned it and disappeared from Venice?"

"Then I would have missed you more than any jewel," he said. As he helped her into the gondola, delivering her into the care of the handsome gondolier, Federico kissed her hand. "But you didn't disappear from Venice, did you?"

Ten

Mino awoke to the music of frying sausage and bickering women. He didn't remember what corner he'd slept in the night before, which restaurant stoop he was soon to be kicked off. He rolled over and felt the surprising softness of a pillow at his cheek, the feather-warm weight of a coverlet over him. His eyes shot open.

He was looking out the window of a second-story room. Outside, big raindrops fell into the canal. There were puddles on the *calle*, water running down the red-and-white awning of a bakery below. He was dry and warm. He was alone in another's bed.

Ana.

He remembered last night, stumbling upstairs, after their walk along canals and beneath the shadows of church towers. He remembered her small hand guiding him and her ripe laughter in his ear, telling him *shhh*, until she closed a door behind them. In the darkness, Mino had stumbled against the bed and Ana pulled him to her.

She had kissed him, and the reality of her firm mouth on his amazed him. He'd felt as if he were kissing a firework. Desire lit her up.

She tasted like oranges.

When his fingers traced her hair, she'd let it down. It spilled like wine past her breasts, a silky web Mino wanted to climb inside.

He didn't realize she was showing him exactly what to do until their bodies moved together. He remembered the damp sweat on her back afterward as they lay still. He found it all hard to believe.

He lifted the sheet, looked down at his nakedness, expecting to appear different from yesterday. The sight brought back a new memory—both her hands wrapped around him at once—and he wanted her again.

He heard her giggle. His head popped out from under the quilt.

She stood in the open doorway in a pretty white nightgown, her hair swooped over one shoulder in a low braid. A wicker tray balanced on her hip.

"You'd better be hungry." Her words were confident but her voice was shy, and this touched Mino and relieved him. From the moment he'd remembered where he was, he'd worried about overstaying his welcome.

"Starving."

She brought the tray to him. He rolled onto his side to face her, and she sat down on the bed in the curve between his chest and knees. He was surprised by how natural it felt to prop himself up on an elbow and open his mouth as Ana raised a fork to his lips. He bit the sausage, crisp and hot. He chewed for a long time. Nothing he had ever eaten had tasted half as good.

"You're too thin," she said. Her voice was as smooth as the sunlight on her shoulders. Mino glanced out the window again. A moment ago it had been raining. Now that Ana was in the room, sun broke through the clouds over the canal and made it shine.

"You must start eating better," she said, drawing him back to the plate.

He took another bite, but as soon as he had swallowed, he called, "Sprezz?"

Mino and Sprezz had had breakfast together every morning for half a year. Some days Sprezz had been the only thing that kept Mino going.

Now the mutt crawled out from under a heap of blankets at the foot of the bed, padding up to Mino's chest and licking his chin. Mino hugged him, ashamed that he had not remembered the dog coming in with them last night. Sprezz eyed the sausage, wagged his tail.

With a blunt knife, Ana sliced off the tapered end of the sausage and tossed it to him, clapping her hands when Sprezz leaped up to catch it. Mino's eyes widened. Who was this magical woman who shared sausage of such quality with the dog of a man she'd met the night before? Sprezz licked his chops and looked at Mino. He, too, could not believe their luck.

"There's plenty more," Ana said. "We make it." She rolled her eyes. "All day long. You've heard of Costanzo's?"

"Your family?"

"My grandfather, and my father after him. Papa died two years ago, and now my mother and my sisters and I handle the shop." The corners of Ana's mouth flicked up, a smile with minor notes of sadness as she glanced around the simple room. "This apartment used to be my grandfather's. Mamma and my sisters and I live across the hall." She nodded her head in the direction of the women's voices. "We rent this place to boarders when we can."

Mino wanted to beg for the apartment. Whatever the price, he would pay it. Imagine seeing Ana every day. This thought surprised him; for years the only person he'd yearned to see was Letta. But when he looked at Ana now, he knew the urge was real. He wanted to see her again. But he didn't want her to know he had no other home, so he stayed quiet.

"Do you like working in the sausage shop?" he asked.

"I used to want to be a governess." She was looking out the window, her fingers soft on Sprezz's ears. "I like children. I should have been the eldest, not the baby. But when Papa died, we all had to help. Well, except for Stella. She already earned money with her violin. Mamma made the rest of us vow to help her, so now I stuff meat bits into intestines every day."

Mino took her hand. "I have never eaten so well."

She kissed him. "Stay for lunch."

Her eyes were like the darkest grains in the cherrywood of his lost violin. Mino found it hard to keep looking at her. She was so pretty, and it had been so long since anyone had talked to him like this. It was too much, too rich, like the sausage already tightening his stomach. A man should not go from famine to feast. He looked away, out the window at the canal.

"I have a confession," Ana said.

"Tell me."

"I have known you since before last night."

Mino's face fell. His stomach lurched. The drunken penniless state in which Ana had met him last night was among the most flattering states he'd assumed this past year.

"Where else?" he asked. What street corner? Which scrap heap? What brothel?

"The *maranzaria*."

"Oranges," Mino said. Her scent, like the first breath after peeling the fruit. He knew it from the sunrise job hauling oranges to the *maranzaria*. This was better than so many other places Ana might have seen him, and yet it pained Mino to think about it. How miserable he'd been each of those mornings, always the last hour before he stumbled off to sleep. He wondered how slumped he must have been under the weight of the crates. How brutish his expression. He had known her for eight hours and already she made him want to be a better man.

"It's near our shop," Ana explained. "I used to see you passing with the crates on your shoulder." Her fingers threaded through his hair. "You looked like you'd come from somewhere exotic."

"I don't," he said.

"Still, I fantasized. I'd try to steal away, to follow you and see where you went after you set down the last crate, took your soldi from the merchant. I always wished to buy an orange while you were there, unloading. But each time, you'd be gone before I could catch up." Her eyes narrowed. "Then one day, you weren't there, and I confess, I missed you."

She covered her face, embarrassed, and Mino gently drew her hands down so they could look at each other. She was flushed but smiling, and Mino admired the way she sat with her discomfort, certain it would pass and brightness return.

"And then?" he asked.

"Last night," she said, "there you were, snapping a hair off my sister's violin bow." She touched his cheek, her palm so light and soft. "I'm not usually like this, but I couldn't let you get away again. What if you never came back?"

Mino put his arms around her waist, pulled her back under the covers, and threaded his leg around hers. With the weight of her settled over him, he felt rooted, as if by staying right here he could grow into something better.

What if he never left?

Eleven

IN THE ANNEX of La Sirena, Violetta studied herself in the mirror. It was October, the first week of *carnevale* and her first night performing at the casino. Nerves kept her fingers busy, smoothing her new gown, tugging at her wig for the thousandth time. She had chosen every aspect of her costume, but taken altogether, her reflection mystified her. She looked like the kind of woman she had long admired, the kind of woman whose confidence was as much on display as her pearls. Now she wondered whether those bold, inspiring women on the *altana* ever felt as unsure as she did beneath her mask.

Her gown shimmered, blue silk woven with shiny threads of silver, created by Federico's seamstress. Her petticoat had a thousand layers, and when she sat it billowed around her like the sea. Her lace gloves reached her elbows, and her lace collar plunged down between her breasts, leaving ample space for the black opal. Her wig she'd chosen carefully—not blond like every other lady's in Venice, but glossy black and curled into long ringlets that cascaded down her back. Most exquisite of all was her mask. Federico had had it painted by the famous *mascareri* Patrice, to resemble the iridescent scales of a fish. It was the same shape as a *bauta*, but at the mouth Federico had requested a rectangle of dark painted mesh instead of the *papier-mâché*. The mesh was indiscernible from the rest, and would let her sing more clearly.

Federico's purse had opened at the first request, and open it had stayed. Nothing was deemed frivolous. Yes to a brand-new corset. Yes to a series of fittings with the dressmaker. Yes to an armoire at the casino, for there was no way she could store her clothing at the Incurables. Yes when she requested a harpist to accompany her performance; the violin would have reminded her too much of Mino. She would have lied if Federico had asked why, but he asked no questions. He only said yes. Anything. Yes. It gave her the confidence to experiment, to make herself beautiful and strange.

The anteroom was drafty and damp, but it was hers and it was quiet, and the candlelight flattered her reflection. She had asked Federico for the librettos to secular operas she had no access to at the Incurables. Of the bounty he provided, she'd selected an aria from Handel's *Giulio Cesare*. She thought that, after Mino's mother's song, this was one of the saddest and most beautiful pieces she knew: imprisoned Cleopatra singing to her brother and betrayer, Tolomeo.

Piangerò la sorte mia,
sì crudele e tanto ria,
finché vita in petto avrò.
Flow my tears, cease not your grieving,
Though my sorrow be past relieving,
While I breathe still let me mourn.

Everything about the aria resonated with Violetta, its minor chords and legato phrasing. Every word of its libretto. She wanted to use the pain it brought her, how it made her think of Mino and the mistakes that had determined their fate. She wanted to sing those words in a sorrowful, hedonistic manner. It would be so unlike anything she'd ever sung through the grille of the *coro*.

The terms of her agreement with Federico were simple: on the one night a week she performed, he would give her fifteen percent of the casino's earnings. It was far more than she'd expected and far more than the five percent all the *coro* girls split at the Incurables. She could stop at any time, on the condition she discussed her leaving with him first.

She could manage one late night a week and still sing at the Incurables as expected. The thrill of these nights out gave her more energy than sleeping. She could keep this secret for now. Not even Laura had guessed.

There were three bottles of perfume on the vanity in her little boudoir, rouges and powders in becoming pinks and golds, fine kohl crayons for lining the eyes behind the mask, for shading the beauty marks. There was even, to Violetta's great amazement, her own *cicisbeo*, a wispy man with a naughty sense of humor. He appeared without warning at Fortunato's side to assist her with her preparations.

His name was Davide, and until Violetta asked him politely to stop, he applauded everything she did—humming, cleaning her fingernails, scratching an itch. But once he relaxed, she did, too. He even sang for her in a startlingly deep baritone, confessing as he powdered her neck and bosom beneath her mask that he once dreamed of becoming a castrato. He brought tea brewed from jasmine that tingled Violetta's throat. When he stirred in the honey, and asked her about her lovers, she demurred and drank while it was still too hot.

He laughed. "I can't tell if you're a virgin or if you love someone you shouldn't."

She tried to smile enigmatically, but he couldn't see it through her mask.

"If you get nervous," Davide coached, arranging ringlets across her back, dabbing her neck with vanilla cologne, "look for me in the audience. I know all the words to every song. I'll cheer you on."

But Violetta wouldn't be nervous. Every day for almost a year, she'd sung before larger, soberer, and more discerning audiences. She had sung before the doge at Easter and had received a card and bounty of white roses with his compliments. She still had the note at her bedside. She had sung before Federico.

She blushed thinking of that first night when he'd found her on his balcony. She'd never asked about his reaction the day he heard her sing at the Incurables, and she still didn't understand it. She would never get used to making people cry with her music, but at least in the church, she could guess why they were moved. They wanted to feel closer to God, and the *coro* helped bring them there. With Federico, she suspected it was something different.

Now the anteroom door opened and there he was, in a suit made of marvelous golden thread. He smelled of ambergris. He came to stand behind her, admiring her through the mirror. She wasn't sure if she should rise to greet him or not; there was something exciting about just watching each other in the mirror. He put his hand on her shoulder. She liked the way it looked in the reflection, and she liked the way it felt through her dress. Now she rose and came to him. She wanted to be closer. They leaned in for the greeting kisses. His lips brushed her mask, and she wished hers could reach his skin. Did he shiver as she did when they touched? He took her hands and held her at a distance to look at her.

"My Sirena." His soft tone made her dizzy. "Are you ready?"

"Let's go."

As they left the anteroom, walking from the hall into the loud casino, Federico's hand slipped from hers. Violetta shivered as if a draft had blown between them, but then he flashed her a smile, and she smiled back. He climbed the stairs to introduce her onstage.

From here, the casino looked different. She had never practiced in this room, for she could never make it to La Sirena before it was filled with guests. The stage was small but high. There was barely room next to the harp for her to stand. She looked out over a dozen tables drawn close, and a dozen more booths beyond. There might have been a hundred people in the casino, far fewer than she usually sang to, but she'd never performed alone before, and she'd never sung from behind a mask. She knew to amplify her voice, but she didn't know how this crowd would receive her music. It was easy for the *coro* girls to be the brightest part of a church service, but at the casino, Violetta's song would be competing with darker pleasures: drink and money and sex.

Perhaps she *was* nervous. She tried to steady her breath. She turned to Federico for comfort. She liked how he looked up there, his dark hair silhouetted, candlelit.

"Gentlemen, I suggest you lash yourself to the mast of your ship," he announced grandly, "for there is no resisting . . . La Sirena!"

Half the crowd applauded tepidly. The other half were occupied in conversations or with their drinks. As Violetta took the stage she reminded herself that Federico believed in her. She stood above her audience, each of them masked and many in shadow. She was ready to sing, to wake them from drunken dreams, and draw them to her.

Then, on the inhale before her first note, she thought of Mino.

She had known from the day he left the Incurables that he would not return, that he would never hear her sing, never know what became of her. She had driven him away. But every time she stepped outside those walls, part of her wondered whether Mino was walking the same street as she. She was always masked, and he would be, too. They would never know if the other was passing.

What if fate had brought him here tonight?

All this passed through Violetta's mind in the time it took to fill her lungs. So when she opened her mouth to sing, the words and the melody that came out were not Handel's *Piangerò*. It was Mino's song.

I am yours, you are mine . . .

She hadn't meant to, but now, all she could do was go on. She heard the harpist pull back, slowing and simplifying his plucking after the unexpected change. She felt the shift in the audience, their attention drawn from games and wine to her. She held them with her voice note after note, minute after minute. She held them as she reached the crescendo. By then she had become the music.

But at the song's end, what Violetta felt was not relief that she had done it, that Federico would be happy. She felt devastated. Mino was not in the room. She would have felt him if he was.

The crowd begged for more, but her face was wet with tears.

Twelve

Mino moved in across from Ana, her mother, her sisters, a precocious five-year-old niece, and a large birdcage of turtledoves. Their apartments were on the third floor of a building wedged into a corner of the Campo San Apostoli in Cannaregio. It was a neighborhood of merchants, close to the *merceria*. The long main street that stretched between Rialto and San Marco bustled with the most famous markets in Venice, among them Ana's family's sausage shop.

It was as far from the Incurables as one could get and still reside in Venice. Mino had slept in that room across the hall since the night Ana brought him home the month before. When she'd made the bed the next morning, Mino had helped her draw up the soft blue coverlet.

"What do your boarders pay?" he asked.

She laughed. "I can't rent to you."

"Why not?" he asked, flushing, remembering how she had paid the bill the night before.

"Mamma would . . ." Ana trailed off. Now her face was red. "She senses things. She's a traditional woman. We work early in the morning. We're not maskers, Mino."

"I will work for you," he said. "Tell me how to address your mother."

"What about your place?" she asked.

"I'd rather be here," he said and took her hands. "Near you."

Ana took a moment. How pretty she was when thinking.

At last, she smiled. "Mamma is Siora Costanzo."

He grinned and kissed her hands.

"Be comfortable," she said. "After Mamma is asleep, I will come to you."

Mino put his arms around her waist. He could not believe his change of fortune. He held Ana close, kissed the top of her dark head, and vowed to make himself valuable to her.

"Has anyone ever told you that you are like the butterfly, floating between the boughs of a lemon tree?" he said. "*Farfalla*." Butterfly.

She laughed, but before Mino could feel embarrassed, she looked up and let him in on her amusement. "I'm no butterfly. More a bee. I protect my hive. But I get more than one sting before I die."

She reached for a pillow and set it on the floor at the foot of Mino's bed. She patted it for Sprezz, who eyed it with suspicion.

"You're used to sleeping with him, aren't you?" she asked the dog.

Mino knew she must be imagining an apartment, at the very least a rented room, and without question, a bed, where man and dog might sleep together. Ana wasn't thinking of alcoves on dark street corners where, if you had something warm to lean into, you held it fast and did not let it go.

"Yes," he answered for the dog.

"From now on, Sprezz, you'll sleep here." Ana patted the pillow. "Agreed?" She held out her hand. Mino was enchanted to see Sprezz raise his paw to meet hers. They shook. "We'll be friends, but your breath smells of fish, and this bed's too small for three."

Sprezz lay down in total comfort, and Mino knew then Ana's gift: she could settle matters in a way that pleased everyone.

❋

HE DID NOT miss nights at the casino with Carlo. He threw himself into work at the sausage shop, and within a week he was fully ensconced in its world. He lightened the family's load by hauling crates to their black-awninged shop in the *merceria*. He cleaved cold meat off bones. At first, Ana's mother made no attempt to hide her skepticism, but Mino learned too quickly for her annoyance to keep up. Soon she was confiding in him about the price of Adriatic salt from the latest ship, about which important customers preferred what ratio of fat to meat. He took home no pay beyond his meals, board, and Ana's arms, and he was rich.

Every morning, he woke to the wonderful scent of frying sausage down the hall, to turtledoves cooing, and the chorus of women arguing over chairs and which of them had chipped the butter dish. He would roll over and smile, then join Ana and her sisters at breakfast. Later on, he would barter a rope of sausage for a vial of resin at the bookbinders to fix the broken butter dish.

He liked doing things like this for Ana. He longed for the look in her eyes when he surprised her with some cleverness. He knew how much he owed her, and it was far more than the fact that after two weeks he could no longer feel Sprezz's ribs through his skin, no longer see his own ribs in his reflection. It was more than the blissfully quiet sleep he now took for granted. Even more than the nights in Ana's arms. She had answered the question he had worried over all his life: Was he worthy of love?

"Will you marry her?" Siora Costanzo asked, one month into his stay. Mino sat in her parlor by the light of a candle, brushing pine resin along the butter dish's crack.

In his shock, Mino nearly dropped the dish, and all the women, even five-year-old Genevieve, laughed.

He wanted for nothing in Ana's company. He yearned all day for the moment she would come to his room in the night and he could hold her. But marriage had not crossed his mind. She seemed a delicacy someone had handed him on a silver platter. He feared the moment it became clear he couldn't pay.

"Mamma, please." Ana's sister Vittoria groaned as she tugged tangles from Genevieve's hair. "It's been too long since she had a man around to torture," she apologized to Mino.

"Poor Angelo couldn't take it." Siora Costanzo sniffed.

"My husband," Vittoria muttered to Mino. "Mino is not a drunk like Angelo was. He is not cruel like Papa."

"What does any of us have if we can't keep men on their toes?" Siora said. "When I was a girl, we knew how to keep a man guessing." She pointed at Mino. "Look at him, Ana. Do you see him guessing?"

Ana smiled and floated over to Mino, taking the repaired dish from his hands and setting it on the windowsill to dry. She put her arms around him. "I see him fixing everything in sight." Then she leaned close, until she was the only thing in Mino's sight. Was she broken? He couldn't tell and he worried over whether he was the man to fix her.

She kissed him in front of the others, which she had never done before.

"Would you like to be married?" he whispered. His heart was racing. He had not thought the words before he spoke them, and now he heard his own fear. What if she said yes?

"Don't worry, Mino," she said. "You'll know what to do."

❦

STELLA CAME TO the apartment in October, on the cold first night of *carnevale*, to borrow one of Vittoria's dresses. She appeared in the kitchen, so much taller and fairer than the rest of the family. She looked more like Mino than her own sisters.

"He's still here?" She laughed, tossing bits of bread into the turtledoves' cage.

"You promised," Ana warned her sister.

"Fine," Stella said, stepping toward Mino with a yellow dress draped over her arm. "Let me see your painting."

"Your half token, Mino," Ana said. "I told Stella about your mother."

Mino rummaged for his half token, embarrassed that his search had languished since he'd been with Ana. How long had it been since he'd taken the painting from his pocket?

He held it out. Stella looked at it a long time. He'd stopped expecting the thoughtful gazes to lead to anything. It was just a beautiful face.

"Does it mean anything to you?" Ana asked Stella, coming to stand beside her sister. Mino saw now how alike they looked. Their bodies and coloring were different, but their heart-shaped faces and the set of their mouths were the same.

"No," Stella said, sounding sorrier than Mino expected. "Though we could ask my friend Elizabeth. She knows every musician in Venice. She's British, but don't let that deter you. Her husband runs the most important opera house in London. I could bring the painting to her tomorrow—"

"No." Mino returned it to his pocket. He couldn't part with it, even for an hour.

"Let us come with you?" Ana asked. "Where are you meeting Elizabeth? Not that casino, I hope?"

"La Sirena?" Mino realized he hadn't been there, hadn't even had a drink since he'd met Ana, and something inside him soared. He hadn't missed the casino until Ana mentioned it. But now he wondered if Carlo was worried about him, and he wondered what new ideas were circulating among the Rosicrucians. Would they see how he was changed, how he was golden now because of Ana?

Ana's expression tightened. "That casino is no place for a man trying to make something of himself."

These were words they'd never discussed, a plan for Mino's life he didn't know about. What was the *something* he was trying to make of himself?

"Ana, you're too rigid," Vittoria called from her bedroom.

"You're not rigid enough," Ana called back sharply, and Mino remembered Ana telling him of the strain Vittoria's husband's drinking had been on the family. She had little patience for debauchery now.

"Don't worry, Ana," Stella said. "I have a proper job at last, at a little *teatro*. Elizabeth is a busy woman, but I'll ask if she would meet you."

"Please," Ana said.

"Did you get your violin fixed?" Mino asked, noticing the case resting on the console near the door.

Stella sighed. "Someday I'll get the money to buy a new one. There's a luthier called Guarneri in Cremona, Elizabeth knows him—"

"What if I fixed it for you?"

Stella shrugged as she moved toward the door. As she left for the party on the streets of Cannaregio, she called over her shoulder, "If you mess it up, I will kill you."

❦

ALL NIGHT, MINO worked on the violin. *Carnevale* exploded on the streets below, and Genevieve begged him to join the rest of the family at the parade downstairs, but Mino declined. He saw nothing but the violin, heard nothing but the music it might make when he was through.

Ana declined to go out, too. She made Mino dinner, then tea; she sat beside him. She seemed drawn to his diligence, doting on him while they had the apartment to themselves for once.

"I don't want to keep you from *carnevale*," he said.

"There's months of *carnevale*," she said. "If you want to stay in every night of it and work like this, I'll stay with you. I prefer watching you work to any party."

"Can you play it?" he asked her, holding out the bow, the violin. "I need to feel around the strings while someone plays so I can find the problem."

"No." She waved her hands, more sheepish than Mino had seen her, and for an instant, he wished it were Letta at his side. "I'm no musician."

"Pluck it then," he said, "forget the bow." With his fingers, he showed her a simple pizzicato. "Nothing to it."

She accepted the instrument, used her narrow middle finger to pluck a few strings. Mino leaned in, his ear close. He pressed his ring finger down on one string at a time as she plucked, satisfied when he heard the buzzing stop.

"It is as I suspected. Her D and G strings need new windings." His mind worked over what spare metal he might use to wrap her strings.

Ana raised her eyebrows as Mino detached the chain from the top of his half token and laid it flat upon the table. Its links were wire thin, pliable. He used to wish they were sturdier, but now he knew just what to do. If only—

Ana rose from the table. "I'll be right back," she said and returned a moment later with a small metal box. Inside were a pair of pliers, a hammer.

"Perfect," Mino said. If he could flatten the links of his broken chain and coil them tight enough with the pliers, he might have enough length to use them as new metal windings at the base of the strings. Stella's violin would sing like a mezzo-soprano.

"Are you sure?" Ana asked.

"Never surer," Mino said as he completely loosened the two lower strings and tightened the fine tuner peg.

When he was finished hours later, when his half token's chain lived in Stella's violin, Mino felt a kind of ecstasy he remembered from his earliest days playing. He looked up, remembering Ana, and the sight of her annoyed him, for she was surely impatient to go to bed. And Mino couldn't go to bed, because he wasn't there in that apartment. He was on the roof of the Incurables, playing as Letta sang.

"I see your mother in your eyes," Ana said.

"What?" Mino asked, brought back to the room.

"All night, you've been so joyful," she said. "The moment you finish working, I see the pain return to your eyes."

It was longing for Letta she had seen, and Mino was ashamed. Ana had been so open with him, but there was much about his past he wished never to tell her. He didn't want to lie.

"What if I never find her, Ana?" he said.

She took his hand. "Maybe you already have."

Mino stared at her, afraid of what she might say next. "I mean," Ana said, "maybe it is not your mother in the flesh that you will find, Mino, but a sign, a guiding hand to shape your life the way a mother's love might do. Tonight you put a piece of her inside this violin. I believe she would have wanted a bright future for you."

"I don't understand," Mino said.

"My family is happy for your help at the shop, but there's more for you, Mino." She held up the instrument. "You have a gift."

He shook his head. "I fixed one violin. I'm not a luthier."

Ana lifted her shoulders, a smile in her eyes. "Every luthier starts somewhere."

"Yes, in an apprenticeship, with a master—"

She put her hand over his to stop him talking. She eased herself onto his lap and draped her arms around his neck. Her kiss was tender, full of love. Mino felt himself relax at last.

"Maybe all you need is someone to believe in you."

THIRTEEN

BY THE END of November, when Violetta had been performing at La Sirena for two months, she needed guards to escort her off the stage. Her audience lined up outside the casino's door hours before her performances. Once inside, they battled to press against her, hungry for a word with the mysterious singer. Each night after she sang, the guards ushered her to Federico's booth in the back room. She never knew whether he would be there.

Tonight in his place was a vast bouquet of flowering jasmine. She hadn't told him she liked jasmine, but she remembered fondling a blossom in one of the casino's vases last week.

"Marvelous, aren't they?" her *cicisbeo* had said, taking note at her side. "Are they your favorite?"

Davide worked for tips.

This jasmine was meticulously arranged, a hundred blooms in an ornate spun-glass vase from Murano. Nothing like the strewn flowers on the bed in Mino's apartment. Along with the flowers, Federico had left champagne and enough steak to feed the entire *coro*. She was always starving after a performance.

"Please sit," Fortunato said as he and a squadron of guards formed a wall around her, dissuading the gamblers wishing to try their luck.

Then they parted again, moments later, and Violetta expected Federico. She was disappointed to see a woman approach her table. She was older than Violetta, though it was hard to tell by how much. She had blond hair, curled and coiled in surprising places above her white *bauta*. Her dress was pale blue, with giant ruffled sleeves and a long elaborate train made of lace and velvet. She had tied a blue ribbon in a giant bow around her neck.

"At last we meet." She curtseyed. "I am Elizabeth Baum, Federico's friend from London, and now, I hope yours, too."

Violetta blinked at the British woman, impressed by her confidence. Normally, Violetta talked to no one after her performances, but tonight she was feeling vulnerable, eager for company. That morning she'd had a bad row with Laura, who had pressed Violetta over a rehearsal Violetta skipped to nap.

"Are you ill?" Laura had asked, dubious.

Violetta had almost told her friend the truth about the other world she lived in. But how, when Laura had found all she'd ever wanted in the *coro*? There was no way to make her friend understand that Violetta *had* to sing at La Sirena. She couldn't let anything come between her and these nights at the casino.

"Tell them I am ill," she instructed Laura, "but do not send a nurse. It's only my time. I'm bleeding."

Laura stared at her, and Violetta understood that her friend knew she'd bled the week before. This made Violetta's lie even worse. She'd never paid attention to the rhythms of Laura's body.

"I can't keep covering for you," Laura said. "It's not like when we were in the music school."

Now she felt ashamed. She wished she could show this place to Laura, drink champagne and eat steak and talk about men in ways that would make the younger orphans blush.

Impossible.

She would make amends with Laura tomorrow, but tonight she didn't want to think about the Incurables. She wanted company that might understand her. So she made room for the elegant woman from London.

"I hope you're hungry," she said. "Federico sends enough food for a party he never graces."

"Indeed, he does," Elizabeth said, wasting no time sawing off a large bite of steak. "But if he lingered over filet with you, who would keep out the republic's rabble?" She pointed her fork across the casino to where a man in a black patrician robe pleaded with Federico, attempting to fend off two guards.

"One game," the man cried to Federico, hands clasped as if before a priest.

Federico's features held a cold distaste, making him almost unrecognizable to Violetta. She saw his lips move: "Out."

When Violetta thought of rabble, she thought—without judgment—of the republic's working people. The men of the *squeri*, men like Mino. She saw plenty of working-class men in this casino, gambling unmolested, surrendering what must be precious soldi to the tables. But Elizabeth was speaking of a nobleman, an older masked gentleman with ornaments of silver dangling from his robe. It confused her.

This foreign woman understood something about Venice that

Violetta didn't. She leaned closer to Elizabeth, keen to see the place through her eyes.

"Who is that man?" she asked Elizabeth.

"He is a *barnabotto*," Elizabeth said, "a nobleman at the end of his family's fortunes. He and a hundred like him sit with Federico on the Great Council. The governing body of your city is now half full of men selling their votes for gambling money. They come to every ball but cannot afford to host them. Federico has no patience for them."

"Because they posture as if they are still rich?"

"Because," Elizabeth said and smiled, "what if noble destitution is catching?" The woman tossed her head with an intelligent mirth that Violetta admired. "What happens when all this money runs dry, too?" She glanced around the casino, finished her wine, dabbed the corners of her mouth with a napkin. "But let us not concern ourselves with the fate of the republic. Have you ever been to London?"

"No." Violetta looked at her hands, felt the distance open back up between her and Elizabeth. "I wish to someday. . . ."

"My husband runs the King's Theatre in London. I design the costumes, and come here for inspiration every *carnevale*. Before tonight I thought the fashions were the most inspiring aspect of Venetian life, but now I've heard you sing, and I've changed my mind. You must visit. Do you have a favorite opera?"

Violetta raised her shoulders, not wanting to mention that she'd seen only part of one opera in her life.

"Does Federico ever visit?" she asked. She was surprised by her own question, but it was easier—and more fun—to imagine one day traveling with him to a place as distant and romantic as London.

Elizabeth gazed through Violetta's mask, taking her aback with their intensity. "Sometimes. But regardless of him, Sirena, you should."

Everything out of this woman's mouth enchanted Violetta, but the practicalities of such a visit still eluded her. She had money now; Federico paid her at the end of every evening, and he'd been right—the two or three sequins she took home from one night at the casino was more than ten times what she made in a week at the church. But still, she wasn't like Elizabeth, who could come and go from the city as she pleased. If Violetta ever left the Incurables—for longer than these few hours at night—she would have to leave it forever. And then, if she still wanted to sing, she would have to leave Venice altogether.

Sometimes she did want to leave it all behind. And sometimes nothing was more terrifying.

Now the guards parted again, and one placed a card before Violetta. She opened it and saw Federico's hand. She shivered with unexpected pleasure at his message.

Your presence is requested for a special performance tomorrow night.
If you agree, Nicoletto will pick you up at half past ten.

F

❋

FOR THE SECOND night in a row, Violetta opened her window and readied her bedsheet to escape. The night was windy, almost December, and she was fatigued from the night before. Her provocative dinner conversation with Elizabeth had kept her up late, thinking of London, imagining walking down real streets, not *calli* bordered by water. She imagined horses and carriages.

She hadn't apologized to Laura yet, and she'd felt the coldness throughout their suite all day. She put it out of her mind. She wouldn't miss the chance to see Federico. Shivering under her cloak, she lowered herself down with the bedsheet, tossed it back up inside her window, now with practiced ease. She leaped down to the street. The night was frigid, but the sky was clear. She hurried for the gondola, but there was no gondola waiting.

Instead, there stood a broad, floral-decked *burchiello*, the kind of boat noblemen took on longer voyages, up the Brenta Canal to Padua. A whistle rang out, and Violetta saw Nicoletto at the helm.

She went to him and took his hand. He helped her onto it wordlessly, as if this majestic, candlelit vessel were her ride every night.

Inside, Fortunato bowed his greeting, and then, the best surprise—Federico. He was seated alone at the polished wooden dining table inside the boat's salon, which could have held two dozen guests.

"Good evening," he said.

"Who am I singing for tonight?" she asked. This was a boat fit for the republic's most distinguished nobility. Violetta felt suddenly nervous.

"For no one," Federico said. He smiled enigmatically, coming forward to greet her with a kiss.

"I don't understand."

The boat began to move. Usually, Violetta traveled inward, up the Dorsoduro toward the casino; tonight Nicoletto steered the *burchiello* south, turning left onto the wide Giudecca Canal.

"Tonight," Federico said, gesturing out the windows of the ship, toward the sky, "there are fireworks in Giudecca, and a hundred illuminated boats to shine like stars. Tonight Fortunato has prepared a feast, and there is no one else for us to share it with. Tonight, Sirena, the republic performs for you."

Violetta blinked at him, a smile spreading across her face. She thought of the girl she'd been in the attic, the old doll she used to press to the window, promising enchanting nights like this. Her throat felt tight as she looked out at the splendor she so rarely got to see.

The sky bloomed with sparkling light she wished would last forever. The way the fireworks faded and reflected on the water was beautiful and sad.

There were many boats on the canal that evening, and as they glided by, Violetta heard bursts of laughter and violin music. She felt like they were all at one big, magical party. Through the windows of other gondolas' wooden *fèlzi*, she saw masks turn to stare at Federico's opulent boat, wondering who was inside.

"What are the fireworks for?" she asked.

"A wedding, I think," Federico said absently. "A member of the *nobiltà da terra ferma*."

Last night she'd learned of *barnabotti*, the fallen noblemen of yore. But she had long known about the *nobiltà da terra ferma*. They were newly rich citizens, relatively speaking in an empire of a thousand years. They had bought their way into the nobility by funding wars two hundred years ago, and no one ever forgot it. Violetta knew of the *nobiltà da terra ferma* because the Incurables gladly took their money, but the prioress reserved her true respect for that closed caste of nobility, the original families of the republic.

"They can hang the sky with jewels for their celebrations," Federico said, his tone gently mocking, "but everyone knows their ancestors sold sugar in the *merceria*."

He was joking, but it made Violetta sad. Wasn't she like the *nobiltà da terra ferma*? Trying to escape her original circumstances and become something new? It made her wonder, in the Republic of Venice, could she ever be anything but an orphan?

Federico's fingers moved to untie the ribbon of her mask, but Violetta pulled away. She could not show her face. Federico came closer, to her side, and nodded in Fortunato's direction. The servant was drawing the curtains closed.

"You can feel at ease with him," Federico said of Fortunato. "He is like family. He would do anything, anything I asked. You're safe here."

She knew Federico had much invested in keeping her identity secret. She trusted that, as well as her own yearning to show herself to him. Slowly, she untied the *bauta,* let it slide to the ground. With her bare face, she looked up at him.

Federico's smile was soft, mostly in his pale blue eyes. She felt his pleasure at the secret of her face. His gaze swept over her eyes, her lips, her cheeks and ears and nose, seeming to savor what he saw. It was so slow and so thrilling Violetta managed to sit still through her embarrassment. She let him look at her even as she blushed. For the first time in her life, she felt beautiful.

"The fish is ready, sir," Fortunato said, placing two silver salvers upon a white tablecloth. Violetta had eaten risotto and salad, drank a mug of watery wine at sundown with the *coro* girls, but she was still hungry, and the fish smelled wonderfully smoky and fresh. They sat down to eat amid a tower of vegetables, an appetizer of beef consommé set in aspic, and an array of little tarts filled with lamb and potatoes and leeks. Fortunato poured amber wine from a green bottle.

"We're not so different, you and I," Federico said as the boat glided on. "I am practically an orphan, raised by servants, just as you were raised by your prioress."

Violetta flinched and her mind went to Mino. What it would have meant to him to know his family.

"But you *knew* them," she said, "you knew the sound of their voices, the scent of their hair, and the touch of their fingers on your face when you were ill."

"Of course." Federico flushed. "I am sorry."

Instantly, she felt a sharper pain at having embarrassed him. "It's all right; I'm not sentimental. I don't think of my parents, just as I don't think they've ever thought of me. I'm happiest on my own. I've always been that way."

"Funny," Federico said, tiling his head. "That's not how I see you."

She felt an invitation in those words, in his expression. She put her fork down, leaned forward. "With you, it's different." How did she explain it? "When I listen to a new oratorio, I can hear, in the slow opening notes of its adagio, the anticipation of the faster allegro that will follow." Her cheeks were warm with nerves but she pressed on. "With you, it's as if I can hear that *something* is coming in the music."

"How does it sound?" he asked. "Will you sing it for me?"

She dropped from her chair to her knees and drew near him. At first, she felt his body welcoming her, her elbows on his thighs, but then he tensed, and she became embarrassed at her forwardness. She withdrew, turned away. She pulled one curtain back a bit and gazed out the window, at the golden sparks igniting the sky.

"Violetta," he said in a low voice, "once I loved a girl with all my heart."

She waited for him to go on.

"But I was a fool," he said, "and I lost her. I don't want to lose you. . . ."

Outside, the sky exploded, the show's finale, golden bands of light sinking in the darkness. Violetta turned from the window to look at Federico. "You won't."

He sighed, and she heard his infinite sadness. How she longed to comfort him and to take comfort in him, too.

"In my experience," he said, choosing his words with special caution, "it is possible to ask too much of one person." His hand cupped her cheek, then his fingers trailed down her face until they were under her chin. He raised it so that she looked into his eyes. He smiled and, though she was still embarrassed, she smiled back.

"We have agreed upon music," he said. "We are gifted with starlight and champagne. For now, Sirena, it's enough."

Fourteen

In the *Merceria,* next door to Costanzo's Sausages, a painted plaque swung in the March air from a metal arm outside a new shop. The plaque was not an exact replica of Mino's half token—Ana had painted it on the floor in her apartment—but it was close. Mino felt a proud ache to see it marking the entrance to his store, to see the words above it:

I Violini della Mamma.

It had been Ana's idea to paint the plaque in the image of his half token, to name the fledgling shop after his mother.

"I do not wish to whore my token out," he'd told her in a series of arguments beginning the night he'd fixed her sister's violin.

"Think of it as a talisman, Mino," she'd said, ever calm and steady, "to draw your family closer to you."

Eventually he saw her wisdom. Between his work in the sausage shop, his renewed devotion to the violin, and Ana, there was less and less time to pursue his mother, especially with no leads to follow. But what could Mino do with the shame he felt at *not* searching for her?

"More people will pass by and see this painting than you could ever show her to," Ana argued. "If anyone pauses to stare, is compelled to step inside, there you'll be. And if they don't know your family, maybe they'll want your business."

While Mino sought out materials—willow and spruce planks, clamps and blades, metal bending straps to shape the instruments' waists—Ana worked on the shop itself. She had convinced her family to spare the storage room adjacent to their storefront. It had its own entrance and was just the right size for a man starting out. She detailed a plan for Mino to pay them rent as soon as his work turned a profit. She scoured the columns of San Marco to round up groups of *facchìni,* men for daily hire waiting near the docks. But for the grace of God and Ana, Mino would have still been one of them. The men brought their axes and their wood, cleared the room, and built a wall and a door between the two establishments.

She had Mino fitted for a periwig, explaining that no merchant wore his own hair. She chose wallpaper, patterned in blue like Mino's eyes, and bought four plush blue receiving chairs on consignment. She threw down rugs and bought an expensive tea set, insisting Mino learn to steep and serve it, making him promise to offer a cup to anyone who stepped inside.

"Venice is small," she said. "Everything you do must suit the gossips."

She was the one who pushed him to open before Easter, kept him up until early in the mornings, constructing a prototype violin for the shop. Privately, Mino wished to model his prototype not on Stella's instrument but on the one he'd rebuilt years ago: his first violin. He spent a week tinkering with the angle of the neck, making the strings arch higher and higher, drawing closer to the sound he remembered could match Letta's voice on the roof.

When it was not ready by Easter, he felt anxious about disappointing Ana. She had invested so much in him. Her happiness was increasingly essential to his own.

Was this love?

She was generous, gave him things he didn't know he wanted. In return she made her expectations clear. There were many, but they were reasonable, and most had to do with his work. He was to be frugal with his expenses. He was to honor the relationships her family had established with the other merchants on the *calle*. He was not to take his earnings to a tavern. Between the two of them, in the little bedroom they shared at night, with Sprezz, life was easy. They could please each other so simply. They could fall asleep fast in each other's arms.

Every day he grew more confident in his work, his blade quicker at the wood, his fingers steadier at fine-tuning the strings. His prototype looked finished, but it still did not approach his first violin.

He sat at the table for two days, staring down at the instrument, mystified. He walked the streets with Sprezz. He avoided Ana's probing questions about opening the shop. He snuck into a tavern. He ordered a drink, and then another, feeling guilty but in need of the jolt. He let his mind travel back to repairing his first violin.

Before that *carnevale* afternoon. Before he'd bought the masks and found the golden ring between cobblestones. Before he'd kissed her for an instant in the apartment.

Back to when he was just agreeing to the terms of his work at the *squero*. For a year before his full apprenticeship began, Mino had volunteered his time at the boatyard one afternoon a week. He was given small tasks, mostly hauling materials to and from the workshops. He watched old men sawing wood for gondolas, waiting for them to break for supper so that he could devote himself to that broken instrument.

Mino remembered varnishing it, but now he wondered why he would have done it. The violin would have already been varnished. Then he remembered the plague of worms that had swept through the *squero*'s store of wood. He remembered being tasked with dousing the shipbuilding oak and fir and elm with a potent, protective brine. When no one was looking, he had submerged the violin in the brine as well. He would not surrender his most prized possession to worms.

The violin had sounded different ever after.

Now, in the tavern in Cannaregio, Mino paid his bill and raced back to Ana's apartment.

"Mino!" Ana sounded shocked when she found the prototype in pieces once again.

But he was heating canal water over the hearth, too consumed with his work to answer.

❁

BY THE BEGINNING of April, two weeks after Easter, Mino was ready to open. Ana wore her best dress and had ordered a new light blue suit for Mino. She brewed tea, brought in oranges and dry sausages on a tray as Mino counted the minutes until his first appointment. Stella was sending her friend Elizabeth and her husband, John, from the opera house in London.

At eleven o'clock, the three of them entered in a whirlwind of high voices and blond hair, flitting about the shop as Ana showed off Mino's prototype.

"The angle of the neck is his signature," Ana said, running her fingers down the instrument's body. They had agreed to let customers know about the neck but not the brining; Mino wished to keep his greatest innovation still a secret. "Notice how high it is. It produces a stronger, far more brilliant sound than the traditional shape."

"What we need is repair," John said. "We have half a dozen violins in need of attention."

Mino was watching Elizabeth, remembering the rumor that she knew every musician in Venice. He stayed close to her as Ana poured tea and led John to a chair, suggesting prices that made the man shift uncomfortably in his seat.

"Your wife is good at this," Elizabeth said to Mino.

He flushed, and Elizabeth raised her chin slightly, understanding his embarrassment. "Never mind, Mino. You can marry anytime, or not at all. This is Venice, isn't it?"

"Yes," Mino said. The idea of marrying anyone but Letta still surprised him sometimes.

"Hmm . . ." Elizabeth smiled and picked up his violin from its stand near the window. She held it expertly and drew the bow across the strings, drawing out a beautiful, trembling C minor. "Wonderful!"

It struck Mino that Elizabeth had played the opening chord of his mother's song. He thought of what Ana had said about the plaque being a talisman. The British woman's candor set him at ease.

"May I ask you something?" he said.

When Elizabeth set down the violin, Mino pulled out the half token. "Maybe you saw this outside."

She nodded. "It's very pretty."

"My mother left it for me. She was a singer, I think, and I . . ."

"You were hoping I would know her," Elizabeth said kindly. "I am sorry."

"Excuse me." Mino put his token away, wishing he had never shown it. He had ruined his first appointment with this personal request. He felt ashamed, watching Ana smoothly serving the tea to John.

"What if Mino made us new violins, John?" Elizabeth called across the shop. "He might spend as much time repairing your old, decrepit instruments as building an orchestra from scratch."

"That's a huge commission, darling," John said. "The man has just opened shop today. Give him a moment to catch his breath."

"Didn't you hear the way it played? If we give him a moment, he'll be booked for years."

John looked at Mino and laughed. "In all of Europe are there two women with stronger convictions than ours?"

Mino pushed Letta from his mind.

"I'll do it," he said.

"In that case, we'll need champagne." Ana grinned at him.

When Mino returned with the bottle, he was still trying to reconcile his gloom over the token with his pleasure over the commission. Ana worked out the financial details with John while Mino popped the cork and filled the glasses. Everyone drank heartily but Ana, who tasted hers and returned to her accounting. Mino wished she would give in to the moment a little more.

At the door, Elizabeth kissed his cheek in parting. "I hope you find her, Mino."

When the English couple left, Ana caught him by the wrist, concerned. "What's wrong with you?"

Was it his mother? Was it Ana? He didn't know, and so he told her, "I wish they were Venetian. I don't like to think about my violins traveling to England, somewhere I'll never see."

"Mino, this is only the beginning. And an incredible one! We must thank Stella." She looked up at him tenderly and kissed him. "There will be many more violins."

He nodded, but something nagged at him.

"I'm off to help Mamma," she said. "I'll be back at closing time."

With Ana gone next door, it puzzled Mino that he had the next year of his life sorted. He glanced around the storage room, where he would now be every day. He felt immense gratitude, but then something else, something stifling that he didn't want to look at too closely for fear of what he might discover.

❈

TWO WEEKS LATER, as Mino was measuring the cut he would make to the ribs of the first violin, the shop door opened. When he looked up from his worktable, his chest constricted. The prioress of the Incurables and Laura stood in the middle of his store.

"Mino?" the prioress said, seeming as struck as he was by their meeting. She rushed forward to embrace him and held him close. Mino could not move. Over her shoulder he saw Laura studying him.

Was Letta nearby? Waiting outside? What would Mino do if she stepped through his door? Would he fall to dust?

"What are you doing here?" he asked, his voice a whisper.

"We've just come from auditioning a trumpeter at San Apostoli," Laura explained. For parts like the trumpet, deemed unsuitable for women players, the *ospedali* commissioned external musicians to play with the *coro*.

"He's good," Mino said. Ana loved the trumpeter at San Apostoli, though Mino had always preferred strings over brass.

"We heard about a new shop in this neighborhood," the prioress said, "but I never dreamed we'd find you." At last she released him, keeping his hands in hers. "Look at you. How marvelous. But—what about the *squero*?"

He shook his head. "Things changed."

The prioress looked stunned, her mind working as she glanced back out the window. "I recognized the painting outside but wasn't sure why. Now, of course, I remember."

"My mother—"

"Your half token—"

"I'm still looking for her." Mino found himself looking at Laura. They did not know each other. They had never spoken in the thirteen years they'd both been at the Incurables. But Letta used to talk about Laura. Mino was surprised to feel Laura looking at him pointedly. What would Letta have told her?

"Did you make this?" Laura asked, approaching his prototype. "The bridge is so unusual."

Mino moved to her side, placed the instrument in her hands. "Please."

She began to play a measure. He closed his eyes, aching to hear the old sacred music again. Ana and Mino went to church in their *sestieri* on Sundays, but the music was nothing compared to that at the Incurables.

"It's remarkable," Laura breathed when she was finished. "I'd love to hear how it sounds in the church."

Mino bowed his head. This was significant praise from an Incurables musician—and from someone Letta had spoken of so highly. "Thank you."

Laura raised an eyebrow, as if getting an idea. "Many of the *coro* violins are in need of repair."

"Laura, I'm not sure we have the funds—" the prioress started to say.

"That violin outplays any I have ever touched. Think of the *Sensa* concert, *siora*. At least let us discuss it with the maestro."

The prioress's face took on a stubborn set. "The Pietà girls do try to outshine us every year." She looked at Mino, raised her shoulders as if helpless. "Come by. We will talk."

Mino's heart was racing. He had been back to the Incurables to hear Letta sing, but anonymously, briefly. He'd had to face no one and left the church feeling shattered. To return at someone else's request, as a merchant, when Letta might see him? He could not trust himself to act professionally in her presence. He would do more harm to his fledgling business than good. Ana would sense something. It was impossible.

"Tomorrow?" Laura said.

"I'll be working."

"Come when you can then," the prioress said.

"It's difficult. My customers—"

"Make us your customers," Laura said. "Your violins could transform our *coro*."

"Sunday," he blurted out against all reason. Before he could change his mind, he added: "After mass."

As soon as they left, chattering excitedly, Mino collapsed in a chair. He closed his eyes and heard Letta's voice. He yearned for her, still, with such ferocity that he could no longer deny he'd yearned for her every moment of these recent months with Ana. That his instruments might accompany Letta's voice, might share the air she breathed, was too much.

He didn't know how long he sat there petting Sprezz, but when Ana returned to the shop and he rose to pretend nothing had changed, it was dark outside.

Fifteen

Spring came late that April. Rain cloaked a cold sky outside the parlor windows where Violetta and Laura sat on a languid Wednesday afternoon. They should have been studying the new sheets for vespers, but Violetta was exhausted. Her eyelids felt weighted as if by sandbags used to barricade doorways during high tide.

She'd had too much champagne last night. When Federico was pouring, Violetta couldn't say no. Now she lay on the floral chaise, stretching her feet toward the fire, holding the libretto up so Laura wouldn't see her eyes drift closed.

A nap would be delicious. She let her mind glide toward Federico, toward the night world of La Sirena, her thoughts lingering on each beguiling detail. He'd been exuberant after her set, his arm around her waist as he introduced her to three visiting French gentlemen.

"Your friend Elizabeth is back in Venice," he'd said to her, nodding toward the back booth, where the English woman sat examining an array of exquisite fans from a vendor's trunk.

Violetta had brightened behind her mask. The women had dined together several times since their first meeting, but when Elizabeth returned to England at Christmas, Violetta was left to eat alone after her performances. Now Elizabeth grinned at Violetta, hiding her face coquettishly behind a black lace fan. Violetta waved, blew Elizabeth a kiss.

"She requested to have dinner with you," Federico said. "Order anything you like."

"Will you dine with us?" she asked, turning to him.

"I have eaten already," he said, and kissed the back of Violetta's hand twice, as he always did when he had business to attend to.

"Which do you prefer?" Elizabeth asked, gesturing at the fans as Violetta slid into the booth. She wore a new red dress that complemented her hair and she sipped champagne, laughing heartily at her own antics with her fan. "Fans make me feel young again, as fresh and lovely as you. I've missed you, Sirena. You were wonderful tonight."

"Thank you." Violetta smiled. "I'm happy to see you, too." She chose the cream-colored fan, flicking it open in front of her as Elizabeth poured them both champagne.

"What brings you back to Venice?" Violetta asked.

"John and I discovered the most brilliant new luthier," she said. "To hear his violins, Sirena, it's as if you've never heard music before."

Violetta was glad her mask hid her expression. She heard exceptional violin music every day, but none compared to Mino's on the roof, long ago.

"You're contradicting yourself," Elizabeth said.

"What?" Violetta said, confused as Elizabeth reached to reposition her collapsing fan.

"Half open and you're beckoning." To demonstrate, Elizabeth turned to survey the room, and Violetta watched a masked man a few tables away notice her. His chin lifted in complicity. "Once you have the gentleman's eye," Elizabeth explained, "open the fan further to let him know *I'm available now.*" But she did not move her fan. "Or close it slowly"—now she demonstrated, the gentleman leaning forward in his seat to watch—"to let him know *I'm available later.*"

"What's the signal for *I'd rather lie with a Byzantine oar at the bottom of the canal*?" Violetta asked.

Elizabeth laughed loudly. "I don't need to tell you that," she said. "It's the message you radiate all the time."

"It is not." Violetta picked up a second fan, slowly clicking it open, delighted by the small painted scene of a woman picnicking with two centaurs.

Elizabeth was so unlike the women at the Incurables. She wasn't modest or quiet or demure. Violetta wanted to be more like her. She hadn't forgotten the woman's offer to visit her in London.

Across the room, Federico glanced up from his conversation with the Frenchmen. He smiled at her. Her heart quickened as she clicked her fan open all the way.

"Oh no," Elizabeth teased. "Don't tell me . . ."

Violetta flushed, tossing down the fan so that it jostled her champagne. Why should Elizabeth be surprised? Why should Violetta be embarrassed? Why wouldn't any woman in La Sirena—or in Venice, for that matter—want Federico? He was like the finest champagne: effervescent, complicated, emboldening, and gone too quickly from each encounter. Elizabeth was married, but surely she'd taken lovers on her trips to Venice, where a beau was as much an accessory as a *bauta*. She had just been flirting with that gambler across the room. She must see the appeal of Federico.

"Tilt your fan elsewhere, Sirena," Elizabeth said.

"Why?"

Elizabeth filled both their glasses, finishing off the bottle and gesturing to the waiter for another. "For one thing," she said, "he's far too old. Any young man in this casino would kill to have you. And almost all of them would treat you better than Federico."

Violetta rolled her eyes. But it was true that men were watching her. All she had to do was look around to catch a dozen glances. She felt watched when she sang in the *coro,* but at the Incurables, gazes threatened to turn into marriage proposals. She'd never thought about what might be different at La Sirena. What she thought about at La Sirena was Federico.

"What if I introduced you to my luthier," Elizabeth said. "He's absolutely—"

"I know what I want," Violetta said. "I don't need anyone to approve."

"Only him," Elizabeth said, nodding in Federico's direction. She clinked her glass against Violetta's. "When you tire of the effort, let me know. I'll take you to London. You won't believe your fortune there."

Violetta's frustration thundered inside her. Her flirtation with Federico, which had once seemed to point in an inevitable direction, had stayed right where he'd left it the night he'd taken her out on the *burchiello*—nearly six months ago. Violetta knew he cared for her. He saw to her every comfort. He watched her from across the room with intense affection. Why did he draw away when she got close?

❁

"ARE YOU SLEEPING?" Laura's voice startled Violetta awake, and she jumped up from the chaise. Her eyes adjusted to the light from the window.

How she wished to take Laura into her confidence. She'd loved talking with Elizabeth, but who knew when she'd see the British woman again? And besides, Elizabeth did not know who Violetta really was. An orphan. A *coro* girl. *Violetta, voce d'angelo.* Laura had known her all her life.

"Violetta?" she asked again.

She couldn't tell Laura everything, but she desperately wanted to tell her something. "I think I am in love."

"Violetta." Laura gasped and rushed to sit beside her. Her eyes dropped and her cheeks flushed. "I confess: I found your bedsheet, your open window. One night. Months ago. I know you have been leaving. But I never suspected . . ."

Both girls laughed with nervous relief. How lucky she was to have a friend as good as Laura. Violetta felt she did not deserve her. Even now as they divulged their secrets, Violetta would still lie. It would be too dangerous for Laura to know about her performances as La Sirena. But she could tell her about Federico. She could use her friend's advice.

"What is he like?" Laura asked. "Will you marry?"

"No," Violetta said quickly. "Of course not. He knows my position on marriage." She was surprised to find herself thinking of Federico's own restrictions on marriage, his status as the second son.

"Your position hasn't changed?" Laura asked, a little teasing. "Even now that you're in love?"

Violetta shook her head. "We meet once a week. It's enough," she lied. "He's very exciting."

They laughed again and Laura squeezed her hands. "It is good you told me. You can trust me, Violetta." She closed her eyes and took a deep breath. "And now I must tell you something."

"Anything," Violetta said lightly, her mind still pondering the mysteries of Federico. She was glad Laura hadn't asked about their intimacy. She had depressingly little to say on the subject.

"Yesterday I saw Mino."

Violetta's hands went slack. Questions rolled into her mind like fog until she couldn't think. She'd heard wrong. Or Laura was mistaken.

Mino was gone.

"You know the prioress and I went to hear the trumpeter in Cannaregio," Laura said, her voice a whisper. "On our way back, through the *merceria*, we passed a little violin shop. Mino owns it, Violetta. He builds them. They are like no instrument I've ever held—"

Violetta meant to say *stop,* but her mouth was too dry. Her skin burned as if near a hot flame.

"There's more," Laura said. "He is coming here for a meeting. Sunday."

Violetta looked up at Laura with terror in her eyes. She felt the need to tear something to shreds—the music in her hands, or Laura, or her own capricious heart.

"Did he ask after me?"

Laura swallowed.

"Oh." Violetta felt as if she had been punched.

"He looks well," Laura said. "Come Sunday. Make amends."

❋

SOMEHOW, SHE WAS there after mass that Sunday, in her best Incurables dress with her hair braided. Laura had requested Violetta join the meeting, lend her opinion in Porpora's absence. The maestro had gone to Vienna to compose an opera for the season; his replacement had yet to be agreed upon. Laura had cited to the prioress Violetta's perfect ear and her position as the *coro*'s lead soprano. The prioress obliged—she could refuse Laura nothing.

Violetta would be limited by what she could say to Mino before the prioress, but her presence could show him that she was sorry. Perhaps it was all she needed him to know.

She felt more exhausted than ever, even though she had stayed in the past few nights. She should have gone out last night—turned up at La Sirena to drink and exhaust her mind. Instead she'd lain awake, tortured by memories.

If Violetta could change what had happened between them, how much would she do differently? She would erase every word she'd said about his mother, of course. But the rest? Would she decline Mino's proposal again?

Yes. She couldn't see another way, even now. Even though he had meant more to her than any other person. Even though she did love him. It was different than the physical ache she felt for Federico; it was its own kind of love and it was still in her heart. She knew she could not marry, could never be any man's wife or any child's mother. But she kept returning to that moment when he'd proposed. She saw his blue eyes when he said *Marry me.* She felt his hands holding her close. She smelled the jasmine on the bed. She felt anew how she'd wrecked the future he dreamed of.

Waiting with Laura before the fire in the downstairs receiving parlor, she was on the brink of tears. She went to the window, wishing she could open it, let in all the rain from outside.

"He isn't coming," she said.

"It's not even half past one," Laura said. "Should we allow him to be late before you write him off?"

"I know he isn't," Violetta said under her breath.

Half past one turned to a quarter to two, and Violetta caught Laura and the prioress exchanging glances. When finally a door opened, Violetta's heart caught in her throat. But the man in the doorway wasn't Mino. It took a moment for Violetta to remember Carlo, the young man she'd met at her first masquerade. She knew him only from the instant he'd lifted his mask. She'd clung to her own all that night.

He must know Mino. How? What if Mino had been there, that night at the party? What if she had ended up dancing in his arms, instead of Carlo's? She would never have met Federico. Where would she be now?

"I'm sorry," Carlo said, bowing. "A personal matter prevents Mino from meeting today. He's sent this letter, and a wish to reschedule."

What personal matter? Violetta didn't believe him.

The prioress took the letter, read it quickly. Then she folded it again and slipped it into her pocket, and Violetta lost the chance to glimpse even his words. She told herself it didn't matter as she fought the urge to plunge her hands into the prioress's skirts.

Regardless of what Mino had written, Violetta knew the truth. She felt incoherent with regret, her mind clear on only one thing: he had not come because of her.

Sixteen

On sunday evening, Ana came to Mino's room earlier than usual, just after her mother retired. She lay down in his arms and closed her eyes before they even made love, a soft smile on her face. How quickly she slept.

The night was mild and clear. Mino breathed her orange-scented skin and listened to the dreaming patterns of her breath. He watched her face as the moon climbed through the sky. Wonder kept him awake now; last night it had been fear. Last night everything had been different. When he held Ana in this same position, she had seemed the only solid ground in Mino's world.

Last night he'd feared the meeting at the Incurables, meant to take place this morning. He had risen early, left before sunrise for his shop to prepare. But then, an hour before, in a single moment, his life had changed forever.

He had made his meeting at the Incurables for when he knew Ana would be at mass and then luncheon. He hated keeping a secret from her, but he hadn't known how to tell her.

Early that morning before the meeting, he'd lit the candles in the shop but left the wooden casements closed. The floor was carpeted with wood shavings, and the smell of varnish had been enough to singe his nostrils. Mino loved it there, particularly alone, late at night or early in the morning. He'd lifted his prototype proudly. He wanted to present it at the Incurables as an example of what he had accomplished. He had made it with his old home in mind.

Would Letta be there? he'd wondered. Would she look upon his violin with her dark, appraising eyes? He'd shivered to imagine it. Her approval would mean so much to him. It would mean not just that his instrument was good—he knew it was—but that she didn't hate him anymore.

He wasn't foolish enough to hope for a moment alone with her. The prioress would be there, perhaps the maestro, and Laura. But he could look at her. They had once shared an entire unspoken language. He could tell her he was sorry with his eyes. He would recognize her silent answer.

What if she forgave him, there in the parlor? What then?

He didn't know. He had to stop. He would drown if he began to wonder what else she might tell him—about *coro* life and the roof, about what freedom looked like to her now. He didn't need to know those things anymore. He had Ana. He had Sprezz. He had his shop.

All he needed was Letta's forgiveness so he could move on.

The back door had creaked open. Mino had looked up, startled by Ana in her pink cloak and hood.

"What time is it?" he'd gasped. Had he lost himself in thoughts for so long that she was already back from lunch? Was he late?

"Early," she'd said, her voice unusually thin. She was a woman who spoke quietly but with a fortitude that showed her intelligence, whether she was talking about the price of artichokes or the war of the Polish Succession. Mino had looked down and saw that beneath her cloak, the hem of her nightgown showed. She'd gone there without dressing.

"What's wrong?" he had asked, feeling his heart quicken. He had only told her of his meeting in passing. He had mentioned the violin maestra from a church orchestra and cast it as preliminary. He had not specified that this church belonged to an *ospedale.* He had gotten nowhere near telling her the *ospedale* was his.

Guilt had flooded him. Did she know?

She'd come close, reached for the violin in his hands and set it gently on his workbench. When she'd taken his hands, hers were clammy. She drew him to the chaise and they sat down. Her smile was broad but flickering.

He felt uneasy.

"Ana—"

"We're going to have a baby, Mino."

She laughed and covered her face, and when he'd drawn her hands away he'd seen tears in her eyes. A baby.

The world stopped. Mino felt a sense of great peace. For so many years, he had sought his mother, thinking she was the answer to all his questions. Now he was looking at a new mother, one he had helped create. Ana. Together they had made someone new.

A child would look to them for everything. His child. He couldn't speak for his amazement.

Suddenly, all there was to life was Ana and this babe. They held hands as if neither would ever let go. Mino dropped to his knees before her. He moved their hands to her belly. He felt the life within.

He would not go to Dorsoduro that day. There could be no meeting at the Incurables. No more *what ifs*. With the British commission, Mino had more work already than he'd hoped to acquire in half a year. He could make his own opportunities. He must stop looking upon his broken past to heal him. He only had to look right here. Here was a baby. Here its mother. Here its father.

"Marry me," he had said.

Ana had dropped to her knees and kissed him. "Yes."

❈

THE LETTER CAME four months later, in September, when pale sunlight faded in the afternoon sky, when Ana wore the rose behind her ear, indicating her betrothal. Her belly had swollen to a beautiful globe, and she sat on the chaise in his shop—the only place she was comfortable—going over his accounting while she ate anchovies for the fifth meal in a row.

"Mino?" She looked up from the paper in her hand. "What meeting did you neglect at the Ospedale degli Incurabili?"

He put down the varnish brush, wiped his face with a rag, and took a breath before he spoke. "What does it say?"

"You had an appointment to discuss an order and never showed up, never rescheduled," Ana said, looking again at the paper, as if perhaps she had misread. "That isn't like you."

"It's my mistake," he said slowly. "The meeting was the day you told me about the baby." He touched her shoulder, knowing she would remember how, after she had told him, they made love on the shop floor for hours. "I forgot about it afterward."

"They are seeking violins for a full *coro*, Mino, and their music school. Do you not think an order of that size has to do with my well-being and the baby's?"

He felt hot and tugged at his collar. "I couldn't have fulfilled it," he said. "I've been working all hours just to meet the Baums' order."

"And now you're halfway done with the commission," she said. "And according to this letter, they are still in need of instruments." She looked at him carefully. "What aren't you telling me?"

Mino came to sit beside her. He breathed her in. Underneath the anchovies was still the reassuring sweetness of oranges. This was Ana. He could tell her.

"I am an orphan of the Incurables. It would be painful for me to return."

"Darling," she said, and put her arms around him. "I wish you'd told me." When she kissed him, he felt how overwhelmingly good she was, how loving. He didn't deserve her. "Shall I go with you?"

Months ago, he wanted to go alone, to look in Letta's eyes and return to Ana stronger. That was before he knew of the baby. With the baby coming, Mino was already stronger. He was bonded to Ana. He could lean on her.

So now he saw it—the meeting, Letta watching him, watching Ana. Would it upset Letta to see him with another? Foolish thought. She had never loved Mino, not as he loved her. Might it be better if Letta didn't have to wonder whether Mino was still in love with her? Ana's presence would make the meeting more comfortable for everyone.

"Thank you," he told her.

"I'll set everything up. I know a member of their council. We'll bring sausages." Ana smiled at him, then down at her belly, addressing the baby. "Your papa is about to work for the most important *coro* in Venice. This will change your life, little one."

"I don't want our life to change," Mino said and kissed her, leaning over her on the chaise until she laughed and pulled him close, making room between her legs.

She would never know how truly he meant it.

Seventeen

Again," Violetta instructed Helena from the parlor chaise. "This time, slow down. Stop worrying about the next note. Stay with the one you are singing. Stay there as if you'll never leave it."

She knew this was difficult advice, but she sighed as Helena ignored her, singing the scale again exactly as she had before. Outside a pale and gray September sky made the parlor gloomy. Violetta couldn't imagine how it was nearly *carnevale* again. Two years already since that last day with Mino. It put her in a sullen mood to think of cycling through the same excruciating anniversaries every year. Why could time never circle back so that she might unsay those words?

"Your tongue is too thick," she told Helena irritably.

"What am I meant to do about that?" Helena asked.

"Stick it out," Violetta said, and when Helena did, Violetta held it between her thumb and forefinger and pulled it forward until Helena's eyes widened. Violetta had learned this trick from Giustina and it had served her well at the casino, where there was never time for a full warm-up before a performance. "Now sing."

As her protégé moved through the exercise, Violetta pushed everything from her mind but the rise and fall of Helena's notes. Ever since Mino had missed that meeting, she had thrown herself into her responsibilities.

For almost as long as she'd been a member of the *coro,* Violetta had secluded herself in the afternoons, claiming a virtuoso's need for private time to rehearse and study while sleeping off her nights as La Sirena. But after Mino didn't come, Violetta had trouble sleeping. Darkness filled her mind. She'd had to find new ways to stay busy.

Helena had a bright, bell-like voice. What the eleven-year-old girl lacked in nuance, she made up for in volume. It might serve her well, as Hasse—the new maestro—composed bold oratorios that begged for a soloist whose voice could cut through an orchestra. Violetta had learned how to sing over the din of La Sirena; Hasse thought she was brilliant.

"Do you have an admirer?" Helena lisped, her tongue still pinched between Violetta's fingers.

Violetta let go. "Pardon me?"

The girl seemed to wither under Violetta's gaze. "It's what some of the other girls are saying."

Violetta raised an eyebrow and waited, trying to give away nothing of the heat flushing her cheeks.

"They say you have an admirer, and you're expecting a proposal. That's why you've started training me, because you're going to leave."

Violetta rolled her eyes, even as she relaxed. This was children's gossip; it had nothing to do with her nighttime realities. "Who do they believe my admirer to be?" She leaned closer to Helena, showing the girl it was okay to speak freely.

"Ava said it was Porpora." Helena laughed, glancing up to confirm this was absurd before going on. "That you're already carrying his child, and that's why his contract wasn't renewed."

"And you?" Violetta asked. "What do you think?"

"I don't think you're going anywhere," Helena said, her large brown eyes holding Violetta's. It was meant to be an expression of faith and loyalty, but it felt like a prophecy Violetta couldn't abide. She stacked up her papers and turned away.

"Again tomorrow," she told Helena before closing herself in her chamber.

Her mood was bitter. She had realized that what she hated most about her life now—more than being cloistered at the Incurables, more than never knowing her own parents—was that she had to admit she had hurt Mino out of spite and jealousy. Even if she fled this city, that would still be true. It crushed her that he hadn't shown up for the meeting with the prioress, that she'd been ready to make amends and he had not. That was all she could make of his absence that day. Nothing, not even fantasies of Federico, could lift the weight.

Only her singing didn't suffer. Both in the church and at the casino, Violetta sang her heartache. She moved her audiences to tears, and she liked it. The moments she was singing were the only ones in which she felt a measure of peace.

❃

WHEN THE LETTER came in late September that Mino would reschedule, Violetta told Laura she would attend the meeting. But when that Saturday arrived, she stole to the roof and hid for hours. She was not strong enough to bear his rejection again. The roof was the only place she could be certain she wouldn't see him, wouldn't be found.

It seemed an eternity that she watched boats disappear over the horizon. Eventually, cold and damp in the evening fog, she crept back inside and knocked on Laura's door.

It swung open. Behind her candlestick, Laura's eyes were huge with relief, then annoyance.

"And?" Violetta said.

Laura shook her head, incredulous. "We waited. I searched for you—"

"I couldn't," Violetta said. "Tell me. Please."

Laura rubbed her eyes and turned back inside her room. She set the candlestick by the bedside. She retied the ribbon at the neck of her nightgown.

"We've commissioned a dozen violins. The expense is high but worthwhile. We've had to advance the funds out of—"

"Laura!" Violetta shouted. "What else?"

Laura sighed and sat down on the bed, patting the space beside her. Violetta climbed in and felt the covers close around her. She lay her head on Laura's breast. It rose and fell. She heard Laura's breath like scales as her friend stroked her hair.

"He is getting married."

Violetta stiffened. Silence swelled around them.

"Tomorrow," Laura said.

Violetta closed her eyes and felt a void open inside her. *Marry someone better than me.* She'd said it. Did he love this woman? It didn't matter. She was so glad she hadn't gone to the meeting.

Laura's fingers brushed her, a calming weight to them. Her voice dropped to a whisper. "He has a baby coming."

Violetta pushed slowly off Laura's chest. She rose from the bed. She looked her friend in the eyes and saw that it was true. Desperation filled her and she swung at a vase of flowers on the table next to Laura's bed. The porcelain crashed to the floor and shattered. The water dripped across the terrazzo. There was so much more she wished to break.

"Calm, Violetta," Laura said. Her voice stayed steady. "He's found love again, just as you have. It's all right—"

Violetta cried out, fell on her knees. She didn't want to be reasoned with. Shards of porcelain cut through her dress, into her legs. The pain felt good. She wanted to be as broken as the vase.

"You're bleeding." Laura gasped. "I'll get the nurse—"

"Don't," Violetta said, finding her feet, not even looking down at her wounds. She made herself breathe, to appear calmer than she was. "I'm very tired. I'm going to bed."

"Violetta, don't do anything tonight—"

"Please. Leave me be." She hugged Laura tightly, briefly. "Good night," she whispered, then closed herself in her room.

❧

SHE HAD NEVER gone out her window before sundown and was surprised to see the Zattere below was crowded. But she knew her people; whatever Venetians thought of a woman scaling a hospital window, they would think on it intensely for a moment, and then the thought would flit away.

Tomorrow was to be a grand regatta, and the Giudecca Canal was already crowded with decorated boats ready for racing. Everyone who had money and access to a boat was heading out for evening picnics on the water. The casino would be crowded later.

She thought of Mino, who once planned to apprentice at the *squero.*

This would have been an important night for his work as a shipbuilder. Instead, he had even more pressing matters on his mind. His wedding. His baby. Violetta imagined him exchanging vows with an unknown woman. Her stomach churned.

She would miss Laura. She would miss the music, always. She would miss the wonder in the eyes of the churchgoers as she sang. But she couldn't stay in the same place any longer.

Mino had moved on. It was past time for her to do the same.

She waited for a family to pass, and then, as quickly as she could, she let down the bedsheet, climbed to the ledge, and for the last time, jumped to the street. She didn't look back to see who was watching. She turned and ran.

Her pockets were heavy with sequins. She wore her mask, an unremarkable white dress, her cloak, and the opal at her neck. She had nothing else she valued, only the freedom she chased. She pushed through the crowds without caring about the eyes she drew. She had to get far from the Incurables, fast.

Venice glowed pink at sunset—the buildings, the water, the air. Big clouds clotted the sky, their edges limned with light. The romance of the city pained Violetta. She needed to slide into the darkness of the casino, to let it take her in its arms.

Halfway there, it began to rain. Violetta hurried, but soon she was soaked. Dipping under the cork bough, dashing up the circular steps, she drew a quizzical look from Fortunato at the door. She tugged down her cloak to bare the glittering stone.

"It's me."

He straightened, turned the key to open the door. "La Sirena. What a surprise."

"Is he here?" she asked.

"Is he expecting you today?"

She shook her head. "I'll wait."

Fortunato bowed. "His table is open. Shall I send some champagne and a towel?"

She thanked him and ducked inside, feeling instantly soothed by the dark walls and early evening quiet. She went to her boudoir and changed into a yellow dress, forgoing her corset since her *cicisbeo* was not yet there to tie it. She went out to find champagne waiting at Federico's table. Free of the Incurables, she should have had much to toast. But as she sat down at the booth and took in the view of the casino, Violetta's whole body was shaking.

She should have been happy for Mino. She had been the one to reject him. For years she had convinced herself she wished him well. But what she felt now was different. Envy roiled through her core. She was jealous of Mino for getting what he wanted. And she was jealous of the woman who would get him for the rest of her life.

"What have I done?" she whispered.

"Do my eyes deceive me?" a voice said over her shoulder.

"Federico—"

He slid into the booth beside her. He was smiling, but his eyes conveyed alarm. "What are you doing here on a Saturday?" He touched her hair. "And all wet? I would have sent Nicoletto to pick you up in the gondola. I hope everything is all right?"

"I want to sing."

She tipped her mask up a little, just above her lips. She wrapped her arms around Federico and kissed him on the mouth. His lips met hers, welcomed them, and Violetta's breast warmed with desire. He took hold of her shoulders. Tenderly and too quickly, he held her back.

"You're drunk."

She should tell him why. Not about Mino, but that she'd left the Incurables for good. But she feared she might weep if she put it into words. "Only a little champagne."

He lifted the bottle and she was surprised to see she'd nearly finished it. "You can't sing in the state you're in."

"I can," she said crossly and turned her back to him, pouring herself the last glass of champagne.

"Violetta," he warned. He whisked her glass away. "Go to your boudoir and freshen up. If you can do that, I'll give you the stage in an hour."

She sat in the booth a moment longer, staging a small, impotent protest even as Federico disappeared. When she finally rose, she felt a man catch her gently by the elbow.

"Do you need to get out of here?"

"Davide," she whispered. Her *cicisbeo*'s deep voice was a relief. "Yes."

"Come on," he said. "There's a door in the back."

❋

IN AN UNKNOWN tavern down a *calle* she'd never seen before, Davide ordered two wines on credit.

"The drinks are terrible here," he apologized, handing her a dingy mug, "but the dancing is the wildest in the republic, and something tells me you need that tonight." He downed his wine. "I need it every night."

Violetta laughed, but soon sadness overwhelmed her. Davide was patient as she wept into his chest. She couldn't tell that the wine was terrible, nor that the dancing was wild. She was drunk and having a wonderful, terrible time.

"Federico won't be happy," she said, feeling both a freedom at having disappeared and a dizzy pull back to the casino.

"Don't worry about him tonight," Davide said recklessly, a little drunk himself. "Tomorrow, if you insist, we can worry about him together."

He introduced her to a dozen friends, using the false name she'd given him months ago—Gelsomina. It charmed her to meet his friends, who were as loud and drunk as she was. She could almost imagine a life for herself where nights like this might be common, if she'd been born a different girl. She might have been boisterous, competitive at drunken games of billiards. She might have kissed strangers in corners. Soon she drifted from Davide and found herself dancing the furlana, caught up in the arms of a gray-suited man. When the music changed, he pressed her up against a wall.

"*Siora*," he said with an amorous purr. The anonymity of his flirtation relieved her; he didn't desire her specifically. As a child, she had always longed to distinguish herself from others, to be loved distinctly. Tonight she wanted to escape herself: as Violetta, she had ambitions and responsibilities; as La Sirena, she had desires and dreams. But she and this stranger were just two bodies. Tonight she didn't want to be known. She only wanted to feel.

"*Sior*," she said and hiccupped.

His mouth moved toward her neck and he kissed her just below her jawline. She was surprised by how exciting it was, a stranger's mouth and touch. A yearning for more coursed through her as she arched her neck in offering. His lips were hot and wet, moving down her skin until they stopped at her necklace. He pulled her cloak open wider.

She didn't want to think about the necklace, but she liked his open admiration and his dark, spellbinding eyes. She lifted her mask just enough to kiss him.

His arms encircled her, drew her close against his body. How she had wanted Federico to do this earlier tonight. How simple it could feel to be taken in someone's arms. She kissed the stranger more deeply. She felt herself opening, surrendering to pleasure as his hand moved between her legs, feeling her through the layers of her clothing, applying a pressure that made her gasp.

"Is that his name," the stranger said with a little laugh. "Mino?"

"What? I didn't—" The name sent a shiver down her spine.

"It's all right." He laughed and kissed her again. "I'll be your Mino tonight."

Violetta wrapped her fingers around his and drew them down again between her legs. He took the invitation eagerly, now hoisting her skirt and reaching under it, touching her through her chemise. He kissed her breasts as he pleased her, until she threw her head back, amazed to feel such a wild sensation in the middle of this tavern.

When she came back to her senses, she gaped at the stranger, needing air, a drink of water.

"Excuse me," she said, and moved to leave him.

"I see," he said, bowing farewell. "Goodbye."

But then, Violetta felt a lightness at her throat, and when she reached for her necklace, it was gone. She pushed through the crowd, seeking the stranger.

"Davide!" she called. Where was her *cicisbeo*?

She could find neither her friend nor the stranger in the crowd, and she panicked as the room began to spin around her. At last, near the door, she saw the man in the gray suit. He was leaving. She rushed him, caught his arm.

"My necklace."

He raised his shoulders in a shrug. "What?"

She launched at him, thrashing her fists against his chest.

"Give it back—"

"Get off me," he shouted, snapping his elbow up and hitting Violetta's cheek. She gasped and cupped her hands against the hot pain through her mask.

"She's crazy," the man said loudly. "I don't know this woman."

"He stole my necklace," she cried. "Search him and you'll find it."

Men surrounded her and she assumed they had come to her aid, but then rough hands took her body, shoved her away from the stranger.

"Gelsomina!" Davide's voice rang out.

"Davide!" she screamed.

At last, she spotted her *cicisbeo* through the crowd. She waved him over. But before he reached her, Violetta felt a blow at the back of her head, and the world dissolved, the horizon caving in.

Eighteen

The voice beckoned but never grew closer. It stayed faint and far away. Mino would have followed that song anywhere, so desperate was he to find the woman singing. But he couldn't move. Something fixed him in place, as if he were an insect pinned under a glass.

He was dreaming. He knew this feeling. He reminded himself that he always awoke. Still, the darkness frightened him. He knew where he was.

The wheel. Again.

He tried to scream. Nothing. He tried to move but could hardly breathe. If the singer would only come closer, he could ask for help.

The song ended, and behind a sudden glowing brightness, he saw Letta. Her beauty slapped him in the face. She appeared precisely as she had on the bridge that last day. She wore her blue cloak inside out. She wore the bright white mask he'd bought her. Her short hair was plaited, loose strands falling about her face. Behind the mask, her large, remarkable eyes were full of wonder. They looked just as they had when she leaned forward, holding his hand, to see the view of the Grand Canal.

Now she reached for him, and at the touch of her hand on his shoulder, he felt a terrible disparity. He was a boy, the same five-year-old who'd been abandoned at the Incurables. But she had grown, matured. She was a woman, responding to a small child in need of help.

Letta, he tried to say, but nothing emerged, and she looked at him as if he were a stranger. She opened her mouth, but the sound that came out was music. Her voice was a violin.

HE SHOT UP in bed. The moon hung low outside the window.

He touched his chest and arms to reassure himself of their size. Ana slept next to him, hands cradling her belly. When the sun rose, it would be their wedding day. They were marrying on the day of a grand regatta. Had he stayed on at the *squero*, this festival would have been as big as *carnevale* to Mino. But here in the inner *calli* of Cannaregio, they were far from the Grand Canal, and farther still from the Giudecca Canal, where most of the races took place.

He had never guessed his life would turn out this way. So much was because of Ana. Her face usually steadied him. But where was her grounding effect tonight?

If Ana was a candle, lighting the amount of space one needed to see, then Letta was a conflagration; she lit up the full night sky, but she burned all she touched along the way. Marrying Ana was what he wanted. Soon they would be a real family. Their child would grow up on love.

Still, Mino couldn't forget how bright Letta's face had been in the dream, and when he put his hand over Ana's belly, he almost felt unfaithful.

Why this dream? Why now? Yes, he had been at the Incurables that afternoon, pretending nothing was wrong when Letta failed to show. Yes, he had wondered all evening whether Letta had heard of his wedding, of his child. But the dream seemed to be about more than Letta, and Mino couldn't understand what it meant.

He needed to clear his mind. He rose, careful not to tug Ana's covers or set his weight on the creaking floorboard, even though at this point in her pregnancy, very little roused her. He took his cloak, slipped from the apartment, and descended the staircase in his slippers.

Sprezz appeared as Mino stepped into a drizzly autumn chill. He rubbed the dog beneath his chin and they began to walk. They crossed the bridge at the bend in the *calle*, and soon they passed his violin shop. They kept going.

Mino missed Venice's stillness. It could only be felt outside, standing motionless, in the middle of the night. Most nights he worked on his violins but never this late, and when he left his shop, he was always tired, hurrying back to the apartment, to Ana. He couldn't remember the last time he had loitered on an empty bridge.

He peered into the dark water and saw his shimmering reflection in the moonlight and soft rain. A grown man, twenty years old next month, tall and muscular, his blond hair shining. He'd finally made something of himself. His life was respectable. But that wasn't what Mino saw. He looked harder. He forced himself to see the truth:

Inside, he was still a boy abandoned by his mother. His heart was still as fragile as it had been when he awoke in the *ospedale* kitchen. He worried that he did not deserve his own child.

In the two years since he'd left the Incurables, he had not come near to finding his mother. She was a void, her elusiveness his deepest shame. Who were his people? Who gave him to this city and this life? His child would know Ana's kin, of course, but Mino had no one to offer.

The baby had changed Mino's understanding of himself. He wanted to earn the child's esteem. He might spend his whole life trying to be half as good as his wife, but would he ever feel worthy?

An answer came to him like a boat along a current: he had dreamed of Letta because she had seen his mother at the wheel. She could tell him what she'd really witnessed that night. He was finally strong enough to listen. And perhaps in knowing how his mother left him, he would understand how to hold on to his child.

He had to find Letta, the one person who knew the truth.

❋

CHURCH BELLS ON Sunday morning. A bottle of champagne. A cake Ana's mother had baked with saffron. Eight varieties of sausage. Her sisters, her mother, the *sestieri* priest. Carlo, who had brought Carina. Ana in her second-best dress, as was tradition, with the waist let out for the baby.

That was their wedding. To Mino, it was perfect. The sun swept out from behind thin clouds after the ceremony, on their walk back to the sausage shop, which had the most space for dancing. Mino played a violin he'd just finished for Elizabeth and John. He played for an hour with intense devotion, and would not have stopped if Stella hadn't begged to take over, insisting Mino dance with his bride.

Ana's dress was white muslin with lace roses at the collar, and he felt the firm swell of her against him as they pressed and twirled. Mino had never danced before. With the gentle pressure of her hands, Ana taught him all he needed to know.

"I'll teach our baby to play the violin," Mino murmured, "if you teach her to dance."

"Her?" Ana lips curved up.

Mino smiled. "It's just a guess."

"Ana," Vittoria called from across the room. "We're out of champagne. We're going across the bridge to the tavern."

Before Ana could argue, Stella had taken her sister by the arm, leading the entire wedding party out of the shop. As they walked, they passed groups of rowers, just back from the races on Giudecca. Mino used to watch the regatta from the roof of the Incurables. Today he watched his new family surround his new wife, making sure she was comfortable as they entered the tavern, patting the mound of her belly.

"You're lucky." Carlo sighed, joining Mino at a table as they watched the women. "I pray you'll never understand the heartbreak that is my life."

"Carlo," Mino said, "I understand."

Carlo looked at him and saw the truth Mino no longer tried to hide.

"Who was she?" Carlo asked, drawing nearer.

"She was everything, once." He raised his shoulders. What else was there to say?

"Does Ana know?" Carlo looked worried.

Mino shook his head. "Why should she? It's over."

"A woman needs to know these things," Carlo said, seeming amazed by Mino's naïveté. "This kind of omission becomes a lie if you're not careful."

"Not to Ana," Mino said. He caught her eye across the table, and she smiled.

"Don't worry—no matter what you tell her of your past, she'll hear what she wants to hear," Carlo said. "Still, it's better if you're plain."

"How do you know how I would tell it?" Mino laughed. "And why wouldn't she hear it that way?"

Carlo thought a moment. "Have you ever tried to give a somber toast at a wedding?"

Mino shook his head. This was his first wedding. Ana's mother had given the toast, which to Mino felt somewhat threatening but which everyone else found heartily amusing.

"Guests want to laugh at a wedding," Carlo said. "Just as wives want to feel that all other women were but stepping-stones on their husbands' paths to them." He paused, looked at Mino. "What really happened between you and this other woman?"

"We were young," Mino said. He placed a hand on Carlo's shoulder and nodded to the back door. Carina was slipping out with the barman. Carlo started toward her, but Mino held him back. "I know what you don't, Carlo. A heart can break and love again."

Carlo smiled with more bitterness than Mino had seen in his friend.

"Maybe women can love again after a broken heart," he said. "Carina? That is something she could do. Even Ana." He nodded at the bride, now making her way toward them. "If one day, Mino, you fell into the canal, your wife would rescue another poor soul and stitch him into another prince." He gazed at Mino intensely. "But fools like us? Once we love, it's forever."

NINETEEN

CHURCH BELLS CRASHED through Violetta's dreams. Pain surged through her before she knew she was awake—but it wasn't the ache at the back of her head nor the bruise at her cheekbone. It wasn't the laudanum Davide had made her drink before he'd tucked her into his bed last night. It wasn't even the loss of the opal necklace.

It was Mino, getting married somewhere in Venice, today. The weight of Violetta's mistakes felt crushing, and she did not know how she could rise and bear them yet again.

She thought of the painting of Saint Ursula in the Incurables cathedral—the bride escorted by eleven thousand virgins, the endless marital caravan snaking through the Bavarian countryside. Ursula was doomed, slaughtered by Huns on her way to her own wedding, yet she was the closest thing to a patron saint of marriage that Violetta knew.

She clasped her hands and invoked the tranquility in the painted woman's face. *Heavenly Saint,* she prayed, *take Mino and his bride under your care. Give them happiness. And give my words meaning in my own heart. Help me to wish them well.*

She lay on Davide's pillow and watched the sun through his thin pink curtains. She listened to his snores on the floor beside her and felt shame at having drawn him into her misery. He was paid to dote on her at the casino. She had seen him counting the money Federico gave him, but he was so good at his job he sometimes fooled her into thinking they were friends. She mustn't expect his affection to extend beyond the job. Vaguely she remembered him asking where she lived last night, how to take her home when they left the party in the rain. She was relieved that she had feigned delirium, leaving him no choice but to bring her here. She could no more let Davide know about the Incurables than she could ever go back. But she couldn't expect to stay here.

She rose and reached for her mask, wincing at the pressure against her cheek as she tied the ribbon. She stood before the glass. Her dress was filthy. She needed fresh clothes, a bath. Her bruise had spread, giving her a purple left eye that looked almost painted through the mask. She kissed Davide's cheek and left.

Winding through the *calli,* she took some time to get her bearings. At last, she found the Grand Canal and moved along its stone passages. Hundreds of boats were docked and ready for the regatta that afternoon. The crowds spilled back onto smaller bridges where spectators might get a glimpse of a floral-crowned ship from their neighborhood.

The streets were damp from last night's rain. The ripeness of the city overwhelmed Violetta—the gleaming vegetables bobbing in crates on boats, the couples walking quickly to church, the scent of chestnuts roasting.

The sun was high when she arrived at Federico's palazzo. A doorkeeper she didn't know leaned against the bars inside the front gate, packing a pipe.

"I need to see Federico."

He glanced up, his silver eyebrows arching for a moment before he went back to his tobacco.

"He's not receiving, *siora*."

In her cheap mask and dirty dress, Violetta no longer looked like someone who could call on this estate. She didn't have the necklace anymore.

"I am La Sirena."

"Where's the stone?"

She leaned close and lowered her voice. "I wonder," she said, "how might Federico punish the man who turned me away?"

Behind her, on the street, a family crossed to the other side, disturbed by the hiss of her voice. But she had the guard's attention. He narrowed his eyes and she watched him take in the blazing purple bruise behind her mask. She pressed two gold sequins into his palm, ten times the standard tip for a favor. "Get Fortunato."

He pocketed the money, then turned up the stone path, weaving among the cypress and statues before disappearing inside the front door. Moments later, it reopened and Fortunato extended his head. Violetta raised her hand in greeting. Her arm trembled.

Know me, she willed the man, who started slowly down the path. He was running by the time he reached her at the gate.

"La Sirena?"

She heard relief in his voice. They'd been expecting her. She exhaled. She didn't need to raise her mask.

"Take me to him?"

Fortunato unlocked the gate. He took her hand and rushed her through the courtyard garden and tall front door.

"Wait here," he said, ringing a bell to call another servant.

"Tea, *siora*?" asked a maid, eyeing Violetta's dress.

She handed Violetta an expensive jasmine bud unfurling in a painted china cup. A lira for these few hot swallows, Violetta thought, half a month's work for a *figli del commun* at the Incurables, a week for a *figli del coro*, a minute or two onstage at the casino. She tasted its worth in each sip.

She remembered the last time she was here, her first masquerade. How this room had thrilled her with its trunks of rich disguises. The palazzo was no less magnificent today, but now it felt warm and welcoming. It felt big enough to hold her pain.

She longed to see Federico. She feared it, too. He'd be angry about her disappearance, last night's abandoned performance. And he didn't even know about the necklace.

She heard slippers on the stairs and looked up. There was scarcely time to put her teacup down before Federico caught her in his arms. He lifted and spun her, holding her against his chest. She wrapped her hands around his neck and could have cried at how good it felt. She ran fingers over his robe, felt the tautness of his shoulders through the silk.

"You're all right," he said. He leaned away and saw her purple eye through the mask. His expression darkened and he lifted her again, this time one arm coming under her knees to carry her up the stairs.

"Lunch, Fortunato," he called. "Send for sausages from Costanzo's."

He brought her to a parlor off a long hall. The curtains were closed and a draft chilled the air, but the paintings and the carpets were lavish. Federico laid her on a sofa in the center of the room.

"I'm all right," she told him.

He knelt before her, his fingers tugging at the ribbon of her mask. She felt it loosen, fall to the ground, the littlest clatter of *papier-mâché* on terrazzo. He swept soft fingers over her bruise.

"Who did this?"

Violetta thought how to describe the man. In her hesitation, a fog of jealousy formed in Federico's eyes.

"I'll kill him."

"Ice would be better," she said, finding herself smiling at his reddened cheeks, his urgent hands on her shoulders.

"If you ever go back to that man—"

"Don't worry," she said, choosing her words. "It's over. Only . . ." She reached up and touched her neck. She watched his eyes run over her bare skin. Her voice hitched. "I'm so sorry."

He embraced her. She could not see his face nor read his tone when he said, "You're here. That's all that matters."

"I'll repay you."

"Don't speak of it," he said. His lips at her cheek had never been so tender. "I thought I'd lost you. I went to mass this morning, and when I didn't see you—"

"I can't go back there, Federico."

He watched her face for explanation. When she said nothing, he cupped her cheek. "You will be safe here," he said, "but you must sing at the casino in two nights' time. It won't do for the star of the *coro* of the Incurabili and the star of La Sirena to have gone missing in the same week. People would wonder at the coincidence."

She couldn't imagine performing on Tuesday, but she understood Federico's point. She nodded.

"You'll rest today and tomorrow. We'll make up your face to cover the bruise." He cupped her other cheek, pausing a moment. "You may stay here as long as you need."

"Here?" She looked around the room, noticing a second door that led to an equally opulent bedroom.

"We'll light a fire," Federico said.

A warmth was already spreading through her. Was this it? Was she home? Gazing at Federico, Violetta felt she'd known him all her life. It had been little more than a year since she'd stepped inside his palazzo and he'd heard her song, but the change in Violetta's circumstances was so great it overwhelmed her. She leaned toward him with a kiss.

He pressed her away gently but firmly.

She touched her face, winced. "I look terrible."

"You're beautiful."

"But you don't want me," she said miserably. She remembered the opera singer, his recent lover. "Is it Lucrezia?"

Federico laughed and shook his head. "Last I heard, she was in Moscow, and that was months ago. But, no, it was never Lucrezia."

"What then, Federico? I am here. I want—"

"What do you want with me?" His sharp tone took her aback. He moved to the window, his back to her, and looked out at the Grand Canal. "I am too old for you to lust after. You could throw a stone and it would ricochet off three men as rich as I. I am no singer, Violetta, no musician who might complement your gifts. So what is it?"

Violetta was astonished. How could anyone justify desire? How could she explain that she adored the smoothness of his walk, his rare smile, the luster of his hair and the creases at his eyes, the neat, round shape of his fingernails, and the way he never hid himself behind a mask? How could she put into words what it felt like when he watched her sing, his eyes full of wonder, even gratitude? Should she admit she liked his somber qualities and his fierce protectiveness of her? That she loved the beguiling woman she became at La Sirena, and that she would never have lived so gloriously from dusk until dawn if it hadn't been for him? And even if she could say all of that, none of it was quite why she desired him. Realizing that he didn't know any of this made her feel alone.

"Don't be cross," he said, glancing back at her.

She was not cross. She was embarrassed.

He sighed. He looked sorry. "I welcome you here. I expect nothing from you in exchange for shelter. We have an agreement. You owe me only your songs."

Violetta remembered the night they'd watched the fireworks over Giudecca. That was the closest Federico had ever come to opening himself to her, speaking of the woman he had asked too much of and lost.

"What was her name?" she asked.

"Who?" he asked, the word like a whip.

"The woman you lost. Is it she who stands between us?"

"Of course not." He was looking out the window again.

How she wished he'd turn to her.

She stood up, went to him, and took his hands, relieved that they held hers fast.

"What was her name?" she pressed. Something about his former love still haunted him. She wanted to understand.

"Antonia," he said, as if the name were always at the tip of his tongue. His voice was calm but his eyes were cold, gazing out the window.

"What happened to her?"

"She disappeared."

Violetta felt his hesitation. There was more he wasn't telling her, but she sensed the story would dissolve if she reached for it, like a reflection in the canal.

A knock startled them both. Federico strode to the door and opened it.

Fortunato entered, studying his master carefully. "Are you all right, sir?"

"Fine," Federico said. "Put the tray down there."

Fortunato set it before Violetta. The tray held ice, wine, a tureen of soup, and a wonderfully aromatic plate of steaming sausages.

"Stay with me?" Violetta asked Federico, reaching for him as he moved toward the door. She had assumed that they would dine together.

"You must rest," he said. "Fortunato will see to anything else you need." He put a hand on the servant's arm.

"Sir?" Fortunato leaned close.

"Find the jewel," Federico said crisply.

Fortunato glanced past Federico and briefly met Violetta's eyes, as if gauging her reaction.

Federico turned back to her. He smiled tenderly, took her hand. "I don't want you to hold out hope. The thief has likely taken the opal outside the republic by now. It's too well known to pawn within Venice. But we will do everything we can to get it back."

Before Violetta could respond, Federico was gone.

Twenty

After christmas, as Venice swayed back into the arms of *carnevale*, Mino danced between two labors in his shop: in the cold, early mornings he applied himself to the cradle commissioned by his wife; afterward, he turned his attention to the first violin for the Incurables.

He had no prototype for the cradle, only Ana's vision, described as she lay in his arms at night, the waxing moon of her belly warm against his ribs. He built it out of willow, sturdy and elegant, with smooth bars spaced just widely enough for him to reach through and meet little fingers.

The violin proved thornier. When he had built the six new violins for the Baums, his effort had felt miraculous, given his lack of formal training. Now that lack pressed on him, and his work lagged. The violin eluded Mino; neither the brine for the wood nor the angle of the neck were ever right. He had sanded, varnished, and resanded ebony more times than he cared to count. And the thing still wouldn't play. It seemed to speak another language than the song of violins.

He was testing it, cursing the whine it produced, when Ana appeared at the shared door between their shops.

"It sounds finished to me," she said, leaning a shoulder against the doorframe. It was earlier than she usually met him to close up, but Ana had been checking in on him more in recent days. She'd made no secret of her impatience for Mino to finish the first Incurables violin. She was certain he would get the blessing of the prioress and the new maestro, and be able to approach the rest of the commission with less anxiety.

"I should begin again from scratch," Mino muttered.

"Madonna," Ana muttered. "And the cradle?"

"It's ready," he said, smiling to himself. Ana held their dreams in such close rein; it was rare he got to surprise her with good news.

She gasped with pleasure and fluttered across the shop.

He watched her move, her lightness still more like a butterfly than a woman with child. Turning the pegs of the violin, he added quickly, "As soon as the varnish dries."

Ana drew her hand back in time to avoid smudging Mino's work. She stood over it for several moments, admiring, and Mino felt proud.

"Just in time." Ana's voice was quieter than usual.

He looked up and his breath caught. His wife's eyes held a bright distance he had never seen before, a joyful preoccupation.

"The baby?" he said, feeling a wash of cold sweep through his body.

"Your girl is coming."

Mino dropped the violin and rushed to his wife. He felt the need to lift her up in his arms and carry her home, but instead of letting herself be lifted, she deftly turned his reach to an embrace. She gazed up at him with her wide smile and kissed him.

When she pulled away, Mino felt her guiding him to a chair, helping him to sit. His body felt heavy, collapsing onto the wood. Only then did he acknowledge his dizziness.

Ana lowered herself, crouching between his legs. She patted his cheek.

"Calm, Mino," she said. "We have time. I feel well."

He tried to speak but found no voice, and Ana laughed and rose to pour water from the jug. He downed the cup, felt thirstier. She refilled it and returned to his side.

"I'll make dinner," he said. "You'll be hungry. I'll—"

"Didn't you smell Mamma boiling the octopus this morning? It's what she ate with each of her babies. It's what my sister ate with Genevieve." She shrugged. "What choice do I have in the matter?"

"How did your mamma know?" Mino asked. Envy crept up in him at the thought of Ana mentioning her labor to her mother half a day ago, leaving Mino out. They could be like that, her family. There were things between them they thought Mino shouldn't know.

"Because she's Mamma," Ana said. "Someday I suppose I'll know the same thing about our girl. She said it has something to do with the moon."

Mino had heard none of this—not his mother-in-law's superstitious speculations, not the preparation of a special meal to nourish Ana during labor. The household often swirled around him, built of its own feminine energy.

"Don't be afraid, Mino," Ana said, squeezing his hand. She closed her eyes and her brow tensed. She was in pain.

Mino studied her, troubled. She made no sound. After a long moment, her expression cleared and she opened her eyes. She smiled at him, then rose as if nothing had happened. She lifted the violin he'd dropped, returning it to its stand near the window.

The baby made him want to finish the violin, for he could imagine walking through the Incurables doors again, this time with the news: he had a family. And in his fantasy, it was not the prioress or Laura who greeted him. It was Letta.

He turned to his wife. She cradled her belly, humming a soft, simple song. He went to her and felt the vibration of her song against his breast.

⁂

AT MIDNIGHT STELLA sent him out for ice.

"I'm not leaving," he argued in the hall.

"What good do you think your pacing is doing?" Stella said. "She wants ice. Go and get it."

He kneeled by Ana, who lay in bed with damp hair and bright eyes.

"You really want ice?" he murmured.

"Yes," she said. "And more than that, I want fresh air for you."

She kissed him, and he thought she'd never looked so beautiful. Not pretty as she always did, but with a new intensity that threw the soft contours of her face into sharper, more dazzling relief. He saw so clearly how motherhood would suit her. It made him wonder whether she saw anything like that in him.

"Ice." He nodded and took Sprezz over the bridge toward the tavern where they'd celebrated after their wedding.

At first he hurried, but when he reached the center of the Apostoli bridge, he stopped and took in the night, knowing he would want to remember it. Clear and cold, stars winking beside the big moon at its zenith in the navy sky. Ana was right. This crisp air and the noise of *carnevale* were relaxing. Mino breathed more deeply than he had since his wife told him of her labor.

Her family's calm unnerved him in the apartment, but out here, away from them, he understood. They had done this all before.

"There's nothing more natural than babies," Siora Costanzo had told him as she served the octopus earlier that evening.

But how could Ana's pain feel natural to Mino? It occurred to him that this was how things were meant to go—a woman surrounded by family, bringing the next generation to life. There was a time when the only woman Mino could imagine having children with was Letta. Now he tried to imagine a night like this with her, and his chest tightened.

He never thought about that apartment he had so briefly lived in, but now, in his mind, he was in it. He was alone with Letta and a midwife neither of them knew. He was frightened. The responsibility to be everything for someone else was colossal.

It wasn't like that with Ana. He was comforted by the fact that his wife was cared for by experienced, loving hands. He felt a new amazement at how he had entered into this family. It made him want to get down on his knees and pray. He knew in his bones his child would thrive. He found himself thinking of Letta.

He imagined her in her bed at the Incurables, and he wondered whether she was lonely. He prayed that her music fulfilled her and brought her peace. She would hate this prayer, find it pitying, but Mino meant it. He wished her joy and love.

Inside the tavern, the bartender raised his brow. He knew Ana well enough to know that Mino didn't belong in there alone.

"What'll it be?" he asked.

"Ice," Mino said. "My baby is coming."

The bartender smiled and brought out his pick. From the back room, he chipped off a brick of ice, wedging it into pieces.

"Some to suck on," he explained, "and the larger ones to wrap and cool her skin."

"You've done this before," Mino said, taking the cloth-wrapped parcel.

"Four times," the bartender said and waved off Mino's soldi. "Good luck, Papa."

❋

HE FOUND ANA in the same position as before, surrounded by sisters and candles. She looked tired, but she smiled at him.

He placed a wedge of ice on her tongue, wrapped another in the thin cloth and brushed it around her face as the bartender had told him to do. He felt Ana's family watching him, quietly surprised. He wanted to climb inside his wife's body and feel each pulse she felt.

"Is it too cold?" he asked.

She shook her head, rolling onto her side, her back to him.

"Do you want another pillow?"

She moaned. Mino tried to stifle his questions. He felt her mother's hand on his shoulder.

The *siora*'s gaze was clear—she wanted him out of the bedroom, away from Ana's side. Never before had he noticed how much his mother-in-law looked like his wife. The set of their jaws were the same. He knew there would be no negotiation.

"First babies take time." She led him to the door with Ana's gentle firmness. She nodded at the sofa. "Rest."

"How?" Mino protested.

"Rest, Mino," Ana murmured from her bed. "The baby will need you in the morning."

He obliged. He didn't think he could sleep, but as soon as he lay down and curled into a blanket, exhaustion swept over him. The turtledoves were quiet in their cage, nestled against one another. He would get more ice in the morning. He knew a tavern that opened close to dawn.

Rest, he heard his wife's plea, and eventually a calming song came into Mino's head. It was his mother's lullaby.

He'd never liked thinking of the song that way. Even after what Letta had told him, he still felt the song was *his*. Tonight he felt different. Tonight this melody was the one thing he could pass down from his mother to his child.

I am yours, you are mine . . .

He sang himself to sleep.

❋

A BABY'S CRY jolted Mino awake. He leaped to his feet, feeling the lateness of the morning, the sun warm on his skin. He spun around the living room, not knowing where he was until his eyes fell on Ana's mother holding his child.

He saw the trembling little mouth, clenched eyelids, the tender wrinkled head swaddled tightly. Tears sprung to his eyes and he reached out, but Ana's mother held the child fast, and when he met her eyes he froze.

"What's wrong?"

"Your daughter is healthy," she said wanly. "Go to Ana now."

He rushed into the bedroom, where Vittoria sat weeping beside her sister. Stella was gathering something scarlet in her arms. Mino realized they were sheets. The bed was red with blood.

"Madonna." Mino got down on his knees before Ana.

"She's resting," Vittoria said, making room for Mino.

He took Ana's hand. It was clammy. Her eyes were closed and she was so pale. She looked tranquil and younger than she'd looked last night. And for a second, Mino smiled. She could rest now. She'd done everything she had to do.

But as he watched her chest rise and fall, he saw that it was over. That soon Ana would leave them.

"Farfalla," he whispered. She had never taken to the nickname, but to Mino, that was what she was. His butterfly. Delicate. Busy. Fleeting.

Her eyes drifted open. "You can do this, Mino."

"No," he begged. "Not without you."

"You can," she said. "Only look for me in the sky." She closed her eyes again.

Mino felt a deep stab, knowing he would never see their brilliance again.

"What will you call her?"

These were Ana's last words. She was gone before he could answer.

TWENTY-ONE

VIOLETTA'S EYES OPENED slowly to the view of the Grand Canal. Soft January light streamed through Federico's bedroom window as she lay on her side, nestled into the down pillow. She loved waking up to the view of masked, black-suited waiters serving coffee at the café across the water.

It looked cold outside. Women tightened fur-lined cloaks about their shoulders as they sipped steaming drinks and watched the gondolas glide by. It was warm in Federico's bed. She lay nude in his pressed linen sheets. She could stay all morning like this.

"Are you awake?"

Violetta startled at Federico's voice. His warm hand glided over her hip, and his fingertips traced a circle around her navel. She smiled.

"I thought you'd left," she said.

In the three months she had spent waking up in Federico's bed, she always rolled over to find him gone, breakfast waiting for her on a silver tray. He would be out most of the day, at the Doge's Palace if the Great Council was voting, or at the casino.

In her first days at his palazzo, Federico brought back word that the *governanti* of the Incurables was searching for their missing lead soprano. She expected this, and yet it unnerved her to hear it confirmed. But Federico knew both spies employed in the search. He could keep them at a distance. For now, he assured her, as long as she took no risks outside, she was safe.

"I'm sorry it has to be this way," he'd said. "It's not forever."

But Violetta agreed with his caution. The last thing she wanted was to be caught, returned to the Incurables, and banned forever from the *coro* and all singing. She did not wish to leave Federico, and she wanted to go on as La Sirena. She had spent most of her life sequestered at the Incurables, so to be confined to this palazzo was an improvement. It was really only Laura that she missed.

Federico's staff was smaller than she expected, and upon her arrival he'd relieved any nonessential servants. They were down to Fortunato and the cook, both trusted friends, so Violetta could go about his house and his garden without her mask, as long as the gate was locked.

It was the first time in her life that she had known leisure. She spent hours before the fire with a Montesquieu novel and a chilled glass of *acqaioli*. She finally taught herself how to braid her own hair, though not as tidily as Laura used to do it. She missed her friend most in the late mornings before Federico returned for dinner. She longed for their conversations and easy laughter. With Federico, meals were quiet and pleasant, the two of them sitting close at his enormous table, facing the water, watching the boats, eating polenta and oranges on painted china.

On Tuesdays, and now on Thursdays and Saturdays, she met him at the casino after sundown to perform. And they always came together in his bed at the end of the night.

The first time they'd made love, a week into her stay, she had visited him in his room as he undressed. His fingers had been loosening his silk cravat. He'd looked up at her in his doorway, in her nightgown, and watched as she drew it over her head, let it fall to her feet. He stood still as she approached him. She was trembling with nerves and desire, but as soon as she pressed herself firmly against him, his arms came around her. He'd whispered her name. She closed her eyes at the bliss of his hands on her skin.

"Now do you believe that I desire you?" she'd asked, her lips brushing his ear.

She'd been terrified that he'd push her away again with another mysterious excuse. But her naked body finally won her what she wanted. Federico kissed her with a passion she was thrilled to match. He lifted her up and carried her to the bed. Laying her down, he kissed her, touching her breasts, her ribs, her thighs. They had kissed until she could bear the wait no longer. He had taken out a skin, the first condom Violetta had ever seen, from a wooden box in his armoire. Every night since then they had made love for hours in his bed.

Now she rolled over and arched her body to his, wrapping her arms around his neck, kissing him deeply, feeling that stir inside.

Federico fingered a strand of her hair, tucking it behind her ear. "You were uneasy in your sleep. I wanted to stay to make sure you were all right."

Violetta was surprised. She remembered no unsettling dreams the night before. She was moved by his concern, but it troubled her to think of him seeing her trapped in a nightmare. The wheel was the only bad dream she had, and it seemed odd that she would have dreamed of it now. Thoughts of Mino had receded since she'd been at Federico's palazzo, in Federico's arms.

Sometimes she thought of Mino, with his wife and child, but her imaginings of his life had grown less painful. She could fantasize about their paths crossing one day, about recognizing him in his child. She wondered what Mino would see in her new life. For years he had listened to her dream of the horizon. Would he believe her if she tried to tell him that what she had in this palazzo was enough? In her mind, she and Mino argued hotly, and she could never make him see.

Do you love him? he would ask.

Of course.

Does he love you?

The truth of Federico's heart was something she wondered about all the time. When they lay in bed on the brink of sleep, she felt an increasing urge to tell Federico that she loved him. More than anything, she wanted to know whether he would say it back.

"I'm fine," she assured him, nuzzling closer.

He kissed her. "Good."

"Can you stay?" She ran her nails over the muscles of his chest. Unclothed he was trim, but very strong. He felt firm beneath her fingers.

"I wish I could," he said, though he made no move to rise from bed. "We vote at the Doge's Palace in half an hour."

"Well, then," Violetta said, sitting up and bringing one leg over to straddle him. "We'd better be quick."

As she sat astride his body, she felt a slight weight at her neck. She reached up and touched the stolen black opal, its gold chain fastened once again about her. Had Federico put it on her in her sleep?

He was watching her closely.

"You got it back," she said, astonished.

"It took some time. And effort. But when I saw how it upset you to lose it, I couldn't stand it. Are you pleased?"

In truth, Violetta had not thought of the necklace in some time. Her feelings were not of loss but of guilt at having been careless with something valuable to him. She thought the stone was beautiful, but she'd never really felt that it was *hers*.

From the way Federico was looking at her, she sensed it mattered to him. She wondered whether he had lingered in bed this morning in part to see her reaction upon its return.

"Of course I'm pleased," she said. "Thank you. But how—"

"Don't worry about how. I would do anything for you."

He kissed her then and drew her close. They made love in a frenzy, so different from their usual leisureliness. As Violetta shuddered over him and called his name, a memory of that man, that night, came to her. The shocking titillation of the stranger's hand under her skirt. He was a thief, and had been brutal with her, but she couldn't help wondering what fate he had met over this necklace. It gave her a heavy feeling in the pit of her stomach.

Afterward, Federico dressed for the Great Council in the long, gathered gown all noblemen wore on official business. She liked being awake to watch him dress, the careful way he tied the ribbons of his garters at his knees. She'd never seen him do that before. His quiet focus charmed her. She stayed unclothed, moving naked toward the mirror on the wall across from his bed. It was huge and extravagantly framed with blown black glass from the island of Murano.

Violetta was pleased by her reflection, how womanly she looked. Her hair was loose and wild, her skin flushed from their passion. She touched the necklace and watched the stone shimmer in the reflection. She was glad to have it back.

She was about to move back to the window when she noticed something sticking out from the bottom corner of the mirror's frame. She reached forward and with her nail slowly teased out a flat, triangular piece of wood about the size of the playing cards at the casino.

When she turned it over, her stomach lurched.

It was a dusty painting of a fishtail. It was the same image that marked the plaque outside the casino door. Violetta had seen it a hundred times by the light of the blue glass lantern. But what caught her eye now, what stopped her cold, was the diagonal cut bisecting the painting. She cleared the dust with her finger, touched the rough grain where the wood was shorn. Goose bumps rose on her skin.

She studied the azure blue of the background, which could have been water or sky. Every time she'd seen the image at the casino, she'd envisioned the head of the fish beneath the water, but now she realized, of course—

"*La Sirena*," she said aloud. A mermaid.

It was the other half of Mino's token.

"Yes," Federico said from behind her, making her jump. She looked up and met his gaze in the reflection. She could not read his expression. He stepped closer. The ermine stole he wore over his *veste* brushed her shoulder. He reached over and lifted the token gently. Turning, she felt her nakedness before him. Why did it suddenly shame her? She moved to the chair by the window where she had left her chemise. She tugged it over her head. Her heart was racing when she returned to Federico's side. He was staring at the token as if he had not looked upon it in some time.

"Where did you get this?" he asked.

"Behind the mirror. What is it?"

He hesitated, and she saw in the set of his jaw that he was trying to control a flare of anger. He clearly wished she had not found it.

"My mother painted it," he said quietly. "She had a fascination with the myth."

"And the other half?" she whispered, touching the air beyond the fishtail where the woman's body should have been.

Where was Mino now?

"I don't know," Federico said.

"You're lying," she said.

His brow furrowed. "You are disturbed. What is it? Come. Sit down, Violetta."

"The other half," she said. Her voice wavered. "What happened to it?"

Federico exhaled, then moved to sit at the foot of his bed. He looked at the painting as he spoke. "I gave this to Antonia when we first fell in love. She returned it, years later, but"—he paused—"only half."

Violetta sat down next to him. She felt faint as she envisioned that woman at the wheel. Mino's mother.

Was she Antonia?

Was Mino's father—

Federico clutched the token in his palm. She remembered Mino's smaller hand clutching its other half. Could it be? Of all the men in Venice, had her life revolved around one father and his son?

"Antonia was an opera singer," Federico said, "the best Venice had heard in many years. We had great dreams together. We would travel abroad, to Naples, Vienna, and Paris. When I gave this to her, she was preparing for the principal role in a new opera of Vivaldi's. She was to play the mythic creature *La Sirena*, yearning for love above the lagoon. But the show never made it to the stage."

"Why not?" Violetta had a guess.

"Antonia fell pregnant."

Mino.

"As you know," Federico said, "I cannot wed. That path was for my elder brother, not me. I could not legitimize the child. By law, I could not write it into the Book of Names. Antonia knew that when we first met. I never hid it from her. There could be no proper life for the babe as a bastard. I urged her to bring it to an *ospedale*, where it would be cared for while she pursued her dreams onstage." He shook his head, his jaw clenched. "She wouldn't hear it. We fought. She left. I didn't see her again for several years."

Violetta struggled to breathe. In Federico's trembling voice, she heard how Antonia had broken Federico, and beneath that, so much anger. It sharpened every word he said.

"I searched for her," he went on, "to no avail. I could not rid myself of thoughts of her betrayal. She had abandoned me. Ruined me. And then, one day, there she was again." He was looking past Violetta now, into the distance, remembering. "I heard her singing. She was masked, but I would know her voice anywhere. I was in my gondola. She was on the *calle*. I passed her from the water. She was washing clothes outside a decrepit building. She was singing a lullaby to a boy some four or five years old."

"Your son," Violetta said hoarsely. She could see them now—mother and child, the same pair she'd witnessed at the wheel.

Federico didn't seem to hear her words. He was transported back to that day. His features tightened. "Our eyes met across the water, but I did not stop my boat." He looked down at the painting, and when he spoke again, there was a subtle shift in his voice, as if he were forcing himself to brighten it.

"The next day, she came here, to see me."

"With the child?" Violetta sat very still. It took all her effort to suppress a thousand other questions.

He tensed his brow. "She came alone," he said, speaking quickly now. "When Fortunato let her in, and I saw her up close, I could tell she was very ill. Her skin was marred by syphilitic lesions. She confessed she had struggled to get by in the years after we parted. By the time she came back to me, it was too late. She was dying. She begged my forgiveness."

He met Violetta's eyes and she was surprised to find them filled with tears.

"I still loved her, even after all those years. I forgave her, of course, but my position on the child had not changed. She begged me to soften my heart toward him. I still believed it best, for his sake, to grow up in an *ospedale*."

He touched her thigh. She fought the impulse to flinch. She could not reconcile this cold man with the one she had lain with all these months, with the one she had so desired.

"Surely you understand," he said. "The *ospedali* are not bad places. They do wonderful things for the city. They gave us you."

"He was your son," she said.

"I saw no other way," Federico said.

There was a distance in his voice that made Violetta's heart ache for Mino. She itched to take the half token into her own hands. She wanted to leave and gather her thoughts. She wanted space from Federico and this story. She knew her face was filled with horror she could no longer hide. He looked at her. He saw it.

"There's more," he said. "Hear me, Violetta. I was too stunned that day to think clearly, but after Antonia died, I did search for him. She left me this token as means to find the boy. Perhaps she knew all along I would change my mind. She told me he would be at the Mendicanti, in Castello, near where I had passed her in my boat. I searched for him there . . . I searched for him at all four *ospedali*, but to no avail."

He met her eyes again, and she saw him searching her briefly, checking for her response. And she knew he was lying. He had never gone to look for Mino at Mendicanti or anywhere else. He'd hid the token away and tried to forget. Except—

She took the token from him and traced the mermaid's tail.

"Why did you use this image for your casino?"

Federico sighed. "What happened with Antonia is my greatest regret. My casino operates in her memory. That plaque honors her and the child, and it reminds me to turn my life in a better direction."

Violetta started crying, small sobs that racked her shoulders.

He reached for her, and she caved in, her head falling onto his shoulder.

"I was a different man," he said.

Church bells chimed outside. They startled Violetta, but Federico didn't seem to hear them.

"The vote, Federico, at the palace," she reminded him. "You'll be late."

His eyes ran over her face, worried. "I don't want to leave you now."

"You don't have to say anything else," she said. He seemed relieved by her words. It sickened her that he could believe she was all right. But she wanted him gone. Silhouetted as he was by the sunlight behind him, she saw how she had made him into a man-shaped horizon, hanging all her dreams on him. What a fool she'd been.

"You're not upset?" he said, doubtful.

"The past is the past," she told him evenly. "I'll see you tonight at La Sirena."

"And afterward," he said, drawing her to him on the bed. "Right here." He looked at her closely, his dark brows arched, and she felt the threat beneath his words. "Promise me."

"Of course," she said and kissed him one more time, though she felt ill inside.

When he closed the door behind him, she was trembling. He'd left the token behind, as if it didn't matter. She clutched it, drawing closer to the mirror again. She looked at herself in terror and shame, running over the details of his story. She knew he was lying about searching for Mino, to make himself look better in her eyes. But something else didn't make sense.

Violetta had a clear memory of Antonia from the night she'd left Mino in the wheel. The timing in Federico's telling matched what she knew—Mino had been nearly five years old when he'd been abandoned—but the woman who had left him had not been dying. Violetta knew the late stages of syphilis. She knew the lesions and the blindness and the bone-deep pain those invalids suffered. She had lived among them at the Incurables, not in close quarters, but close enough to know. Antonia had not been diseased that night. What other reason would she have had to abandon Mino?

Violetta thought back to the last portion of Federico's story that had felt true to her. It was the moment Federico said he'd seen Antonia, masked and singing, from his gondola, and their eyes had locked.

A cold bolt of fear ran through Violetta. It was as if she saw through Antonia's eyes the rage on Federico's passing face. Violetta had seen his dark side at the casino—with the *barnabotti*, with the spy who'd tried to touch her. She'd written off those incidents. So Federico had a temper; it was the other side of his passion. He had never turned his rage on her, not even when she lost the necklace.

But it was in him. It was possible. And if she ever betrayed him, as he felt Antonia had . . .

Why would a mother give up her child? Violetta had seen with her own eyes that night how deeply Antonia loved Mino. Only death would part them.

Or the fear of it.

The day Federico saw Antonia singing on the *calle*, he discovered her hideout, the apartment where she had sought sanctuary from him. She would have known what kind of man he was, and how her betrayal became a disease Federico would never be cured of. She would have known she was in danger. She would have taken measures to protect her child.

Now, in her reflection, Violetta saw the necklace anew. Suddenly she remembered: Mino's mother had worn a similar stone that night. She stared at it. She knew. The black opal at Violetta's neck had been Antonia's.

If the stone had come back into Federico's possession, along with this half token . . . Maybe Antonia had not come back to visit Federico at all. Maybe she had not begged him to look after their child.

Violetta was seized by the conviction that Federico had done her harm, perhaps even with his own hands. How else could these two spoils have been reclaimed from Mino's mother's body?

Violetta turned from the mirror and ran down the hall to her bedroom. She had to get out of there. She had to find Mino.

Twenty-two

On a dark morning in January, Mino stood at the rain-spotted window next to the turtledove cage. He held his baby in his arms. "It should have been me," he told her.

How old was his daughter—three days? A dozen? Since her birth, since Ana's death, time had fallen away from Mino.

When Farfalla was calm, she fit in Mino's cupped palms. But she was not calm. She wailed. She swung her limbs in spastic fits. She was ferociously distraught except for the precious time she spent at the breast of the laundress who lived down the *calle* and had given birth to her own son two months before.

Every day Mino carried Farfalla, thickly swaddled, down the dismal, rainy *calle* to see the laundress, who lived in a damp room above her shop. She'd set down her huge wooden spoon next to her murky, steaming bucket of sheets, and Mino would release the baby to her, then wait in the hall while she lowered her bodice.

His back pressed against the stone, he would listen to his daughter's sounds. She was anxious with hunger at first, then briefly content before becoming anxious again as her tiny stomach filled. Back in his arms, Farfalla writhed and reddened, arching her back until she vomited and fell into a fitful, abbreviated sleep.

Every challenge of her fresh, new soul staggered Mino, and the onslaught was continuous. Ana's family helped, but their help was a torture to Mino. So dutiful were these women in both their grief and their competency. Mino failed at both. He had neither the time nor the energy to wonder what it might have been like if his wife had lived. When he thought of Ana, it was not in a kindly manner. He was angry with her for dying, for leaving him alone. He envied her sudden, permanent disappearance. He was the last man who should be charged with the responsibility of this tiny, struggling being. And in his heart he also felt guilty. It was his fault Ana was dead.

Mino wanted to die. His grief felt so deep it might kill him. He took no comfort in his helpless daughter, and this brought him more guilt. When he looked upon her face, he saw a stranger, and he felt a dark fear that he would never know her.

How did the others bear it, orbiting him in the apartment? Vittoria cried so quietly as she changed the baby's cloths. Siora cooed like the turtledoves and smiled as she lifted the child from Mino's grasp, pretending she wasn't afraid he might crush her fragile granddaughter. Their calm enraged him, made him feel ashamed of himself. What foolish optimism had led him here? He was not like this family. He did not belong. He never had.

In the darkness—listening to rain fall and his daughter's cries—Mino wondered about his own mother. If he had found any evidence of the woman, of his family, would he be stronger? Would life's traumas not destroy him? Would he be standing strong despite Ana's death, understanding the right way to provide for his daughter?

Mino believed that, yes, he would have been a better, more capable man, and so he blamed himself for failing to find his mother, for giving up the search when he met Ana. He was weak to let another woman fill that empty place.

And now? He could do nothing for his own child. It would be best to offer her the same chance at a better life his mother had offered him. The wheel spun round and round; there was no getting off.

His absence would mark his daughter forever. He knew that. But it would be better than weighting her with his guilt and dark fortune. He was no good for anyone.

"Mino." Siora put a hand on his arm, gathering Farfalla from him. The child had been fussing, but she settled into the wide crook of her grandmother's arm.

In the glow of the hearth, Mino looked at Siora Costanzo, seeing so much of his wife in her face. Now he saw the differences, too. Beneath the extra years and the recent grief and exhaustion, there was another distinction. It made Mino sad to realize it: Ana's face had been lit by the faith she had in others. It gave her a spark and a grace that were absent in her mother. Mino felt he could be frank with the woman.

"I can't do this," he said.

"I know."

It stung to have her acknowledge it so readily. Just when Mino didn't think he possessed a capacity to bear more pain, here it was. There were always new ways to hurt.

Siora Costanzo touched the baby's nose. The child's eyelids fluttered open.

"Your mamma could make anyone feel strong," Siora told her granddaughter. "I never could determine whether this was a blessing or a curse." She looked up at Mino then. "We plan to raise her, Mino."

Mino winced and his hands moved to his heart, but to his horror no argument sprang to his lips.

How could he walk away from his only kin?

He couldn't stay. He couldn't go. He couldn't raise the child. He couldn't leave her. He couldn't go on like this.

"It's better this way, Mino," Siora said. It was a goodbye. He stood and watched her take the baby to her room and close the door.

❀

STRUGGLING BENEATH A driving rain, Mino was crossing the bridge to La Sirena when he realized Sprezz was still at the apartment. The dog had been sleeping at the base of the cradle, and in Mino's creeping shame it had not occurred to him to wake Sprezz up.

For the first time since Ana died, Mino cried. He slumped to his knees on the wet bridge. He hung his head in his hands, and he wept. Sobs choked him. His hot tears were a balm on his frozen hands. He could feel revelers dart past him, but he didn't care.

He wept for his dog, his child, his wife. He wept for his mother. And he wept for Letta—how right she had been about the dark reach of orphandom. All these years, he had never wanted to look directly at who he was—and who he wasn't. A son. A brother. The person someone in this lonesome world loved without question, and loved most of all.

He wiped his eyes. "I'm sorry, Sprezz. You'll be better off without me."

He entered the casino with his hat slung low, not that the doorkeeper would have recognized him; it had been more than a year since he'd darkened this door. He squinted at the dimness and the noise, which throbbed with clinking glasses and coins. He could not remember having slept or eaten recently, and he staggered as he moved toward the center table. Once, right there, the alchemists had allowed Mino to believe he might turn his dull life to gold. What a hoax.

A figure approached from the shadowy corner near the bar. At first, Mino flinched and raised his arms to fend off an assault. But then he recognized the man.

Carlo wore his curled white wig, white stockings, and new red silk britches with a matching jacket. He flung his arms around Mino, who hugged him back with all the desperation in his heart.

"Friend," Carlo said, wiping away tears that were always at the ready.

Tonight, in Mino's state, he could see at last how his friend's emotions were genuine, only bigger than most other men's. This moved Mino, and he knew he had come to the only place he could bear to be.

"I came to see you as soon as I heard," Carlo said.

Mino hadn't known Carlo tried to visit the apartment. It rankled but did not surprise him that Siora had turned his friend away.

"I haven't been fit for visitors," he said.

Carlo waved him off. "What can I do?"

Mino glanced toward the bar. "A drink?"

Carlo was already pouring wine from a bottle at the table. He slid it before Mino and offered him his chair, crouching to be next to him. "Drink and only nod when you want more."

Mino nodded as he took his first sip, and Carlo laughed and squeezed his shoulder. "I'm glad you're here."

Carlo's gaze felt unexpectedly intense, and Mino realized no one had really looked at him since Ana died. Siora, Vittoria, even little Genevieve seemed unnerved by the power of his pain.

Not Carlo. He studied Mino awhile, and then something lit up his face. With one hand, he gently steered Mino's shoulders until they faced the stage at the back of the casino.

"You are lucky."

"Lucky?" Mino said bitterly.

"Yes," Carlo said, his head gesturing toward the small stage, empty except for a large golden harp. "She performs tonight."

Mino glanced around the casino, confused. "Who?"

Carlo wagged a finger. "La Sirena herself. The namesake singer. Don't fool me, Mino. You've heard of her. She sings songs no one knows. She wears a mask with painted fish scales, and a sparkling opal around her neck."

An image flashed in Mino's mind of the glowing stone. Had he seen the singer on a night he no longer remembered? The opal in Mino's mind felt like an older memory. It was made of blue-green stars, ever changing in the light. He felt he had touched the stone before, wrapped his hands around it. He could almost smell the metallic tinge of its gold chain. He looked at Carlo and felt embarrassed, as if he were inventing some connection with this singer.

"I don't know her."

"Everyone knows her," Carlo said. "They come from England, boys straight out of Oxford commencing the Grand Tour of Europe. And this"—he poked the table where they sat—"is their first stop. There's one itinerary, few deviations: a residence in Rome, certainly. A tour through Florence's museums, yes. But first, ah"—Carlo smiled and closed his eyes—"first, music and wonder, right here in Venice. They used to go to hear the *coro* singers at the *ospedali*," he said, leaning close, "but recently, the ones who *know* come here. To La Sirena."

Mino shrugged, part of him still thinking of that necklace. But he had not been to La Sirena since the night Ana led him out its door and into another life.

"I've been in my shop. I've been with my wife." He closed his eyes, fought against his sorrow. He would not be able to speak of his daughter without crying.

"You've been away too long."

"And not long enough," Mino said.

"Or perhaps your timing is perfect." Carlo grinned. "If you'd come last night, you would have missed her."

"Does she perform miracles?" Mino asked. There was only one singer's voice that had ever interested Mino.

"Indeed, she is miraculous," Carlo said. "La Sirena is the only woman I've ever known to make Carina jealous. One note escapes her lips and every woman in the room feels inadequate, every man immortal."

Mino finished his second glass of wine and poured himself a third. He was distantly aware of a table of gamblers cheering, of a trio of blond Scandinavians charming a courtesan with their rough approximation of Venetian. Money, sex, delirium, what was the point of any of it? Life seemed to Mino a cosmic waste.

"The last thing I wish to feel is immortal," he said.

By the bottom of his third glass, Mino dared La Sirena to take the stage and draw even a fraction of his interest. But she was late, the stage stayed dark, and in her absence the cacophonic music of gamblers and maskers composed its own hateful oratorio.

By the bottom of his fifth glass, the stage was still dark, and Mino and Carlo had both passed out, too broke to pay their bill, too drunk to notice that the famous singer wasn't coming.

Twenty-Three

Violetta fled the palazzo an hour before she was to perform. Her mind was racing. She was terrified as she stole deeper into the city, unable to flee fast enough. Her footfalls made loud slaps on the damp cobblestones. Her silk slippers were soaked, but she ignored the cold. She hurried across the Grand Canal at the Rialto Bridge, where the narrow houses looked like blades beneath their iron roofs. She berated herself for her naïveté. How had it taken her so long to *know*?

Something about Federico had always felt familiar. Why else would she have been drawn to a stranger so swiftly? How could she have believed she loved such a monster?

Everything she had just learned was unfathomable, but there was one part that shone hottest in her mind. Mino had a father. A living, breathing relative. And it would destroy him to know what kind of man his father was.

Why hadn't Violetta trusted the love she saw between Antonia and Mino that night? Back then, she hadn't known how to believe in love. And now? Now, when she thought of love, she thought of Mino.

She had to find him, retell the story she'd seen through the attic window. She had to bring him peace. She would be brief but honest.

And what else? Would he introduce her to his wife and child? She wouldn't stay long. There was nothing left for her in this city. She would go her own way. Maybe she would visit London.

But how would she find him? She didn't even know where her feet carried her now. She had never tread upon these dark *calli* or crossed these *ponti* before. When she rested in the shadows of a quiet church's eave, she looked up at the bell tower, but didn't recognize the sky above. After so many months of not seeing the world beyond Federico's palazzo or the casino, all this open starlight, all this glittering water, staggered Violetta.

As soon as morning broke, she would need a new disguise. At this very moment, Nicoletto might be knocking on her door at the palazzo, and when she didn't answer, he'd be forced to knock it down. He would find the open window, the silk bedsheet knotted like a ladder.

She knew what Federico's guards could do. She'd seen their violence at La Sirena, tossing out men who couldn't pay. She felt certain they had tracked the thief who'd stolen the necklace. She felt in her bones the awful fate that had befallen Antonia.

Federico's vengeance would come for her, too, if she did not get out of Venice soon. She gripped the other half of Mino's token, hidden in the heavy pouch where she kept her gold. She drew strength from it.

All night she stayed in darkness, close to the walls, not sleeping. She had always taken precautions on the street, but now she had to go further. Federico's resources, his cunning, and his jealousy and desperation were of another timber. His words came back to her.

I saw no other way . . .

He'd been talking about giving up the baby to an *ospedale,* but Violetta believed he was also talking about what he'd done to Antonia. There would be one response to her betrayal; it was absolute.

❧

THE FIRST RAYS of sun brought pink light to the cobblestones and fresh terror to her breast. Violetta felt unexpected sorrow as she took in the beauty of the dawn-lit canals. She would miss this maze of water and stone, the masks and the parties, the echo of her voice in the church of the Incurables. But she wanted to live. She didn't want to hide anymore. As soon as she'd given Mino back his token, she'd go.

She found a dressmaker opening shop in the *merceria.* She stepped inside, closed the door, and breathed more easily. Her fingers ran over cloaks and gowns, touched feathered edges of masks. The shop smelled musty and sweet. She bought a hooded black cloak trimmed in lace, a green silk gown with a narrowing bodice, long white wool gloves, a three-cornered black hat, and a wide white mask to render her fully anonymous. Not the flashy clothes of a casino singer but those of a subdued aristocrat. She bought a wig with long, golden-blond curls. When she looked in the glass she did not recognize herself. She prayed that no one would.

For six days she walked in search of Mino's shop, knowing it was in Cannaregio but not where Cannaregio was. She would speak to no one, only listened to the music of strangers' clues around her. Six nights she took a different room at a different boardinghouse, ate her meals alone, removed her mask only in absolute privacy, with the door bolted and shutters closed. When she lay in lumpy beds amid strange sounds and scents, she prayed that tomorrow she would find him.

On the seventh day, Violetta did not find the shop so much as it found her. Swinging from the iron post was a painted sign bearing the image of Mino's half token.

"*I Violini della Mamma*," Violetta read the sign. She wished to take the other half of the token from her velvet pouch and hold it up so that they formed a whole. Not now. Once she found Mino, she would try to make everything whole for him.

His shop was closed, perhaps for lunch, but Violetta touched the windows, lay her hands upon the panes. As soon as she did, she *felt* him through the glass.

"Mino," she whispered.

She moved to the door. She knocked. Then louder, longer. She would wait as long as it took.

"This shop is closed." A voice jarred Violetta. She turned around to find an unmasked woman a few years older than she holding two heavy crates in her arms.

"I can wait. I'm looking for a someone," she said, feeling obliged to help the woman. She reached beneath a crate to share some of the load.

"Thank you." The woman nodded toward a doorway. "Here."

They set the boxes in the doorway next to the violin shop and the woman righted herself, rubbing the small of her back. "That shopkeeper is gone."

"Mino?" Violetta said.

The woman leveled her gaze at Violetta, taking in her fine clothes. She seemed confused. "Yes. Mino."

Violetta stepped close, took the woman by her sleeve. "You know him?"

The woman's eyes shifted; pain flickered through them. "My sister's husband."

She squinted at Violetta, trying to make sense of her. "Are you from the *ospedale*?"

"Yes," Violetta said without thinking.

"I'll get the violin. The first is finished. Wait here." She disappeared and came back a few moments later, holding a beautiful instrument. It was no ordinary violin. This was a masterwork. The woman held it out to her.

Violetta took it in her hands and shivered, feeling him.

"I must confess something," the woman said. "Mino is missing. I don't know if he'll be back to complete the work."

"Missing?" Violetta's chest seized.

"My sister—his wife—she died three weeks ago," the woman said quietly.

Violetta exhaled slowly. How had she missed the woman's mourning clothes? "I'm sorry." She looked down at the violin again, her thoughts whirling. She knew she had to hand it back—but what if she never found Mino? What if this was her last chance to touch him? "What is the balance due on this violin?"

"I don't know."

"The maestra put down twenty percent, I believe?" she guessed. She remembered Laura saying they commissioned each violin for five gold sequins. What would Laura say now, at the sight of Violetta fishing into her purse, putting four sequins in the woman's hand?

"What about the baby?" she asked.

"Yes," the woman said, and finally a smile broke across her face. She was very pretty, with fragile features and dark, clear eyes. Violetta imagined that her sister, Mino's wife, had been pretty in much the same way. "The child is well. Nearly one month old."

"No," Violetta said. How could it be? "The child lived yet Mino is gone?" It didn't seem possible.

"He was not well after Ana died."

"I see," Violetta said, but she didn't. Mino, who desired nothing more than family, had finally got one and then abandoned it?

She thought of her horrible words to him—that an orphan like her should never have children. She hadn't meant Mino. She had meant herself. Everyone knew Mino was different. She had thought she was protecting him from the mistake of loving her. What effect had her words had on him?

No, Violetta dismissed the notion. The man's wife had just died. What was wrong with her that she thought his desperation and disappearance might be something to do with her?

The woman shifted, glanced at her crates, and Violetta felt the end of the conversation advancing with terrible speed.

"Can I meet her?" she asked quickly.

"Who?"

"The baby." Violetta's voice was a whisper.

The woman looked wary. She could make no sense of Violetta's interest in the child.

"Please."

The woman hesitated. Violetta could not bear missing this chance. For years, she had been vigilant about preserving her anonymity—hiding first that she was a *coro* girl, and now that she was La Sirena. But no one hunting Violetta knew that she had a third identity. She could show it to this woman now; she could tell the truth.

"Mino was my dearest friend." The words rushed out of her. "I was so hoping to see him and the child today."

The woman heard Violetta's sincerity and she softened. "My mother won't like it," she said slowly, "but she is away for the hour."

They stepped inside a sausage shop and Violetta was assaulted by the rich scent of meat. She saw the unusual, narrow sausages, the same as Fortunato had brought her when she was recovering at Federico's. How close she'd been to Mino yet again. It filled her with an even stronger need to find him.

"Your family owns this place?"

"My grandfather, then my father, now my mother. Ana would have taken over, but I suspect now it will be me. My name is Vittoria. And my daughter, Genevieve." She called into the back of the shop. "Genevieve, bring Farfalla."

From a back door, a little girl appeared. She had plaited black hair and a red-checked dress, bright eyes and a charming gap-toothed smiled. In her arms she carried a tiny bundle. She passed the baby to her mother, who cooed and kissed the sleeping child before holding her up for Violetta to see.

Violetta caught her breath at the baby's beauty. She was round and bright with soft pink lips and thick dark eyelashes. She felt a rush inside of her and reached out to hold the child. Vittoria put the baby into her arms. Violetta felt tears well in her eyes.

Suddenly, she couldn't bear the mask blocking her face. She wanted to see the child wholly, to have the little girl see her. She took the risk and raised her mask. Despite everything, her face broke into a grin.

Mino's daughter. His *family.* A miracle.

"Oh, Mino," she said.

"I don't think he was prepared for those early days. Lord knows my husband couldn't take it. He left after two weeks, just as Mamma predicted he would. Mino did the same." She put up a hand, as if arguing with herself. "I know that isn't fair to Mino. He was also grieving his wife. All my husband grieved was the loss of his nights at a tavern. But I did see those early days wear Mino to the bone. You know how it is. How old are your children?" Vittoria asked.

Violetta looked up, blinked. "I don't have children."

"Forgive me," she said. "The way you held her, I thought . . ." Vittoria laughed apologetically and stroked the baby's cheek with her finger. "She is special." She swallowed and was quiet for a moment, and Violetta sensed a hesitation in her.

"What is it?" she asked.

"My sister told me her last wish was for Mino to raise the child up. I think she knew he'd leave, but I think she thought he'd take the baby with him. She wanted me to know that was all right with her."

"Does Mino know that?" Violetta asked.

Vittoria shook her head. "My mother would never tell him. She helped him pack."

Violetta didn't want to hand the baby back. Farfalla's small, warm weight made her want to stay still. For the first time in her life she felt whole, without a yearning for more. How could she surrender it? How cold would the space in her arms feel? How must Mino be feeling right now? Where was he?

She longed to take the baby with her on her journey to find him, but it wasn't her place. She knew that every moment she waited would make it harder for her to let go. She released the child, and lifted the violin again. The need to find Mino was absolutely dire.

"He'll come back for her," she told Vittoria. "I know he will."

Vittoria put a hand on Violetta's arm. "Good luck."

TWENTY-FOUR

A HARD BOOT TO the ribs awoke Mino.

"Out of the way," a street hawker called, pushing past with his cart.

"Ass," Mino shouted, scrambling back against a low wall he didn't remember falling asleep against. "You'll kill a man." He clutched his side and curled in on himself at the stabbing pain.

"The men I know work for a living," the man called over his shoulder. "Rats like you crawl along bridges." He nodded in Mino's direction, where a smattering of soldi shone dully in the cloudy light.

A new low. While he slept off last night's misery, Mino had been taken as an outright beggar. He hated himself for how greedy he felt sweeping the coins into his palm. He hated his relief at having secured at least another meal. Without Sprezz, free food was hard to come by.

The depths of his indignity continued to amaze him. He straightened his mask, tightened the bindings. He knew no one anymore; still he did not wish to be seen even by a stranger. He rolled to his knees, pulled himself up, and took in his surroundings.

"Madonna." He muttered. What cruel force had led him here last night? Of all bridges, what had driven him to rest his head upon *this* one?

For two years, Mino had avoided this inconspicuous cobblestoned crossing at the northwest edge of Dorsoduro. Now no broken rib nor battered pride could compare to the pain of his nostalgia. This was the site of his last lovely moment with Letta. When the two of them had walked back down this bridge, it had been the end of everything Mino had imagined for his life.

He looked out at the water, tracing the foolish optimism that marked his past. He saw Violetta's beauty that day, how it crested to a new height in the light of their rebellion. He saw the short, gorgeous tenure of their freedom. It had seemed eternal on this bridge.

Now he saw Ana, dead in her red coffin. He saw his tiny, struggling child wailing in her crib, unable to fathom the source of her pain. Shame cut through him. He couldn't go back for her. He was not fit to raise a child. But how could he live with himself? How could he go on?

He gripped the cool stone of the bridge's parapet. Had he come here last night to die? To drown himself at the site of his original failure? His stomach churned and he leaned over the bridge, lifting his mask slightly just in time to heave last night's sour wine into the canal. His throat burned. He braced himself on the bridge, sweating and sick.

Someone beside him inched away, and Mino was glad. He wished to be found so deplorable that no one else would share this bridge with him. But the masked woman wasn't leaving, only getting a bit of space. He glanced at her out of the corner of his eye. She was a patrician, likely a senator's wife. It was rare to see a woman of stature alone, standing still on a bridge. For any distance over half a *calle*, they preferred passage by boat over the common use of feet. He felt the churning again in his stomach and foresaw the woman would not linger much longer.

❧

VIOLETTA WISHED THE beggar would take himself away. She wanted the bridge to herself. She wanted to be alone.

She opened her mouth to speak, just as the beggar pointed at her violin case. He seemed too captivated by it.

"Where did you get that?" His voice was hoarse, a whisper.

Violetta looked down at the case in her hands, then up at the beggar. She clutched it closely. Was he figuring how much he could pawn it for?

The man began to approach. She considered fleeing, glanced about her. Would she recognize one of Federico's spies if he stepped onto this bridge?

❧

MINO'S MIND SPUTTERED. How had this violin ended up in the hands of anyone except the prioress at the Incurables? Had Ana's mother pawned it? Or had this woman somehow stolen it? Was that why she seemed so nervous?

He wanted to hold it. He wanted to—

He felt the noblewoman flinch as he reached out. His cheeks flushed.

❧

VIOLETTA TOOK A step backward, hugging the violin. Couldn't she simply give him money? She could invent a little task so as not to make him feel like a beggar. Perhaps she could ask for directions and tip him five lire. She'd seen Federico do it. It was the fastest way to get rid of a vagrant.

"I'll be careful," the man said, still focused on the violin, his hands reaching out.

Violetta held the instrument tighter. The violin was all she had of Mino.

"I used to play," he said.

Something in his voice struck her as familiar. She heard a longing in his words that made her wonder: If someone were to take away her voice, what would she do to get it back? Even just for a moment, what would she do to sing? She found she didn't want to stand between a musician and music. She decided to trust that instinct and put the case into his hands.

❈

MINO GASPED. IT felt like a lifetime since he'd held the instrument. He opened the case and lifted the neck, the bow. He turned the pegs, winding himself back in time, not to the shop where he had built this violin but to the roof where long ago he'd played the only song he knew.

He placed his fingers on the strings, closed his eyes, and lowered the bow.

❈

VIOLETTA HELD HER breath as he began to play. For several moments, she couldn't see. She could only hear the man before her playing Mino's mother's song.

His song. How could it be possible?

Mino.

Around them, people stopped to stare. Violetta's heart thundered in her chest. She wanted to sing. More than anything she wanted to meet him in the song and have him know her. But she knew the danger. She could not expose herself in public. She stood silent, trembling as he played.

※

AT THE LAST glide of his bow across the strings, Mino's feet were obscured under a blanket of coins. His desire to scoop up the money and run embarrassed him. Then he saw the woman reaching for him.

※

WITH HER HEART in her throat, Violetta untied Mino's mask. It fell atop the pile of coins. When he looked up, she saw him—his youthful beauty matured, battered, and bruised. How handsome he'd become. But she also saw in his eyes her own terrible words, the way they had marked him over the years. And she saw Federico's blood in Mino's features. He was dark to Mino's blond, forty-five to Mino's twenty, but so much between them was the same. At last, she saw her own blindness, and what was really underneath her desire for Federico. A shiver ran through her.

All along, this was the man she'd been seeking.

Here he was. Not the boy she'd refused, unable to take seriously. Back then, she'd assumed Mino's ideas of love were naive. If he knew all there was to know about Violetta, he wouldn't love her. No one would.

When she looked at Mino now, she saw how he wore his mistakes and his shortcomings in his eyes. They made him Mino. And she felt she was seeing him at last as openly and as lovingly as he had always seen her.

It made her think of the violin he had repaired. He hadn't tried to hide the hole in the bout, the wrongly angled neck; instead his unique attention had made these imperfections sing. This, Violetta realized, was love.

֍

MINO SQUINTED AT the noblewoman. She had untied his mask. She was crying behind hers. He watched the bearing of her shoulders when she sobbed. The way they lifted, shuddered. He had held these shoulders before. How many times?

He gaped at the impossibility. He reached for the ribbon behind her mask.

Her arm shot up to stop him. She caught his hand in the air only a hairbreadth from her face. And he knew then. He knew from the electric touch of her skin on his. He didn't even have to see her.

"Letta?" he whispered.

What was she doing outside the Incurables with no chaperone? What was she doing in a noblewoman's disguise?

"Not here," she told him.

As soon as possible Violetta had to get Mino somewhere discreet where she could show him the painting. She felt it burning in her pocket. But with his destitution, his fresh grief for his wife and daughter . . . could he withstand the horrors of his history?

"It can't be," Mino said, though he knew it was. He was mortified at being seen by Letta in his condition. How many times had he fantasized about encountering her at the Incurables, bringing his violins for her to see how he had made something of himself? And now—he couldn't bear that *this* was what she would think of him.

He pressed a hand to his forehead. "No," he said. "I'm dreaming."

Violetta smiled at his words, for the reunion felt as surreal to her.

"Don't wake up," she told him now. *Don't leave me.* She saw doubt in his eyes. She felt him wanting to pull away, to run and disappear. She realized he was still angry with her. Of course. Why wouldn't he be? She had to explain, quickly, before he got away again.

"I must speak to you. Where can we be alone?" she asked.

"No—"

"Mino, please."

"I'm sorry," he said, ill with himself. What was there to speak of? What could Mino tell her of his life that wouldn't disgust her? "I can't."

"Mino." Violetta stepped closer, until their shoulders were nearly touching. She turned her body toward the canal. With one hand she turned him with her so their backs were to the passersby on the bridge. Inside her pocket, her fingers toyed with the silk tie of her purse. She drew out the lower half of Mino's token and pressed it into his hand, closing his fingers around it carefully so that only he could see what he held.

Mino's hands shook as his finger ran the length of the diagonally shorn wood. A moment ago, he had needed to run. Now stillness came over him. He looked up at Letta with tears in his eyes, his shame replaced by wonder.

Life was like music; if you changed a single note, you changed the entire song. Mino had made mistakes. He had hurt those he cared for and given up too soon. He had been a fool, a coward, a failure—and if he hadn't been each of those things in precisely the ways he had, he wouldn't be standing on this bridge right now with Letta and the other half of his token in his hand.

"How?" he whispered.

"Come with me," she said.

TWENTY-FIVE

MINO RATTLED THE bucket against the window of Carlo's apartment one floor above the pharmacist. Letta stiffened as they waited, sneaking only darting glances up from the ground, as if she couldn't stand to look at their surroundings for too long. Suddenly he saw through her eyes the cramped and filthy *calle* with its squalid apartments stacked on either side. He'd spent only one night in Carlo's apartment and its lowliness had hardly occurred to him, but now he felt ashamed that he could think of no finer place to bring her. He knew, of course, that she had risen in prosperity, in access to Venice's splendor. But judging from her gown—and her intense present discomfort—there was even more he did not know.

"It's not the Doge's Palace," he said apologetically, "but my friend will take us in and ask no questions."

Hearing embarrassment in Mino's voice, Violetta squeezed his arm. "All we need is a door that closes." She would have retired to a chicken coop if it meant the two of them could be alone and safe. Besides, she didn't even have a friend to turn to. Laura couldn't help them, and Violetta didn't even know if Elizabeth was in Venice or London, much less where the woman might stay when she was in town. Violetta would have no complaints about where Mino took her. But she knew he sensed her discomfort, and she could not yet tell him its cause: Mino's friend's apartment was around the corner—a stone's throw—from La Sirena, and she could scarcely breathe through her fear of being caught.

"Is he coming?" she whispered, her eyes glued to the cobblestones.

"I have a better idea," Mino said, as relieved as he was surprised with himself. The old urge to impress Letta was making him bolder than he'd felt in some time. He took her hand and led her along one *calle*, then another, toward the church of the Frari. Months ago he had delivered his first commission of violins to his original client, Elizabeth Baum. He remembered the tea she'd served him, and the conversation about Hasse and Vivaldi. He remembered her admiration of his work. They were not friends, but Elizabeth might be polite enough not to let that on to Letta. Mino would feel like less of a vagrant if she would just let them in for tea so he could hear what Letta had to say.

In ten minutes, they had reached Elizabeth's palazzo. When the servant answered the door, Mino remembered her. He watched her face as she tried to recognize him in his unseemly state, as she glanced at Letta, disguised by her gown and wig, her mask and hat. At last Mino raised the violin case, and the servant's eyes shifted with recognition.

"Is *siora* in?" he asked. "I've come to check the condition of her instruments."

The woman led them both inside and closed the gate behind them.

Violetta heard the click of the bolt and exhaled. They walked along a loggia facing a small garden with a little fountain. They waited at the front door.

When Elizabeth Baum descended the stairs moments later, Violetta nearly fell into her arms.

"Mino," Elizabeth said with kind confusion, glancing at his wild hair and ragged clothes. "Is everything all right?"

"I'm afraid I must ask a favor," Mino said. He was greatly relieved he did not have to remind her who he was. "I wasn't sure where else to turn."

Elizabeth stepped close. "What can I do?"

Violetta knew Elizabeth well enough to see in her eyes that she was fond of Mino, though not intimate. At the Incurables, Mino's social confidence had made Violetta envious—but now she found it remarkable. She wished she were more like Mino in this way; it was clear Elizabeth was flattered to have been asked for help.

"And who's this?" Elizabeth asked, turning her gaze on Violetta. How strange that if Violetta were to untie her mask right now, Elizabeth still wouldn't know her. The English woman had never seen her features behind her *bauta*. Violetta had to decide right now whether she could trust Elizabeth. The woman had known Federico far longer than she'd known the singer La Sirena.

She glanced at Mino and felt his trust in the woman. He reached for her hand and said, "This is my dearest friend—"

"Elizabeth," Violetta said, "it's me."

Elizabeth's bearing changed. She leaned so close her lips touched Violetta's mask. "La Sirena?"

Before Violetta could answer, Elizabeth swiftly drew the two of them into her parlor, a small room filled with bookshelves, embroidered furniture, and leather-paneled walls. She closed and locked the door.

"You're in danger," Elizabeth said.

"I know," Violetta said, feeling Mino's curiosity. Her face flushed at the understanding of how widespread Federico's search for her must be if Elizabeth knew of it. It was worse than she thought, which would make all she had to tell Mino more dangerous.

Mino was racing to catch up. Elizabeth had called Letta La Sirena—the singer whom Carlo had wanted him to hear at the casino. But how? Performing onstage at a casino was forbidden to *coro* girls.

Then again, when had the rules stopped Letta before?

When he looked at her admiringly, he saw something dark hovering over her, and he knew that breaking the Incurables vows was not the danger Elizabeth spoke of. Letta was in far more trouble than he could guess.

"You must leave Venice," Elizabeth said.

"I know," Violetta said.

"What is she talking about?" Mino asked Letta. "Who threatens you?"

Letta inhaled and shook her head. "Mino—"

"I can help you," Elizabeth said. "We can take my boat, but it must be done quickly, before . . ." She paused and cracked a rueful smile at Letta. "I don't even know your name."

"Violetta," she said. Slowly, she took off her mask.

"Violetta." Elizabeth came close and studied her features. She smiled and kissed Violetta's cheek. She blinked rapidly, taking in her friend's face for the first time.

Tears filled Violetta's eyes. It felt so good to be seen for who she was.

"I've been so afraid for you," Elizabeth said. "Let me help."

Violetta nodded, clasping Elizabeth's hand.

"Tonight," Elizabeth said.

"London?" Violetta whispered.

"Letta, tell me what's going on," Mino said. Inside him churned an impotent rage. He could not stand to see the fear in Letta's eyes and not know the source of it or how to make it stop.

"I don't know where to start," Violetta said.

"Start with a bath," Elizabeth said. "Both of you look as if you've been dragged through the canal. You'll want to clean up and rest some, Violetta, before the journey."

"Mino." Violetta turned to him and took his hands in hers. "Will you come with me to London? I know it sounds mad, but—"

"Yes." Mino gazed at her and saw the bright unknown of the future. He had so many questions. But if he had Letta, there was only one thing to say. "Yes."

❦

AFTER A BATH, a tray of breakfast, and a change of borrowed clothes, Violetta lingered near the door of her guest room. The bed beckoned. She had scarcely slept in the week since she'd left Federico, but she was less tired than she was anxious about all she had to tell Mino. She longed to see him, to be with him, but she feared what her words might do to him. She could hardly stomach them herself. She put on her mask to cross the hall. She didn't want the servants to see her, and also she needed the strength its shield brought to her. She hadn't realized how much she'd come to rely on it.

She knocked on his door but got no answer. After a moment, she tried the knob. It was unlocked. Mino sat before a fire on the far side of the room. He had bathed, shaved, and dressed in an older man's clean clothes. His eyes were fixed on the table before him so intently he did not see her come in. She knew what he was looking at.

Mino was aware that a story of his provenance was coming, and he knew it was not the lovely tale he used to dream of as a boy. He would understand the truth in good time, but for now, it was enough to gaze upon his half token made whole.

Violetta came close, and together they stared at the two pieces lined up to make the siren.

"Mino." She touched his arm.

He looked up at her. Letta, luminous, a little wild. She still made him nervous. He used to feel his life's work was earning her esteem. Then, after their split, when he met Ana, he put the same energy into earning hers. He had done all he could to deserve his wife's love, which was honest and loyal and good. But he had never loved her like this.

"Before you speak," he said, a tremor in his voice, "there is something you must know."

Violetta sat in the chair beside him. She took his hand. "Go on."

"I have a daughter. I cannot leave. I cannot leave her."

Violetta slid onto Mino's lap and wrapped her arms around him, threading her fingers through the hair at the back of his neck. It felt so good to touch him again.

"Mino," she said, her face tipped close, her lips brushing his. "We're not leaving Farfalla. We're going to take her with us."

Mino's eyes widened. His heart swelled with relief and amazement. "You know?"

Violetta nodded. "I went to look for you. I held her in my arms today." Her throat tightened. "She is beautiful. She is waiting for you."

Tears streamed down Mino's cheeks. Violetta wiped them with her thumbs.

"It will be all right, Mino."

He could not speak through his emotion. He needed to see Letta's face. He reached for the ribbon to untie her mask.

She pulled away. "Let's wear them. Put yours on," she said. It was too much at once. Soon she would tell Mino every secret she knew—Federico, La Sirena, his mother. She felt a need to hold on to some of her mystery, her mask.

He shook his head. "Let me see you."

"I'm not the Letta you used to know."

"You are the Letta you are today, and tomorrow you'll be different. I won't try to stop you changing. I only wish to see you." He pulled the ribbon.

She let the mask fall, tears in her eyes.

His gaze swept over her face. "Why are you crying?"

He reached for her. He held the back of her head with one hand, the curve of her hip with the other. She felt their bodies come together as he kissed her tears, softly, then her lips, firmly. She opened her mouth to him. She felt his tongue on hers. She put her arms around him, and her touch at the back of his neck made him moan, and his moan made her shiver. Their kiss was deep and heavy. The touch of their skin as electric as the first time they'd touched years ago on the roof. But it transported neither of them back there. They were here, now, together at last, as hungry for each other as they'd been then, only this time their hunger did not scare them. All this desire, and they knew what to do with it. Violetta took off his shirt, ran her hands over his shoulders, the muscles of his arms. Mino's skin pricked with goose bumps as his mouth trailed down her neck.

Back on the roof, they used to speak a secret language made of music. They were older now, so different from the orphans they had been. They fell on the bed in a tangle, a new music between them building to crescendo.

Twenty-six

Violetta rolled over in bed, reaching for Mino through half sleep. Her skin tingled with the memory of their bodies twined together. The pleasure had not been in the transgression of the act, but in the unparalleled wholeness she had felt. She remembered his mouth on the back of her neck. The calluses on his fingers. Her thumb in the notch of his collarbone. The heat of him, how it filled her until she cried out. And afterward, those kisses. That blissful, exhausted peace.

She wanted to draw against his warmth and stay there. Always.

But his place in the bed was empty.

She bolted up. His clothes were gone from the floor where he'd shed them. She suddenly remembered the rest. Their conversation as they'd shared one pillow, facing each other in bed. He hadn't wanted to believe her words. It wasn't the story he'd imagined. He'd argued bitterly that the other half of the token alone did not prove his mother's murder. He'd reminded her that Federico had confessed to nothing. What if she was wrong?

She was not wrong.

"You don't know him like I know him," she said.

"If you knew him like that, then why did you stay? Why were you with him?"

She'd stiffened, and he'd caressed her face, then closed his eyes and shuddered.

"I'm sorry," he said. "You make me feel as if we've never been apart."

"Speak to me as if we haven't," she insisted. "That's how I'm speaking to you."

She drew the necklace out from her dress pocket, and Mino remembered it. He held it in his hands and wept. It broke her heart.

"We'll get Farfalla," she'd said, holding him to her. "After sundown. Then we'll be gone from all of this."

She'd felt him nod and hold her tighter, too exhausted to respond.

When they'd fallen asleep soon after, it had been the middle of the day. Now dusk painted the sky rosy and the fire in the hearth had burned low. Violetta didn't think Mino would have gone for his daughter without her, but where else would he be?

The answer came to her like a punch in the stomach, and she was out of the bed, hurrying back into her clothes and her mask. She bounded down the stairs of the palazzo.

"Violetta."

"Elizabeth—"

"The boat is ready. John will meet us—"

"First we have to go to La Sirena."

"What?" Elizabeth said. "It's too dangerous."

Violetta took hold of Elizabeth's elbows. "Mino is there."

Elizabeth blanched, her eyes losing their sparkle. "Madonna," she whispered. "Let's go."

❖

IT HAD COME to Mino in Letta's arms. The only way out was the most unfathomable. All his life, he'd sought his family. And now? His father lived and breathed just down the *calle*. Federico. The dark-haired, unmasked, fearsome proprietor of the casino, whom he had seen in passing at the bar.

At first, Mino hadn't wanted to accept the darkest parts of Letta's story, but then he'd held that opal and remembered. It had been his mother's. He had a memory of his hands around the back of her neck—the feel of her hair above the thick gold chain. His fingers used to trace the chain down to that blue-black stone at her breast.

She had cherished it. She would have to be dead for someone to take it from her.

So. The same man who had murdered his mother now threatened Letta. What other choice did Mino have? He had to kill his father.

If he didn't, Federico would come for them. No borders could stop a man like that from pursuing a woman like Letta. Even if they went to London, even if they started everything anew, they would always be looking over their shoulders. Unless Mino ended it tonight.

He must prepare himself to break the dark chain of his family's past. Then flee the city he loved. He would be haunted no more.

He hurried past the boy lighting the *calle* rushlights, past the fishermen coming home with their full buckets. He could still smell Letta on him, could still feel her under his fingertips. He would return to her as soon as this was done.

Mino's whole life had been preparing him to love her, not as a child but as a man. Now he had loved her in that bed, and he trembled to recall it. Again he desired her. Again and again. He wanted all the time in the world. But he was no man if he could not put her peace above all else, if he could not protect her.

What if she woke while he was gone? This thought troubled him, but then, he couldn't have risked waking her. She would never have let him go.

Farewell, Venice. Farewell, one thousand moons on the canals. He knew nothing but this city, yet he felt no sorrow at leaving. If he had Letta and his daughter, if he had Sprezz, he'd have all he desired. If he could end the fear he'd seen in Letta's eyes, he would feel worthy of loving her.

At the entrance to the casino, the doorkeeper glanced at Mino's simple mask and fine clothes. Elizabeth's husband's shirt had lace at the wrists and throat, and his wool britches were cut in the French fashion. The doorkeeper nodded Mino in. The blue glass lantern cast a spell over the siren's tail, and Mino traced it with his fingertips as he entered.

It was early yet, and the casino was quiet. He scanned the dark room's velvet cushions, then the bar, uncertain where to find Federico. He had anticipated nothing but the brute rage that would carry him through the act. But now, drifting alone in the place where he had spent so many evenings, his confidence waned. Discreetly, he lifted a mostly empty bottle of wine off a table. He tucked it behind his back.

At the rear of the room, barmaids moved in and out of the door to the storerooms and back exit. Mino had been led out of it twice when he couldn't pay his bill, on nights when the barmaid had been feeling kind and Federico had been elsewhere. He knew there were anterooms back there, offices. He needed to find Federico alone.

The next time he noticed both barmaids engaged with customers, Mino slipped through the door. He stood alone in the candlelit hall.

He passed a storeroom, then another, and then, before the exit, he came upon a closed door. His brow dampened. He swigged the last of the wine from the bottle. He could feign drunkenness, claim he was looking for the door to step outside and piss.

He shattered the bottle against the wall until he held a jagged shard. The sound shocked him: he was actually going to do this. With his other hand he turned the knob.

❋

BY THE TIME Violetta and Elizabeth got to La Sirena in the *burchiello*, the sky was just growing dark. She hadn't been expecting the small crowd already outside the casino.

"Do you want me to come in?" Elizabeth asked.

"No," Violetta said quickly, rising from the sofa in the boat's cabin. "Wait for me here. Be ready to leave as soon as I find Mino."

She kissed Elizabeth quickly and moved to the back of the line, eyeing the group at the casino door. It was a performance night, and surely some among these maskers expected to hear her sing inside. How hot would Federico's anger toward her be by now? How much money had she cost him?

She could not think what darkness would transpire if she didn't reach Mino before he found Federico. She shifted miserably, watching the doorkeeper argue with two *barnabotti*.

Violetta considered revealing herself to get inside. She could say her stage name and the doorkeeper would make the crowd part for her. But then the guards would be upon her. Even if she found Mino more quickly, they'd never make it out. There had to be another way.

From the *burchiello*, she saw Elizabeth's white-gloved wave. She glanced about her—no one watching—and approached the boat again.

"The back door," Elizabeth said.

❦

Federico looked up from a stack of books when Mino opened his door. His expression was weary, and in the moment it took for displeasure to cloud it, Mino saw the resemblance. The set of his eyes and his long, slender face, his jaw—all of this was mirrored on Mino like a cloud upon a canal. Uncanny that he had not seen this parity before. He had never known to look. How undeniable it was.

Warmth spread through his chest. He tried to extinguish it, but it overwhelmed him.

"Father," he whispered.

"Get out," Federico said automatically. Then he looked again at Mino, narrowing his eyes. He rose slowly from his chair.

In one hand Mino held the broken bottle. In the other, he reached into his pocket for the proof. He held the token out, against all reason, for the man to see.

Federico's jaw tensed. "Where is she?"

"This is between you and me."

Federico swallowed, his expression enigmatic. He seemed to be waiting for Mino to make the next move, but Mino felt paralyzed. It was one thing to plan to kill a man. It was another to look your father in the eyes and raise a shard of glass.

"You look like your mother," Federico said in a quiet, distant voice. "Do you know that? There is much I could tell you about her. Antonia. There was no one like her."

Mino wanted to nod but couldn't move. Looking closely at Federico's face, he remembered his mother more clearly than he had in years. He felt a sweetness that predated his memory, one he had not known since his mother held him as a child. He was not no one. His daughter was not no one. He was the descendent of this brutal man, but he had come from a good woman, and Farfalla had, too. A tear slipped down his cheek.

Federico watched it patiently. "Put the bottle down, son. A man needs both hands to embrace." He extended his arms.

Mino felt a slow, undeniable pull toward his father. He looked at the glass in his hands. He stepped closer.

❋

VIOLETTA RACED UP the dock toward the back entrance. Before she reached it, the door flung open. Fortunato stood before her.

On instinct she recoiled, ready to run, but he caught her by the wrist. She felt his brute strength and shuddered. She fought against him. She was terrified—until she looked in his eyes.

"La Sirena," he whispered. His face was ghostly white. "I'm sorry."

"What happened?" She gripped his elbows. "Where is he?"

He took a breath, visibly struggling for composure. "He is dead."

Violetta cried out in anguish. She was too late. She staggered, barely standing, as a memory assaulted her, heavy and bright:

Mino on the roof that first day. His knee touching hers. His laughter, like he didn't know what worry was. She remembered the shock of his hair against her fingers. She hadn't wanted to let go of him then. She never should have.

How could it be that she'd gotten him back only to lose him forever?

Farfalla. She thought of his daughter, that beautiful baby. How close Mino had been to returning for her. To claiming his family at last.

I will go to her, she told him in her heart. *I will be her family, and in that way, I'll still have you.*

She wanted to run from Fortunato, down the dock, straight for the child. If she stepped inside this casino, she'd never get free. But she couldn't leave Mino in there.

"Come," Fortunato said, taking her arm more gently than she expected. Nausea swept her as he helped her down the hall. When she saw Federico's open door, her feet picked up speed and she swerved inside. In the doorway, she stopped short.

Two men lay on the floor. Father and son, each curled toward the other. There was blood everywhere. Violetta fell to her knees. She put her hands on Mino's feet as she came closer. His legs. His hips. Elbow. Cheek. His eyes were closed. Federico's were open, staring up, and that's when she knew he was dead. He held a dagger in his hand, but no blood stained its blade. What had happened? She fell upon Mino's breast and clutched him, racked by sobs.

"My love," she said.

And then she felt Mino shift beneath her. His arm came around her and his eyes opened. She gasped.

"Where are you hurt?" she asked, her hands probing his chest, his stomach.

He pressed his hand to his heart. There was no wound.

"He tried to . . ." he whispered, and Violetta followed Mino's eyes to the knife in Federico's hand. "What have I done?"

Now Violetta saw the base of the wine bottle protruding from Federico's gut, the wheel-shaped wound in his core. His face—the frozen, dead outrage—sickened her more. She turned away, telling herself to breathe, that it was over. Mino was alive.

"Come away," she told him. She kissed his cheek.

"I can't," he said. "My father."

Violetta pressed her face to Mino's, turned him away from Federico.

"Farfalla," she said.

His daughter's name seemed to wake Mino from the nightmare. Silently, he rose. He helped Violetta up, but there was no strength in his touch. His face was drained of color and emotion. It frightened her.

"Sirena?" Fortunato spoke from the doorway, barely audible.

She looked up at Federico's servant. She had forgotten about him, and now her body tensed. What would it cost to get free now? Her eyes returned to the glass bottle shoved into Federico's belly. What lengths would she go to for Mino?

It confused her that Fortunato had not attacked Mino, that she had found the two of them lying alone, still in the aftermath.

She raised her mask and looked at Fortunato. She saw the conflict in his eyes.

"You've done worse at his request," she guessed.

"I was not an orphan like you," Fortunato said, "but Federico was the closest thing I had to family, despite the awful things he . . . we—"

"Have mercy on us," Violetta begged him. She put her hand in Mino's. "This is Antonia's son. Let us go in peace. I will pay you—"

Fortunato waved her off. "Leave now. Be free."

She kissed his cheek. "Thank you, Fortunato."

"Farewell, Sirena."

❋

MINO STAGGERED DOWN the hall, numb, blind, and nauseated. He leaned on Letta, grateful for her strength, for his had fled.

"What's wrong?" he asked when she stopped before an open door next to Federico's office. She didn't answer, only drew him with her into the small room. He glanced about it, at the gowns and perfumes, and he understood this to be her boudoir from her performing days. On the table before the mirror, there was a mask painted to look like fish scales. Letta pressed it to her breast, then turned back toward the door.

"Let's go," she said.

As they stepped outside the back door, a cry escaped his mouth. It was over, but he no longer knew whether he'd been right or wrong. Was he free now? Was Letta? Was this a story he would want to tell his daughter? He did not know. He knew the night was cold, starlit, and still. He knew a light wind rippled the canal, and that a lantern shone in Elizabeth's boat, growing brighter as Letta led him closer. He knew Letta's strong arms. He prayed that every time he was haunted by the memory of his father, she would be close enough to hold him.

At the sound of his footfall on the wooden dock, Mino knew they were really leaving. His mind sent desperate prayers of hope and love in every direction, to every corner of this city. To his mother at the wheel. To Ana in the *maranzaria*. To Carlo at the Rosicrucians' table. To everyone at the Incurables, and the rooftop where he had grown into himself.

For the past two years, Mino had been sending prayers to Letta. Now he held her hand. He felt it play within his body like a song. He could give her more than prayers. He could give her everything. He would never let her go.

By the time they boarded the boat, Mino felt a physical need for his violin. He needed to put this night to music. All that had just happened, all that lay ahead. A single measure, round and rich as a black opal.

And somehow, his violin case was there on the long bench of the boat. Letta had brought it for him.

"Let's go," he heard her tell Elizabeth, who told the boatman. The smooth confidence in their voices made Mino think, for the first time in such a long time, that maybe things would be all right.

At the sound of the violin, Violetta spun around. She had brought the instrument and her few small possessions when she left Elizabeth's palazzo, but it stunned her to hear Mino playing it now. He'd seemed so weak as they'd left the casino. She'd thought he would need to rest.

But now he stood with the violin at his breast, and he looked strong again. He looked like Mino. Even though he was bathed in his father's blood, balancing in the center of a *burchiello*, sailing away from everything they knew.

The first song Violetta had heard Mino play had determined her life. It had been the source of her nightmares. It had taught her how to sing. She remembered embracing him after they played together, amazed by how their song had felt like a physical force.

Tonight a new melody poured out of him, slow and open, profoundly bittersweet. She listened, as she always listened, with a deep desire to join him in the song.

"Beautiful," she said when he lifted the bow and looked up with tears in his eyes.

"Will you give it words?" he asked. "I don't know what it's about."

She smiled and came close, lyrics already swirling in her mind. She would sing of a horizon, a little girl, of ships gliding in the night, and true love.

"It's about us," she said, and she kissed him. She would never let him go.

London

June 1821

"Nonna farfalla." My granddaughter taps me. "You fell asleep again."

"Don't you know the rest, child?" I murmur through half dreams, settling back in my bed in my son's London flat. I am eighty-one years old and tired. I have birthed five children, who have given me eighteen grandchildren and, at last count, two tiny great-grandchildren, one named in my honor. I have sung on opera stages in London, Vienna, and Naples. Twenty years ago I buried my father next to Violetta's London grave; they passed within six months of each other. I buried my own husband twelve years later. But somehow it has taken me this long to tell my story—all of it—to someone who would listen.

Violet, my granddaughter, twenty years old and just as plucky as her namesake. They have the same dark, beguiling eyes.

"I know they picked you up in the *burchiello* from the sausage shop," Violet says, reciting the more commonly known portion of our family lore, "and that you sailed along the Brenta Canal to Padua. You took a coach north, then another ship across the Channel. You came to London and grew up singing." She shakes her head. "But all this time, I never knew Letta and Mino were orphans."

"We are all orphans at some point or another. I am one now that my parents are dead." I take her hand in mine and meet her eyes. "In every generation, there's a storyteller. Tell the real story of the Incurables to your children. And if they won't listen, be patient. One day, you'll have grandchildren, too."

"I'm not a storyteller," she says, "not like you."

I draw her hand close before my face. My vision isn't what it used to be, but I can still see color. Violet is a painter, studying at the Royal Academy of Arts. Her hands always bear memories of the canvas she brings to life.

I trace a dash of green along her thumb. "What is this? Grass?"

She smiles. "Willow frond."

I find the blue nearby, on the joint of her forefinger. "A creek for the willow to weep in?"

"You're good, Nonna."

There's white paint on her nail. I rub at it with my finger. "Cloudy day?"

She shakes her head. "Clear skies. That's lace. The dress of a woman on a picnic."

"You see?" I say. "You are a storyteller."

"Mozart!" she says suddenly, sharply. "Get down."

"It's all right," I tell her, patting the space beside me on the bed for the little spotted dog to sit. "Let him stay."

The beast is the descendant of the original Sprezzatura, who traveled with us from Venice to London long ago. Each in his line has been pampered and spoiled by my family, their lineage as Venetian street mutts not forgotten but elevated into lore.

"So now," I whisper to Violet, aware of her father, my middle son, passing in the hallway, "will you grant my request? I know your papa thinks it morbid, but I don't care. *You* understand me—"

"Shh, Nonna," Violet says, reaching beneath her chair at my bedside. My heart lifts when she raises the mask. It's worn, yellow at the edges, the black ribbon frayed. She's had it with her all along. She puts it in my hands.

I close my eyes, wrap my fingers around it.

"Thank you." My voice surprises me, choked with emotion. I could not make it to the attic to retrieve the *bauta* on my own.

It is the one my father gave Violetta on that *carnevale* afternoon. No one in my family—no one except for Violet—could understand why I need it now at the end.

When Venice finally fell to the Austrians some twenty years ago, *carnevale* ceased to exist. I am told masks are forbidden there now, though it's impossible to imagine. The once-ubiquitous *baute* are considered strange today. Restrictive. Even foreboding. My own children have come around to this unfortunate way of thinking.

I never had the chance to take them back to Venice. They never got to see it as I did. It was only one trip, but it changed me forever. My father, Violetta, and I spent two wondrous days there when I was twelve years old. We were always masked, whirling through a party that never seemed to end. They took the risk because they wanted me to know where we had come from. To this day that trip is my most precious memory. I used to make them wear the masks around our home in London as often as they would indulge me.

Now I press the *bauta* to my face and travel back to Venice. I lift my head off the pillow so Violet can tie the ribbon. This small effort exhausts me, and I know I've managed just in time.

Violetta left this *bauta* to me. It always seemed to charm her that I preferred the simple white mask to the painted one she wore as La Sirena. She was buried in that mask, my father in his original white *bauta*. I want to meet them wearing mine. I want them to know me through it.

I meet my granddaughter's eyes again. When she smiles, it is enough. I close my eyes and hear the lullaby my father used to sing.

Acknowledgments

With thanks to Tara Singh Carlson, whose generosity and intellect let me find the book I hoped to write. To Helen Richard, Sally Kim, and the distinguished team at Putnam, for your commitment and ingenuity. To Laura Rennert, beautiful ally.

To Federica Fresch, for two spellbinding journeys into Venice's past. To Dr. Nelli-Elena Vanzan Marchini, for your passionate discussion of a Serene Republic. To Agata Brusegan, for the dive into archives of the *ospedali*. To Guiseppe Ellero, fellow writer and keeper of the orphans' secrets. To Don Giovanni, for revealing Tintoretto's *Ursula and the Eleven Thousand Virgins*, original art of the Incurables. To Giordano Aterini and Giulia Taddeo from Rizzoli, for warmth and wisdom. To Hanbyul Jang, for violin lessons. To Leonard Bryan, voice coach. To Addison Timlin, for tattooed inspiration. To Soundis Azaiz Passman and September Rea, sundial and compass.

To *Idomeneo* at the Teatro La Fenice. To spritzes to go from the

Corner Pub in Dorsoduro. To alleys too narrow for double strollers. To the Aqua Palace Hotel, for letting us know.

To my parents, Harriet and Vic, and my family and friends, with love. To Matilda, my teacher. To Venice, love is here. And to Jason, everything.